# GREAT SEA STORIES

# GREAT
# SEA STORIES

EDITED BY

JOSEPH L. FRENCH

FOREWORD BY

ADMIRAL WILLIAM V. PRATT, U.S.N. RET.

TUDOR PUBLISHING CO.

NEW YORK

1943

PRINTED IN THE UNITED STATES OF AMERICA
BY THE VAIL-BALLOU PRESS, INC., BINGHAMTON, N. Y.

# PUBLISHER'S FOREWORD

Some years ago, that remarkable anthologist, the late Joseph Lewis French, set about compiling two volumes which were published under the title "Great Sea Stories." This present book, which combines the two, is largely his work, with such additions from today's stirring tales of the sea as carry on the spirit in which the original stories were gathered together.

# CONTENTS

# Contents

# Contents

# FOREWORD

IN this book, "Great Sea Stories," the reader, if he be not such a confirmed land lubber that mention of the sea causes nausea, will find a collection of sea tales, twenty-nine in all, which from start to finish should hold him fascinated.

The sea scope of the stories covers the seven seas. The reader sails with the writers in the waters of the South Pacific, the China Seas, the Solomons, the Straits of Malacca, and the Malayan Coast. He braves the dangers of Cape Wrath with its storms, and even ventures to Iceland in the north. The waters of California welcome him, and he may in thought run the waters of the South Atlantic, past the bight of Brazil, until he drops anchor in the quiet haven of Martha's Vineyard.

The waters off the coast of African Guinea, Spain, France, the Azores, Ireland, and the North Atlantic will whisper to him or throw the spume of storm-tossed waves in his face. He even peeks into the Caribbean, and harks back to the days of old Spain and the exploits in those waters.

In the North Sea, he ventures forth with the fringes of the fleet and partakes of adventure. In the Black Sea, he follows some of the sea operations off Sevastopol. Amongst the coral isles of the Pacific, he follows the fate of air men shot down and their long trek to safety on a raft. Even the expendables give him a glimpse into Subic Bay.

They are all there, the old ships of the line, with their tapering spars and white sails, down to the latest ships of the fleet. Heavy guns thunder, and airplanes swoop down like hawks. The past blends into the present. Mutineers, slavers, whalers, storms and derelicts all find roles in these stories. There is fiction, to be sure, but many of the stories are based on fact. And the list of authors, tops in their class, but too numerous to cite by name, is one to conjure with, and proof of the interest these sea tales should arouse.

While the book appeals first to the seaman's heart, even the man who prefers to sleep soundly in his bed on land will find in it much to stir the imagination and arouse keen interest.

WILLIAM V. PRATT
Admiral, U.S.N., *Retired*

# INTRODUCTION

THE theme of the sea is heroic—epic. Since the first stirrings of the imagination of man the sea has enthralled him; and since the dawn of literature he has chronicled his wanderings upon its vast bosom.

It is one of the curiosities of literature, a fact that old Isaac Disraeli might have delighted to linger over, that there have been no collectors of sea-tales; that no man has ever, as in the present instance, dwelt upon the topic with the purpose of gathering some of the best work into a single volume. And yet men have written of the sea since 2500 B. C. when an unknown author set down on papyrus his account of a struggle with a sea-serpent. This account, now in the British Museum, is the first sea-story on record. Our modern sea-stories begin properly with the chronicles of the early navigators—in many of which there is an unconscious art that none of our modern masters of fiction has greatly surpassed. For delightful reading the lover of sea stories is referred to Best's account of Frobisher's second voyage—to Richard Chancellor's chronicle of the same period —to Hakluyt, an immortal classic—and to Purchas' "Pilgrimage."

But from the earliest growth of the art of fiction the sea was frankly accepted as a stirring theme, comparatively rarely handled because voyages were fewer then, and the subject still largely unknown. To the general reader it may seem a rather astounding fact that in "Robinson Crusoe" we have the first classic of this period and in "Colonel Jack" another classic of much the same type. These two stories by the immortal Defoe may be accepted as the foundation of the sea-tale in literary art.

A century, however, was to elapse before the sea-tale came into its own. It was not until a generation after Defoe that Smollett, in "Roderick Random," again stirred the theme into life. Fielding in his "Voyage to Lisbon" had given some account of a personal experience, but in the general category it must be set down as simply episodal. Foster's "Voyages," a translation from the German published in England at the beginning of the third quarter of the eighteenth century, a compendium of monumental importance, continued the tradition of Hakluyt and Purchas. By this time the sea-power of England had become supreme,—Britannia ruled the waves, and a native sea-literature was the result. The sea-songs of Thomas Dibdin and other writers were the first fruits of this newly created literary nationalism.

Shortly after the beginning of the nineteenth century the sea-writer established himself with Michael Scott in "Tom Cringle's Log," a forgotten, but ever-fresh classic. Then came Captain Marryat, who was to the sea what Dickens and Thackeray were to land folk. America, too, contributed to this literary movement. Even before Marryat, our own Cooper had essayed the sea with a masterly hand, while in "Moby Dick," as in his other stories, Herman Melville glorified the theme. Continental writers like Victor Hugo and the Hungarian, Maurus Jokai, who had little personal knowledge of the subject, also set their hands to tales of marine adventure.

Such work as this has established a succession which has been continuous and progressive ever since. The literature of the sea of the past half-century is voluminous, varied and universally known, and whether in the form of personal adventure, or in purely fictional shape, it has grown to be an art cultivated with great care by the best contemporary writers.

The noble band of singers of the sea, from the days of the Elizabethans to the sublime Swinburne, belongs to another volume. It is the sincere hope of the compiler that the present collection offers undisputable evidence that the prose tradition has been fully sustained and that the reader will find in these pages living testimony to the marvelous interest of the theme—its virility and its beauty.

JOSEPH LEWIS FRENCH

# GREAT SEA STORIES

# NARRATIVE OF
# THE MUTINY OF THE *BOUNTY*

From "Chambers' Miscellany," ANONYMOUS

ABOUT the year 1786, the merchants and planters interested in the West India Islands became anxious to introduce an exceedingly valuable plant, the bread-fruit tree, into these possessions, and as this could best be done by a government expedition, a request was preferred to the crown accordingly. The ministry at the time being favorable to the proposed undertaking, a vessel, named the *Bounty*, was selected to execute the desired object. To the command of this ship Captain W. Bligh was appointed, Aug. 16, 1787. The burden of the *Bounty* was nearly two hundred and fifteen tons. The establishment of men and officers for the ship was as follows:—1 lieutenant to command, 1 master, 1 boatswain, 1 gunner, 1 carpenter, 1 surgeon, 2 master's mates, 2 midshipmen, 2 quarter-masters, 1 quarter-master's mate, 1 boatswain's mate, 1 gunner's mate, 1 carpenter's mate, 1 carpenter's crew, 1 sailmaker, 1 armorer, 1 corporal, 1 clerk and steward, 23 able seamen—total, 44. The addition of two men appointed to take care of the plants, made the whole ship's crew amount to 46. The ship was stored and victualled for eighteen months.

Thus prepared, the *Bounty* set sail on the 23d of December, and what ensued will be best told in the language of Captain Bligh.

*Monday, 27th April 1789.*—The wind being northerly in the evening, we steered to the westward, to pass to the south of Tofoa. I gave directions for this course to be continued during the night. The master had the first watch, the gunner the middle watch, and Mr. Christian the morning watch.

*Tuesday, 28th.*—Just before sunrising, while I was yet asleep, Mr. Christian, with the master-at-arms, gunner's mate, and Thomas Burkitt, seaman, came into my cabin, and seizing me, tied my hands with a cord behind my back, threatening me with instant death if I spoke or made the least noise. I, however, called as loud as I could, in hopes of assistance; but they had already secured the officers who were not of their party, by placing sentinels at their doors. There were three men at my cabin door, besides the four within; Christian had only a cutlass in his hand, the others had muskets and bayonets. I was pulled out of bed, and forced on deck in my shirt, suffering great pain from the tightness with which they had tied my hands. I demanded the reason of such violence, but received no other answer than abuse for not holding my tongue. The master, the gunner, the surgeon, Mr. Elphinstone, master's mate, and Nelson, were kept confined below, and the fore-hatchway was guarded by sentinels. The boatswain and carpenter, and also the clerk, Mr. Samuel, were allowed to come upon deck. The boatswain was ordered to hoist the launch out, with a threat if he did not do it instantly to take care of himself.

When the boat was out, Mr. Hayward and Mr. Hallett, two of the midshipmen, and Mr. Samuel, were ordered into it. I demanded what their intention was in giving this order, and endeavored to persuade the people near me not to persist in such acts of violence; but it was to no effect. Christian changed the cutlass which he had in his hand for a bayonet that was brought to him, and holding me with a strong grip by the cord that tied my hands, he with many oaths threatened to kill me immediately if I would not be quiet; the villains round me had their pieces cocked and bayonets fixed. Particular people were called on to go into the boat, and were hurried over the side, whence I concluded that with these people I was to be set adrift. I therefore made another effort to bring about a change, but with no other effect than to be threatened with having my brains blown out.

The boatswain and seamen who were to go in the boat were allowed to collect twine, canvas, lines, sails, cordage, an eight-and-twenty-gallon cask of water, and Mr. Samuel got a hundred and fifty pounds of bread, with a small quantity of rum and wine, also a quadrant and compass; but he was forbidden, on pain of death, to touch either map, ephemeris, book of astronomical observations, sextant, time-keeper, or any of my surveys or drawings.

The officers were next called upon deck, and forced over the side into the boat, while I was kept apart from every one abaft the mizzen-mast.

Isaac Martin, one of the guard over me, I saw had an inclination to assist me, and, as he fed me with shaddock (my lips being quite parched), we explained our wishes to each other by our looks; but this being observed, Martin was removed from me. He then attempted to leave the ship, for which purpose he got into the boat; but with many threats they obliged him to return. The armorer, Joseph Coleman, and two of the carpenters, M'Intosh and Norman, were also kept contrary to their inclination; and they begged of me, after I was astern in the boat, to remember that they declared that they had no hand in the transaction. Michael Byrne, I am told, likewise wanted to leave the ship.

It appeared to me that Christian was some time in doubt whether he should keep the carpenter or his mates; at length he determined on the latter, and the carpenter was ordered into the boat. He was permitted, but not without some opposition, to take his tool-chest. The officers and men being in the boat, they only waited for me, of which the master-at-arms informed Christian; who then said, "Come, Captain Bligh, your officers and men are now in the boat, and you must go with them; if you attempt to make the least resistance, you will instantly be put to death:" and without further ceremony, with a tribe of armed ruffians about me, I was forced over the side, where they untied my hands. Being in the boat, we were veered astern by a rope. A few pieces of pork were thrown to us, and some clothes, also four cutlasses; and it was then that the armorer and carpenters called out to me to remember that they had no hand in the transaction. After having undergone a great deal of ridicule, and having been kept some time to make sport for these unfeeling wretches, we were at length cast adrift in the open ocean.

I had eighteen persons with me in the boat. There remained on board the *Bounty* twenty-five hands, the most able men of the ship's company. Having little or no wind, we rowed pretty fast towards Tofoa, which bore north-east about ten leagues from us. While the ship was in sight, she steered to the west-north-west; but I considered this only as a feint; for when we were sent away, "Huzza for Otaheite!" was frequently heard among the mutineers.

It will very naturally be asked, What could be the reason for a such a revolt? In answer to which, I can only conjecture that the mutineers had flattered themselves with the hopes of a more happy life among the Otaheitans than they could possibly enjoy in England; and this, joined to some female connections, most probably occasioned the whole transaction. The women at Otaheite are handsome, mild and cheerful in their manners and conversation, possessed of great sensibility, and have sufficient delicacy to make them admired and beloved. The chiefs were so much attached to our people, that they rather encouraged their stay among them than otherwise, and even made them promises of large possessions. Under these, and many other attendant circumstances equally desirable, it is now perhaps not so much to be wondered at, though scarcely possible to have been foreseen, that a set of sailors, most of them void of connections, should be led away: especially when, in addition to such powerful inducements, they imagined it in their power to fix themselves in the midst of plenty, on one of the finest islands in the world, where they need not labor, and where the allurements of dissipation are beyond anything that can be conceived.

### FATE OF THE CASTAWAYS

My first determination was to seek a supply of bread-fruit and water at Tofoa, and afterwards to sail for Tongataboo, and there risk a solicitation to Poulaho, the king, to equip our boat, and grant us a supply of water and provisions, so as to enable us to reach the East Indies. The quantity of provisions I found in the boat was a hundred and fifty pounds of bread, sixteen pieces of pork, each piece weighing two pounds, six quarts of rum, six bottles of wine, with twenty-eight gallons of water, and four empty barrecoes.

We got to Tofoa when it was dark, but found the shore so steep and rocky that we could not land. We were obliged, therefore, to remain all night in the boat, keeping it on the lee-side of the island, with two oars. Next day (Wednesday, April 29) we found a cove, where we landed. I observed the latitude of this cove to be 19 degrees 41 minutes south. This is the northwest part of Tofoa, the north-westernmost of the Friendly Islands. As I was resolved to spare the small stock of provisions we had in the boat, we endeavored to procure something towards our support on the island itself. For two days we ranged through the island in parties, seeking for water, and anything in the shape of provisions, subsisting, meanwhile, on morsels of what we had brought with us. The island at first seemed uninhabited, but on Friday, May 1, one of our exploring parties met with two men, a woman, and a child: the men came with them to the cove, and brought two cocoanut shells of water. I endeavored to make friends of these people, and sent them away for bread-fruit, plantains, and water. Soon after, other natives came to us; and by noon there were thirty about us, from whom we obtained a small supply. I was much puzzled in what manner to account to the natives for the loss of my ship: I knew they had too much sense to be amused with a story that the ship was to join me, when she was not in sight from the hills. I was at first doubtful whether I should tell the real fact, or say that the ship had overset and sunk, and that we only were saved: the latter appeared to be the most proper and advantageous for us, and I accordingly instructed my people, that we might all agree in one story. As I expected, inquiries were made about the ship, and they seemed readily satisfied with our account; but there did not appear the least symptom of joy or sorrow in their faces, although I fancied I discovered some marks of surprise. Some of the natives were coming and going the whole afternoon.

Towards evening, I had the satisfaction to find our stock of provisions somewhat increased; but the natives did not appear to have much to spare. What they brought was in such small quantities, that I had no reason to hope we should be able to procure from them sufficient to stock us for our voyage. At night, I served a quarter of a bread-fruit and a cocoanut to each person for supper; and a good fire being made, all but the watch went to sleep.

*Saturday, 2d.*—As there was no certainty of our being supplied with water by the natives, I sent a party among the gullies in the mountains, with empty shells, to see what could be found. In their absence the natives came about us, as I expected, and in greater numbers; two canoes also came in from round the north side of the island. In one of them was an elderly chief, called Macca-ackavow. Soon after, some of our foraging party returned, and with them came a good-looking chief, called Egi-jeefow, or Eefow.

Their affability was of short duration, for the natives began to increase in number, and I observed some symptoms of a design against us. Soon after, they attempted to haul the boat on shore, on which I brandished my cutlass in a threatening manner, and spoke to Eefow to desire them to desist: which they did, and everything became quiet again. My people, who had been in the mountains, now returned with about three gallons of water. I kept buying up the little bread-fruit that was brought to us, and likewise some spears to arm my men with, having only four cutlasses, two of which were in the boat.

As we had no means of improving our situation, I told our people I would wait till sunset, by which time, perhaps, something might happen in our favor; for if we attempted to go at present, we must fight our way through, which we could do more advantageously at night; and that, in the meantime, we would endeavor to get off to the boat what we had bought. The beach was lined with the natives, and we heard nothing but the knocking of stones together, which they had in each hand. I knew very well this was the sign of an attack. At noon I served a cocoanut and a bread-fruit to each person for dinner, and gave some to the chiefs, with whom I continued to appear intimate and friendly. They frequently importuned me to sit down, but I as constantly refused; for it occurred both to Nelson and myself that they intended to seize hold of me, if I gave them such an opportunity. Keeping, therefore, constantly on our guard, we were suffered to eat our uncomfortable meal in some quietness.

After dinner, we began, by little and little, to get our things into the boat, which was a troublesome business, on account of the surf. I carefully watched the motions of the natives, who continued to increase in number; and found that, instead of their intention being to leave us, fires were made, and places fixed on for their stay during the night. Consultations were also held among them, and everything assured me we should be attacked. I sent orders to the master that, when he saw us coming down, he should keep the boat close to the shore, that we might the more readily embark.

The sun was near setting when I gave the word, on which every person who was on shore with me boldly took up his proportion of things and carried them to the boat. The chiefs asked me if I would not stay with them all night. I said "No, I never sleep out of my boat; but in the morning we will again trade with you, and I shall remain till the weather is moderate, that we may go, as we have agreed, to see Poulaho, at Tongataboo." Macca-ackavow then got up and said, "You will not sleep on shore, then, Mattie?" (which directly signifies, we will kill you); and he left me. The onset was now preparing: every one, as I have described before, kept knocking stones together; and Eefow quitted me. All but two or three things were in the boat, when we walked down the beach, every one in a silent kind of horror. We all got into the boat, except one man, who, while I was getting on board, quitted it, and ran up the beach to cast the sternfast off, notwithstanding the master and others called to him to return, while they were hauling me out of the water.

I was no sooner in the boat than the attack began by about two hundred men; the unfortunate poor man who had run up the beach was knocked down, and the stones flew like a shower of shot. Many Indians got hold of the stern rope, and were near hauling the boat on shore, which they would certainly have effected, if I had not had a knife in my pocket, with which I cut the rope. We then hauled off to the grapnel, every one being more or less hurt. At this time I saw five of the natives about the poor man they had killed, and two of them were beating him about the head with stones in their hands.

We had no time to reflect, for, to my surprise, they filled their canoes with stones, and twelve men came off after us to renew the attack; which they did so effectually, as to nearly disable us all. We were obliged to sustain the attack without being able to return it, except with such stones as lodged in the boat. I adopted the expedient of throwing overboard some clothes, which, as I expected, they stopped to pick up; and as it was by this time almost dark, they gave over the attack, and returned towards the shore, leaving us to reflect on our unhappy situation.

The poor man killed by the natives was John Norton: this was his second voyage with me as a quarter-master, and his worthy character made me lament his loss very much. He has left an aged parent, I am told, whom he supported.

We set our sail, and steered along shore by the west side of the island of Tofoa, the wind blowing fresh from the eastward. My mind was employed in considering what was best to be done, when I was solicited by all hands to take them towards home; and when I told them that no hopes of relief for us remained, except what might be found at New Holland, till I came to Timor, a distance of full twelve hundred leagues, where there was a Dutch settlement, but in what part of the island I knew not, they all agreed to live on one ounce of bread and a quarter of a pint of water per day. Therefore, after examining our stock of provisions, and recommending to them, in the most solemn manner, not to depart from their promise, we bore away across a sea where the navigation is but little known, in a small boat, twenty-three feet long from stem to stern, deep laden with eighteen men. I was happy, however, to see that every one seemed better satisfied with our situation than myself.

Our stock of provisions consisted of about one hundred and fifty pounds of bread, twenty-eight gallons of water, twenty pounds of pork, three bottles of wine, and five quarts of rum. The difference between this and the quantity we had on leaving the ship was principally owing to our loss in the bustle and confusion of the attack. A few cocoanuts were in the boat, and some bread-fruit, but the latter was trampled to pieces.

*Sunday, 3d.*—At daybreak the gale increased; the sun rose very fiery and red—a sure indication of a severe gale of wind. At eight it blew a violent storm, and the sea ran very high, so that between the seas the sail was becalmed, and when on the top of the sea, it was too much to have set; but we could not venture to take in the sail, for we were in very imminent danger and distress, the sea curling over the stern of the boat, which obliged us to bail with all our might. A situation more distressing has perhaps seldom been experienced.

Our bread was in bags, and in danger of being spoiled by the wet: to be starved to death was inevitable, if this could not be prevented. I therefore began to examine what clothes there were in the boat, and what other things could be spared; and having determined that only two suits should be kept for each person, the rest was thrown overboard, with some rope and spare sails, which lightened the boat considerably, and we had more room to bail the water out.

Fortunately the carpenter had a good chest in the boat, in which we secured the bread the first favorable moment. His tool-chest also was cleared, and the tools stowed in the bottom of the boat, so that this became a second convenience.

I served a teaspoonful of rum to each person (for we were very wet and cold), with a quarter of a bread-fruit, which was scarce eatable, for dinner. Our engagement was now strictly to be carried into execution, and I was fully determined to make our provisions last eight weeks, let the daily proportion be ever so small.

*Monday, 4th.*—At daylight our limbs were so benumbed, that we could scarcely find the use of them. At this time I served a teaspoonful of rum to each person, from which we all found great benefit. Just before noon, we discovered a small flat island, of a moderate height, bearing west-south-west four or five leagues. I observed our latitude to be 18 degrees 58 minutes south; our longitude was, by account, 3 degrees 4 minutes west from the island of Tofoa, having made a north 72 degrees west course, distance ninety-five miles, since yesterday noon. I divided five small cocoanuts for our dinner, and every one was satisfied. During the rest of that day we discovered ten or twelve other islands, none of which we approached. At night I served a few broken pieces of bread-fruit for supper, and performed prayers.

*Tuesday, 5th.*—The night having been fair, we awoke after a tolerable rest, and contentedly breakfasted on a few pieces of yams that were found in the boat. After breakfast we examined our bread, a great deal of which was damaged and rotten; this, nevertheless, we were glad to keep for use. We passed two islands in the course of the day. For dinner I served some of the damaged bread, and a quarter of a pint of water.

*Wednesday, 6th.*—We still kept our course in the direction of the North of New Holland, passing numerous islands of

various sizes, at none of which I ventured to land. Our allowance for the day was a quarter of a pint of cocoanut milk, and
the meat, which did not exceed two ounces to each person. It
was received very contentedly, but we suffered great drought.
To our great joy we hooked a fish, but we were miserably
disappointed by its being lost in trying to get it into the boat.

As our lodgings were very miserable, and confined for want
of room, I endeavored to remedy the latter defect by putting
ourselves at watch and watch; so that one-half always sat up
while the other lay down on the boat's bottom, or upon a
chest, with nothing to cover us but the heavens. Our limbs
were dreadfully cramped, for we could not stretch them out;
and the nights were so cold, and we so constantly wet, that
after a few hours' sleep, we could scarcely move.

*Thursday, 7th.*—Being very wet and cold, I served a spoon-
ful of rum and a morsel of bread for breakfast. We still kept
sailing among the islands, from one of which two large canoes
put out in chase of us; but we left them behind. Whether these
canoes had any hostile intention against us must remain a doubt:
perhaps we might have benefited by an intercourse with them;
but, in our defenceless situation, to have made the experiment
would have been risking too much.

I imagine these to be the islands called Feejee, as their extent,
direction, and distance from the Friendly Islands answer to the
description given of them by those islanders. Heavy rain came
on at four o'clock, when every person did their utmost to
catch some water, and we increased our stock to thirty-four
gallons, besides quenching our thirst for the first time since
we had been at sea; but an attendant consequence made us pass
the night very miserably, for, being extremely wet, and having
no dry things to shift or cover us, we experienced cold shiverings scarcely to be conceived. Most fortunately for us, the
forenoon, Friday 8th, turned out fair, and we stripped and
dried our clothes. The allowance I issued to-day was an ounce
and a half of pork, a teaspoonful of rum, half a pint of cocoanut
milk, and an ounce of bread. The rum, though so small in

quantity, was of the greatest service. A fishing-line was generally towing from the stern of the boat, but though we saw great numbers of fish, we could never catch one.

In the afternoon we cleaned out the boat, and it employed us till sunset to get everything dry and in order. Hitherto I had issued the allowance by guess, but I now made a pair of scales with two cocoanut shells, and having accidentally some pistol-balls in the boat, twenty-five of which weighed one pound, or sixteen ounces, I adopted one ball as the proportion of weight that each person should receive of bread at the times I served it. I also amused all hands with describing the situation of New Guinea and New Holland, and gave them every information in my power, that, in case any accident happened to me, those who survived might have some idea of what they were about, and be able to find their way to Timor, which at present they knew nothing of more than the name, and some not even that. At night I served a quarter of a pint of water and half an ounce of bread for supper.

*Saturday, 9th.*—About nine in the evening the clouds began to gather, and we had a prodigious fall of rain, with severe thunder and lightning. By midnight we caught about twenty gallons of water. Being miserably wet and cold, I served to the people a teaspoonful of rum each, to enable them to bear with their distressed situation. The weather continued extremely bad, and the wind increased; we spent a very miserable night, without sleep, except such as could be got in the midst of rain. The day brought no relief but its light. The sea broke over us so much, that two men were constantly bailing; and we had no choice how to steer, being obliged to keep before the waves, for fear of the boat filling.

The allowance now regularly served to each person was 1-25th of a pound of bread, and a quarter of a pint of water, at eight in the morning, at noon, and at sunset. To-day I gave about half an ounce of pork for dinner, which, though any moderate person would have considered only as a mouthful, was divided into three or four.

All Sunday, Monday, Tuesday, Wednesday, Thursday, and Friday, the wet weather continued, with heavy seas and squalls. As there was no prospect of getting our clothes dried, my plan was to make every one strip, and wring them through the salt water, by which means they received a warmth that, while wet with rain, they could not have. We were constantly shipping seas and bailing, and were very wet and cold during the night. The sight of the islands which we were always passing served only to increase the misery of our situation. We were very little better than starving, with plenty in view; yet to attempt procuring any relief was attended with so much danger, that prolonging of life, even in the midst of misery, was thought preferable, while there remained hopes of being able to surmount our hardships. For my own part, I consider the general run of cloudy weather to be a blessing of Providence. Hot weather would have caused us to have died with thirst, and probably being so constantly covered with rain or sea protected us from that dreadful calamity.

*Saturday, 16th.*—The sun breaking out through the clouds gave us hopes of drying our wet clothes; but the sunshine was of short duration. We had strong breezes at south-east by south, and dark gloomy weather, with storms of thunder, lightning, and rain. The night was truly horrible, and not a star to be seen, so that our steerage was uncertain.

*Sunday, 17th.*—At dawn of day I found every person complaining, and some of them solicited extra allowance, which I positively refused. Our situation was miserable; always wet, and suffering extreme cold during the night, without the least shelter from the weather. Being constantly obliged to bail, to keep the boat from filling, was perhaps not to be reckoned an evil, as it gave us exercise.

The little rum we had was of great service. When our nights were particularly distressing, I generally served a teaspoonful or two to each person; and it was always joyful tidings when they heard of my intentions.

The night was dark and dismal, the sea constantly breaking

over us, and nothing but the wind and waves to direct our steerage. It was my intention, if possible, to make to New Holland, to the southwest of Endeavor Straits, being sensible that it was necessary to preserve such a situation as would make a southerly wind a fair one; that we might range along the reefs till an opening should be found into smooth water, and we the sooner be able to pick up some refreshments.

Monday and Tuesday were terrible days, heavy rain with lightning. We were always bailing. On Wednesday the 20th, at dawn of day, some of my people seemed half dead. Our appearance was horrible, and I could look no way but I caught the eye of some one in distress. Extreme hunger was now too evident; but no one suffered from thirst, nor had we much inclination to drink—that desire, perhaps, being satisfied through the skin. The little sleep we got was in the midst of water, and we constantly awoke with severe cramps and pains in our bones.

Thursday, Friday and Saturday, we were in the same distressed condition, and I began to fear that such another night or two would put an end to us. On Saturday, however, the wind moderated in the evening, and the weather looked much better, which rejoiced all hands, so that they ate their scanty allowance with more satisfaction than for some time past. The night also was fair; but being always wet with the sea, we suffered much from the cold.

*Sunday, 24th.*—A fine morning, I had the pleasure to see produce some cheerful countenances; and the first time, for fifteen days past, we experienced comfort from the warmth of the sun. We stripped, and hung our clothes up to dry, which were by this time become so threadbare, that they would not keep out either wet or cold.

This afternoon we had many birds about us which are never seen far from land, such as boobies and noddies. As the sea began to run fair, and we shipped but little water, I took the opportunity to examine into the state of our bread, and found that, according to the present mode of issuing, there was a sufficient quantity remaining for twenty-nine days' allowance, by which time I hoped we should be able to reach Timor; but as this was very uncertain, and it was possible that, after all, we might be obliged to go to Java, I determined to proportion the allowance so as to make our stock hold out six weeks. I was apprehensive that this would be ill received, and that it would require my utmost resolution to enforce it; for small as the quantity was which I intended to take away for our future good, yet it might appear to my people like robbing them of life; and some, who were less patient than their companions, I expected would very ill brook it. However, on my representing the necessity of guarding against delays that might be occasioned in our voyage by contrary winds or other causes, and promising to enlarge upon the allowance as we got on, they cheerfully agreed to my proposal. It was accordingly settled that every person should receive 1-25th of a pound of bread for breakfast, and the same quantity for dinner; so that, by omitting the proportion for supper, we had forty-three days' allowance.

*Monday, 25th.*—At noon some noddies came so near to us, that one of them was caught by hand. This bird was about the size of a small pigeon. I divided it, with its entrails, into eighteen portions and by a well-known method at sea, of "Who shall have this?" [1] it was distributed, with the allowance of bread and water for dinner, and ate up, bones and all, with salt water for sauce. I observed the latitude 13 degrees 32 minutes south; longitude made 35 degrees 19 minutes west, course north 89 degrees west, distance one hundred and eight miles.

In the evening, several boobies flying very near to us, we had the good fortune to catch one of them. This bird is as large as a duck. I directed the bird to be killed for supper, and the blood to be given to three of the people who were most distressed for want of food. The body, with the entrails, beak,

---

[1] One person turns his back on the object that is to be divided; another then points separately to the portions, at each of them asking aloud, "Who shall have this?" to which the first answers by naming somebody. This impartial method of division gives every man an equal chance of the best share.

and feet, I divided into eighteen shares, and, with an allowance of bread, which I made a merit of granting, we made a good supper, compared with our usual fare.

Sailing on Tuesday, Wednesday, and Thursday, I at length became satisfied that we were approaching New Holland. This was actually the case; and after passing the reefs which bound that part of the coast, we found ourselves in smooth water. Two islands lay about four miles to the west by north, and appeared eligible for a resting-place, if for nothing more; but on our approach to the nearest island, it proved to be only a heap of stones, and its size too inconsiderable to shelter the boat. We therefore proceeded to the next, which was close to it, and towards the main. We landed to examine if there were any signs of the natives being near us: we saw some old fireplaces, but nothing to make me apprehend that this would be an unsafe situation for the night. Every one was anxious to find something to eat and it was soon discovered that there were oysters on these rocks, for the tide was out; but it was nearly dark, and only a few could be gathered. I determined, therefore, to wait till the morning, when I should know better how to proceed.

*Friday, 29th.*—As there were no appearances to make me imagine that any of the natives were near us, I sent out parties in search of supplies, while others of the people were putting the boat in order. The parties returned, highly rejoiced at having found plenty of oysters and fresh water. I had also made a fire by the help of a small magnifying glass; and, what was still more fortunate, we found among a few things which had been thrown into the boat, and saved, a piece of brimstone and a tinder-box, so that I secured fire for the future.

One of the people had been so provident as to bring away with him from the ship a copper pot: by being in possession of this article, we were enabled to make a proper use of the supply we now obtained; for, with a mixture of bread, and a little pork, we made a stew that might have been relished by people of far more delicate appetites, and of which each person received a full pint. The general complaints of disease among us were a dizziness in the head, great weakness of the joints, and violent tenesmus.

The oysters which we found grew so fast to the rocks, that it was with difficulty they could be broken off, and at length we discovered it to be the most expeditious way to open them where they were fixed. They were of a good size, and well tasted. To add to this happy circumstance, in the hollow of the land there grew some wire-grass, which indicated a moist situation. On forcing a stick about three feet long into the ground, we found water, and with little trouble dug a well, which produced as much as our necessities required.

As the day was the anniversary of the restoration of King Charles II., I named the island Restoration Island. Our short stay there, with the supplies which it afforded us, made a visible alteration for the better in our appearance. Next day, Saturday the 30th, at four o'clock, we were preparing to embark, when about twenty of the natives appeared, running and hallooing to us, on the opposite shore. They were each armed with a spear or lance, and a short weapon which they carried in their left hand. They made signs for us to come to them, but I thought it prudent to make the best of our way. They were naked, and apparently black, and their hair or wool bushy and short.

*Sunday, 31st.*—Many small islands were in sight to the northeast. We landed at one of a good height, bearing north one-half west. The shore was rocky, but the water was smooth, and we landed without difficulty. I sent two parties out, one to the northward, and the other to the southward, to seek for supplies, and others I ordered to stay by the boat. On this occasion fatigue and weakness so far got the better of their sense of duty, that some of the people expressed their discontent at having worked harder than their companions, and declared that they would rather be without their dinner than go in search of it. One person, in particular, went so far as to tell me, with a mutinous look, that he was as good a man as myself. It was not possible for me to judge where this might have an end, if not stopped in time; therefore, to prevent such disputes in future, I determined either to preserve my command, or die in the attempt; and seizing a cutlass, I ordered him to take hold of another and defend himself, on which he called out that I was going to kill him, and immediately made concessions. I did not allow this to interfere further with the harmony of the boat's crew and everything soon became quiet. We here procured some oysters and clams, also some dog-fish caught in the holes of the rocks, and a supply of water.

Leaving this island, which I named Sunday Island, we continued our course towards Endeavor Straits. During our voyage Nelson became very ill, but gradually recovered. Next day we landed at another island, to see what we could get. There were proofs that the island was occasionally visited by natives from New Holland. Encamping on the shore, I sent out one party to watch for turtle, and another to try to catch birds. About midnight the bird party returned, with only twelve noddies, birds which I have already described to be about the size of pigeons; but if it had not been for the folly and obstinacy of one of the party, who separated from the other two, and disturbed the birds, they might have caught a great number. I was so much provoked at my plans being thus defeated, that I gave this offender a good beating. This man afterwards confessed that, wandering away from his companions, he had eaten nine birds raw. Our turtling party had no success.

Tuesday and Wednesday we still kept our course northwest, touching at an island or two for oysters and clams. We had now been six days on the coast of New Holland, and but for the refreshment which our visit to its shore afforded us, it is all but certain that we must have perished. Now, however, it became clear that we were leaving it behind, and were commencing our adventurous voyage through the open sea to Timor.

On Wednesday, June 3rd, at eight o'clock in the evening, we once more launched into the open ocean. Miserable as our situation was in every respect, I was secretly surprised to see that it did not appear to affect any one so strongly as myself. I encouraged every one with hopes that eight or ten days would bring us to a land of safety; and after praying to God for a continuance of His most gracious protection, I served an allowance of water for supper, and directed our course to the west-south-west, to counteract the southerly winds in case they should blow strong. For six days our voyage continued; a dreary repetition of those sufferings which we had experienced before reaching New Holland. In the course of the night we were constantly wet with the sea, and exposed to cold and shiverings; and in the daytime we had no addition to our scanty allowance, save a booby and a small dolphin that we caught, the former on Friday the 5th, and the latter on Monday the 8th. Many of us were ill, and the men complained heavily. On Wednesday the 10th, after a very comfortless night, there was a visible alteration for the worse in many of the people, which gave me great apprehensions. An extreme weakness, swelled legs, hollow and ghastly countenances, a more than common inclination to sleep, with an apparent debility of understanding, seemed to me the melancholy presages of an approaching dissolution.

*Thursday, 11th.*—Every one received the customary allowance of bread and water, and an extra allowance of water was given to those who were most in need. At noon I observed in latitude 9 degrees 41 minutes south; course south 77 degrees west, distance 109 miles; longitude made 13 degrees 49 minutes west. I had little doubt of having now passed the meridian of the eastern part of Timor, which is laid down in 128 degrees east. This diffused universal joy and satisfaction.

*Friday, 12th.*—At three in the morning, with an excess of joy, we discovered Timor bearing from west-south-west to west-north-west, and I hauled on a wind to the north-north-east till daylight, when the land bore from south-west by south to north-east by north; our distance from the shore two leagues. It is not possible for me to describe the pleasure which the blessing of the sight of this land diffused among us. It appeared scarcely credible to ourselves that, in an open boat, and so poorly provided, we should have been able to reach the coast of Timor in forty-one days after leaving Tofoa, having in that time run, by our log, a distance of 3,618 miles and that, notwithstanding our extreme distress, no one should have perished in the voyage.

I have already mentioned that I knew not where the Dutch settlement was situated, but I had a faint idea that it was at the south-west part of the island. I therefore, after daylight, bore away along shore to the south-south-west, which I was the more readily induced to do, as the wind would not suffer us to go towards the north-east without great loss of time.

We coasted along the island in the direction in which I conceived the Dutch settlement to lie, and next day, about two o'clock, I came to a grapnel in a small sandy bay, where we saw a hut, a dog, and some cattle. Here I learned that the Dutch governor resided at a place called Coupang, which was some distance to the north-east. I made signs for one of the Indians who came to the beach to go in the boat and show us the way to Coupang, intimating that I would pay him for his trouble; the man readily complied, and came into the boat. The Indians, who were of a dark tawny color, brought us a few pieces of dried turtle and some ears of Indian corn. This last was the most welcome, for the turtle was so hard, that it could not be eaten without being first soaked in hot water. They offered to bring us some other refreshments, if I would wait; but, as the pilot was willing, I determined to push on. It was about half-past four when we sailed.

*Sunday, 14th.*—At one o'clock in the morning, after the most happy and sweet sleep that ever men enjoyed, we weighed, and continued to keep the east shore on board, in very smooth water. The report of two cannon that were fired gave new life to every one; and soon after, we discovered two square-rigged vessels and a cutter at anchor to the eastward. After hard rowing, we came to a grapnel near daylight, off a small fort and town, which the pilot told me was Coupang.

On landing, I was surrounded by many people, Indians and Dutch, with an English sailor among them. A Dutch captain, named Spikerman, showed me great kindness, and waited on the governor, who was ill, to know at what time I could see him. Eleven o'clock having been appointed for the interview, I desired my people to come on shore, which was as much as some of them could do, being scarce able to walk; they, however, were helped to Captain Spikerman's house, and found tea, with bread and butter, provided for their breakfast.

The abilities of a painter, perhaps, could seldom have been displayed to more advantage than in the delineation of the two groups of figures which at this time presented themselves to each other. An indifferent spectator would have been at a loss which most to admire—the eyes of famine sparkling at immediate relief, or the horror of their preservers at the sight of so many spectres, whose ghastly countenances, if the cause had been unknown, would rather have excited terror than pity. Our bodies were nothing but skin and bone, our limbs were full of sores, and we were clothed in rags: in this condition, with tears of joy and gratitude flowing down our cheeks, the people of Timor beheld us with a mixture of horror, surprise, and pity.

The governor, Mr. William Adrian Van Este, notwithstanding extreme ill health, became so anxious about us, that I saw him before the appointed time. He received me with great affection, and gave me the fullest proofs that he was possessed of every feeling of a humane and good man. Though his infirmity was so great that he could not do the office of a friend himself, he said he would give such orders as I might be certain would procure us every supply we wanted. A house should be immediately prepared for me, and with respect to my people, he said that I might have room for them either at the hospital or on board of Captain Spikerman's ship, which lay in the road. . . .

FATE OF THE MUTINEERS—COLONY OF
PITCAIRN'S ISLAND

The intelligence of the mutiny, and the sufferings of Bligh and his companions, naturally excited a great sensation in England. Bligh was immediately promoted to the rank of commander, and Captain Edwards was despatched to Otaheite, in the *Pandora* frigate, with instructions to search for the *Bounty* and her mutinous crew, and bring them to England. The *Pandora* reached Matavai Bay on the 23d of March, 1791; and even before she had come to anchor, Joseph Coleman, formerly armorer of the *Bounty*, pushed off from shore in a canoe, and came on board. In the course of two days afterwards, the whole of the remainder of the *Bounty's* crew (in number sixteen) then on the island surrendered themselves, with the exception of two, who fled to the mountains where, as it afterwards appeared, they were murdered by the natives.

Nearly twenty years elapsed after the period of the above occurrences, and all recollection of the *Bounty* and her wrecked crew had passed away, when an accidental discovery, as interesting as unexpected, once more recalled public attention to that event. The captain of an American schooner having, in 1808, accidentally touched at an island up to that time supposed to be uninhabited, called Pitcairn's Island, found a community speaking English, who represented themselves as the descendants of the mutineers of the *Bounty*, of whom there was still one man, of the name of Alexander Smith, alive amongst them. Intelligence of this singular circumstance was sent by the American captain (Folger) to Sir Sydney Smith at Valparaiso, and by him transmitted to the Lords of the Admiralty. But the government was at that time perhaps too much engaged in the events of the continental war to attend to the information, nor was anything further heard of this interesting little society until 1814. In that year two British men-of-war, cruising in the Pacific, made Pitcairn's Island, and on nearing the shore, saw plantations regularly and orderly laid out. Soon afterwards they observed a few natives coming down a steep descent, with their canoes on their shoulders, and in a few minutes perceived one of these little vessels darting through a heavy surf, and paddling off towards the ships. But their astonishment may be imagined when, on coming alongside, they were hailed in good English with, "Won't you heave us a rope now?" This being done, a young man sprang up the side with extraordinary activity, and stood on the deck before them. In answer to the question "Who are you?" he replied that his name was Thursday October Christian, son of the late Fletcher Christian, by an Otaheitan mother; that he was the first born on the island, and was so named because he was born on a Thursday in October. All this sounded singular and incredible in the ears of the British captains, Sir Thomas Staines and Mr. Pipon; but they were soon satisfied of its truth. Young Christian was at this time about twenty-four years old, a tall handsome youth, fully six feet high, with black hair, and an open interesting English countenance. As he wore no clothes, except a piece of cloth round his loins, and a straw-hat ornamented with black cock's feathers, his fine figure and well-shaped muscular limbs were displayed to great advantage, and attracted general admiration. His body was much tanned by exposure to the weather; but although his complexion was somewhat brown, it wanted that tinge of red peculiar to the natives of the Pacific. He spoke English correctly both in grammar and pronunciation; and his frank and ingenuous deportment excited in every one the liveliest feelings of compassion and interest. His companion was a fine handsome youth, of seventeen or eighteen years of age, named George Young, son of one of the *Bounty's* midshipmen.

The youths expressed great surprise at everything they saw, especially a cow, which they supposed to be either a huge goat or a horned sow, having never seen any other quadrupeds. When questioned concerning the *Bounty*, they referred the captains to an old man on shore, the only surviving Englishman, whose name, they said, was John Adams, but who proved to be the identical Alexander Smith before-mentioned, having changed his name from some caprice or other. The officers went ashore with the youths, and were received by old Adams (as we shall now call him), who conducted them to his house, and treated them to an elegant repast of eggs, fowl, yams, plantains, bread-fruit, etc. They now learned from him an account of the fate of his companions, who, with himself, preferred accompanying Christian in the *Bounty* to remaining at Otaheite—which account agreed with that he afterwards gave at greater length to Captain Beechey in 1828. Our limits will not permit us to detail all the interesting particulars at length, as we could have wished, but they are in substance as follows:—

It was Christian's object, in order to avoid the vengeance of the British law, to proceed to some unknown and uninhabited island, and the Marquesas Islands were first fixed upon. But Christian, on reading Captain Cartaret's account of Pitcairn's Island, thought it better adapted for the purpose, and shaped his course thither. Having landed and traversed it, they found it every way suitable to their wishes, possessing water, wood, a good soil, and some fruits. Having ascertained all this, they returned on board, and having landed their hogs, goats, and poultry, and gutted the ship of everything that could be useful to them, they set fire to her, and destroyed every vestige that might lead to the discovery of their retreat. This was on the 23d of January 1790. The island was then divided into nine equal portions amongst them a suitable spot of neutral ground being reserved for a village. The poor Otaheitans now found themselves reduced to the condition of mere slaves; but they patiently submitted, and everything went on peacefully for two years. About that time Williams, one of the seamen, having the misfortune to lose his wife, forcibly took the wife of one of the Otaheitans, which, together with their continued ill-usage, so exasperated the latter that they formed a plan for murdering the whole of their oppressors. The plot, however, was discovered, and revealed by the Englishmen's wives, and

two of the Otaheitans were put to death. But the surviving
natives soon afterwards matured a more successful conspiracy,
and in one day murdered five of the Englishmen, including
Christian. Adams and Young were spared at the intercession of
their wives, and the remaining two, M'Koy and Quintal (two
desperate ruffians), escaped to the mountains, whence, however, they soon rejoined their companions. But the further
career of these two villains was short. M'Koy, having been
bred up in a Scottish distillery, succeeded in extracting a bottle
of ardent spirits from the *tee root;* from which time he and
Quintal were never sober, until the former became delirious,
and committed suicide by jumping over a cliff. Quintal being
likewise almost insane with drinking, made repeated attempts
to murder Adams and Young, until they were absolutely compelled, for their own safety, to put him to death, which they
did by felling him with a hatchet.

Adams and Young were at length the only surviving males
who had landed on the island, and being both of a serious turn
of mind, and having time for reflection and repentance, they
became extremely devout. Having saved a Bible and prayer-
book from the *Bounty*, they now performed family worship
morning and evening, and addressed themselves to training up
their own children and those of their unfortunate companions
in piety and virtue. Young, however, was soon carried off by
an asthmatic complaint, and Adams was thus left to continue
his pious labors alone. At the time Captain Staines and Pipon
visited the island, this interesting little colony consisted of about
forty-six persons, mostly grown-up young people, all living in
harmony and happiness together; and not only professing, but
fully understanding and practicing, the precepts and principles
of the Christian religion. Adams had instituted the ceremony
of marriage, and he assured his visitors that not one instance of
debauchery and immoral conduct had occurred amongst them.

The visitors having supplied these interesting people with
some tools, kettles, and other articles, took their leave. The
account which they transmitted home of this newly-discovered

colony was, strange to say, as little attended to by government as that of Captain Folger, and nothing more was heard of Adams and his family for nearly twelve years, when, in 1825, Captain Beechey, in the *Blossom*, bound on a voyage of discovery to Behring Strait, touched at Pitcairn's Island. On the approach of the *Blossom*, a boat came off under all sail towards the ship, containing old Adams and ten of the young men of the island. After requesting and obtaining leave to come on board, the young men sprung up the side, and shook every officer cordially by the hand. Adams, who was grown very corpulent, followed more leisurely. He was dressed in a sailor's shirt and trousers, with a low-crowned hat, which he held in his hand in sailor fashion, while he smoothed down his bald forehead when addressed by the officers of the *Blossom*. The little colony had now increased to about sixty-six, including an English sailor of the name of John Buffett, who, at his own earnest desire, had been left by a whaler. In this man the society luckily found an able and willing schoolmaster. He instructed the children in reading, writing, and arithmetic, and devoutly co-operated with old Adams in affording religious instruction to the community. The officers of the *Blossom* went ashore, and were entertained with a sumptuous repast at young Christian's, the table being spread with plates, knives and forks. Buffett said grace in an emphatic manner; and so strict were they in this respect, that it was not deemed proper to touch a morsel of bread without saying grace both before and after it. The officers slept in the house all night, their bedclothing and sheets consisting of the native cloth made of the native mulberry-tree. The only interruption to their repose was the melody of the evening hymn, which was chanted together by the whole family after the lights were put out; and they were awakened at early dawn by the same devotional ceremony. On Sabbath the utmost decorum was attended to, and the day was passed in regular religious observances.

In consequence of a representation made by Captain Beechey, the British government sent out Captain Waldegrave in 1830, in the *Seringapatam*, with a supply of sailors' blue jackets and trousers, flannels, stockings and shoes, women's dresses, spades, mattocks, shovels, pickaxes, trowels, rakes, etc. He found their community increased to about seventy-nine, all exhibiting the same unsophisticated and amiable characteristics as we have before described. Other two Englishmen had settled amongst them; one of them, called Nobbs, a low-bred, illiterate man, a self-constituted missionary, who was endeavoring to supersede Buffett in his office of religious instruction. The patriarch Adams, it was found, had died in March, 1829, aged sixty-five. While on his deathbed, he had called the heads of families together, and urged upon them to elect a chief; which, however, they had not yet done; but the greatest harmony still prevailed amongst them, notwithstanding Nobb's exertions to form a party of his own. Captain Waldegrave thought that the island, which is about four miles square, might be able to support a thousand persons, upon reaching which number they would naturally emigrate to other islands.

Such is the account of this most singular colony, originating in crime and bloodshed. Of all the repentant criminals on record, the most interesting, perhaps, is John Adams; nor do we know where to find a more beautiful example of the value of early instruction than in the history of this man, who, having run the full career of nearly all kinds of vice, was checked by an interval of leisurely reflection, and the sense of new duties awakened by the power of natural affections.

# THE SINKING OF THE *REPULSE* *

From "Suez to Singapore," BY CECIL BROWN

THE *Repulse* is going down.

The torpedo-smashed *Prince of Wales*, still a half to three-quarters of a mile ahead, is low in the water, half shrouded in smoke, a destroyer by her side.

Japanese bombers are still winging around like vultures, still attacking the *Wales*. A few of those shot down are bright splotches of burning orange on the blue South China Sea.

Men are tossing overboard rafts, lifebelts, benches, pieces of wood, anything that will float. Standing at the edge of the ship, I see one man (Midshipman Peter Gillis, an eighteen-year-old Australian from Sydney) dive from the Air Defense control tower at the top of the main mast. He dives 170 feet and starts to swim away.

Men are jumping into the sea from the four or five defense control towers that segment the main mast like a series of ledges. One man misses his distance, dives, hits the side of the *Repulse*, breaks every bone in his body and crumples into the sea like a sack of wet cement. Another misses his direction and dives from one of the towers straight down the smokestack.

Men are running all along the deck of the ship to get further astern. The ship is lower in the water at the stern and their jump therefore will be shorter. Twelve Royal Marines run back too far, jump into the water and are sucked into the propeller.

The screws of the *Repulse* are still turning. There are five or six hundred heads bobbing in the water. The men are being swept astern because the *Repulse* is still making way and there's a strong tide here, too.

* Reprinted by courtesy of Random House, Inc.

On all sides of me men are flinging themselves over the side. I sit down on the edge of the *Repulse* and take off my shoes. I am very fond of those shoes. A Chinese made them for me just a few days ago in Singapore. They are soft, with a buckle, and they fit well. I carefully place them together and put them down as you do at the foot of your bed before going to sleep.

I have no vision of what is ahead, no concrete thoughts of how to save myself. It is necessarily every man for himself. As I sit there, it suddenly comes to me, the overwhelming, dogmatic conviction. I actually speak the words: "Cecil, you are never going to get out of this."

I see one man jump and land directly on another man. I say to myself: "When I jump I don't want to hurt anyone."

Down below is a mess of oil and debris, and I don't want to jump into that either. I feel my mind getting numb. I look across at the *Wales*. Its guns are flashing and the flames are belching through the grayish-black smoke.

My mind cannot absorb what my eyes see. It is impossible to believe that these two beautiful, powerful, invulnerable ships are going down. But they are. There's no doubt of that.

Men are sliding down the hull of the *Repulse*. Extending around the edge of the ship is a three-inch bulge of steel. The men hit that bulge, shoot off into space and into the water. I say to myself: "I don't want to go down that way. That must hurt their backsides something terrible."

About eight feet to my left there is a gaping hole in the side of the *Repulse*. It is about thirty feet across, with the plates twisted and torn. The hull of the *Repulse* has been ripped open as though a giant had torn apart a tin can. I see an officer dive over the side, dive into the hole underneath the line, dive back inside the ship.

I half turn to look back on the crazy-angled deck of the ship. The padre is beside one of the pom-poms, administering the final rites to a gunner dying beside his gun. The padre seems totally unconcerned by the fact that the *Repulse* is going down at any moment.

*About forty-two men have made their way through the tangled, destroyed, burning interior of the ship, crept, stumbled and scrambled and have clambered through the inside of the dummy smokestack to the top. They find the wire screen across the top of the stack is fastened on the outside. Someone hears their cries, but by then it is too late. The men are trapped.*

*Midshipman Christopher Bros, from St. Andrews, is in the fifteen-inch transmitting station, at the very bottom of the ship. There are twenty-five men with him in the small room, and the sharp list of the ship is making it difficult to get out. The water is pouring in.*

*"Fall in, everyone! March. Up you go," Bros orders.*

*The men start streaming out, starting a climb up six decks. One by one they pass out of the room. The water is coming higher. The water comes in faster than twenty-five men can get out. The twenty-sixth man is trapped. Midshipman Kit Bros, tall, slim, Rugby graduate from Scotland gets all his men out. He is the twenty-sixth man.*

I slide down the hull of the *Repulse* about five feet. There I brace myself in a porthole, take off my tin hat and white cloth anti-flash hood and place them at my feet in the porthole. I lie on the side of the *Repulse*, watching this incredible scene—men bobbing in the water, black oil spreading over the debris-filled, blue sea, the *Wales* obviously sinking, the sky still filled with aircraft and black puffs of anti-aircraft fire.

I don't want to jump, to leave the relative security of this steel for that mess down below. I have no panic in me, no particular fear, just this numbness. I know I'll have to jump sooner or later. I know I cannot lie here and let the water come over me without fighting back somehow. There's no hurry. To jump into the water will hasten the inevitable.

*Captain Tennant on the bridge turns to the navigating officer: "It looks a bit different from this angle, doesn't it, pilot?"*

*The navigating officer nods, but says nothing. The group of officers on the bridge look at each other, and at the skipper.*

*"Well, gentlemen," Captain Tennant says quietly, "you had better get out of it now."*

*"Aren't you coming with us, sir?" two or three eagerly demand simultaneously.*

*The captain smiles, shakes his head negatively, then says impatiently: "Off you go now. There's not much time." They are all hanging on to something, one leg braced to keep an even keel as the ship heels over more and more.*

*"But, Captain," the lieutenant commander says, "you must come with us. You've done all you could for this ship. More than most men could."*

*Captain Tennant does not budge. The men are getting restive. Almost by pre-arrangement they all move toward their skipper. They push him forcibly through the narrow doorway and onto the deck. The* Repulse *is almost on her beam ends. Captain Tennant will go no farther. The officers and men of the bridge seize Captain Tennant and push him over the side. Then they jump into the sea.*

I seem to be glued to the hull of the *Repulse.* Just my head is loose. I turn it from side to side, watching the last-minute evacuation of the ship. Someone slides down the hull, pauses for a moment at the bulge, stands up and makes a beautiful swan dive. That galvanizes me, and I stand up in the porthole and jump, the camera wildly swinging from its strap around my neck.

The jump is about twenty feet. The water is warm; it is not water, but thick oil. My first action is to look at my stop watch. It is smashed at 12.35, one hour and twenty minutes after the first Japanese bomb came through 12,000 feet to crash into the catapult deck of the *Repulse.*

It doesn't occur to me to swim away from the ship until I see others striking out. Then I realize how difficult it is. The oil soaks into my clothes weighting them and I think underwater demons are tugging at me, trying to drag me down. The airless life belt, absorbing oil too, tightens and tautens the preserver cords around my neck. I say to myself: "I'm going to choke to death, I'm going to choke to death."

Next to confined places, all my life, I've been afraid of choking to death. This is the first moment of fear.

I have a ring on my left hand which Martha bought for me on the *Ponte Vecchio* in Florence when we were on our honeymoon. It is rather loose on my finger. With oil on my hands, I'm afraid I will lose it. I clench my fist so that it won't slip off.

I start swimming away with the left hand clenched. With my right hand I make one stroke, tug at the cord around my neck in a futile effort to loosen it, then make another stroke to get away from the ship.

That ring helps save my life. Something like it must have helped save the lives of hundreds of men. Your mind fastens itself on silly, unimportant matters, absorbing your thoughts and stifling the natural instinct of man to panic in the face of death.

I see a life preserver eighteen inches long and four inches thick. It is like a long sausage and I tuck it to me. A small piece of wood appears inviting and I take that too. A barrel comes near, but I reject that because the oil prevents me getting a grip on it. All around me men are swimming, men with blood streaking down their oil-covered faces.

The oil burns in my eyes as though someone is jabbing hot pokers into the eyes. That oil in the eyes is the worst thing. I've swallowed a bit of oil already, and it's beginning to sicken me.

Fifty feet from the ship, hardly swimming at all now, I see the bow of the *Repulse* swing straight into the air like a church steeple. Its red under plates stand out as stark and as gruesome as the blood on the faces of the men around me. Then the tug and draw of the suction of 32,000 tons of steel sliding to the bottom hits me. Something powerful, almost irresistible, snaps at my feet. It feels as though someone were trying to pull my legs out by the hip sockets. But I am more fortunate than some others. They are closer to the ship. They are sucked back.

When the *Repulse* goes down it sends over a huge wave, a wave of oil. I happen to have my mouth open and I take aboard considerable oil. That makes me terribly sick at the stomach.

As I swim in the water, other men are hanging on to pieces of wood, floating life belts and debris. Four or five times I see blood- and oil-covered hands loosen their grip and slide beneath the water.

I do not see Gallagher anywhere. It is difficult to recognize anyone through the oil on his face. About fifteen yards away I see someone struggling and fighting in the water. I finally recognize Sub-Lieutenant Page. There are two men near by. The injured Page is struggling to get out of the two life belts wrapped around him, the belts he had on when he was tossed overboard.

*"I'm hurt,"* Page is crying. *"I'm hurt. I'm no good any more. You take the belts."*

*The men can't swim, but Page is insisting and sobbing, peeling out of the belts. "Take them; I'm no good any more."*

Page prevails on the two men to accept the belts. They are saved, and Sub-Lieutenant Page slips underneath the water.

Someone calls to me, "Are you all right, War Correspondent?"

"Yes," I say, opening my mouth to say it, and I take aboard more oil. I decide if anyone asks me any more questions I will wave my hand, if I have the strength. I am terribly tired.

A small table, about three feet square, floats by. I grab hold of one leg, but it is too slippery and I know I will lose it. I scramble up on top and lay there for a moment. And then I watch the *Prince of Wales* go down, a big, dark thing sliding into nothingness.

Now the sea seems really deserted, with just men and mess floating on the surface.

As I swim I hear one man yell, "An electric eel just shocked me!"

There are no sharks that I can see, although this area of the South China Sea is usually filled with sharks.

There is a Carley float about three-quarters of a mile away, and a destroyer about two miles distant. I have no intention of trying to reach them. I only want to rest on top of the small table. The conviction that this is my finish is still strong within me. Besides, I want to conserve my strength, want jealously to guard it during the hours before death comes.

I say to myself, "I've gotta remember all this; I gotta remember all this." And the next minute, "What the hell's the use? I will never be able to report this story."

It's so easy to close your eyes, shut out this sight, and fiercely forget what the eyes already have seen.

Strangely enough, I don't think of my wife, my family, or my childhood. I constantly glance around to see if I recognize any of the men, and I am especially watching for Gallagher. I don't see him but I do recognize two or three officers and we smile wanly at each other.

As I lie on the table I pull off my heavy cotton khaki socks. They are soaked and weighted by oil, as heavy as iron. I let the soaked socks slip into the water and feel five pounds lighter. As the warmth of the South China Sea slushes between my toes I think, "That feels wonderful on my feet."

The effort, little as it is, exhausts me. The drag of the camera around my neck and the choking by the life-preserver cord convince me I ought to do something about them. But the water-and-oil-soaked cord of the preserver is knotted and I can't unfasten it. As for the camera, I feel I'd rather drown than throw it away.

I know that I should somehow try to get rid of some of my clothes. The oil makes their weight feel like tons. Tears are pouring out of my eyes from the oil, and I sense tiny salty rivulets running down my oil-covered face.

That oil! It coagulates around each body, around the debris, around the men. One officer in the water shouts, "Spread out a bit, men, and let's get out of this oil." Some of the men do it;

others are reluctant to get away from pieces of wood. Others depend on absorbing some strength from men around them. Not only miserable but drowning men love company.

One officer swims by me and says, "Let's make for that raft." I shake my head no, and he swims on.

About ten yards from me I see two youngsters—they must be about eighteen—laughing and joking, and I hear one say, "I'll race you to Singapore." We are fifty miles from shore and one hundred and fifty miles north of the city those youngsters are talking about.

It's the tide, not my efforts, that brings me near the Carley float. The Carley contraptions are rafts, fifteen feet long, ten feet wide, and bounded on all sides by a foot-high bulge. Extending around the bulge is a rope on which men can grab hold.

The raft toward which the tide carries me is jammed. There are men inside, men sitting solid on the bulge at the edge, and every handhold on the rope is occupied. Obviously there is no room for me, so I make no effort whatsoever, letting the tide carry me where it wants. It carries me to that raft.

A Royal Marine sitting on the edge calls to me when I am ten feet away, "Just a bit more, just a bit more." I don't answer, just look at him across that ten-foot chasm.

Gradually I draw nearer. He extends his hand as far as he can and I stretch out my hand. For five minutes our hands are three inches apart, but I don't have the energy to bridge that tiny gap. Once again the tide does it for me. Our hands meet, clasp and I'm yanked toward the raft, leaving the small table which thus far has saved my life.

The twenty-year-old marine, Morris Graney, pushes one of the men sitting on the bulge back inside the raft, on top of another man, to make way for me. Then he pulls me onto the bulge and holds me there.

His first remark is: "My Lord, do you still have your camera?"

"Yes."

"Are you all right?"

I nod.

"Can you sit here?"

I say, "Yes, I am all right."

Actually I'm not, and almost fall face forward into the water. Graney grabs me, takes one of my hands—my right hand, since my left is still clenched to prevent my ring from falling off—and forces it to grasp the lifebelt of a man inside the raft.

"Hang onto him," Graney says.

I hang on.

The raft tosses and heaves with the swell of the sea. Men are bobbing and swimming on all sides near the raft, some trying to reach it, some hoping eventually to get a hand hold on it. We want to reach a destroyer which is stationary about a mile or a mile and a half away. There is one paddle on board, and some one inside, using the paddle, is calling, "Heave ho, heave ho, heave ho!"

Graney says, "Let's all sing." Not many voices join in his choice, "When Irish Eyes Are Smiling," but the voices that do are cheerful.

Graney wears only shorts and his thick chest is covered with oil. His brown hair hangs over his forehead and into his eyes. I think just the sight of Graney helps many a man. He is almost six feet tall, husky, almost barrel-chested. Above a square jaw he has a slim, delicate mustache and blue, kind, shy eyes. All the time the only one definable emotion expressed in those eyes is amusement. Graney's amusement is enough, though, as the raft tosses. I am deathly sick at the stomach, and dizzy, too, and again almost fall forward. Graney grabs me.

"You stay right here," he says, slapping me on the shoulder.

"I am very tired," I say, "and I want to rest down there."

Graney slaps me across the face, saying, "Now, none of that. You stay right here with me."

"No. Those other men aren't on the raft," I say. "I am tired, and I can rest better in the water."

Graney's hand is digging into my arm and shoulder. It hurts, but somehow I don't protest. I just know it hurts.

"We're watching those other men," Graney says sharply. "They're all right. You stay right here with us."

I'm not convinced, and twist my head around to look inside the raft. It's the wrong time to do that. Men inside are vomiting and glassy-eyed, all of them black with oil. Two men have just died and their bodies are being gently hustled over the side to make room for more men. I feel a twinge of pity at the sight of it, but it seems an eminently practical thing to do.

Six or seven Jap bombers are roaring over again at about 5,000 feet.

"They're coming over to machine-gun us!" someone says.

"Shut up that guff!" Graney growls, because we all feel bad enough as it is.

"If they come over to machine-gun us," a voice suggests, "dive under the water."

I think to myself: "If I have to dive under the water, I'm never coming up again."

They don't swoop down on us and they don't drop bombs. They just go on. It isn't Japanese chivalry or Bushido. They're just out of bombs and ammunition. With the planes gone and heads turned from the sky to the horizon, we get the impression that the destroyer is getting farther and farther away. In fact, we see one of our destroyers steam away. Someone calls in panic, "They're all going." A reply comes from somewhere inside the raft: "They'll wait for us, don't worry."

Men hanging onto the rope around the side are kicking furiously. One man says, "I'm going to swim for it." He starts out, but when he is ten yards away he calls, "I can't make it—I'm coming back." And he does. Men near me slip off the raft to go to the help of men who can be seen going under. They do it several times.

As the minutes go on and we seem to be getting no nearer to the destroyer, the morale on the raft begins to slip lower and lower. Graney is one of the first to recognize this. "Keep kicking, keep paddling!" he shouts. "We will soon be there!"

As we drew near the destroyer he said, "All right, now, it's

'Anchors Aweigh'!" And again he starts singing. Almost every one joins in then, because for the first time we seem to have a chance of rescue.

Rafts and men are converging on the destroyer from all directions. We can already see dripping figures being hauled onto the deck of the ship. Through a megaphone an officer on the bridge is shouting something at us, but we can't make it out.

"They want us to hurry," one man in our raft says. "Anyway, that's what I'd be calling if I was on the bridge."

The oil around the destroyer seems about two feet thick, solid oil. To me it looks like dirty black castor oil. And it tastes the same.

A rope with a loop at the end is tossed thirty feet from the destroyer to us. We miss it. The rope is hauled back and again is hurled. Someone grabs it, but Graney tears it out of his hands and roughly passes the loop over me. "We have an American war correspondent here," he shouts at the destroyer. Then he waves and shouts, "Heave up, heave up!"

He asks solicitously, "Can you hold onto the rope?"

"Of course. Don't worry about me. I'm all right."

And the men on the destroyer pull me off the edge of the Carley float. I sink underneath the oil, and for ten feet while I'm dragged underneath the surface I feel I'm plowing my way through some kind of a solid wall. The pressure pounds at my head like a great rubber hammer.

Then I'm beside the destroyer. A wooden ladder hangs over the side.

"Grab hold—hurry!" someone on the destroyer yells down.

I try to reach the bottom rung and can't. It is four feet above the water. The gentle undulation of the oily waves brings me nearer. I make a lunge and get my right hand on the bottom rung.

"You'll have to help yourself," a man on the destroyer calls.

Down the side of the destroyer there are other ladders, and rope mats and nets; but I am afraid if I lose my grip this time I can never make another try.

A frenzied voice calls, "Hang on, hang on! But hurry!"

I get up the ladder and four men drag me over the taffrail. The deck is burning hot on my bare feet. They strip off my clothes and someone hands me a heavy woolen parka. I put it on, and one of the officers says, "Are you all right?"

"I'm fine," I say. "Who has a camera on board this ship?"

The officer doesn't know, but he calls over another man, saying, "Find this man a camera. There must be one on board."

The rating scoots off, and I stand there while Graney, who has just been brought on board, keeps urging me to sit down and rest.

"There's plenty of time for that," I insist. "I've got to get a camera."

Graney empties the pockets of my cover-alls, bush jacket and shorts, and hands over the precious notebook in which I kept this account of the battle. I open the notebook, and see every page is water-and-oil-soaked but still legible.

About a half dozen men are dead on the deck of the destroyer. Others are being sick from the oil. Some men are laughing and joking and inquiring after their special buddies.

The hospital of the sick bay is jammed, and some of the dead are being carried out and laid on the deck. Men with blood on their faces are being carried back to the sick bay for attention. Still more survivors are being brought on board, and I snap pictures. I use up all the film. They find me another camera and I use all that film.

By then my feet are blistered from the hot deck, and I'm leaping from hot deck plate to hatch, to another hot plate, to another hatch, as though playing hopscotch.

The destroyer's chief engineer, Frank McLeod of Southsea, Hampshire, comes up and says, "I have a pair of shoes for you." He hands over a pair of the "Suitcase Simpson" caliber. "Those shoes," he says, "were last worn by one of the three survivors of the *Hood*. I gave them to a midshipman when I pulled *him* out of the water." He gives me an Engineers' Log Book, too, for taking notes, and I scurry about the ship, talking with survivors of the *Repulse* and the *Prince of Wales,* fitting the details of their personal experiences together.

The destroyer is the *Electra,* which took 1,100 men out of the hell of Dunkirk to England.

There is no bitterness among these men this afternoon about the absence of aircraft protection, just regret that they've lost their ship. One man is wailing that he'd lost the pictures of his girl friend, his mother, his dad.

Another says he's lost his penknife, to which a third replies, "Now quit your grousing. Each of us lost exactly the same thing—everything!"

After about an hour, three Brewster Buffaloes come roaring over, sweeping ten feet from the ship. The Japs are long gone by now.

In the steaming hot wardroom of the *Electra* forty or fifty officers are drinking tea, most all naked to the waist. The heat is stifling, and as we sit there—I taking notes—the sweat pours out of us as though we are under a shower.

As the sweat drips from me, I remember how exactly twenty-four hours before I sat in the comfortable wardroom of the *Repulse,* talking with the officers of the battle cruiser, and thinking of the British tendency to underestimate the enemy, to look at them solely through British eyes. "It's better," I said, "to consider your enemy twice as good as you are and twice as smart. Then you won't be surprised."

The British officers, twenty-four hours before had been amiable, cheerful and skeptical. Now in that smelling, sweltering wardroom of the *Electra,* one of the officers of the *Repulse* comes up with a rueful smile on his face and says: "You told us not to underestimate the enemy."

"Yes, I know," I say, "but I take no satisfaction in that now —not even grim satisfaction."

Some men sit at the table, their heads buried in their arms. A number of them have bandages on their heads. Men are asking each other, "Did you see So-and-So?"

The remarks I hear are these:

"The first thing I'm going to do is send a cable home."

"This is a terrible blow."

"I hope they've learned their lesson. We must have aircraft protection."

"Those Japs were bloody good."

"This shows that if a determined attack is pressed home, you can sink battleships."

"They'll get you every time without escort and aircraft."

"Did you enjoy your swim?"

"I owe him two dollars. If he's alive I'll give it to him. If he's dead he won't want it."

"I hear they're going to form us into a naval brigade, give us rifles and tell us to kill some Japs."

"We'll handle those Japs yet."

I want to know about Captain Tennant. One man speaks up: "I saw him floating face down in the water." I can find no one who has seen the other war correspondent. Gallagher gone? I can't believe it.

Down there in the wardroom I am told the sequence of attacks on the *Prince of Wales*.

The attack was similar to our own. High-level bombers and torpedo-carrying bombers. With four torpedoes in the *Wales*, Admiral Phillips said: "Tell the *Express* [which was then alongside the *Wales*] to signal to Singapore for tugs to tow us home."

It was obvious the Admiral hadn't yet made up his mind that the ship was going to sink.

I ask a lieutenant commander from the *Wales* about Admiral Phillips and Captain Leach.

They were last seen standing on the bridge of the *Prince of Wales*.

"The admiral and the captain stood there together," the officer says. "They would not go. As we started away, Captain Leach waved, and called out: 'Good-bye. Thank you. Good luck. God bless you.'"

Then the water rose up to meet them, meeting and then covering them.

# BLOW UP WITH THE BRIG

## From "After Dark," by Wilkie Collins

I have got an alarming confession to make. I am haunted by a Ghost.

If you were to guess for a hundred years, you would never guess what my ghost is. I shall make you laugh to begin with—and afterward I shall make your flesh creep. My Ghost is the ghost of a Bedroom Candlestick. Yes, a bedroom candlestick and candle, or a flat candlestick and candle—put it which way you like—that is what haunts me. I wish it was something pleasanter and more out of the common way; a beautiful lady, or a mine of gold and silver, or a cellar of wine and a coach and horses, and such like. But, being what it is, I must take it for what it is, and make the best of it; and I shall thank you kindly if you will help me out by doing the same.

I am not a scholar myself, but I make bold to believe that the haunting of any man with anything under the sun begins with the frightening of him. At any rate, the haunting of me with a bedroom candlestick and candle began with the frightening of me with a bedroom candlestick and candle—the frightening of me half out of my life; and, for the time being, the frightening of me altogether out of my wits. That is not a very pleasant thing to confess before stating the particulars; but perhaps you will be the readier to believe that I am not a downright coward, because you find me bold enough to make a clean breast of it already, to my own great disadvantage so far.

Here are the particulars, as well as I can put them:

I was apprenticed to the sea when I was about as tall as my own walking-stick; and I made good enough use of my time to be fit for a mate's berth at the age of twenty-five years.

It was in the year eighteen hundred and eighteen, or nine-

teen, I am not quite certain which, that I reached the before-
mentioned age of twenty-five. You will please to excuse my
memory not being very good for dates, names, numbers, places,
and such like. No fear, though, about the particulars I have
undertaken to tell you of; I have got them all ship-shape in my
recollection; I can see them, at this moment, as clear as noonday
in my own mind.

Well, in eighteen hundred and eighteen, or nineteen, when
there was peace in our part of the world—and not before it
was wanted, you will say—there was fighting, of a certain
scampering, scrambling kind, going on in that old battlefield
which we seafaring men know by the name of the Spanish
Main.

The possessions that belonged to the Spaniards in South
America had broken into open mutiny and declared for themselves years before. There was plenty of bloodshed between
the new government and the old; but the new had got the best
of it, for the most part, under one General Bolivar—a famous
man in his time, though he seems to have dropped out of people's memories now. Englishmen and Irishmen with a turn for
fighting, and nothing particular to do at home, joined the general as volunteers; and some of our merchants found it a good
venture to send supplies across the ocean to the popular side.
There was risk enough, of course, in doing this; but where one
speculation of the kind succeeded, it made up for two, at the
least, that failed. And that's the true principle of trade, wherever I have met with it, the world over.

Among the Englishmen who were concerned in this Spanish-
American business, I, your humble servant, happened in a small
way to be one.

I was then mate of a brig belonging to a certain firm in the
city, which drove a sort of general trade, mostly in queer out-
of-the-way places, as far from home as possible; and which
freighted the brig, in the year I am speaking of, with a cargo of
gunpowder for General Bolivar and his volunteers. Nobody
knew anything about our instructions, when we sailed, except

the captain; and he didn't half seem to like them. I can't rightly say how many barrels of powder we had on board, or how much each barrel held—I only know we had no other cargo. The name of the brig was the *Good Intent*—a queer name enough, you will tell me, for a vessel laden with gunpowder, and sent to help a revolution. And as far as this particular voyage was concerned, so it was. I mean that for a joke, and I hope you will encourage me by laughing at it.

The *Good Intent* was the craziest old tub of a vessel I ever went to sea in, and the worst found in all respects. She was two hundred and thirty, or two hundred and eighty tons burden, I forget which; and she had a crew of eight, all told—nothing like as many as we ought by rights to have had to work the brig. However, we were well and honestly paid our wages; and we had to set that against the chance of foundering at sea, and, on this occasion, likewise the chance of being blown up into the bargain.

In consideration of the nature of our cargo, we were harassed with new regulations, which we didn't at all like, relative to smoking our pipes and lighting our lanterns; and, as usual in such cases, the captain, who made the regulations, preached what he didn't practice. Not a man of us was allowed to have a bit of lighted candle in his hand when he went below—except the skipper; and he used his light, when he turned in, or when he looked over his charts on the cabin table, just as usual.

This light was a common kitchen candle or "dip," and it stood in an old battered flat candlestick, with all the japan worn and melted off, and all the tin showing through. It would have been more seamanlike and suitable if he had had a lamp or a lantern; but he stuck to his old candlestick; and that same old candlestick has ever afterward stuck to *me*.

Well (I said "well" before, but it's a word that helps a man on like), we sailed in the brig, and shaped our course first for the Virgin Islands in the West Indies; and, after sighting them, we made for the Leeward Islands next, and then stood on due south, till the lookout at the masthead hailed the deck and said he saw land. That land was the coast of South America. We had had a wonderful voyage so far. We had lost none of our spars or sails, and not a man of us had been harassed to death at the pumps. It wasn't often the *Good Intent* made such a voyage as that, I can tell you.

I was sent aloft to make sure about the land, and I did make sure of it.

When I reported the same to the skipper, he went below, and had a look at his letter of instructions and the chart. When he came on deck again, he altered our course a trifle to the eastward—I forgot the point on the compass, but that don't matter. What I do remember is, that it was dark before we closed in with the land. We kept the lead going, and hove the brig to in from four to five fathoms water, or it might be six—I can't say for certain. I kept a sharp eye to the drift of the vessel, none of us knowing how the currents ran on that coast. We all wondered why the skipper didn't anchor; but he said No, he must first show a light at the foretopmasthead, and wait for an answering light on shore. We did wait, and nothing of the sort appeared. It was starlight and calm. What little wind there was came in puffs off the land. I suppose we waited, drifting a little to the westward, as I made it out, best part of an hour before anything happened—and then, instead of seeing the light on shore, we saw a boat coming toward us, rowed by two men only.

We hailed them, and they answered "Friends!" and hailed us by our name. They came on board. One of them was an Irishman, and the other was a coffee-colored native pilot, who jabbered a little English.

The Irishman handed a note to our skipper, who showed it to me. It informed us that the part of the coast we were off was not oversafe for discharging our cargo, seeing that spies of the enemy (that is to say, of the old government) had been taken and shot in the neighborhood the day before. We might trust the brig to the native pilot; and he had his instructions to take us to another part of the coast. The note was signed by the proper parties; so we let the Irishman go back alone in the boat, and allowed the pilot to exercise his lawful authority over the brig. He kept us stretching off from the land till noon the next day—his instructions, seemingly, ordering him to keep us well out of sight of the shore. We only altered our course in the afternoon, so as to close in with the land again a little before midnight.

This same pilot was about as ill-looking a vagabond as ever I saw; a skinny, cowardly, quarrelsome mongrel, who swore at the men in the vilest broken English, till they were every one of them ready to pitch him overboard. The skipper kept them quiet, and I kept them quiet; for the pilot being given us by our instructions, we were bound to make the best of him. Near nightfall, however, with the best will in the world to avoid it, I was unlucky enough to quarrel with him.

He wanted to go below with his pipe, and I stopped him, of course, because it was contrary to orders. Upon that he tried to hustle by me, and I put him away with my hand. I never meant to push him down; but somehow I did. He picked himself up as quick as lightning, and pulled out his knife. I snatched it out of his hand, slapped his murderous face for him, and threw his weapon overboard. He gave me one ugly look, and walked aft. I didn't think much of the look then, but I remembered it a little too well afterward.

We were close in with the land again, just as the wind failed us, between eleven and twelve that night, and dropped our anchor by the pilot's directions.

It was pitch-dark, and a dead, airless calm. The skipper was on deck, with two of our best men for watch. The rest were below, except the pilot, who coiled himself up, more like a snake than a man, on the forecastle. It was not my watch till four in the morning. But I didn't like the look of the night, or the pilot, or the state of things generally, and I shook myself down on deck to get my nap there, and be ready for anything at a moment's notice. The last I remember was the skipper whispering to me that he didn't like the look of things either, and that he would go below and consult his instructions again. That is the last I remember, before the slow, heavy, regular roll of the old brig on the groundswell rocked me off to sleep.

I was waked by a scuffle on the forecastle and a gag in my mouth. There was a man on my breast and a man on my legs, and I was bound hand and foot in half a minute.

The brig was in the hands of the Spaniards. They were swarming all over her. I heard six heavy splashes in the water, one after another. I saw the captain stabbed to the heart as he came running up the companion, and I heard a seventh splash in the water. Except myself, every soul of us on board had been murdered and thrown into the sea. Why I was left, I couldn't think, till I saw the pilot stoop over me with a lantern and look, to make sure of who I was. There was a devilish grin on his face, and he nodded his head at me, as much as to say, "*You* were the man who hustled me down and slapped my face, and I mean to play the game of cat and mouse with you in return for it!"

I could neither move nor speak, but I could see the Spaniards take off the main hatch and rig the purchases for getting up the cargo. A quarter of an hour afterward I heard the sweeps of a schooner, or other small vessel, in the water. The strange craft was laid alongside of us, and the Spaniards set to work to discharge our cargo into her. They all worked hard except the pilot; and he came from time to time, with his lantern, to have another look at me, and to grin and nod always in the same devilish way. I am old enough now not to be ashamed of confessing the truth, and I don't mind acknowledging that the pilot frightened me.

The fright, and the bonds, and the gag, and the not being able to stir hand or foot, had pretty nigh worn me out by the time the Spaniards gave over work. This was just as the dawn broke. They had shifted a good part of our cargo on board their vessel, but nothing like all of it, and they were sharp enough to be off with what they had got before daylight.

I need hardly say that I had made up my mind by this time

to the worst I could think of. The pilot, it was clear enough, was one of the spies of the enemy, who had wormed himself into the confidence of our consignees without being suspected. He, or more likely his employers, had got knowledge enough of us to suspect what our cargo was; we had been anchored for the night in the safest berth for them to surprise us in; and we had paid the penalty of having a small crew, and consequently an insufficient watch. All this was clear, but what did the pilot mean to do with *me?*

On the word of a man, it makes my flesh creep now, only to tell you what he did with me.

After all the rest of them were out of the brig, except the pilot and two Spanish seamen, these last took me up, bound and gagged as I was, lowered me into the hold of the vessel, and laid me along on the floor, lashing me to it with ropes' ends, so that I could just turn from one side to the other, but could not roll myself fairly over, so as to change my place. They then left me. Both of them were the worse for liquor; but the devil of a pilot was sober—mind that!—as sober as I am at the present moment.

I lay in the dark for a little while, with my heart thumping as if it was going to jump out of me. I lay about five minutes or so when the pilot came down into the hold alone.

He had the captain's cursed flat candlestick and a carpenter's awl in one hand, and a long thin twist of cotton-yarn, well oiled, in the other. He put the candlestick, with a new "dip" candle lighted in it, down on the floor about two feet from my face, and close against the side of the vessel. The light was feeble enough; but it was sufficient to show a dozen barrels of gunpowder or more left all round me in the hold of the brig. I began to suspect what he was after the moment I noticed the barrels. The horrors laid hold of me from head to foot, and the sweat poured off my face like water.

I saw him go next to one of the barrels of powder standing against the side of the vessel in a line with the candle, and about three feet, or rather better, away from it. He bored a hole in the side of the barrel with his awl, and the horrid powder came trickling out, as black as hell, and dripped into the hollow of his hand, which he held to catch it. When he had got a good handful, he stopped up the hole by jamming one end of his oiled twist of cotton yarn fast into it, and he then rubbed the powder into the whole length of the yarn till he had blackened every hairbreadth of it.

The next thing he did—as true as I sit here, as true as the heaven above us all—the next thing he did was to carry the free end of his long, lean, black, frightful slow-match to the lighted candle alongside my face. He tied it (the bloody-minded villain!) in several folds round the tallow dip, about a third of the distance down, measuring from the flame of the wick to the lip of the candlestick. He did that; he looked to see that my lashings were all safe; and then he put his face close to mine, and whispered in my ear, "Blow up with the brig!"

He was on deck again the moment after, and he and the two others shoved the hatch on over me. At the furthest end from where I lay they had not fitted it down quite true, and I saw a blink of daylight glimmering in when I looked in that direction. I heard the sweeps of the schooner fall into the water—splash! splash! fainter and fainter, as they swept the vessel out in the dead calm, to be ready for the wind in the offing. Fainter and fainter, splash, splash! for a quarter of an hour more.

While those sounds were in my ears, my eyes were fixed on the candle.

It had been freshly lighted. If left to itself, it would burn for between six and seven hours. The slow-match was twisted round it about a third of the way down, and therefore the flame would be about two hours reaching it. There I lay, gagged, bound, lashed to the floor; seeing my own life burning down with the candle by my side—there I lay, alone on the sea, doomed to be blown to atoms, and to see that doom drawing on, nearer and nearer with every fresh second of time, through nigh on two hours to come: powerless to help myself, and speechless to call for help to others. The wonder to me is that

I didn't cheat the flame, the slow-match, and the powder, and die of the horror of my situation before my first half-hour was out in the hold of the brig.

I can't exactly say how long I kept the command of my senses after I had ceased to hear the splash of the schooner's sweeps in the water. I can trace back everything I did and everything I thought, up to a certain point; but, once past that, I get all abroad, and lose myself in my memory now, much as I lost myself in my own feelings at the time.

The moment the hatch was covered over me, I began, as every other man would have begun in my place, with a frantic effort to free my hands. In the mad panic I was in, I cut my flesh with the lashings as if they had been knife-blades, but I never stirred them. There was less chance still of freeing my legs, or of tearing myself from the fastenings that held me to the floor. I gave in when I was all but suffocated for want of breath. The gag, you will please to remember, was a terrible enemy to me; I could only breathe freely through my nose— and that is but a poor vent when a man is straining his strength as far as ever it will go.

I gave in and lay quiet, and got my breath again, my eyes glaring and straining at the candle all the time. While I was staring at it, the notion struck me of trying to blow out the flame by pumping a long breath at it suddenly through my nostrils. It was too high above me, and too far away from me, to be reached in that fashion. I tried, and tried, and tried; and then I gave in again, and lay quiet again, always with my eyes glaring at the candle, and the candle glaring at *me*. The splash of the schooner's sweeps was very faint by this time. I could only just hear them in the morning stillness. Splash! splash!— fainter and fainter—splash! splash!

Without exactly feeling my mind going, I began to feel it getting queer as early as this. The snuff of the candle was growing taller and taller, and the length of tallow between the flame and the slow-match, which was the length of my life, was getting shorter and shorter. I calculated that I had rather less than an hour and a half to live.

An hour and a half! Was there a chance in that time of a boat pulling off to the brig from shore? Whether the land near which the vessel was anchored was in possession of our side, or in possession of the enemy's side, I made out that they must, sooner or later, send to hail the brig merely because she was a stranger in those parts. The question for *me* was, how soon? The sun had not risen yet, as I could tell by looking through the chink in the hatch. There was no coast village near us, as we all knew, before the brig was seized, by seeing no lights on shore. There was no wind, as I could tell by listening, to bring any strange vessel near. If I had had six hours to live, there might have been a chance for me, reckoning from sunrise to noon. But with an hour and a half, which had dwindled to an hour and a quarter by this time—or, in other words, with the earliness of the morning, the uninhabited coast, and the dead calm all against me—there was not the ghost of a chance. As I felt that, I had another struggle—the last—with my bonds, and only cut myself the deeper for my pains. I gave in once more, and lay quiet, and listened for the splash of the sweeps.

Gone! Not a sound could I hear but the blowing of a fish now and then on the surface of the sea, and the creak of the brig's crazy old spars, as she rolled gently from side to side with the little swell there was on the quiet water.

An hour and a quarter. The wick grew terribly as the quarter slipped away, and the charred top of it began to thicken and spread out mushroom-shape. It would fall off soon. Would it fall off red-hot, and would the swing of the brig cant it over the side of the candle and let it down on the slow-match? If it would, I had about ten minutes to live instead of an hour.

This discovery set my mind for a minute on a new tack altogether. I began to ponder with myself what sort of death blowing up might be. Painful! Well, it would be, surely, too sudden for that. Perhaps just one crash inside me, or outside me, or both; and nothing more! Perhaps not even a crash; that and death and the scattering of this living body of mine into millions of fiery sparks, might all happen in the same instant! I couldn't make it out; I couldn't settle how it would be. The minute of calmness in my mind left it before I had half done thinking; and I got all abroad again.

When I came back to my thoughts, or when they came back to me (I can't say which), the wick was awfully tall, the flame was burning with a smoke above it, the charred top was broad and red, and heavily spreading out to its fall.

My despair and horror at seeing it took me in a new way, which was good and right, at any rate, for my poor soul. I tried to pray—in my own heart, you will understand, for the gag put all lip-praying out of my power. I tried, but the candle seemed to burn it up in me. I struggled hard to force my eyes from the slow, murdering flame, and to look up through the chink in the hatch at the blessed daylight. I tried once, tried twice; and gave it up. I next tried only to shut my eyes, and keep them shut—once—twice—and the second time I did it. "God bless old mother, and sister Lizzie; God keep them both, and forgive *me*." That was all I had time to say, in my own heart, before my eyes opened again, in spite of me, and the flame of the candle flew into them, flew all over me, and burned up the rest of my thoughts.

I couldn't hear the fish blowing now; I couldn't hear the creak of the spars; I couldn't think; I couldn't feel the sweat of my own death agony on my face—I could only look at the heavy, charred top of the wick. It swelled, tottered, bent over to one side, dropped—red-hot at the moment of its fall—black and harmless, even before the swing of the brig had canted it over into the bottom of the candlestick.

I caught myself laughing.

Yes! laughing at the safe fall of the bit of wick. But for the gag, I should have screamed with laughing. As it was, I shook with it inside me—shook till the blood was in my head, and I was all but suffocated for want of breath. I had just sense enough left to feel that my own horrid laughter at that awful moment was a sign of my brain going at last. I had just sense enough left to make another struggle before my mind broke loose like a frightened horse, and ran away with me.

One comforting look at the blink of daylight through the hatch was what I tried for once more. The fight to force my eyes from the candle and to get that one look at the daylight was the hardest I had had yet; and I lost the fight. The flame had hold of my eyes as fast as the lashings had hold of my hands. I couldn't look away from it. I couldn't even shut my eyes, when I tried that next, for the second time. There was the wick growing tall once more. There was the space of un-burned candle between the light and the slow-match shortened to an inch or less.

How much life did that inch leave me? Three-quarters of an hour? Half an hour? Fifty minutes? Twenty minutes? Steady! an inch of tallow-candle wouldn't burn longer than twenty minutes. An inch of tallow! the notion of a man's body and soul being kept together by an inch of tallow! Wonderful! Why, the greatest king that sits on a throne can't keep a man's body and soul together; and here's an inch of tallow that can do what the king can't! There's something to tell mother when I get home which will surprise her more than all the rest of my voyages put together. I laughed inwardly again at the thought of that, and shook and swelled and suffocated myself, till the light of the candle leaped in through my eyes, and licked up the laughter, and burned it out of me, and made me all empty and cold and quiet once more.

Mother and Lizzie. I don't know when they came back; but they did come back—not, as it seemed to me, into my mind this time, but right down bodily before me, in the hold of the brig.

Yes: sure enough, there was Lizzie, just as light-hearted as usual, laughing at me. Laughing? Well, why not? Who is to blame Lizzie for thinking I'm lying on my back, drunk in the cellar, with the beer-barrels all round me? Steady? She's crying now—spinning round and round in a fiery mist, wringing her hands, screeching out for help—fainter and fainter, like the splash of the schooner's sweeps. Gone—burned up in the fiery mist! Mist? Fire? no; neither one nor the other. It's mother makes the light—mother knitting, with ten flaming points at the ends of her fingers and thumbs, and slow-matches hanging in bunches all round her face instead of her own gray hair. Mother in her old arm-chair, and the pilot's long skinny hands hanging over the back of the chair, dripping with gunpowder. No! no gunpowder, no chair, no mother—nothing but the pilot's face, shining red-hot, like a sun, in the fiery mist; turning upside down in the fiery mist; running backward and forward along the slow-match, in the fiery mist; spinning millions of miles in a minute, in the fiery mist—spinning itself smaller and smaller into one tiny point, and that point darting on a sudden straight into my head—and then, all fire and all mist—no hearing, no seeing, no thinking, no feeling—the brig, the sea, my own self, the whole world, all gone together!

After what I've just told you, I know nothing and remember nothing, till I woke up in a comfortable bed, with two rough-and-ready men like myself sitting on each side of my pillow, and a gentleman standing watching me at the foot of the bed. It was about seven in the morning. My sleep (or what seemed like my sleep to me) had lasted better than eight months—I was among my own countrymen in the island of Trinidad—the men at each side of my pillow were my keepers, turn and turn about—and the gentleman standing at the foot of the bed was the doctor. What I said and did in those eight months, I never have known, and never shall.

It was another two months or more before the doctor thought it safe to answer the questions I asked.

The brig had been anchored, just as I had supposed, off a part of the coast which was lonely enough to make the Spaniards pretty sure of no interruption, so long as they managed their murderous work quietly under cover of night.

My life had not been saved from the shore, but from the sea. An American vessel, becalmed in the offing, had made out the brig as the sun rose; and the captain having his time on his hands in consequence of the calm, and seeing a vessel anchored where no vessel had any reason to be, had manned one of his boats and sent his mate with it, to look a little closer.

What he saw, when he and his men found the brig deserted and boarded her, was the gleam of candlelight through the chink in the hatchway. The flame was within about a thread's breadth of the slow-match when he lowered himself into the hold; and if he had not had the sense and coolness to cut the match in two with his knife before he touched the candle, he and his men might have been blown up along with the brig as well as me. The match caught, and turned into sputtering red fire, in the very act of putting the candle out; and if the communication with the powder-barrel had not been cut off, the Lord only knows what might have happened.

What became of the Spanish schooner and the pilot, I have never heard from that day to this.

As for the brig, the Yankees took her, as they took me, to Trinidad, and claimed their salvage, and got it, I hope, for their own sakes. I was landed just in the same state as when they rescued me from the brig—that is to say, clean out of my senses. But please to remember, it was a long time ago; and, take my word for it, I was discharged cured, as I have told you.

# THE WRECK OF THE *ROYAL CAROLINE*

From "The Red Rover," BY JAMES FENIMORE COOPER

OUR watchful adventurer captain was not blind to these sinister omens. No sooner did the peculiar atmosphere by which the mysterious image that he so often examined was suddenly surrounded, catch his eye, than his voice was raised in the clear, powerful, and exciting notes of warning.

"Stand by," he called aloud, "to in-all-studding-sails! Down with them!" he added, scarcely giving his former words time to reach the ears of his subordinates. "Down with every rag of them, fore and aft the ship! Man the top-gallant clew-lines, Mr. Earing. Clew up, and clew down! In with every thing, cheerily, men!—In!"

This was a language to which the crew of the *Caroline* were no strangers, and it was doubly welcome, since the meanest seaman amongst them had long thought that his unknown commander had been heedlessly trifling with the safety of the vessel, by the hardy manner in which he disregarded the wild symptoms of the weather. But they undervalued the keen-eyed vigilance of Wilder. He had certainly driven the Bristol trader through the water at a rate she had never been known to go before; but, thus far, the facts themselves gave evidence in his favour, since no injury was the consequence of what they deemed temerity. At the quick sudden order just given, however, the whole ship was in an uproar. A dozen seamen called to each other, from different parts of the vessel, each striving to lift his voice above the roaring ocean; and there was every appearance of a general and inextricable confusion; but the same authority which had so unexpectedly aroused them into activity, produced order from their ill-directed though vigorous efforts.

Wilder had spoken, to awaken the drowsy and to excite the torpid. The instant he found each man on the alert, he resumed his orders with a calmness that gave a direction to the powers of all, and yet with an energy that he well knew was called for by the occasion. The enormous sheets of duck, which had looked like so many light clouds in the murky and threatening heavens, were soon seen fluttering wildly, as they descended from their high places, and, in a few minutes, the ship was reduced to the action of her more secure and heavier canvas. To effect this object, every man in the ship exerted his powers to the utmost, under the guidance of the steady but rapid mandates of their commander. Then followed a short and apprehensive pause. All eyes were turned towards the quarter where the ominous signs had been discovered; and each individual endeavored to read their import, with an intelligence correspondent to the degree of skill he might have acquired, during his particular period of service on that treacherous element which was now his home.

The dim tracery of the stranger's form had been swallowed by the flood of misty light, which, by this time, rolled along the sea like drifting vapour, semi-pellucid, preternatural, and seemingly tangible. The ocean itself appeared admonished that a quick and violent change was nigh. The waves ceased to break in their former foaming and brilliant crests, and black masses of the water lifted their surly summits against the eastern horizon, no longer shedding their own peculiar and lucid atmosphere around them. The breeze which had been so fresh, and which had even blown with a force that nearly amounted to a gale, was lulling and becoming uncertain, as it might be awed by the more violent power that was gathering along the borders of the sea, in the direction of the neighbouring continent. Each moment, the eastern puffs of air lost their strength, becoming more and more feeble, until, in an incredibly short period, the heavy sails were heard flapping against the masts. A frightful and ominous calm succeeded. At this instant, a gleam flashed from the fearful obscurity of the ocean, and a roar, like that of a sudden burst of thunder, bellowed along the waters. The seamen turned their startled looks on each other, standing aghast, as if a warning of what was to follow had come out of the heavens themselves. But their calm and more sagacious commander put a different construction on the signal. His lip curled, in high professional pride, and he muttered with scorn,—

"Does he imagine that we sleep? Ay, he has got it himself, and would open our eyes to what is coming? What does he conjecture we have been about, since the middle watch was set?"

Wilder made a swift turn or two on the quarter-deck, turning his quick glances from one quarter of the heavens to another; from the black and lulling water on which his vessel was rolling, to the sails; and from his silent and profoundly expectant crew, to the dim lines of spars that were waving above his head, like so many pencils tracing their curvilinear and wanton images over the murky volumes of the superincumbent clouds.

"Lay the after-yards square!" he said, in a voice which was heard by every man on deck, though his words were apparently spoken but little above his breath. The creaking of the blocks, as the spars came slowly and heavily round to the indicated position, contributed to the imposing character of the moment, sounding like notes of fearful preparation.

"Haul up the courses!" resumed Wilder with the same eloquent calmness of manner. Then, taking another glance at the threatening horizon, he added slowly but with emphasis, "Furl them—furl them both. Away aloft, and hand your courses!" he continued in a shout; "roll them up, cheerily; in with them, boys, cheerily; in!"

The conscious seamen took their impulses from the tones of their commander. In a moment, twenty dark forms were leaping up the rigging, with the alacrity of so many quadrupeds. In another minute, the vast and powerful sheets of canvas were effectually rendered harmless, by securing them in tight rolls to their respective spars. The men descended as swiftly as they had mounted to the yards; and then succeeded another breathing pause. At this appalling moment, a candle would have sent its flame perpendicularly towards the heavens. The ship, missing the steadying power of the wind, rolled heavily in the troughs of the seas, which began to lessen at each instant, as if the startled element was recalling into the security of its own vast bosom that portion of its particles which had so lately been permitted to gambol madly over its surface. The water washed sullenly along the side of the ship, or, as she labouring rose from one of her frequent falls into the hollows of the waves, it shot back into the ocean from her decks in glittering cascades. Every hue of the heavens, every sound of the element, and each dusky and anxious countenance, helped to proclaim the intense interest of the moment. In this brief interval of expectation and inactivity, the mates again approach their commander.

"It is an awful night, Captain Wilder!" said Earing, presuming on his rank to be the first to speak.

"I have known far less notice given of a shift of wind," was the answer.

"We have had time to gather in our kites, 'tis true, sir; but there are signs and warnings that come with this change which the oldest seaman must dread!"

"Yes," continued Knighthead, in a voice that sounded hoarse and powerful, even amid the fearful accessories of that scene; "yes, it is no trifling commission that can call people that I shall not name out upon the water in such a night as this. It was in just such weather that I saw the *Vesuvius* ketch go to a place so deep, that her own mortar would not have been able to have sent a bomb into the open air, had hands and fire been there fit to let it off!"

"Ay; and it was in such a time that the *Greenlandman* was cast upon the Orkneys, in as flat a calm as ever lay on the sea."

"Gentlemen," said Wilder, with a peculiar and perhaps an ironical emphasis on the word, "what would ye have? There is not a breath of air stirring and the ship is naked to her topsails!"

It would have been difficult for either of the two malcontents to give a very satisfactory answer to this question. Both were secretly goaded by mysterious and superstitious apprehensions, that were powerfully aided by the more real and intelligible aspect of the night; but neither had so far forgotten his manhood, and his professional pride, as to lay bare the full extent of his own weakness, at a moment when he was liable to be called upon for the exhibition of qualities of a more positive and determined character. The feeling that was uppermost betrayed itself in the reply of Earing, though in an indirect and covert manner.

"Yes, the vessel is snug enough now," he said, "though eyesight has shown us it is no easy matter to drive a freighted ship through the water as fast as one of those flying craft aboard which no man can say who stands at the helm, by what compass she steers, or what is her draught!"

"Ay," resumed Knighthead, "I call the *Caroline* fast for an honest trader. There are few square-rigged boats who do not wear the pennants of the king, that can eat her out of the wind on a bowline, or bring her into their wake with studding-sails set. But this is a time and an hour to make a seaman think. Look at yon hazy light, here in with the land, that is coming so fast down upon us, and then tell me whether it comes from the coast of America, or whether it comes from out of the stranger who has been so long running under our lee, but who has got, or is fast getting, the wind of us at last, while none here can say how, or why. I have just this much, and no more, to say: give me for consort a craft whose captain I know, or give me none!"

"Such is your taste, Mr. Knighthead," said Wilder, coldly; "mine may, by some accident, be different."

"Yes, yes," observed the more cautious and prudent Earing, "in time of war, and with letters of marque aboard, a man may honestly hope the sail he sees should have a stranger for her master; or otherwise he would never fall in with an enemy. But, though an Englishman born myself, I should rather give the ship in that mist a clear sea, seeing that I neither know her nation nor her cruise. Ah, Captain Wilder, this is an awful sight for the morning watch! Often and often have I seen the sun rise in the east, and no harm done; but little good can come of a day when the light first breaks in the west. Cheerfully would I give the owners the last month's pay, hard as it has been earned, did I but know under what flag the stranger sails."

"Frenchman, Don, or Devil, yonder he comes!" cries Wilder. Then, turning towards the attentive crew, he shouted, in a voice that was appalling by its vehemence and warning, "Let run the after-halyards! round with the fore-yard; round with it, men, with a will!"

These were cries that the startled crew but too well understood. Every nerve and muscle were exerted to execute the orders, to be in readiness for the tempest. No man spoke; but each expended the utmost of his power and skill in direct and manly efforts. Nor was there, in verity, a moment to lose, or a particle of human strength expended here, without a sufficient object.

The lurid and fearful-looking mist, which, for the last quarter of an hour, had been gathering in the north-west, was driving down upon them with the speed of a race-horse. The air had already lost the damp and peculiar feeling of an easterly breeze; and little eddies were beginning to flutter among the masts—precursors of the coming squall. Then, a rushing, roaring sound was heard moaning along the ocean, whose surface was first dimpled, next ruffled, and finally covered with a sheet of clear, white, and spotless foam. At the next moment, the power of the wind fell upon the inert and labouring Bristol trader.

While the gust was approaching, Wilder had seized the slight opportunity afforded by the changeful puffs of air to get the ship as much as possible before the wind; but the sluggish movement of the vessel met neither the wishes of his own impatience nor the exigencies of the moment. Her bows slowly and heavily fell off from the north, leaving her precisely in a situation to receive the first shock on her broadside. Happy it was, for all who had life at risk in that defenceless vessel, that she was not fated to receive the whole weight of the tempest at a blow. The sails fluttered and trembled on their massive yards, bellying and collapsing alternately for a minute, and then the rushing wind swept over them in a hurricane.

The *Caroline* received the blast like a stout and buoyant ship as she was, yielding to its impulse until her side lay nearly incumbent on the element; and then, as if the fearful fabric were conscious of its jeopardy, it seemed to lift its reclining masts again, struggling to work its way through the water.

"Keep the helm a-weather! Jam it a-weather, for your life!" shouted Wilder, amid the roar of the gust.

The veteran seaman at the wheel obeyed the order with steadiness, but in vain did he keep his eyes on the margin of his head sail, to watch the manner in which the ship would obey its power. Twice more, in as many moments, the giddy masts fell towards the horizon, waving as often gracefully upward, and then they yielded to the mighty pressure of the wind, until the whole machine lay prostrate on the water.

"Be cool!" said Wilder, seizing the bewildered Earing by the arm, as the latter rushed madly up the steep of the deck; "it is our duty to be calm; bring hither an axe."

Quick as the thought which gave the order, the admonished mate complied, jumping into the mizzen-channels of the ship, to execute with his own hands the mandate that he knew must follow.

"Shall I cut?" he demanded, with uplifted arms, and in a voice that atoned for his momentary confusion, by its steadiness and force.

"Hold!—Does the ship mind her helm at all?"

"Not an inch, sir."

"Then cut," Wilder clearly and calmly added.

A single blow sufficed for the discharge of this important duty. Extended to the utmost powers of endurance, by the vast weight it upheld, the lanyard struck by Earing no sooner parted, than each of its fellows snapped in succession, leaving the mast dependent on its wood for the support of all the ponderous and complicated hamper it upheld. The cracking of the spar came next; and the whole fell, like a tree that had been snapped at its foundation.

"Does she fall off?" called Wilder, to the observant seaman at the wheel.

"She yielded a little, sir; but this new squall is bringing her up again."

"Shall I cut?" shouted Earing from the main-rigging, whither he had leaped, like a tiger who had bounded on his prey.

"Cut."

A louder and more imposing crash succeeded this order, though not before several heavy blows had been struck into the massive mast itself. As before, the sea received the tumbling maze of spars, rigging, and sails; the vessel surging at the same instant, from its recumbent position, and rolling far and heavily to windward.

"She rights! she rights!" exclaimed twenty voices which had been mute, in a suspense that involved life and death.

"Keep her dead away!" added the calm but authoritative voice of the young commander. "Stand by to furl the fore-top-sail—let it hang a moment to drag the ship clear of the wreck—cut, cut—cheerily, men—hatchets and knives—cut *with* all, and cut *off* all!"

As the men now worked with the vigour of hope, the ropes that still confined the fallen spars to the vessel were quickly severed; and the *Caroline*, by this time dead before the gale, appeared barely to touch the foam that covered the sea. The wind came over the waste in gusts that rumbled like distant thunder, and with a power that seemed to threaten to lift the ship from its proper element. As a prudent and sagacious seaman had let fly the halyards, of the solitary sail that remained, at the moment the squall approached, the loosened but lowered topsail was now distended in a manner that threatened to drag after it the only mast which still stood. Wilder saw the necessity of getting rid of the sail, and he also saw the utter impossibility of securing it. Calling Earing to his side, he pointed out the danger, and gave the necessary order.

"The spar cannot stand such shocks much longer," he concluded; "should it go over the bows, some fatal blow might be given to the ship at the rate she is moving. A man or two must be sent aloft to cut the sail from the yards."

"The stick is bending like a willow whip," returned the mate, "and the lower mast itself is sprung. There would be great danger in trusting a hand in that top, while these wild squalls are breathing around us."

"You may be right," returned Wilder, with a sudden conviction of the truth of what the other had said. "Stay you then here; if any thing befall me, try to get the vessel into port as far north as the Capes of Virginia, at least;—on no account attempt Hatteras, in the present condition of—"

"What would you do, Captain Wilder?" interrupted the mate, laying his hand on the shoulder of his commander, who had already thrown his sea-cap on the deck, and was preparing to divest himself of some of his outer garments.

"I go aloft to ease the mast of that topsail, without which we lose the spar, and possibly the ship."

"I see that plain enough; but, shall it be said that another did the duty of Edward Earing? It is your business to carry the vessel into the Capes of Virginia, and mine to cut the topsail adrift. If harm comes to me, why, put it in the log, with a word or two about the manner in which I played my part. That is the most proper epitaph for a sailor."

Wilder made no resistance. He resumed his watchful and reflecting attitude, with the simplicity of one who had been too long trained to the discharge of certain obligations himself, to manifest surprise that another should acknowledge their imperative character. In the mean time, Earing proceeded steadily to perform what he had just promised. Passing into the waist of the ship, he provided himself with a suitable hatchet, and then, without speaking a syllable to any of the mute but attentive seamen, he sprang into the fore-rigging, every strand and rope-yarn of which was tightened by the strain nearly to snapping. The understanding eyes of his observers comprehended his intention; and with precisely the same pride of station as had urged him to the dangerous undertaking four or five of the oldest mariners jumped upon the rattlings, to mount into an air that apparently teemed with a hundred hurricanes.

"Lie down out of that fore-rigging," shouted Wilder, through a deck trumpet; "lie down; all, but the mate, lie down!" His words were borne past the inattentive ears of the excited and mortified followers of Earing, but for once they failed of their effect. Each man was too earnestly bent on his purpose to listen to the sounds of recall. In less than a minute, the whole were scattered along the yards, prepared to obey the signal of their officer. The mate cast a look about him; perceiving that the time was comparatively favorable, he struck a blow upon the large rope that confined one of the lower angles of the distended and bursting sail to the yard. The effect was much the same as would be produced by knocking away the keystone of an ill-cemented arch. The canvas broke from its fastenings with a loud explosion, and, for an instant, it was seen sailing in the air ahead of the ship, as if it were sustained on wings. The vessel rose on a sluggish wave—the lingering remains of the former breeze—and settled heavily over the rolling surge, borne down alike by its own weight and the renewed violence of the gusts. At this critical instant, while the seamen aloft were still gazing in the direction in which the little cloud of canvas had disappeared, a lanyard of the lower rigging parted, with a crack that reached the ears of Wilder.

"Lie down!" he shouted wildly through his trumpet; "down by the backstays; down for your lives; every man of you, down!"

A solitary individual profited by the warning gliding to the deck with the velocity of the wind. But rope parted after rope, and the fatal snapping of the wood followed. For a moment, the towering maze tottered, seeming to wave towards every quarter of the heavens; and then, yielding to the movements of the hull, the whole fell, with a heavy crash, into the sea. Cord, lanyard, and stay snapped like thread, as each received in succession the strain of the ship, leaving the naked and despoiled hull of the *Caroline* to drive before the tempest, as if nothing had occurred to impede its progress.

A mute and eloquent pause succeeded the disaster. It seemed as if the elements themselves were appeased by their work, and something like a momentary lull in the awful rushing of the winds might have been fancied. Wilder sprang to the side of the vessel, and distinctly beheld the victims, who still clung to their frail support. He even saw Earing waving his hand in adieu with a seaman's heart, like man who not only felt how desperate was his situation, but who knew how to meet it with resignation. Then the wreck of spars, with all who clung to it, was swallowed up in the body of the frightful, preter-natural-looking mist which extended on every side of them, from the ocean to the clouds.

"Stand by, to clear away a boat!" shouted Wilder, without pausing to think of the impossibility of one's swimming, or of effecting the least good, in so violent a tornado.

But the amazed and confounded seamen who remained needed no instruction in this matter. Not a man moved, nor was the smallest symptom of obedience given. The mariners looked wildly around them, each endeavouring to trace in the dusky countenance of some shipmate his opinion of the extent of the evil; but not a mouth opened among them all.

"It is too late—it is too late!" murmured Wilder; "human skill and human efforts could not save them!"

"Sail, ho!" Knighthead shouted in a voice that was teeming with superstitious awe.

"Let him come on," returned his young commander, bitterly; "the mischief is ready done to his hands!"

"Should this be a true ship, it is our duty to the owners and the passengers to speak her, if a man can make his voice heard in this tempest," the second mate continued, pointing, through the haze, at the dim object that was certainly at hand.

"Speak her!—passengers!" muttered Wilder, involuntarily repeating his words. "No; any thing is better than speaking her. Do you see the vessel that is driving down upon us so fast?" he sternly demanded of the watchful seaman who still clung to the wheel of the *Caroline*.

"Ay, ay, sir."

"Give her a berth—sheer away hard to port—perhaps he may pass us in the gloom, now we are no higher than our decks. Give the ship a broad sheer, I say, sir."

The usual laconic answer was given; and, for a few moments, the Bristol trader was seen diverging a little from the line in which the other approached; but a second glance assured Wilder that the attempt was useless. The strange ship (every man on board felt certain it was the same that had so long been seen hanging in the northwestern horizon) came on through the mist, with a swiftness that nearly equalled the velocity of the tempestuous winds themselves. Not a thread of canvas was seen on board her. Each line of spars, even to the tapering and delicate top-gallant masts, was in its place, preserving the beauty and symmetry of the whole fabric; but nowhere was the smallest fragment of a sail opened to the gale. Under her bows rolled a volume of foam that was even discernible amid the universal agitation of the ocean; and, as she came within sound, the sullen roar of the water might have been likened to the noise of a cascade. At first, the spectators on the decks of the *Caroline* believed they were not seen, and some of the men called madly for lights, in order that the disasters of the night might not terminate in an encounter.

"Too many see us there already!" said Wilder.

"No, no," muttered Knighthead; "no fear but we are seen; and by such eyes, too, as never yet looked out of mortal head!"

The seamen paused. In another instant, the long-seen and mysterious ship was within a hundred feet of them. The very power of that wind, which was wont usually to raise the billows, now pressed the element, with the weight of mountains, into its bed. The sea was every where a sheet of froth, but the water did not rise above the level of the surface. The instant a wave lifted itself from the security of the vast depths, the fluid was borne away before the tornado in glittering spray. Along this frothy but comparatively motionless surface, then, the stranger came booming with the steadiness and grandeur with which a cloud is seen sailing in the hurricane. No sign of life was discovered about her. If men looked out from their secret places, upon the straitened and discomfited wreck of the Bristol trader, it was covertly, and as darkly as the tempest before which they drove. Wilder held his breath, for the moment the stranger was nighest, in the very excess of suspense, but, as he saw no signal of recognition, no human form, nor any intention to arrest, if possible, the furious career of the other, a smile gleamed across his countenance, and his lips moved rapidly, as if he found pleasure in being abandoned to his distress. The stranger drove by, like a dark vision; and, ere another minute, her form was beginning to grow less distinct, in the body of spray to leeward.

"She is going out of sight in the mist!" exclaimed Wilder, when he drew his breath, after the fearful suspense of the few last moments.

"Ay, in mist or clouds," responded Knighthead, who now kept obstinately at his elbow, watching with the most jealous distrust, the smallest movement of his unknown commander.

"In the heavens, or in the sea, I care not, provided he be gone."

"Most seamen would rejoice to see a strange sail, from the hull of a vessel shaved to the deck like this."

"Men often court their destruction, from ignorance of their own interests. Let him drive on, say I, and pray I! He goes four feet to our one; and I ask no better favour than that this hurricane may blow until the sun shall rise."

Knighthead started, and cast an oblique glance, which resembled denunciation, at his companion. To his superstitious mind, there was profanity in thus invoking the tempest, at a moment when the winds seemed already to be pouring out their utmost wrath.

"This is a heavy squall, I will allow," he said, "and such a one as many mariners pass whole lives without seeing; but he knows little of the sea who thinks there is not more wind where this comes from."

"Let it blow!" cried the other, striking his hands together a little wildly; "I pray for wind!"

All the doubts of Knighthead, as to the character of the young stranger who had so unaccountably got possession of the office of Nicholas Nichols, if any remained, were now removed. He walked forward among the silent and thoughtful crew, with the air of a man whose opinion was settled. Wilder, however, paid no attention to the movements of his subordinate, but continued pacing the deck for hours; now casting his eyes at the heavens, and now sending frequent and anxious glances around the limited horizon, while the *Royal Caroline* still continued drifting before the wind, a shorn and naked wreck.

# A BURIAL AT SEA

From "Two Years Before the Mast," BY RICHARD HENRY DANA

THIS was a black day in our calendar. At seven o'clock in the morning, it being our watch below, we were aroused from a sound sleep by the cry of "All hands ahoy! a man overboard!" This unwonted cry sent a thrill through the heart of every one, and, hurrying on deck, we found the vessel hove flat aback, with all her studding-sail set; for, the boy who was at the helm leaving it to throw something overboard, the carpenter, who was an old sailor, knowing that the wind was light, put the helm down and hove her aback. The watch on deck were lowering away the quarter-boat, and I got on deck just in time to fling myself into her as she was leaving the side; but it was not until out upon the wide Pacific, in our little boat, that I knew whom we had lost. It was George Ballmer, the young English sailor, whom I have before spoken of as the life of the crew. He was prized by the officers as an active and willing seaman, and by the men as a lively, hearty fellow, and a good shipmate. He was going aloft to fit a strap round the main topmasthead, for ringtail halyards, and had the strap and block, a coil of halyards, and a marline-spike about his neck. He fell from the starboard futtock shrouds, and, not knowing how to swim, and being heavily dressed, with all those things round his neck, he probably sank immediately. We pulled astern, in the direction in which he fell, and though we knew that there was no hope of saving him, yet no one wished to speak of returning, and we rowed about for nearly an hour, without an idea of doing anything, but unwilling to acknowledge to ourselves that we must give him up. At length we turned the boat's head and made towards the brig.

Death is at all times solemn, but never so much so as at sea.

A man dies on shore; his body remains with his friends, and "the mourners go about the streets"; but when a man falls overboard at sea and is lost, there is a suddenness in the event, and a difficulty in realizing it, which give to it an air of awful mystery. A man dies on shore,—you follow his body to the grave, and a stone marks the spot. You are often prepared for the event. There is always something which helps you to realize it when it happens, and to recall it when it has passed. A man is shot down by your side in battle, and the mangled body remains an object, and a real evidence; but at sea, the man is near you,—at your side,—you hear his voice, and in an instant he is gone, and nothing but a vacancy shows his loss. Then, too, at sea—to use a homely but expressive phrase—you *miss* a man so much. A dozen men are shut up together in a little bark upon the wide, wide sea, and for months and months see no forms and hear no voices but their own, and one is taken suddenly from among them, and they miss him at every turn. It is like losing a limb. There are no new faces or new scenes to fill up the gap. There is always an empty berth in the forecastle, and one man wanting when the small night-watch is mustered. There is one less to take the wheel, and one less to lay out with you upon the yard. You miss his form, and the sound of his voice, for habit had made them almost necessary to you, and each of your senses feels the loss.

All these things make such a death peculiarly solemn, and the effect of it remains upon the crew for some time. There is more kindness shown by the officers to the crew, and by the crew to one another. There is more quietness and seriousness. The oath and the loud laugh are gone. The officers are more watchful, and the crew go more carefully aloft. The lost man is seldom mentioned, or is dismissed with a sailor's rude eulogy, —"Well, poor George is gone! His cruise is up soon! He knew his work, and did his duty, and was a good shipmate." Then usually follows some allusion to another world, for sailors are almost all believers, in their way; though their notions and opinions are unfixed and at loose ends. They say, "God won't be hard upon the poor fellow," and seldom get beyond the common phrase which seems to imply that their sufferings and hard treatment here will be passed to their credit in the books of the Great Captain hereafter,—"*To work hard, live hard, die hard, and go to hell after all, would be hard indeed!*" Our cook, a simple-hearted old African, who had been through a good deal in his day, and was rather seriously inclined, always going to church twice a day when on shore, and reading his Bible on a Sunday in the galley, talked to the crew about spending the Lord's Days badly, and told them that they might go as suddenly as George had, and be as little prepared.

Yet a sailor's life is at best but a mixture of a little good with much evil, and a little pleasure with much pain. The beautiful is linked with the revolting, the sublime with the commonplace, and the solemn with the ludicrous.

Not long after we had returned on board with our sad report, an auction was held of the poor man's effects. The captain had first, however, called all hands aft and asked them if they were satisfied that everything had been done to save the man, and if they thought there was any use in remaining there longer. The crew all said that it was in vain, for the man did not know how to swim, and was very heavily dressed. So we then filled away and kept the brig off to her course.

The laws regulating navigation make the captain answerable for the effects of a sailor who dies during the voyage, and it is either a law or a custom, established for convenience, that the captain should soon hold an auction of his things, in which they are bid off by the sailors, and the sums which they give are deducted from their wages at the end of the voyage. In this way the trouble and risk of keeping his things through the voyage are avoided, and the clothes are usually sold for more than they would be worth on shore. Accordingly, we had no sooner got the ship before the wind, than his chest was brought up upon the forecastle, and the sale began. The jackets and trousers in which we had seen him dressed so lately were exposed and bid off while the life was hardly out of his body, and his chest was taken aft and used as a store-chest, so that there was nothing left which could be called *his*. Sailors have an unwillingness to wear a dead man's clothes during the same voyage, and they seldom do so, unless they are in absolute want.

As is usual after a death, many stories were told about George. Some had heard him say that he repented never having learned to swim, and that he knew that he should meet his death by drowning. Another said that he never knew any good to come of a voyage made against the will, and the deceased man shipped and spent his advance, and was afterwards very unwilling to go, but, not being able to refund, was obliged to sail with us. A boy, too, who had become quite attached to him, said that George talked to him, during most of the watch on the night before, about his mother and family at home, and this was the first time that he had mentioned the subject during the voyage.

# FIREBRAND

From "Sea-Hounds," BY LEWIS R. FREEMAN, R.N.

It was a little incident which occurred one night when the Grand Fleet was returning to Base from one of its periodical sweeps through the North Sea that set Able-seaman Melton talking of the things he had seen and felt and heard the time he was standing anti-submarine watch in the *Firebrand*, when her flotilla of destroyers mixed itself up with a squadron of German cruisers in the course of the "dog-fight" which concluded the battle of Jutland.

I had found him, muffled to the eyes and dancing a jangling jig on a sleet-slippery steel plate to keep warm, when I picked my precarious way along the coco-matted deck and climbed up to the after searchlight platform of the Flotilla Leader I chanced to be in at the time. A fairly decent day was turning into a dirty night, and the steadily thickening mistiness which accompanied a sodden rain in process of transformation into soft snow had reduced the visibility to a point where the Commander-in-chief deemed it safer for the Fleet to put back to open sea and take no further chances among the treacherous currents and rock islands that beset the approaches to the Northern Base.

The Flagship, which had received the order by wireless, flashed "Destroyers prepare to take station for screening when Fleet alters to easterly course at nine o'clock," and shortly before that hour the Flotilla Leader made the signal to execute. Almost immediately I felt the hull of the *Flyer* take on an accelerated throb as her speed was increased, and a moment later the wake began to boil higher as the helm was put hard-a-starboard to bring her round. We were steaming a cable's length on the starboard bow of the *Olympus*, the leading ship of the squadron at the time, and the carrying out of the manœuvre involved the *Flyer's* leading her division across the head of the battleship line and down the other side on an opposite course, so that the destroyers would be in a position to resume night-screening formation when the fleet had finished turning.

Just how the captain of the *Flyer* happened to cut his course so fine I never learned, but the patchiness of the drifting mist must have had a good deal to do with making him misjudge his distance. At any rate, just as we had turned through nine or ten points, I suddenly saw the ominously bulking bows of the *Olympus* come juggernauting out of the night, with the amorphous loom of the bridge and foretop towering monstrously above. The *Flyer* seemed fairly to jump out of the water at the kick her propellers gave her as the turbines responded to the bridge's call for "More steam," and a spinning puff of smoke darkened the glow above the funnels for a moment as fresh oil was sprayed upon the fires beneath the boilers.

It was a good deal like a cat scurrying in front of a speeding motor-car, and the consequences would have been more or less similar had not one of the *Olympus's* swarming lookouts, peering into the darkness from his screened nest, gathered hint of the disaster that menaced in time to warn the forebridge. The great super-dreadnought responded to her helm very smartly considering her tonnage, and she turned just far enough to starboard to avoid grinding us under. I could almost look up through the port hawse-pipe as the flare of her bow loomed above my head, and the man standing by the depth-charges on the all-but-grazed stern of the *Flyer* might well have been pardoned even if the story his mates afterwards told of his action on this occasion were true—that he had tried to fend off one of the largest battleships afloat with a boat-hook.

A silhouette against the barely perceptible glow at the back of the forebridge of a "brass-hatted" officer shaking his fist as though in the act of ramping and roaring like a true British sailor moved by righteous anger; a forty or fifty degree heel to starboard as the curling bow-wave of the *Olympus* thwacked resoundingly along her port side, and the *Flyer* drove on into the sleet-shot darkness to blow off accumulated steam in rolling clouds, allow her fluttering pulse to become normal, and resume the even tenor of her way.

Melton, A.B., whistling over and over the opening bars of the chorus of "Do You Want Us to Lose the War?" started his metallically clanking jig again, but presently, like a man with something on his mind, sidled over and shoved his Balaklava-bordered face against the outside of the closely-reefed hood of my "lammy" coat, and muttered thickly something about being afraid he had got himself into trouble. When I had pulled loose a snap and improved communications by un-muffling a lee ear, I learned that it had just occurred to the good chap that he failed to report to the bridge the battleship he had sighted "fifty yards to the port beam," and he was wondering whether there would be a "strafe" coming from the skipper about it.

"Fact is, sir," he said, speaking brokenly as the galloping gusts every now and then forced a word back into his mouth, "that that rip-rarin' stem, with the white foam flyin' off both sides of it, bearing down right for where I was standin'—all that was so like what I saw the night of Jutland in the *Firebrand* that—that the turn it give me took my mind right back and—and I wasn't thinkin' o' anything else till the '*Lympus* was gone by."

I assured him that, since the *Olympus* had doubtless been sighted from the bridge several winks before she had been visible from his less-favourable vantage, they would probably have been too busy to respond to his call at the voice-pipe even had he tried to report what he saw.

"If I were you," I said, "I would forget all about that, and try to explain how a cruiser that the *Firebrand* was about to ram bow-to-bow" (I had, of course, already heard something of that dare-devilish exploit) "could have looked to you like the *Olympus* ramping down on a right-angling course and threatening to slice off the *Flyer's* stern with all her depth-charges. I quite understand that one ramming is a good deal like another, as far as a big ship hitting a destroyer fair and square is concerned, but—"

" 'Twasn't that *first* cru'ser 'tall, sir," Melton interrupted, nuzzling into my "lammy" hood again to make himself heard. " 'Twas 'nother 'un, sir—a wallopin' big un. The seas was stiff wi' cru'sers fer a minnit, sir, an' no sooner was we clear o' the first un than the second come tearin' down on us, tryin' to cut us in two amidships. An' that last un was a battl' cru'ser nigh as big as the *'Lympus,* all shot up in the funnels and runnin' wild an' bloody-minded like a mad bull. We were pretty nigh to bein' stopped dead, an' if she hadn't been slower'n cold grease wi' her helm she'd ha' eat us right up."

There had been nothing of malice aforethought in my action in cornering Melton on the searchlight platform that night, for, as it chanced, I had failed to learn up to that moment that he had been in the famous *Firebrand* at Jutland. Nor, with the wind and sea getting up as fast as the glass and the thermometer were going down, was the time or the place quite what a man would have chosen for anything in the way of cosy fireside reminiscence. But, both these facts notwithstanding, I felt that, since I was leaving the *Flyer* to go to another base directly she arrived in harbour on the morrow, it would be criminal to neglect the opportunity of hearing what was perhaps the most sportingly spectacular of all the Jutland destroyer actions related by one who was actually in it. I did not dare to distract Melton's attention from his lookout by drawing him into talking while he was still on watch, but, when he was relieved at ten o'clock, I waylaid him at the foot of the ladder with a pot of steaming hot ship's cocoa (foraged from the galley by a sympathetic ward-room steward) and both pockets of my "lammy" coat filled with the remnants of a box of assorted Yankee "candy" looted from the American submarine in which I had been on patrol the week before.

Melton rose to the lure instantly—or perhaps I should say

"fell to the bribe"—for the British bluejacket, if only he were given a chance to develop, is quite as sweet of tooth as his brother Yank. Because I could hardly take him to the captain's cabin, which I was occupying for the moment, for a yarn, and because he, likewise, could not take me down to the mess deck to disturb the off-watch sleepers with our chatter, there was nothing to do but carry on as best we could in the friendly lee of one of the funnels.

It was a night of infernal inkiness by now, and only clinging patches of soft snow and their blanker blankness revealed the dimly guessable lines of whaler and cowls and torpedo tubes and the loom of the loftier bridge. The battleship line was masked completely by the double curtain of the darkness and the snow, and only a tremulous greyness, barely discernible in the intervals of the flurries of flakes where the starboard bow-wave curled back from the *Olympus*, gave an intermittent bearing to help in keeping station. Underfoot was the blackness of the pit, not the faintest gleam reflecting from the waves washing over the weather side to swirl half-knee high about our sea boots. Even overhead all that was visible were fluttering patches of snow flakes dancing through the haloes of pale rose radiance that crowned the tops of the funnels. The wail of the wind in the wireless aerials, the crash of the surging beam seas, the throb of the propellers, and the pussy-cat purr of the spinning turbines—these were the fit accompaniment to which Melton A.B. recited to me the epic of the *Firebrand* at Jutland.

The cocoa I quaffed mug for mug with Melton, down to the last of the sweet, sustaining "settlings" in the bottom of the pot; but the candy I kept in reserve to draw on from time to time as it was needed to lubricate his tongue and stoke the smouldering fires of his memory. I started him off with a red-and-white "barber's pole" stick, which took not a little fumbling with mittened hands to extract from its greased tissue paper wrapper, and the seductive fragrance of crunched peppermint mingled with the acrid fumes of burning petroleum as he leaned close and began to tell how the ——th Flotilla, to which the *Firebrand* belonged, screening the ——th B.S. of the Battle Fleet, came upon the scene toward the end of the long summer afternoon. He had witnessed Beatty's consummate manœuvre of "crossing the T" of the enemy line with the four that remained of his battered First Battle Cruiser Squadron, and he had seen the main Battle Fleet baulked of its action by the lowering mists and the closing in of darkness; but it was not until full night had clapped down its lid that the fun for the *Firebrand* really began.

"It was 'twixt daylight an' dark," he said, reaching me a steadying hand in the darkness as the *Flyer* teetered giddily down the back of a receding sea, "that the flotilla dropped back to take stashun 'stern the battl'ships we was screenin'. The *Killarney* was leadin' an' after her came the *Firebran'*, *Seagull*, *Wreath*, an' *Consort*, makin' up the First Divishun. *Wreath* an' *Consort* sighted some Hun U-boats and 'stroyers while this move was on, an' plunk'd off a few shots at 'em. Don't think wi' any fatal consequence. Then there come the rattle of light gun fire from the south'ard, like from cru'sers or battleships repellin' T.B.D.'s. Then it was all serene for mor'n an 'our, an' then all hell opens up."

I suspected, from the sounds he made, that Melton had bitten into a block of milk chocolate without removing its wrapping of foil and paper, but presently his enunciation grew less explosive and more intelligible.

"It was Hun cru'sers drivin' down on us from the starboard quarter that started the monkey-show," he said, "an' that bein' the nor'west it was hardly where we'd reason to expect 'em from. It looks like we had 'em clean cut off, wi' the 'hole Battl' Fleet steamin' 'tween 'em an' their way back home, an' that they was tryin' to sneak through in the darkness. The *Wreath*, at the end o' the line nearest 'em, spotted 'em first, and she, 'cause she didn't want to give herself 'way wi' flashin', reported what she'd seen by low-power W.T. to the rest o' the flotilla. Course I—standin' watch aft—didn't know nothin' 'bout that signal, so that the first I hears o' the Huns was when they all opened up on the poor ol' *Killarney*, 'cause she was the leader, I s'pose, and she started firin' back at their flashes.

"The leadin' Hun flashed his searchlight on the *Killarney* as he opened up, but shut off sharp when *Killarney* came back at him. I could see some o' the projes flittin' right down the light beam until it blinked off, an' it was a flock of two or three of these that I kept my eye on all the way till they bashed into the *Killarney's* bridge and busted. She was zigzaggin' a coupl' o' points on *Firebrand's* starboard bow just then, so my standin' aft didn't prevent my gettin' a good look at what was happenin'. I could see the bodies o' four or five men flyin' up wi' the wreckage o' the explosion, an' then, all in a minnit, she was rollin' in flames from the funnels right for'ard. By the light o' it I could see the crews o' the 'midships and after guns workin' 'em like devils, an' twice anyhow, an' I think three times, I saw a bright, shiny slug slip over the side, an' knew they were loosin' mouldies to try to get their own back from the Hun.

"The sea was boilin' up red as blood where the light from the burnin' *Killarney* fell on the spouts the Huns' projes was throwin' up all round her. She was the fairest mark ever a gun trained on, and p'raps that was what tempted the Hun to keep pumpin' projes at her instead o' givin' more attenshun to the rest o' the divishun trailin' astern. That was what gave *Firebran'* her first chance o' alterin' the Hun navy list that night.

"The second cru'ser in the Hun line was bearin' right abeam to starboard by now, an' I could see by her gunflashes she was of good size, wi' four long funnels fillin' up all the deck 'tween her two masts. She was firing fast in salvoes wi' all the guns that would bear on the burnin' *Killarney*. I could just make out by the light from the *Killarney*, which was growin' stronger every minnit, that the crew of our after torpedo tube was gettin' busy, an' while I was watchin' 'em, over flops the mouldie and starts to run. I knew it was aimed for one or t'other o' the two leadin' Huns, but wasn't dead sure which till I saw the after funnels an' mainmast o' the second toppl' over an' a big flash o' fire take their place. Then it looked like there was exploshuns right off fore an' aft, and then fires broke out all over her from stem to stern. Next thing I knows, she takes a big list to starboard, an' over she goes, wi' more exploshuns throwin' up spouts o' steam, as she rolls under. The second mouldie—it got away right after the first—was never needed to finish the job. The *Firebran'* had evened up the score for the *Killarney*, wi' a good margin over.

"The captain turned away to reload mouldies after that, an' just as we swung out o' line I saw a salvo straddle the *Killarney*, and two or three shells hit square 'tween her funnels an' after sup'rstruct'r'. They must have gone off in her engine room, for there was more steam than fire risin' from her as we turned an' left her astern, an' she looked stopped dead. A Hun cru'ser was closin' the blazin' wreck o' her, firin' hard; but, by Gawd, what d'you think I saw? The only patch on the ol' *Killarney* that was free o' the ragin' fires was her stern, an' from there the steady flashes of her after gun showed it was bein' worked as fast an' reg'lar as ever I seen it done at any night-firin' practice. I looked to see her blow up every minnit, but she was still spittin' wi' that littl' after gun when the sudden flashin' up of the fightin' lights for'ard turned my attenshun nearer home.

"I could just make out a line of what looked like 'stroyers headin' cross our bows, an' thought we'd stumbled into 'nother nest o' Huns till they answered back wi' the signal o' the day, an' I knew it was one of our own flotillas we'd been catchin' up to. That flashin' up o' lights come near to doin' for us tho', for it showed us up to a big Hun steamin' three or four miles off on the port beam, an' he claps a searchlight on us an' chases it up wi' a sheaf o' shells. The only proj that hit us bounced off wi'out doin' much hurt to the ship, but some flyin' hunks o' it smashed the mouldie davit and knocked out most o' the crews o' the after tubes, includin' the T.G.M.[1] That put a stop to reloadin' operashuns wi' a mouldie in only one o' the tubes. By good luck we managed to zigzag out o' the searchlight beam

[1] Torpedo Gunner's Mate.

right after that, an' was free to turn back an' try to start a divershun for the poor ol' *Killarney*.

"Her fires looked to be dyin' down when we first picked her up, but right after that some more projes bust on her an' she started blazin' harder than ever. I watched for the spittin' o' that littl' after gun, but when it come it looked to spurt right out o' the heart o' a blazin' furnace, showin' the fire was now burnin' from stem to stern. One more salvo plastered over her, an' that one got no reply. The good ol' *'Killy'* had shot her bolt, an' her finish looked a matter o' minnits.

"It was plain enough if anyone was still livin' they was goin' to need pickin' up in a hurry, an' the captain put the *Firebran'* at full speed to close her an' stan' by to give a han'. Just then I saw a Hun searchlight turned on and start feelin' its way up to where the *Killarney* was burning, wi' a cru'ser followin' up the small end o' the beam, seemin' to be nosin' in to end the mis'ry. She did not bear right for a mouldie, but we opened up wi' the foremost gun, an' I saw the shells bustin' on her bridge and fo'c'sl' like rotten apples chucked 'gainst a wall. The light blinked off as the first proj hit home, but there was no way to tell if it was shot away or no. It was the second time that night that we'd done our bit to ease off the hell turned loose on the *Killarney*. Likewise it was the last. From then on we had our own partic'lar hell to wriggle out of, wi' no time left to play 'Venging Nemisus' to our stricken sisters. Just a big bon-fire sittin' on the sea an' lickin' a hole in the night wi' its flames —that was the last I saw of the ol' *Killarney*."

Melton paused for a moment as if engrossed in the memories conjured up by his narrative, and I took advantage of the in-terval to hand him one of those most loved lollipops of Yankee youngsterhood, a plump, hard ball of toothsome saccharinity called—obviously from its resistent resiliency—an "All-Day Sucker." When he spoke again I knew in an instant that a sure instinct had led him to make the proper disposition of the succulent dainty—that it was stowed snugly away in a bulging cheek like a squirrel's nut, to melt away in its own good time.

" 'Tween the glare of the burnin' *Killarney*," Melton went on after thrashing his hands across his shoulders for a minute to warm them up, "the gleam o' the Hun cru'ser's searchlight an' the flash o' our own gun-fire, we must all have been more or less blinded in the *Firebrand*, for we had run close to what may have been a part of the main en'my battl' line wi'out nothin' bein' reported. Our firin' had give us away, o' course, an' the nearest ships must have had their guns trained on us, waitin' to be sure what we was. One o' 'em must have made up his mind we was en'my even before we spotted 'em at all, for the first thing I saw was the white o' the bow wave an' wake as she turned toward us, prob'ly to ram. She'd have caught us just about 'midships if the bridge hadn't sighted her an' done the only thing open to do—turned to meet her head on.

"I don't remember that either she or us switched on recognition lights, but the Hun opened with ev'rything that would bear just before we slammed together. It must have been by the gun-flashes that I saw she had three funnels, wi' what looked like some kind o' marks painted on 'em in red. I saw our second funnel give a jump and crumple up as a proj hit it, an' then a spurt o' flame—from a big gun fired almost point-blank— looked to shoot right on to the bridge. I thought that it must have killed ev'ry man there an' carried away all the steering gear. But no.

"The old *Firebrand* wi' helm hard-a-port, went swingin' right on thro' the point or two more that saved her life. I could feel by the way she jumped an' gathered herself that last second that the ol' girl was still under control. Then we struck wi' a horrible grind an' crash, an' I went sprawlin' flat.

"If the Hun had hit us half a wink sooner, or if we had turned half a point less, we'd have been swallowed alive and split up in small hunks. As it was, we didn't have a lot the worst o' it, an' p'raps we more than broke even. It was like a mastiff an' terrier runnin' into each other in the dark, an' the terrier only gettin' run over an' the mastiff gettin' a piece bit clean out o' his neck. It was our port bows that come together, an' for only a sort o' glancin' blow. But it was the stem o' the *Firebran'* that was turned in sharpest, an' it was her that was hittin' up—by a good ten knots—the most speed. She was left in a terribl' mess, but most o' the damage was from her rammin' the Hun, not from the Hun rammin' her. While as for what she did to the Hun, the best proof o'·it was the more'n twenty feet of her side-plantin'—an upper strake, wi' scuttl' holes in it an' pieces o' gutterway deck hangin' to it—that we found in the wreck of our fo'c'sl'. If the hole that hunk of steel left behind it didn't put that Hun out o'. bus'ness as a fightin' unit till she got back to port an' had a refit, I'll eat it."

I wasn't quite clear in my mind whether Melton meant to imply that he would eat the hole in the Hun cruiser or the hunk of steel that came out of it, but there *was* no room for doubt that the violent crunch with which he emphasised the assertion had put a period to the life of his "All-Day Sucker," which was never intended to be treated like chewing toffy. Dipping into the grab-bag of my "lammy" coat pocket for something with which to replace it, therefore, I brought up a stick of chewing gum, and he resumed his story in an atmosphere sweet with the ineffable odour of spearmint and escaping steam.

"How much the Hun was shook up by that smash," Melton continued, "you can reckon from this: We was almost dead stopped for some minnits, an' all out o' control from the time of rammin' till we started connin' her from the engine-room. There was one fire flickerin' in the wreckage o' the fore-bridge, an' another somewhere 'midships, while there was also a big glare throwin' up where the foremost funnel was shot away. We was as soft an' easy a target as even a Hun could ask for; an' yet that one was in too much of a funk wi' his own hurts to let off a singl' other gun at us in all the time that he must have been flounderin' on at not much more'n point-blank range. Mebbe he was knocked up even more'n we thought. Nothin' else would account for him not havin' 'nother go at us.

"Just one wild bally mess—that was what the *Firebran'*

looked like when I got my feet again an' cast an eye for'ard. There was too much smoke an' steam to see clear, an' it was mostly flickers o' red light where the fires were startin', an' big, black shadows full o' wreckage. As it looked to *me* from aft—tho', o' course, the full effects wasn't vis'bl' till daylight, the bridge an' searchlight platform an' mast was shoved right back an' piled up on the foremost funnel. The whaler an' dingy was carried away, an' my first thought, for I was sure she was sinkin', was that we had no boats to put off in. I could see two or three wounded crawlin' out o' the raffle, but I knew that the most to be dished would be in the wreck o' the bridge. The queerest thing o' all was the flashes o' green an' blue light flutterin' thro' the tangled steel o' the wreckage. At first I thought I was sort o' seein' things; but fin'lly I figgered it out as the juice from the busted 'lectric wires short-circuitin'. It meant, I tol' myself, that the men under them tons o' steel was bein' 'lectrocuted on top o' bein' crushed.

"It looked like any one o' three or four things would be enough to finish the ol' *Firebran'*. I remember thinkin' that if she didn't blow up, she was sure to burn up; an' that if, by chance, she missed doin' one o' them, she was goin' to founder anyhow. She was already well down by the head, an'—leastways, it looked so to me at the time—still settlin' fast. An' I was just reflectin' that, even if she was lucky enough not to burn up, or blow up, or founder, she was still too easy pickin' for the Huns to miss doin' her in one way or 'nother, when, thunderin' out o' the darkness an' headin' up to crumpl' underfoot what was left o' the stopped an' helpless *Firebran'*, come a hulking big battl' cru'ser, the one I was just tellin' you the *'Lympus* set me thinkin' on a while back.

"Starin' at our own fires must have blinded me a good bit, or I'd have seen him sooner'n I did. He looked like he been gettin' no end o' a hammerin', for his second funnel was gone, an' out of the hole it left a big spurt o' flame an' smoke was rushin' that would have showed him up for miles. There was a red hot fire ragin' under his fo'c'sl', too, an' I saw the flames lashin' round thro' some jagged shell holes in his port bow. Lucky for us, he was runnin' for his life, an' had no time to more than try to run us down in passin'.

"It must have been just from habit I yelled down my voice-pipe, for I knew they was no longer controllin' her from the bridge; but the roarin' o' a fire an' the clank of bangin' metal was the only sounds that come back. When I looked up again the Hun was right on top of us, an' I must have just stood there —froze—like to-night wi' the '*Lympus*. By the grace o' Gawd, he hadn't been abl' to alter course enough to do the trick. His stem shot by wi' twenty feet or more clearance, an' it was only the fat bulge of him that kissed us off in passin'. It was by the glare o' his fires, not ours, which throwed no light abaft the superstructure I was on, that I saw some of the hands was already workin' to rig a jury steerin' gear aft. Then he was gone, an' much too full o' his own troubles to turn back, or even send the one heavy proj that would have cooked us for good an' all. A few minnits more, an' the wreck o' the *Fire-bran'* begun gatherin' way again, an' when I saw her come round to her nor'westerly course an' push ahead wi'out settlin' any deeper, I knew that the bulkheads were holdin' an' that—always providin' we run into no more Huns—there was a fightin' chance o' pullin' thro'.

"There was about a hundred jobs that needed doin' all at once, an' 'tween the loss o' dead an' wounded—only about half of the reg'lar ship's company was fit for work. The bulkheads had to be shored, for, wi' the fo'c'sl' crumpled up like a con-certina an' the deck an' side platin' ripped off from the stem right back to the capstan engine, she was open to the whole North Sea from the galley right for'ard. This made the first an' second bulkheads o' no use, an' made the third bulkhead all that stood 'tween us an' goin' to the bottom. Then there was the fires—'bove an' 'tween decks—that had to be put out 'fore they got to the magazines, an' the engines to be kept goin', an' the ship to be navigated, an' the wounded to be looked to. An' on top o' all this, the ship had to be got into some kind o' fightin' trim in case any more Huns come pokin' her way. I won't be havin' to tell you it was one bally awful job, carryin' on like that in the dark, an' wi' half the ship's company knocked out.

"When I saw it was the first lieutenant that seemed to be directin' things, I took it the captain was done for, an' that was what everyone thought till, all o' a sudden, he come wrigglin' out o' the wreck o' the bridge—all messed up an' covered wi' blood, but not much hurt otherways—an' began carryin' on just as if it was 'Gen'ral Quarters.' Some cove wi' the stump o' his hand tied up wi' First Aid dressin' was sent up to relieve me on the lookout, an' I was put to fightin' fires an' clearin' up the wreck 'bove decks. As there ain't much to burn on a 'stroyer if the cordite ain't started, we were not long gettin' the fires in han', even wi' havin'—'cause the hoses an' the fire-mains was knocked out—to dip up water in buckets throwed over the side. Wi' the wreckage, the most we could do was to dig out the dead an' wounded an' rig up for connin' ship from aft.

"It was a nasty job when we started in on the wreck o' the forebridge, for the witch-lights o' the short-circuit were still dancin' a cancan in the smashed an' twisted steel plates an' girders, an' it kept a cove lookin' lively to keep from switchin' some of the blue-green lightnin' into his own frame by way o' his ax or saw. No one that had been on any part o' the bridge was wi'out some kind o' hurt, but the three dead was a deal less than was to be expected. There was also three very bad knocked up, an' on one o' them the surgeon—a young pro-bashuner R.N.V.R.—performed an operashun in the dark. It was a cove he was 'fraid to move wi'out tinkerin' up a bit, an' he pulled him thro' all right in the end. One o' the crew of the foremost gun never turned up, an' we figured he must have been lost overboard when she rammed.

"Pois'nous as it was workin' on deck, that wasn't a circum-stance to what it must have been carryin' on below. I didn't see nothin' o' that end o' the show, thank Gawd, but every man as come out o' it alive said it was just one livin' bloomin' hell, no less. There was a good number o' coves who did things off han' that saved the ship from blowin' up, or burnin' up, or sinkin', an' three o' the best o' 'em was a engine-room art'ficer, a stoker P.O., and a stoker that was in the fore stokehold when the bridge was pushed back an' carried away that funnel. They ducked into their resp'rators, stuck to their posts an' kept the fans goin' till the fumes was all cleared away. Nothin' else would have saved the foremost boiler—an' wi' it the ship her-self—blowin' up right then an' there. Same way, gettin' on the jump in backin' up Number 3 bulkhead—the one that was holding back the whole North Sea—was all that kept it from bulgin' in an' floodin' right back into the stokeholds. It was the chief art'ficer engineer that took on that job, an' it was him, too, that stopped up the gaps left by the knocking down o' the first and second funnels.

"Even after it at last seemed like we was goin' to keep her from sinkin' or blowin' up, things still looked so bad to the captain that he ditched the box o' secret books for fear o' their fallin' into the hands o' the Hun. As we'd have been more hindrance than help to the Fleet, he did not try to rejoin the flotilla, but turned west an' headed for the coast o' England on the chance of makin' the nearest base while she still hung together. All night she went slap-bangin' along, wi' the engines shakin' out a few more rev'lushuns just as fast as it seemed the bulkhead was shored strong enough to stand the push o' the sea.

"Mornin' found her still goin', but what a sight she was! My first good look at what was left o' her give me the same kind o' shock I got the first time I had a peep at my mug in a glass after havin' small-pox in Singapore. She wasn't a ship at all, any more'n my face was a face. She was just a mess, that's all, an' clinkin' an' clankin' an' wheezin' an' sneezin' an' yawin' all over the sea. An' the sea was empty all the way roun', wi' no ship in sight to pass us a tow-line or pick us up if she chucked in her hand an' went down.

"We had our hands so full keepin' her afloat an' under weigh, that it wasn't till four in the afternoon—more'n sixteen hours after we rammed the Hun cru'ser—that we found time to bury our dead. It was like gettin' a turribl' load off your chest when we dropped 'em over in their hammocks wi' a fire-bar stitched in alongside 'em to take 'em down. Nothin' is so depressin' to a sailor as bein' shipmates wi' a mate that ain't a mate no longer. Even the ol' *Firebran'* 'peared to ride easier an' more b'oyant after the buryin' was over, as if she knowed the worst o' her sorrer was left behind.

"Luck took a turn against us again just after dark, for the wind shifted six or seven points an' started blowin' strong from dead ahead. We had to alter course some to ease off the bang o' the seas a bit, an' fin'ly the speed had to be slowed even slower'n before to keep the bulkhead from being driv' in. But she weathered it, by Gawd she did, an' next mornin' the goin' was easier. We made the Tyne at noon. It was just a heap o' ol' scrap-iron so far as the eye could see, that they let into the Middle Dock the next day, but it was scrap-iron that had come all the way from Jutland under its own steam, an' wi' no help from no one save what was left o' the lads as once manned a 'stroyer called the *Firebran'*.

"It hadn't taken long to reduce her from a 'stroyer to scrap-iron, an' it didn't seem like it took much longer—time goes fast on home leave—to turn that scrap-iron back into a 'stroyer again. The ol' *Firebran's* got many a good kick in her yet, so they say, an' I'd ask for nothin' better'n to be finishin' the war in her."

I thanked Melton for his yarn, bade him good night, and was about to start picking my way to my cabin to turn in, when I sensed rather than saw that there was something further that he wanted to say, perhaps some final tribute to his officers and mates of the *Firebrand*, I thought. There was a shuffling of sea-booted feet on the steel deck, a nervous pulling off and on of woolen mittens, and it was out.

"I just wanted to say, sir," he said, "that I likes the Yankee Jackies very much; 'specially their candy an' chewin' gum. I was just wonderin' if that last stick you give me was all—"

I emptied both pockets before I renewed my thanks to Melton and bade him a final good night. There are strange ingredients entering into the composition of the cement that is binding Britain and America together, and if there is any objection to chewing gum it certainly cannot be on the ground that it lacks adhesiveness.

# HIGH-WATER MARK

From "The Luck of Roaring Camp," BY BRET HARTE

WHEN the tide was out on the Dedlow Marsh, its extended dreariness was patent. Its spongy, low-lying surface, sluggish, inky pools, and tortuous sloughs, twisting their slimy way, eel-like, toward the open bay, were all hard facts. So were the few green tussocks, with their scant blades, their amphibious flavor, and unpleasant dampness. And if you choose to indulge your fancy,—although the flat monotony of the Dedlow Marsh was not inspiring,—the wavy line of scattered drift gave an unpleasant consciousness of the spent waters, and made the dead certainty of the returning tide a gloomy reflection, which no present sunshine could dissipate. The greener meadow-land seemed oppressed with this idea, and made no positive attempt at vegetation until the work of reclamation should be complete. In the bitter fruit of the low cranberry-bushes one might fancy he detected a naturally sweet disposition curdled and soured by an injudicious course of too much regular cold water.

The vocal expression of the Dedlow Marsh was also melancholy and depressing. The sepulchral boom of the bittern, the shriek of the curlew, the scream of passing brent, the wrangling of quarrelsome teal, the sharp, querulous protest of the startled crane, and syllabled complaint of the "killdeer" plover were beyond the power of written expression. Nor was the aspect of these mournful fowls at all cheerful and inspiring. Certainly not the blue heron standing midleg deep in the water, obviously catching cold in a reckless disregard of wet feet and consequences; nor the mournful curlew, the dejected plover, or the low-spirited snipe, who saw fit to join him in his suicidal contemplation; nor the impassive kingfisher—an ornithological

Marius—reviewing the desolate expanse; nor the black raven that went to and fro over the face of the marsh continually, but evidently couldn't make up his mind whether the waters had subsided, and felt low-spirited in the reflection that, after all this trouble, he wouldn't be able to give a definite answer. On the contrary, it was evident at a glance that the dreary expanse of Dedlow Marsh told unpleasantly on the birds, and that the season of migration was looked forward to with a feeling of relief and satisfaction by the full-grown, and of extravagant anticipation by the callow, brood. But if Dedlow Marsh was cheerless at the slack of the low tide, you should have seen it when the tide was strong and full. When the damp air blew chilly over the cold, glittering expanse, and came to the faces of those who looked seaward like another tide; when a steel-like glint marked the low hollows and the sinuous line of slough; when the great shell-incrusted trunks of fallen trees arose again, and went forth on their dreary, purposeless wanderings, drifting hither and thither, but getting no farther toward any goal at the falling tide or the day's decline than the cursed Hebrew in the legend; when the glossy ducks swung silently, making neither ripple nor furrow on the shimmering surface; when the fog came in with the tide and shut out the blue above, even as the green below had been obliterated; when boatmen, lost in that fog, paddling about in a hopeless way, started at what seemed the brushing of mermen's fingers on the boat's keel, or shrank from the tufts of grass spreading around like the floating hair of a corpse, and knew by these signs that they were lost upon Dedlow Marsh, and must make a night of it, and a gloomy one at that,—then you might know something of Dedlow Marsh at high water.

Let me recall a story connected with this latter view which never failed to recur to my mind in my long gunning excursions upon Dedlow Marsh. Although the event was briefly recorded in the county paper, I had the story, in all its eloquent detail, from the lips of the principal actor. I cannot hope to catch the varying emphasis and peculiar coloring of feminine delineation, for my narrator was a woman; but I'll try to give at least its substance.

She lived midway of the great slough of Dedlow Marsh and a good-sized river, which debouched four miles beyond into an estuary formed by the Pacific Ocean, on the long sandy peninsula which constituted the southwestern boundary of a noble bay. The house in which she lived was a small frame cabin raised from the marsh a few feet by stout piles, and was three miles distant from the settlements upon the river. Her husband was a logger,—a profitable business in a country where the principal occupation was the manufacture of lumber.

It was the season of early spring, when her husband left on the ebb of a high tide, with a raft of logs for the usual transportation to the lower end of the bay. As she stood by the door of the little cabin when the voyagers departed she noticed a cold look in the southeastern sky, and she remembered hearing her husband say to his companions that they must endeavor to complete their voyage before the coming of the southwesterly gale which he saw brewing. And that night it began to storm and blow harder than she had ever before experienced, and some great trees fell in the forest by the river, and the house rocked like her baby's cradle.

But however the storm might roar about the little cabin, she knew that one she trusted had driven bolt and bar with his own strong hand, and that had he feared for her he would not have left her. This, and her domestic duties, and the care of her little sickly baby, helped to keep her mind from dwelling on the weather, except, of course, to hope that he was safely harbored with the logs at Utopia in the dreary distance. But she noticed that day, when she went out to feed the chickens and look after the cow, that the tide was up to the little fence of their garden-patch, and the roar of the surf on the south beach, though miles away, she could hear distinctly. And she began to think that she would like to have some one to talk with about matters, and she believed that if it had not been so far and so stormy, and the trail so impassable, she would have taken the baby and have gone over to Ryckman's, her nearest neighbor. But then, you see, he might have returned in the storm, all wet, with no one to see to him; and it was a long exposure for baby, who was croupy and ailing.

But that night, she never could tell why, she didn't feel like sleeping or even lying down. The storm had somewhat abated, but she still "sat and sat," and even tried to read. I don't know whether it was a Bible or some profane magazine that this poor woman read, but most probably the latter, for the words all ran together and made such sad nonsense that she was forced at last to put the book down and turn to that dearer volume which lay before her in the cradle, with its white initial leaf as yet unsoiled, and try to look forward to its mysterious future. And, rocking the cradle, she thought of everything and everybody, but still was wide awake as ever.

It was nearly twelve o'clock when she at last laid down in her clothes. How long she slept she could not remember, but she awoke with a dreadful choking in her throat, and found herself standing, trembling all over, in the middle of the room, with her baby clasped to her breast, and she was "saying something." The baby cried and sobbed, and she walked up and down trying to hush it, when she heard a scratching at the door. She opened it fearfully, and was glad to see it was only old Pete, their dog, who crawled, dripping with water, into the room. She would like to have looked out, not in the faint hope of her husband's coming, but to see how things looked; but the wind shook the door so savagely that she could hardly hold it. Then she sat down a little while, and then walked up and down a little while, and then she lay down again a little while. Lying close by the wall of the little cabin, she thought she heard once or twice something scrape slowly against the clapboards, like the scraping of branches. Then there was a little gurgling sound, "like the baby made when it was swallowing"; then something went "click-click" and "cluck-cluck," so that she sat up in bed. When she did so she was attracted by something else that seemed creeping from the back door towards the centre of the room. It wasn't much wider than her little finger, but soon it swelled to the width of her hand, and began spreading all over the floor. It was water.

She ran to the front door and threw it wide open, and saw nothing but water. She ran to the back door and threw it open, and saw nothing but water. She ran to the side window, and, throwing that open, she saw nothing but water. Then she remembered hearing her husband once say that there was no danger in the tide, for that fell regularly, and people could calculate on it, and that he would rather live near the bay than the river, whose banks might overflow at any time. But was it the tide? So she ran again to the back door, and threw out a stick of wood. It drifted away towards the bay. She scooped up some of the water and put it eagerly to her lips. It was fresh and sweet. It was the river, and not the tide!

It was then—O, God be praised for his goodness! she did neither faint nor fall; it was then—blessed be the Saviour for it was his merciful hand that touched and strengthened her in this awful moment—that fear dropped from her like a garment, and her trembling ceased. It was then and thereafter that she never lost her self-command, through all the trials of that gloomy night.

She drew the bedstead towards the middle of the room, and placed a table upon it and on that she put the cradle. The water on the floor was already over her ankles, and the house once or twice moved so perceptibly, and seemed to be racked so, that the closet doors all flew open. Then she heard the same rasping and thumping against the wall, and, looking out, saw that a large uprooted tree, which had lain near the road at the upper end of the pasture, had floated down to the house. Luckily its long roots dragged in the soil and kept it from moving as rapidly as the current, for had it struck the house in its full career, even the strong nails and bolts in the piles could not have withstood the shock. The hound had leaped upon its knotty surface, and crouched near the roots shivering and whining. A ray of hope flashed across her mind. She drew a heavy blanket from the bed, and, wrapping it about the babe, waded in the deepening waters to the door. As the tree swung again, broadside on, making the little cabin creak and tremble, she leaped on to its trunk. By God's mercy she succeeded in obtaining a footing on its slippery surface, and, twining an arm about its roots, she held in the other her moaning child. Then something cracked near the front porch, and the whole front of the house she had just quitted fell forward,—just as cattle fall on their knees before they lie down,—and at the same moment the great redwood-tree swung round and drifted away with its living cargo into the black night.

For all the excitement and danger, for all her soothing of her crying babe, for all the whistling of the wind, for all the uncertainty of her situation, she still turned to look at the deserted and water-swept cabin. She remembered even then, and she wondered how foolish she was to think of it at that time, that she wished she had put on another dress and the baby's best clothes; and she kept praying that the house would be spared so that he, when he returned, would have something to come to, and it wouldn't be quite so desolate, and—how could he ever know what had become of her and baby? And at the thought she grew sick and faint. But she had something else to do besides worrying, for whenever the long roots of her ark struck an obstacle, the whole trunk made half a revolution, and twice dipped her in the black water. The hound, who kept distracting her by running up and down the tree and howling, at last fell off at one of these collisions. He swam for some time beside her, and she tried to get the poor beast upon the tree, but he "acted silly" and wild, and at last she lost sight of him forever. Then she and her baby were left alone. The light which had burned for a few minutes in the deserted cabin was quenched suddenly. She could not then tell whither she was drifting. The outline of the white dunes on the peninsula showed dimly ahead, and she judged the tree was moving in a line with the river. It must be about slack water, and she had probably reached the eddy formed by the confluence of the tide and the overflowing

waters of the river. Unless the tide fell soon, there was present
danger of her drifting to its channel, and being carried out to
sea or crushed in the floating drift. That peril averted, if she
were carried out on the ebb toward the bay, she might hope to
strike one of the wooded promontories of the peninsula, and
rest till daylight. Sometimes she thought she heard voices and
shouts from the river, and the bellowing of cattle and bleating
of sheep. Then again it was only the ringing in her ears and
throbbing of her heart. She found at about this time that she
was so chilled and stiffened in her cramped position that she
could scarcely move, and the baby cried so when she put it to
her breast that she noticed the milk refused to flow; and she was
so frightened at that, that she put her head under her shawl, and
for the first time cried bitterly.

When she raised her head again, the boom of the surf was
behind her, and she knew that her ark had again swung round.
She dipped up the water to cool her parched throat, and found
that it was salt as her tears. There was a relief, though, for by
this sign she knew that she was drifting with the tide. It was
then the wind went down, and the great and awful silence oppressed her. There was scarcely a ripple against the furrowed
sides of the great trunk on which she rested, and around her all
was black gloom and quiet. She spoke to the baby just to hear
herself speak, and to know that she had not lost her voice. She
thought then,—it was queer, but she could not help thinking it,
—how awful must have been the night when the great ship
swung over the Asiatic peak, and the sounds of creation were
blotted out from the world. She thought, too, of mariners clinging to spars, and of poor women who were lashed to rafts, and
beaten to death by the cruel sea. She tried to thank God that
she was thus spared, and lifted her eyes from the baby who had
fallen into a fretful sleep. Suddenly, away to the southward, a
great light lifted itself out of the gloom, and flashed and flickered, and flickered and flashed again. Her heart fluttered
quickly against the baby's cold cheek. It was the lighthouse at
the entrance of the bay. As she was yet wondering, the tree

suddenly rolled a little, dragged a little, and then seemed to lie quiet and still. She put out her hand and the current gurgled against it. The tree was aground, and, by the position of the light and the noise of the surf, aground upon the Dedlow Marsh.

Had it not been for her baby, who was ailing and croupy, had it not been for the sudden drying up of that sensitive fountain, she would have felt safe and relieved. Perhaps it was this which tended to make all her impressions mournful and gloomy. As the tide rapidly fell, a great flock of black brent fluttered by her, screaming and crying. Then the plover flew up and piped mournfully, as they wheeled around the trunk, and at last fearlessly lit upon it like a gray cloud. Then the heron flew over and around her, shrieking and protesting, and at last dropped its gaunt legs only a few yards from her. But, strangest of all, a pretty white bird, larger than a dove,—like a pelican, but not a pelican,—circled around and around her. At last it lit upon a rootlet of the tree, quite over her shoulder. She put out her hand and stroked its beautiful white neck, and it never appeared to move. It stayed there so long that she thought she would lift up the baby to see it, and try to attract her attention. But when she did so, the child was so chilled and cold, and had such a blue look under the little lashes which it didn't raise at all, that she screamed aloud, and the bird flew away, and she fainted.

Well, that was the worst of it, and perhaps it was not so much, after all, to any but herself. For when she recovered her senses it was bright sunlight, and dead low water. There was a confused noise of guttural voices about her, and an old squaw, singing an Indian "hushaby," and rocking herself from side to side before a fire built on the marsh, before which she, the recovered wife and mother, lay weak and weary. Her first thought was for her baby, and she was about to speak, when a young squaw, who must have been a mother herself, fathomed her thought and brought her the "mowitch," pale but living, in such a queer little willow cradle all bound up, just like the squaw's own young one, that she laughed and cried together, and the young squaw and the old squaw showed their big white teeth and glinted their black eyes and said, "Plenty get well, skeena mowitch," "wagee man come plenty soon," and she could have kissed their brown faces in her joy. And then she found that they had been gathering berries on the marsh in their queer, comical baskets, and saw the skirt of her gown fluttering on the tree from afar, and the old squaw couldn't resist the temptation of procuring a new garment, and came down and discovered the "wagee" woman and child. And of course she gave the garment to the old squaw, as you may imagine, and when *he* came at last and rushed up to her, looking about ten years older in anxiety, she felt so faint again that they had to carry her to the canoe. For, you see, he knew nothing about the flood until he met the Indians at Utopia, and knew by the signs that the poor woman was his wife. And at the next high-tide he towed the tree away back home, although it wasn't worth the trouble, and built another house, using the old tree for the foundation and props, and called it after her, "Mary's Ark!" But you may guess the next house was built above High-Water Mark. And that's all.

Not much, perhaps, considering the malevolent capacity of the Dedlow Marsh. But you must tramp over it at low water, or paddle over it at high tide, or get lost upon it once or twice in the fog, as I have, to understand properly Mary's adventure, or to appreciate duly the blessings of living beyond High-Water Mark.

# THE CORVETTE *CLAYMORE*

From "Ninety-three," by Victor Hugo

The corvette, instead of sailing south, in the direction of St. Catherine, headed to the north, then, veering towards the west, had boldly entered that arm of the sea between Sark and Jersey called the Passage of the Déroute. There was then no lighthouse at any point on either coast. It had been a clear sunset; the night was darker than summer nights usually are; it was moonlight, but large clouds, rather of the equinox than of the solstice overspread the sky, and, judging by appearances, the moon would not be visible until she reached the horizon at the moment of setting. A few clouds hung low near the surface of the sea and covered it with vapor.

All this darkness was favorable. Gacquoil, the pilot, intended to leave Jersey on the left, Guernsey on the right, and by boldly sailing between Hanois and Dover, to reach some bay on the coast near St. Malo, a longer but safer route than the one through Minquiers; for the French coaster had standing orders to keep an unusually sharp lookout between St. Hélier and Granville.

If the wind were favorable, and nothing happened, by dint of setting all sail Gacquoil hoped to reach the coast of France at daybreak.

All went well. The corvette had just passed Gros Nez. Towards nine o'clock the weather looked sullen, as the sailors express it, both wind and sea rising; but the wind was favorable, and the sea was rough, yet not heavy, the waves now and then dashing over the bow of the corvette. "The peasant" whom Lord Balcarras had called general, and whom the Prince de La Tour d'Auvergne had addressed as cousin, was a good sailor, and paced the deck of the corvette with calm dignity. He did not seem to notice that she rocked considerably. From time to time he took out of his waistcoat pocket a cake of chocolate, and breaking off a piece, munched it. Though his hair was gray, his teeth were sound.

He spoke to no one, except that from time to time he made a few concise remarks in an undertone to the captain, who listened to him deferentially, apparently regarding his passenger as the commander, rather than himself. Unobserved in the fog, and skilfully piloted, the *Claymore* coasted along the steep shore to the north of Jersey, hugging the land to avoid the formidable reef of Pierres-de-Leeq, which lies in the middle of the strait between Jersey and Sark. Gacquoil, at the helm, sighting in turn Grève de Leeq, Gros Nez, and Plérmont, making the corvette glide in among those chains of reefs, felt his way along to a certain extent but with the self-confidence of one familiar with the ways of the sea.

The corvette had no light forward, fearing to betray its passage through these guarded waters. They congratulated themselves on the fog. The Grande Etape was reached; the mist was so dense that the lofty outlines of the Pinnacle were scarcely visible. They heard it strike ten from the belfry of Saint-Ouen, —a sign that the wind was still aft. All was going well; the sea grew rougher, because they were drawing near La Corbière.

A little after ten, the Count Boisberthelot and the Chevalier de la Vieuville escorted the man in the peasant garb to the door of his cabin, which was the captain's own room. As he was about to enter, he remarked, lowering his voice:—

"You understand the importance of keeping the secret, gentlemen. Silence up to the moment of explosion. You are the only ones here who know my name."

"We will carry it to the grave," replied Boisberthelot.

"And for my part, I would not reveal it were I face to face with death," remarked the old man.

And he entered his stateroom.

The commander and the first officer returned on deck, and began to pace up and down side by side, talking as they walked.

The theme was evidently their passenger; and this was the substance of the conversation which the wind wafted through the darkness. Boisberthelot grumbled half audibly to La Vieuville,—

"It remains to be seen whether or no he is a leader."

La Vieuville replied,—

"Meanwhile he is a prince."

"Almost."

"A nobleman in France, but a prince in Brittany."

"Like the Trémouilles and the Rohans."

"With whom he is connected."

Boisberthelot resumed,—

"In France and in the carriages of the king he is a marquis, —as I am a count, and you a chevalier."

"The carriages are far away!" exclaimed Vieuville. "We are living in the time of the tumbril."

A silence ensued.

Boisberthelot went on,—

"For lack of a French prince we take one from Brittany."

"For lack of thrushes—No: since an eagle is not to be found, we take a crow."

"I should prefer a vulture," remarked Boisberthelot.

La Vieuville replied,—

"Yes, indeed, with a beak and talons."

"We shall see."

"Yes," replied Vieuville, "it is time there was a leader. I agree with Tinténiac,—a leader and gunpowder! See here, commander, I know nearly all the possible and impossible leaders, —those of yesterday, those of to-day, and those of to-morrow. Not one of them has the head required for war. In this cursed Vendée a general is needed who would be a lawyer as well as a leader. He must harass the enemy, dispute every bush, ditch, and stone; he must force unlucky quarrels upon him, and take advantage of everything; vigilant and pitiless, he must watch incessantly, slaughter freely, and make examples. Now, in this army of peasants there are heroes, but no captains. D'Elbée is a nonentity, Lescure an invalid; Bonchamps is merciful,—he is kind, and that implies folly; La Rochejaquelein is a superb sub-lieutenant; Silz is an officer good for the open field, but not suited for a war that needs a man of expedients; Cathelineau is a simple teamster; Stofflet is a crafty game-keeper; Bérard is inefficient; Boulainvilliers is absurd; Charette is horrible. I make no mention of Gaston the barber. Mordemonbleu! What is the use of opposing revolution, and what is the difference between ourselves and the republicans, if we set barbers over the heads of noblemen! The fact is, that this beastly revolution has contaminated all of us."

"It is the itch of France."

"It is the itch of the Tiers état," rejoined Boisberthelot. "England alone can help us."

"And she will, captain, undoubtedly."

"Meanwhile it is an ugly state of affairs."

"Yes,—rustics everywhere. A monarchy that has Stofflet, the game-keeper of M. de Maulevrier, for a commander has no reason to envy a republic whose minister is Pache, the son of the Duke de Castries' porter. What men this Vendean war brings face to face—on one side Santerre the brewer; on the other Gaston the hairdresser!"

"My dear La Vieuville, I feel some respect for this Gaston. He behaved well in his command of Guémenée. He had three hundred Blues neatly shot after making them dig their own graves."

"Well enough done; but I could have done quite as well as he."

"Pardieu, to be sure; and I too."

"The great feats of war," said Vieuville, "require noble blood in those who perform them. These are matters for knights, and not for hairdressers."

"But yet there are estimable men in this 'Third Estate,'" rejoined Vieuville. "Take that watchmaker, Joly, for instance. He was formerly a sergeant in a Flanders regiment; he becomes a Vendean chief and commander of a coast band. He has a son, a republican; and while the father serves in the ranks of the Whites, the son serves in those of the Blues. An encounter, a battle: the father captures the son and blows out his brains."

"He did well," said La Vieuville.

"A royalist Brutus," answered Boisberthelot. "Nevertheless, it is unendurable to be under the command of a Coquereau, a Jean-Jean, a Moulin, a Focart, a Bouju, a Chouppes!"

"My dear chevalier, the opposite party is quite as indignant. We are crowded with plebeians; they have an excess of nobles. Do you think the sansculottes like to be commanded by the Count de Canclaux, the Viscount de Miranda, the Viscount de Beauharnais, the Count de Valence, the Marquis de Custine, and the Duke de Biron?"

"What a combination!"

"And the Duke de Chartres!"

"Son of Egalité. By the way, when will he be king?"

"Never!"

"He aspires to the throne, and his very crimes serve to promote his interests."

"And his vices will injure his cause," said Boisberthelot.

Then, after another pause, he continued,—

"Nevertheless, he was anxious to be reconciled. He came to see the king. I was at Versailles when some one spit on his back."

"From the top of the grand staircase?"

"Yes."

"I am glad of it."

"We called him Bourbon le Bourbeaux."

"He is bald-headed; he has pimples; he is a regicide. Poh!"

And La Vieuville added:—

"I was with him at Ouessant."

"On the *Saint Esprit?*"

"Yes."

"Had he obeyed Admiral d'Orvillier's signal to keep to the windward, he would have prevented the English from passing."

"True."

"Was he really hidden in the bottom of the hold?"

"No; but we must say so all the same."

And La Vieuville burst out laughing.

Boisberthelot continued:—

"Fools are plentiful. Look here, I have known this Boulain-villiers of whom you were speaking; I knew him well. At first the peasants were armed with pikes; would you believe it, he took it into his head to form them into pike-men. He wanted to drill them in crossing pikes and repelling a charge. He dreamed of transforming these barbarians into regular soldiers. He undertook to teach them how to round in the corners of their squares, and to mass battalions with hollow squares. He jabbered the antiquated military dialect to them; he called the chief of a squad a *cap d'escade*,—which was what corporals under Louis XIV, were called. He persisted in forming a regiment of all those poachers. He had regular companies whose sergeants ranged themselves in a circle every evening, and, receiving the sign and countersign from the colonel's sergeant, repeated it in a whisper to the lieutenant's sergeant, who repeated it to his next neighbor, who in his turn transmitted it to the next man, and so on from ear to ear until it reached the last man. He cashiered an officer for not standing bareheaded to receive the watchword from the sergeant. You may imagine how he succeeded. This simpleton could not understand that peasants have to be led peasant fashion, and that it is impossible to transform rustics into soldiers. Yes, I have known Boulainvilliers."

They walked along a few steps, each one engrossed in his own thoughts.

Then the conversation was resumed:—

"By the way, has the report of Dampierre's death been confirmed?"

"Yes, commander."

"Before Condé?"

"At the camp of Pamars; he was hit by a cannon-ball."

Boisberthelot sighed.

"Count Dampierre,—another of our men, who took sides with them."

"May he prosper wherever he may be!" said Vieuville.

"And the ladies,—where are they?"

"At Trieste."

"Still there?"

"Yes."

"Ah, this republic!" exclaimed La Vieuville. "What havoc from so slight a cause! To think that this revolution was the result of a deficit of only a few millions!"

"Insignificant beginnings are not always to be trusted."

"Everything goes wrong," replied La Vieuville.

"Yes; La Rouarie is dead. Du Dresnay is an idiot. What wretched leaders are all those bishops,—this Coucy, bishop of La Rochelle; Beaupoil Saint-Aulaire, bishop of Poitiers; Mercy, bishop of Luzon, a lover of Madame de l'Eschasserie—"

"Whose name is Servanteau, you know, commander. Eschasserie is the name of an estate."

"And that false bishop of Agra, who is a curé of I know not what!"

"Of Dol. His name is Guillot de Folleville. But then he is brave, and knows how to fight."

"Priests when one needs soldiers! bishops who are no bishops at all! generals who are no generals!"

La Vieuville interrupted Boisberthelot.

"Have you the *Moniteur* in your stateroom, commander?"

"Yes."

"What are they giving now in Paris?"

" 'Adèle and Pauline' and 'La Caverne.' "

"I should like to see that."

"You may. We shall be in Paris in a month."

Boisberthelot thought a moment, and then added:

"At the latest,—so Mr. Windham told Lord Hood."

"Then, commander, I take it affairs are not going so very badly?"

"All would go well, provided that the Breton war were well managed."

La Vieuville shook his head.

"Commander," he said, "are we to land the marines?"

"Certainly, if the coast is friendly, but not otherwise. In some cases war must force the gates; in others it can slip through them. Civil war must always keep a false key in its pocket. We will do all we can; but one must have a chief."

And Boisberthelot added thoughtfully,—

"What do you think of the Chevalier de Dieuzie, La Vieuville?"

"Do you mean the younger?"

"Yes."

"For a commander?"

"Yes."

"He is only good for a pitched battle in the open field. It is only the peasant who knows the underbrush."

"In that case, you may as well resign yourself to Generals Stofflet and Cathelineau."

La Vieuville mediated for a moment; then he said,—

"What we need is a prince,—a French prince, a prince of the blood, a real prince."

"How can that be? He who says 'prince'—"

"Says 'coward.' I know it, commander. But we need him for the impression he would produce upon the herd."

"My dear chevalier, the princes don't care to come."

"We will do without them."

Boisberthelot pressed his hand mechanically against his forehead, as if striving to evoke an idea. He resumed,—

"Then let us try this general."

"He is a great nobleman."

"Do you think he will do?"

"If he is one of the right sort," said La Vieuville.

"You mean relentless?" said Boisberthelot.

The count and the chevalier looked at each other.

"Monsieur Boisberthelot, you have defined the meaning of

the word. Relentless,—yes, that's what we need. This is a war that shows no mercy. The bloodthirsty are in the ascendant. The regicides have beheaded Louis XVI; we will quarter the regicides. Yes, the general we need is General Relentless. In Anjou and Upper Poitou the leaders play the magnanimous; they trifle with generosity, and they are always defeated. In the Marais and the country of Retz, where the leaders are ferocious, everything goes bravely forward. It is because Charette is fierce that he stands his ground against Parrein,—hyena pitted against hyena."

Boisberthelot had no time to answer. Vieuville's words were suddenly cut short by a desperate cry, and at the same instant they heard a noise unlike all other sounds. This cry and the unusual sounds came from the interior of the vessel.

The captain and the lieutenant rushed to the gun-deck, but were unable to enter. All the gunners came running up, beside themselves with terror.

A frightful thing had just happened.

One of the carronades of the battery, a twenty-four pound cannon, had become loose.

This is perhaps the most dreadful thing that can take place at sea. Nothing more terrible can happen to a man-of-war under full sail.

A cannon that breaks loose from its fastenings is suddenly transformed into a supernatural beast. It is a monster developed from a machine. This mass runs along on its wheels as easily as a billiard ball; it rolls with the rolling, pitches with the pitching, comes and goes, stops, seems to meditate, begins anew, darts like an arrow from one end of the ship to the other, whirls around, turns aside, evades, rears, hits out, crushes, kills, exterminates. It is a ram battering a wall at its own pleasure. Moreover, the battering-ram is iron, the wall is wood. It is matter set free; one might say that this eternal slave is wreaking its vengeance; it would seem as though the evil in what we call inanimate objects had found vent and suddenly burst forth; it has the air of having lost its patience, and of taking a mysterious, dull revenge; nothing is so inexorable as the rage of the inanimate. The mad mass leaps like a panther; it has the weight of an elephant, the agility of a mouse, the obstinacy of the axe; it takes one by surprise, like the surge of the sea; it flashes like lightning; it is deaf as the tomb; it weighs ten thousand pounds, and it bounds like a child's ball; it whirls as it advances, and the circles it describes are intersected by right angles. And what help is there? How can it be overcome? A calm succeeds the tempest, a cyclone passes over, a wind dies away, we replace the broken mass, we check the leak, we extinguish the fire; but what is to be done with this enormous bronze beast? How can it be subdued? You can reason with a mastiff, take a bull by surprise, fascinate a snake, frighten a tiger, mollify a lion; but there is no resource with the monster known as a loosened gun. You cannot kill it,—it is already dead; and yet it lives. It breathes a sinister life bestowed on it by the Infinite. The plank beneath sways it to and fro; it is moved by the ship; the sea lifts the ship, and the wind keeps the sea in motion. This destroyer is a toy. Its terrible vitality is fed by the ship, the waves, and the wind, each lending its aid. What is to be done with this complication? How fetter this monstrous mechanism of shipwreck? How foresee its comings and goings, its recoils, its halts, its shocks? Any one of those blows may stave in the side of the vessel. How can one guard against these terrible gyrations? One has to do with a projectile that reflects, that has ideas, and changes its direction at any moment. How can one arrest an object in its course, whose onslaught must be avoided? The dreadful cannon rushes about, advances, recedes, strikes to right and to left, flies here and there, baffles their attempts at capture, sweeps away obstacles, crushing men like flies.

The extreme danger of the situation comes from the unsteadiness of the deck. How is one to cope with the caprices of an inclined plane? The ship had within its depths, so to speak, imprisoned lightning struggling for escape; something like the rumbling of thunder during an earthquake. In an instant the crew was on its feet. It was the chief gunner's fault, who had neglected to fasten the screw-nut of the breeching chain, and had not thoroughly chocked the four trucks of the carronade, which allowed play to the frame and the bottom of the gun-carriage, thereby disarranging the two platforms and parting the breeching. The lashings were broken, so that the gun was no longer firm on its carriage. The stationary breeching which prevents the recoil was not in use at that time. As a wave struck the ship's side the cannon, insufficiently secured, had receded, and having broken its chain, began to wander threateningly over the deck. In order to get an idea of this strange sliding, fancy a drop of water sliding down a pane of glass.

When the fastening broke, the gunners were in the battery, singly and in groups, clearing the ship for action. The carronade, thrown forward by the pitching, dashed into a group of men, killing four of them at the first blow; then, hurled back by the rolling, it cut in two an unfortunate fifth man, and struck and dismounted one of the guns of the larboard battery. Hence the cry of distress which had been heard. All the men rushed to the ladder. The gun-deck was empty in the twinkling of an eye.

The monstrous gun was left to itself. It was its own mistress, and mistress of the ship. It could do with it whatsoever it wished. This crew, accustomed to laugh in battle, now trembled. It would be impossible to describe their terror.

Captain Boisberthelot and Lieutenant la Vieuville, brave men though they were, paused at the top of the ladder, silent, pale, and undecided, looking down on the deck. Some one pushed them aside with his elbow, and descended. It was their passenger, the peasant, the man about whom they were talking a moment ago.

Having reached the bottom of the ladder he halted.

The cannon was rolling to and fro on the deck. It might have been called the living chariot of the Apocalypse. A dim wavering of lights and shadows was added to this spectacle by the marine lantern, swinging under the deck. The outlines of the cannon were indistinguishable, by reason of the rapidity of its motion; sometimes it looked black when the light shone upon it, then again it would cast pale, glimmering reflections in the darkness.

It was still pursuing its work of destruction. It had already shattered four other pieces, and made two breaches in the ship's side, fortunately above the water-line, but which would leak in case of rough weather. It rushed frantically against the timbers; the stout riders resisted,—curved timbers have great strength; but one could hear them crack under this tremendous assault brought to bear simultaneously on every side, with a certain omnipresence truly appalling.

A bullet shaken in a bottle could not produce sharper or more rapid sounds. The four wheels were passing and repassing over the dead bodies, cutting and tearing them to pieces, and the five corpses had become five trunks rolling hither and thither; the heads seemed to cry out; streams of blood flowed over the deck, following the motion of the ship. The ceiling, damaged in several places, had begun to give way. The whole ship was filled with a dreadful tumult.

The captain, who had rapidly recovered his self-possession, had given orders to throw down the hatchway all that could abate the rage and check the mad onslaught of this infuriated gun; mattresses, hammocks, spare sails, coils of rope, the bags of the crew, and bales of false assignats, with which the corvette was laden,—that infamous stratagem of English origin being considered a fair trick in war.

But what availed these rags? No one dared to go down to arrange them, and in a few moments they were reduced to lint.

There was just sea enough to render this accident as complete as possible. A tempest would have been welcome. It might have upset the cannon, and with its four wheels once in the air, it could easily have been mastered. Meanwhile the havoc increased. There were even incisions and fractures in the masts, that stood like pillars grounded firmly in the keel, and piercing the several decks of the vessel. The mizzen-mast was split, and even the main-mast was damaged by the convulsive blows of the cannon. The destruction of the battery still went on. Ten out of the thirty pieces were useless. The fractures in the side increased, and the corvette began to leak.

The old passenger, who had descended to the gun-deck, looked like one carved in stone as he stood motionless at the foot of the stairs and glanced sternly over the devastation. It would have been impossible to move a step upon the deck.

Each bound of the liberated carronade seemed to threaten the destruction of the ship. But a few moments longer, and ship-wreck would be inevitable.

They must either overcome this calamity or perish; some decisive action must be taken. But what?

What a combatant was this carronade!

Here was this mad creature to be arrested, this flash of light-ning to be seized, this thunderbolt to be crushed. Boisberthelot said to Vieuville:—

"Do you believe in God, chevalier?"

"Yes and no, sometimes I do!" replied La Vieuville.

"In a tempest?"

"Yes, and in moments like these."

"Truly God alone can save us," said Boisberthelot.

All were silent, leaving the carronade to its horrible uproar.

The waves beating the ship from without answered the blows of the cannon within, very much like a couple of hammers striking in turn.

Suddenly in the midst of this inaccessible circus, where the escaped cannon was tossing from side to side, a man appeared, grasping an iron bar. It was the author of the catastrophe, the chief gunner, whose criminal negligence had caused the acci-dent,—the captain of the gun. Having brought about the evil, his intention was to repair it. Holding a handspike in one hand, and in the other a tiller rope with the slip-noose in it, he had jumped through the hatchway to the deck below.

Then began a terrible struggle; a titanic spectacle; a combat between cannon and cannoneer; a contest between mind and matter; a duel between man and the inanimate. The man stood in one corner in an attitude of expectancy, leaning on the rider and holding in his hands the bar and the rope; calm, livid, and tragic, he stood firmly on his legs, that were like two pillars of steel.

He was waiting for the cannon to approach him.

The gunner knew his piece, and he felt as though it must know him. They had lived together a long time. How often had he put his hand in its mouth. It was his domestic monster. He began to talk to it as he would to a dog. "Come," said he. Possibly he loved it.

He seemed to wish for its coming, and yet its approach meant sure destruction for him. How to avoid being crushed was the question. All looked on in terror.

Not a breath was drawn freely, except perhaps by the old man, who remained on the gun-deck gazing sternly on the two combatants.

He himself was in danger of being crushed by the piece; still he did not move.

Beneath them the blind sea had command of the battle. When, in the act of accepting this awful hand-to-hand struggle, the gunner approached to challenge the cannon, it happened that the surging sea held the gun motionless for an instant, as though stupefied. "Come on!" said the man. It seemed to listen.

Suddenly it leaped towards him. The man dodged. Then the struggle began,—a contest unheard of; the fragile wrestling with the invulnerable; the human warrior attacking the brazen beast; blind force on the one side, soul on the other.

All this was in the shadow. It was like an indistinct vision of a miracle.

A soul!—strangely enough it seemed as if a soul existed within the cannon, but one consumed with hate and rage. The blind thing seemed to have eyes. It appeared as though the monster were watching the man. There was, or at least one might have supposed it, cunning in this mass. It also chose its opportunity. It was as though a gigantic insect of iron was endowed with the will of a demon. Now and then this colossal grasshopper would strike the low ceiling of the gun-deck, then falling back on its four wheels, like a tiger on all fours, rush upon the man. He—supple, agile, adroit—writhed like a serpent before these lightning movements. He avoided encounters; but the blows from which he escaped fell with destructive force upon the vessel. A piece of broken chain remained attached to the carronade. This bit of chain had twisted in some incomprehensible way around the breech button.

One end of the chain was fastened to the gun-carriage; the other end thrashed wildly around, aggravating the danger with every bound of the cannon. The screw held it as in a clenched hand, and this chain, multiplying the strokes of the battering-ram by those of the thong, made a terrible whirlwind around the gun,—a lash of iron in a fist of brass. This chain complicated the combat.

Despite all this, the man fought. He even attacked the cannon at times, crawling along by the side of the ship and clutching his handspike and the rope; the cannon seemed to understand his movements, and fled as though suspecting a trap. The man, nothing daunted, pursued his chase.

Such a struggle must necessarily be brief. Suddenly the cannon seemed to say to itself: Now, then, there must be an end to this. And it stopped. A crisis was felt to be at hand. The cannon, as if in suspense, seemed to meditate, or—for to all intents and purposes it was a living creature—it really did mediate, some furious design. All at once it rushed on the gunner, who sprang aside with a laugh, crying out, "Try it again!" as the cannon passed him. The gun in its fury smashed one of the larboard carronades; then, by the invisible sling in which it seemed to be held, it was thrown to the starboard, towards the man, who escaped. Three carronades were crushed by its onslaught; then, as though blind and beside itself it turned from the man, and rolled from stern to stem, splintering the latter, and causing a breach in the walls of the prow. The gunner took refuge at the foot of the ladder, a short distance from the old man, who stood watching. He held his handspike in readiness. The cannon seemed aware of it, and without taking the trouble to turn, it rushed backward on the man, as swift as the blow of an axe. The gunner, if driven up against the side of the ship, would be lost.

One cry arose from the crew.

The old passenger—who until this moment had stood motionless—sprang forward more swiftly than all those mad swirls. He had seized a bale of the false assignats, and at the risk of being crushed succeeded in throwing it between the wheels of the carronade. This decisive and perilous manœuvre could not have been executed with more precision and adroitness by an adept in all the exercises given in the work of Durosel's "Manual of Naval Gunnery."

The bale had the effect of a plug. A pebble may block a log; a branch sometimes changes the course of an avalanche. The carronade stumbled, and the gunner, availing himself of the perilous opportunity, thrust his iron bar between the spokes of the back wheels. Pitching forward, the cannon stopped; and the man, using his bar for a lever, rocked it backward and forward. The heavy mass upset, with the resonant sound of a bell that crashes in its fall. The man, reeking with perspiration, threw himself upon it, and passed the slip-noose of the tiller-rope around the neck of the defeated monster.

The combat was ended. The man had conquered. The ant had overcome the mastodon; the pygmy had imprisoned the thunderbolt.

The soldiers and sailors applauded.

The crew rushed forward with chains and cables, and in an instant the cannon was secured.

Saluting the passenger, the gunner exclaimed,—

"Sir, you have saved my life!"

The old man had resumed his impassible attitude, and made no reply.

The man had conquered; but it might be affirmed that the cannon also had gained a victory. Immediate shipwreck was averted; but the corvette was still in danger. The injuries the ship had sustained seemed irreparable. There were five breaches in the sides, on of them—a very large one—in the bow, and twenty carronades out of thirty lay shattered in their frames. The recaptured gun, which had been secured by a chain, was itself disabled. The screw of the breech-button being wrenched, it would consequently be impossible to level the cannon. The battery was reduced to nine guns; there was a leakage in the hold. All these damages must be repaired without loss of time, and the pumps set in operation. Now that the gun-deck had become visible, it was frightful to look upon. The interior of a mad elephant's cage could not have been more thoroughly devastated. However important it might be for the corvette to avoid observation, the care for its immediate safety was still more imperative. They were obliged to light the deck with lanterns placed at intervals along the sides.

In the meantime, while this tragic entertainment had lasted, the crew, entirely absorbed by a question of life and death, had not noticed what was going on outside of the ship. The fog had thickened, the weather had changed, the wind had driven the vessel at will; they were out of their course, in full sight of Jersey and Guernsey, much farther to the south than they ought to have been, and confronting a tumultuous sea. The big waves kissed the wounded sides of the corvette with kisses that savored of danger. The heaving of the sea grew threatening; the wind had risen to a gale; a squall, perhaps a tempest, was brewing. One could not see four oars' length before one.

While the crew made haste with their temporary repairs on the gun-deck, stopping the leaks and setting up the cannons that had escaped uninjured, the old passenger returned to the deck.

He stood leaning against the main-mast.

He had taken no notice of what was going on in the ship. The Chevalier de la Vieuville had drawn up the marines on either side of the main-mast, and at a signal-whistle of the boatswain the sailors, who had been busy in the rigging, stood up on the yards. Count Boisberthelot approached the passenger. The captain was followed by a man, who, haggard and panting, with his dress in disorder, still wore on his countenance an expression of content.

It was the gunner who had so opportunely displayed his power as a tamer of monsters, and gained the victory over the cannon.

The count made a military salute to the old man in the peasant garb, and said to him:—

"Here is the man, general."

The gunner, with downcast eyes, stood erect in a military attitude.

"General," resumed Count Boisberthelot, "considering what this man has done, do you not think that his superiors have a duty to perform?"

"I think so," replied the old man.

"Be so good as to give your orders," resumed Boisberthelot.

"It is for you to give them; you are the captain."

"But you are the general," answered Boisberthelot.

The old man looked at the gunner.

"Step forward," he said.

The gunner advanced a step.

Turning to Count Boisberthelot, the old man removed the cross of Saint Louis from the captain's breast, and fastened it on the jacket of the gunner. The sailors cheered, and the marines presented arms.

Then pointing to the bewildered gunner he added:

"Now let the man be shot!"

Stupor took the place of applause.

Then, amid a tomb-like silence, the old man, raising his voice, said:—

"The ship has been endangered by an act of carelessness, and may even yet be lost. It is all the same whether one be at sea or face to face with the enemy. A ship at sea is like an army in battle. The tempest, though unseen, is ever present; the sea is an ambush. Death is the fit penalty for every fault committed when facing the enemy. There is no fault that can be retrieved. Courage must be rewarded and negligence be punished."

These words fell one after the other slowly and gravely, with a certain implacable rhythm, like the strokes of the axe upon an oak-tree. Looking at the soldiers, the old man added,—

"Do your duty!"

The man on whose breast shone the cross of Saint Louis bowed his head, and at a sign of Count Boisberthelot two sailors went down to the gun-deck, and presently returned bringing the hammock-shroud; the two sailors were accompanied by the ship's chaplain, who since the departure had been engaged in saying prayers in the officers' quarters. A sergeant detached from the ranks twelve soldiers, whom he arranged in two rows, six men in a row. The gunner placed himself between the two lines. The chaplain, holding a crucifix, advanced and took his place beside the man. "March!" came from the lips of the sergeant; and the platoon slowly moved towards the bow, followed by two sailors carrying the shroud.

A gloomy silence fell on the corvette. In the distance a hurricane was blowing. A few moments later, a report echoed through the gloom; one flash, and all was still. Then came the splash of a body falling into the water. The old passenger, still leaning against the main-mast, his hands crossed on his breast, seemed lost in thought. Boisberthelot, pointing towards him with the forefinger of his left hand, remarked in an undertone to La Vieuville,—

"The Vendée has found a leader."

# SPANISH BLOODHOUNDS AND ENGLISH
# MASTIFFS

From "Westward Ho!" BY CHARLES KINGSLEY

WHEN the sun leaped up the next morning, and the tropic light flashed suddenly into the tropic day, Amyas was pacing the deck, with disheveled hair and torn clothes, his eyes red with rage and weeping, his heart full—how can I describe it? Picture it to yourselves, you who have ever lost a brother; and you who have not, thank God that you know nothing of his agony. Full of impossible projects, he strode and staggered up and down, as the ship thrashed and close-hauled through the rolling seas. He would go back and burn the villa. He would take Guayra, and have the life of every man in it in return for his brother's. "We can do it, lads!" he shouted. "If Drake took Nombre de Dios, we can take La Guayra." And every voice shouted, "Yes."

"We will have it, Amyas, and have Frank too, yet," cried Cary; but Amyas shook his head. He knew, and knew not why he knew, that all the ports in New Spain would never restore to him that one beloved face.

"Yes, he shall be well avenged. And look there! There is the first crop of our vengeance." And he pointed toward the shore, where between them and the now distant peaks of the Silla, three sails appeared, not five miles to windward.

"There are the Spanish bloodhounds on our heels, the same ships which we saw yesterday off Guayra. Back, lads, and welcome them, if they were a dozen."

There was a murmur of applause from all around; and if any young heart sank for a moment at the prospect of fighting three ships at once, it was awed into silence by the cheer which rose from all the older men, and by Salvation Yeo's stentorian voice.

"If there were a dozen, the Lord is with us, who has said, 'One of you shall chase a thousand.' Clear away, lads, and see the glory of the Lord this day."

"Amen!" cried Cary; and the ship was kept still closer to the wind.

Amyas had revived at the sight of battle. He no longer felt his wounds or his great sorrow as he bustled about the deck; and ere a quarter of an hour had passed, his voice cried firmly and cheerfully as of old—

"Now, my masters, let us serve God, and then to breakfast, and after that clear for action."

Jack Brimblecombe read the daily prayers, and the prayers before a fight at sea, and his honest voice trembled, as, in the Prayer for all Conditions of Men (in spite of Amyas's despair), he added, "and especially for our dear brother Mr. Francis Leigh, perhaps captive among the idolaters;" and so they rose.

"Now, then," said Amyas, "to breakfast. A Frenchman fights best fasting, a Dutchman drunk, an Englishman full, and a Spaniard when the devil is in him, and that's always."

"And good beef and the good cause are a match for the devil," said Cary. "Come down, captain; you must eat too."

Amyas shook his head, took the tiller from the steersman, and bade him go below and fill himself. Will Cary went down, and returned in five minutes with a plate of bread and beef, and a great jack of ale, coaxed them down Amyas's throat, as a nurse does with a child, and then scuttled below again with tears hopping down his face.

Amyas stood still steering. His face was grown seven years older in the last night. A terrible set calm was on him. Woe to the man who came across him that day!

"There are three of them, you see, my masters," said he, as the crew came on deck again. "A big ship forward, and two galleys astern of her. The big ship may keep; she is a race ship, and if we can but recover the wind of her, we will see whether our height is not a match for her length. We must give her the slip, and take the galleys first."

"I thank the Lord," said Yeo, "who has given so wise a heart to so young a general; a very David and Daniel, saving his presence, lads. Silas Staveley, smite me that boy over the head, the young monkey; why is he not down at the powder-room door?"

And Yeo went about his gunnery, as one who knew how to do it, and had the most terrible mind to do it thoroughly, and the most terrible faith that it was God's work.

So all fell to; and though there was comparatively little to be done, the ship having been kept as far as could be in fighting order all night, yet there was "clearing of decks, lacing of nettings, making of bulwarks, fitting of waistcloths, arming of tops, tallowing of pikes, slinging of yards, doubling of sheets and tacks." Amyas took charge of the poop, Cary of the forecastle, and Yeo, as gunner, of the main-deck, while Drew, as master, settled himself in the waist; and all was ready, and more than ready, before the great ship was within two miles of them.

She is now within two musket-shots of the *Rose*, with the golden flag of Spain floating at her poop; and her trumpets are shouting defiance up the breeze, from a dozen brazen throats, which two or three answer lustily from the *Rose*, from whose poop flies the flag of England, and from her fore the arms of Leigh and Cary side by side, and over them the ship and bridge of the good town of Bideford. And then Amyas calls—

"Now, silence trumpets, waits, play up! 'Fortune my foe!' and God and the Queen be with us!"

Whereon (laugh not, reader, for it was the fashion of those musical, as well as valiant days) up rose that noble old favorite of good Queen Bess, from cornet and sackbut, fife and drum; while Parson Jack, who had taken his stand with the musicians on the poop, worked away lustily at his violin.

"Well played, Jack; thy elbow flies like a lamb's tail," said Amyas, forcing a jest.

"It shall fly to a better fiddle-bow presently, sir, and I have the luck—"

"Steady, helm!" said Amyas. "What is he after now?"

The Spaniard, who had been coming upon them right down the wind under a press of sail, took in his light canvas.

"He don't know what to make of our waiting for him so bold," said the helmsman.

"He does though, and means to fight us," cried another. "See, he is hauling up the foot of his mainsail: but he wants to keep the wind of us."

"Let him try, then," quoth Amyas. "Keep her closer still. Let no one fire till we are about. Man the starboard guns; to starboard, and wait, all small arm men. Pass the order down to the gunner, and bid all fire high, and take the rigging."

Bang went one of the Spaniard's bow guns, and the shot went wide. Then another and another, while the men fidgeted about, looking at the priming of their muskets, and loosened their arrows in the sheaf.

"Lie down, men, and sing a psalm. When I want you I'll call you. Closer still, if you can, helmsman, and we will try a short ship against a long one. We can sail two points nearer the wind than he."

As Amyas had calculated, the Spaniard would gladly enough have stood across the *Rose's* bows, but knowing the English readiness dare not for fear of being raked; so her only plan, if she did not intend to shoot past her foe down to leeward, was to put her head close to the wind, and wait for her on the same tack.

Amyas laughed to himself. "Hold on yet awhile. More ways of killing a cat than choking her with cream. Drew, there, are your men ready?"

"Ay, ay, sir!" and on they went, closing fast with the Spaniard, till within a pistol-shot.

"Ready about!" and about she went like an eel, and ran upon the opposite tack right under the Spaniard's stern. The Spaniard, astonished at the quickness of the maneuver, hesitated a moment, and then tried to get about also, as his only chance; but it was too late, and while his lumbering length was still hanging in the wind's eye, Amyas's bowsprit had all but scraped his quarter, and the *Rose* passed slowly across his stern at ten yards' distance.

"Now, then!" roared Amyas. "Fire, and with a will! Have at her, archers: have at her, muskets all!" and in an instant a storm of bar and chain-shot, round and canister, swept the proud Don from stem to stern, while through the white cloud of smoke the musket-balls, and the still deadlier clothyard arrows, whistled and rushed upon their venomous errand. Down went the steersman, and every soul who manned the poop. Down went the mizzen topmast, in went the stern-windows and quarter-galleries; and as the smoke cleared away, the golden flag of Spain, which the last moment flaunted above their heads, hung trailing in the water. The ship, her tiller shot away, and her helmsman killed, staggered helplessly a moment, and then fell up into the wind.

"Well done, men of Devon!" shouted Amyas, as cheers rent the welkin.

"She has struck," cried some, as the deafening hurrahs died away.

"Not a bit," said Amyas. "Hold on, helmsman, and leave her to patch her tackle while we settle the galleys."

On they shot merrily, and long ere the armada could get herself to rights again, were two good miles to windward, with the galleys sweeping down fast upon them.

And two venomous-looking craft they were, as they shot through the short chopping sea upon some forty oars apiece, stretching their long sword-fish snouts over the water, as if snuffing for their prey. Behind this long snout, a strong square forecastle was crammed with soldiers, and the muzzles of cannon grinned out through port-holes, not only in the sides of the forecastle, but forward in the line of the galley's course, thus enabling her to keep up a continual fire on a ship right ahead.

The long low waist was packed full of the slaves, some five or six to each oar, and down the center, between the two banks, the English could see the slave-drivers walking up and down a long gangway, whip in hand. A raised quarter-deck at the stern held more soldiers, the sunlight flashing merrily upon their armor and their gun-barrels; as they neared, the English could hear plainly the cracks of the whips, and the yells as of wild beasts which answered them; the roll and rattle of the oars, and the loud "Ha!" of the slaves which accompanied every stroke, and the oaths and curses of the drivers; while a sickening musky smell, as of a pack of kenneled hounds, came down the wind from off those dens of misery. No wonder if many a young heart shuddered as it faced, for the first time, the horrible reality of those floating hells, the cruelties whereof had rung so often in English ears from the stories of their own countrymen, who had passed them, fought them, and now and then passed years of misery on board of them. Who knew but what there might be English among those sun-browned, half-naked masses of panting wretches?

"Must we fire upon the slaves?" asked more than one, as the thought crossed him.

Amyas sighed.

"Spare them all you can, in God's name: but if they try to run us down, rake them we must, and God forgive us."

The two galleys came on abreast of each other, some forty yards apart. To out-maneuver their oars as he had done the ship's sail, Amyas knew was impossible. To run from them was to be caught between them and the ship.

He made up his mind, as usual, to the desperate game.

"Lay her head up in the wind, helmsman, and we will wait for them."

They were now within musket-shot, and opened fire from their bow-guns; but, owing to the chopping sea, their aim was wild. Amyas, as usual, withheld his fire.

The men stood at quarters with compressed lips, not knowing what was to come next. Amyas, towering motionless on the quarter-deck, gave his orders calmly and decisively. The men saw that he trusted himself, and trusted him accordingly.

The Spaniards, seeing him wait for them, gave a shout of joy—was the Englishman mad? And the two galleys converged rapidly, intending to strike him full, one on each bow.

They were within forty yards—another minute, and the shock would come. The Englishman's helm went up, his yards creaked round, and gathering way, he plunged upon the larboard galley.

"A dozen gold nobles to him who brings down the steersman!" shouted Cary, who had his cue.

And a flight of arrows from the forecastle rattled upon the galley's quarter-deck.

Hit or not hit, the steersman lost his nerve, and shrank from the coming shock. The galley's helm went up to port, and her beak slid all but harmless along Amyas's bow; a long dull grind, and then loud crack on crack, as the *Rose* sawed slowly through the bank of oars from stem to stern, hurling the wretched slaves in heaps upon each other; and ere her mate on the other side could swing round to strike him in his new position, Amyas's whole broadside, great and small, had been poured into her at pistol-shot, answered by a yell which rent their ears and hearts.

"Spare the slaves! Fire at the soldiers!" cried Amyas; but the work was too hot for much discrimination; for the larboard galley, crippled but not undaunted, swung round across his stern, and hooked herself venomously on to him.

It was a move more brave than wise; for it prevented the other galley from returning to the attack without exposing herself a second time to the English broadside; and a desperate attempt of the Spaniards to board at once through the stern-ports and up the quarter was met with such a demurrer of shot and steel that they found themselves in three minutes again upon the galley's poop, accompanied, to their intense disgust, by Amyas Leigh and twenty English swords.

Five minutes' hard cutting, hand to hand, and the poop was

clear. The soldiers in the forecastle had been able to give them no assistance, open as they lay to the arrows and musketry from the *Rose's* lofty stern. Amyas rushed along the central gangway, shouting in Spanish, "Freedom to the slaves! death to the masters!" clambered into the forecastle, followed close by his swarm of wasps, and set them so good an example how to use their stings that in three minutes more there was not a Spaniard on board who was not dead or dying.

"Let the slaves free!" shouted he. "Throw us a hammer down, men. Hark! there's an English voice!"

There is indeed. From amid the wreck of broken oars and writhing limbs, a voice is shrieking in broadest Devon to the master, who is looking over the side.

"Oh, Robert Drew! Robert Drew! Come down, and take me out of hell!"

"Who be you, in the name of the Lord?"

"Don't you mind William Prust, that Captain Hawkins left behind in the Honduras, years and years agone? There's nine of us aboard, if your shot hasn't put 'em out of their misery. Come down, if you've a Christian heart, come down!"

Utterly forgetful of all discipline, Drew leaps down hammer in hand, and the two old comrades rush into each other's arms.

Why make a long story of what took but five minutes to do? The nine men (luckily none of them wounded) are freed, and helped on board, to be hugged and kissed by old comrades and young kinsmen; while the remaining slaves, furnished with a couple of hammers, are told to free themselves and help the English. The wretches answer by a shout; and Amyas, once more safe on board again, dashes after the other galley, which has been hovering out of reach of his guns: but there is no need to trouble himself about her; sickened with what she has got, she is struggling right up wind, leaning over to one side, and seemingly ready to sink.

"Are there any English on board of her?" asks Amyas, loth to lose the chance of freeing a countryman.

"Never a one, sir, thank God."

So they set to work to repair damages; while the liberated slaves, having shifted some of the galley's oars, pull away after their comrade; and that with such a will that in ten minutes they have caught her up, and careless of the Spaniard's fire, boarded her en masse, with yells as of a thousand wolves. There will be fearful vengeance taken on those tyrants, unless they play the man this day.

And in the meanwhile half the crew are clothing, feeding, questioning, caressing those nine poor fellows thus snatched from living death; and Yeo, hearing the news, has rushed up on deck to welcome his old comrades, and—

"Is Michael Heard, my cousin, here among you?"

Yes, Michael Heard is there, white-headed rather from misery than age; and the embracings and questionings begin afresh.

"Where is my wife, Salvation Yeo?"

"With the Lord."

"Amen!" says the old man, with a short shudder. "I thought so much; and my two boys?"

"With the Lord."

The old man catches Yeo by the arm.

"How, then?" It is Yeo's turn to shudder now.

"Killed in Panama, fighting the Spaniards; sailing with Mr. Oxeham; and 'twas I led 'em into it. May God and you forgive me!"

"They couldn't die better, cousin Yeo."

The old man covers his face with his hands for a while.

"Well, I've been alone with the Lord these fifteen years, so I must not whine at being alone awhile longer—'twon't be long."

"Put this coat on your back, uncle," says some one.

"No; no coats for me. Naked came I into the world, and naked I go out of it this day, if I have a chance. You'm better go to your work, lads, or the big one will have the wind of us yet."

"So she will," said Amyas, who had overheard; but so great

is the curiosity of all hands that he has some trouble in getting the men to quarters again; indeed, they only go on condition of parting among themselves with them the newcomers, each to tell his sad and strange story. How after Captain Hawkins, constrained by famine, had put them ashore, they wandered in misery till the Spaniards took them; how, instead of hanging them (as they at first intended), the Dons fed and clothed them, and allotted them as servants to various gentlemen about Mexico, where they throve, turned their hands (like true sailors) to all manner of trades, and made much money; so that all went well, until the fatal year 1574, when, much against the minds of many of the Spaniards themselves, that cruel and bloody Inquisition was established for the first time in the Indies; and how from that moment their lives were one long tragedy; how they were all imprisoned for a year and a half, racked again and again, and at last adjudged to receive publicly, on Good Friday, 1575, some three hundred, some one hundred stripes, and to serve in the galleys for six or ten years each; while as the crowning atrocity of the Moloch sacrifice, three of them were burnt alive in the market-place of Mexico.

The history of the party was not likely to improve the good feeling of the crew towards the Spanish ship which was two miles to leeward of them, and which must be fought with, or fled from, before a quarter of an hour was past. So, kneeling down upon the deck, as many a brave crew in those days did in like case, they "gave God thanks devoutly for the favor they had found," and then with one accord, at Jack's leading, sang one and all the ninety-fourth Psalm:

> "Oh, Lord, thou dost revenge all wrong;
> Vengeance belongs to thee," etc.

And then again to quarters; for half the day's work, or more than half, still remained to be done; and hardly were the decks cleared afresh, and the damage repaired as best it could be, when she came ranging up to leeward, as closehauled as she could.

She was, as I said, a long flush-decked ship of full five hundred tons, more than double the size, in fact, of the *Rose,* though not so lofty in proportion; and many a bold heart beat loud, and no shame to them, as she began firing away merrily, determined, as all well knew, to wipe out in English blood the disgrace of her late foil.

"Never mind, my merry masters," said Amyas, "she has quantity and we quality."

"That's true," said one, "for one honest man is worth two rogues."

"And one culverin three of their footy little ordnance," said another. "So when you will, captain, and have at her."

"Let her come abreast of us, and don't burn powder. We have the wind, and can do what we like with her. Serve the men out a horn of ale all round, steward, and all take your time."

So they waited five minutes more, and then set to work quietly, after the fashion of English mastiffs, though, like whose mastiffs, they waxed right mad before three rounds were fired, and the white splinters (sight beloved) began to crackle and fly.

Amyas, having, as he had said, the wind, and being able to go nearer it than the Spaniard, kept his place at easy point-blank range for his two-eighteen-pounder culverins, which Yeo and his mate worked with terrible effect.

"We are lacking her through and through every shot," said he. "Leave the small ordnance alone yet awhile, and we shall sink her without them."

"Whing, whing," went the Spaniard's shot, like so many humming-tops, through the rigging far above their heads; for the ill-constructed ports of those days prevented the guns from hulling an enemy who was to windward, unless close alongside.

"Blow, jolly breeze," cried one, "and lay the Don over all thou canst.—What, the murrain is gone, aloft there?"

Alas! a crack, a flap, a rattle; and blank dismay! An unlucky shot had cut the foremast (already wounded) in two, and all forward was a mass of dangling wreck.

"Forward, and cut away the wreck!" said Amyas, unmoved. "Small arm men, be ready. He will be aboard of us in five minutes!"

It was true. The *Rose*, unmanageable from the loss of her head-sail, lay at the mercy of the Spaniard; and the archers and musqueteers had hardly time to range themselves to leeward, when the *Madre Dolorosa's* chains were grinding against the *Rose's*, and grapples tossed on board from stem to stern.

"Don't cut them loose!" roared Amyas. "Let them stay and see the fun! Now, dogs of Devon, show your teeth, and hurrah for God and the Queen!"

And then began a fight most fierce and fell: the Spaniards, according to their fashion, attempted to board: the English, amid fierce shouts of "God and the Queen!" "God and St. George for England!" sweeping them back by showers of arrows and musket balls, thrusting them down with pikes, hurling grenades and stink-pots from the tops; while the swivels on both sides poured their grape, and bar, and chain, and the great main-deck guns, thundering muzzle to muzzle, made both ships quiver and recoil, as they smashed the round shot through and through each other.

So they roared and flashed, fast clenched to each other in that devil's wedlock, under a cloud of smoke beneath the cloudless tropic sky; while all around, the dolphins gamboled, and the flying-fish shot on from swell to swell, and the rainbow-hued jellies opened and shut their cups of living crystal to the sun.

So it raged for an hour or more, till all arms were weary, and all tongues clove to the mouth. And sick men, rotting with scurvy, scrambled up on deck, and fought with the strength of madness: and tiny powder-boys, handing up cartridges from the hold, laughed and cheered as the shots ran past their ears; and old Salvation Yeo, a text upon his lips, and a fury in his heart as of Joshua or Elijah in old time, worked on, calm and grim, but with the energy of a boy at play. And now and then an opening in the smoke showed the Spanish captain, in his suit of black steel armor, standing cool and proud, guiding and pointing, careless of the iron hail, but too lofty a gentleman to soil his glove with aught but a knightly sword-hilt: while Amyas and Will, after the fashion of the English gentlemen, had stripped themselves nearly as bare as their own sailors, and were cheering, thrusting, hewing, and hauling, here, there, and everywhere, like any common mariner, and filling them with a spirit of self-respect, fellow-feeling, and personal daring, which the discipline of the Spaniards, more perfect mechanically, but cold and tyrannous, and crushing spiritually, never could bestow. The black-plumed Señor was obeyed; but the golden-locked Amyas was followed, and would have been followed through the jaws of hell.

The Spaniards, ere five minutes had passed, poured en masse into the *Rose's* waist: but only to their destruction. Between the poop and forecastle (as was then the fashion) the upper-deck beams were left open and unplanked, with the exception of a narrow gangway on either side; and off that fatal ledge the boarders, thrust on by those behind, fell headlong between the beams to the main-deck below, to be slaughtered helpless in that pit of destruction, by the double fire from the bulkheads fore and aft; while the few who kept their footing on the gangway, after vain attempts to force the stockades on poop and forecastle, leaped overboard again amid a shower of shot and arrows. The fire of the English was as steady as it was quick.

Thrice the Spaniards clambered on board, and thrice surged back before that deadly hail. The decks on both sides were very shambles; and Jack Brimblecombe, who had fought as long as his conscience would allow him, found, when he turned to a more clerical occupation, enough to do in carrying poor wretches to the surgeon, without giving that spiritual consolation which he longed to give, and they to receive. At last there was a lull in that wild storm. No shot was heard from the Spaniard's upper-deck.

Amyas leaped into the mizzen rigging and looked through

the smoke. Dead men he could descry through the blinding veil, rolled in heaps, laid flat; dead men and dying; but no man upon his feet. The last volley had swept the deck clear; one by one had dropped below to escape that fiery shower: and alone at the helm, grinding his teeth with rage, his mustachios curling up to his very eyes, stood the Spanish captain.

Now was the moment for a counter stroke. Amyas shouted for the boarders, and in two minutes more he was over the side, and clutching at the Spaniard's mizzen rigging.

What was this? The distance between him and the enemy's side was widening. Was she sheering off? Yes—and rising, too, growing bodily higher every moment, as if by magic. Amyas looked up in astonishment and saw what it was. The Spaniard was heeling fast over to leeward away from him. Her masts were all sloping forward, swifter and swifter—the end was come, then!

"Back! in God's name back, men! She is sinking by the head!" And with much ado some were dragged back, some leaped back—all but old Michael Heard.

With hair and beard floating in the wind, the bronzed naked figure, like some weird old Indian fakir, still climbed on steadfastly up the mizzen-chains of the Spaniard, hatchet in hand.

"Come back, Michael! Leap while you may!" shouted a dozen voices. Michael turned—

"And what should I come back for, then, to go home where no one knoweth me? I'll die like an Englishman this day, or I'll know the reason why!" and turning, he sprang in over the bulwarks, as the huge ship rolled up more and more, like a dying whale, exposing all her long black hulk almost down to the keel, and one of her lower-deck guns as if in defiance exploded upright into the air, hurling the ball to the very heavens.

In an instant it was answered from the *Rose* by a column of smoke, and the eighteen-pound ball crashed through the bottom of the defenseless Spaniard.

"Who fired! Shame to fire on a sinking ship!"

"Gunner Yeo, sir," shouted a voice from the main-deck. "He's like a madman down here."

"Tell him if he fires again, I'll put him in irons, if he were my own brother. Cut away the grapples aloft, men. Don't you see how she drags us over? Cut away, or we shall sink with her."

They cut away, and the *Rose*, released from the strain, shook her feathers on the wave-crest like a freed seagull, while all men held their breaths.

Suddenly the glorious creature righted herself, and rose again, as if in noble shame, for one last struggle with her doom. Her bows were deep in the water, but her after-deck still dry. Righted: but only for a moment, long enough to let her crew come pouring wildly up on deck, with cries and prayers, and rush aft to the poop, where, under the flag of Spain, stood the tall captain, his left hand on the standard-staff, his sword pointed in his right.

"Back men!" they heard him cry, "and die like valiant mariners."

Some of them ran to the bulwarks, and shouted "Mercy! We surrender!" and the English broke into a cheer and called to them to run her alongside.

"Silence!" shouted Amyas. "I take no surrender from mutineers. Señor," cried he to the captain, springing into the rigging and taking off his hat, "for the love of God and these men, strike; and surrender *á buena guerra*."

The Spaniard lifted his hat and bowed courteously, and answered. "Impossible, Señor. No *guerra* is good which stains my honor."

"God have mercy on you, then!"

"Amen!" said the Spaniard, crossing himself. She gave one awful lunge forward, and dived under the coming swell, hurling her crew into the eddies. Nothing but the point of her poop remained, and there stood the stern and steadfast Don, cap-à-pie in his glistening black armor, immovable as a man of iron, while over him the flag, which claimed the empire of both worlds, flaunted its gold aloft and upwards in the glare of the tropic noon.

"He shall not carry that flag to the devil with him; I will have it yet, if I die for it!" said Will Cary, and rushed to the side to leap overboard, but Amyas stopped him.

"Let him die as he lived, with honor."

A wild figure sprang out of the mass of sailors who struggled and shrieked amid the foam, and rushed upward at the Spaniard. It was Michael Heard. The Don, who stood above him, plunged his sword into the old man's body: but the hatchet gleamed, nevertheless: down went the blade through the headpiece and through head; and as Heard sprang onward, bleeding, but alive, the steel-clad corpse rattled down the deck into the surge. Two more strokes, struck with the fury of a dying man, and the standard-staff was hewn through. Old Michael collected all his strength, hurled the flag far from the sinking ship, and then stood erect one moment and shouted, "God save Queen Bess!" and the English answered with a "Hurrah!" which rent the welkin.

Another moment and the gulf had swallowed his victim, and the poop, and him; and nothing remained of the *Madre Dolorosa* but a few floating spars and struggling wretches, while a great awe fell upon all men, and a solemn silence, broken only by the cry

> "Of some strong swimmer in his agony."

And then, suddenly collecting themselves, as men awakened from a dream, half-a-dozen desperate gallants, reckless of sharks and eddies, leaped overboard, swam towards the flag, and towed it alongside in triumph.

"Ah!" said Salvation Yeo, as he helped the trophy up over the side; "ah! it was not for nothing that we found poor Michael! He was always a good comrade. And now, then, my masters, shall we inshore again and burn La Guayra?"

"Art thou never glutted with Spanish blood, thou old wolf?" asked Will Cary.

"Never, sir," answered Yeo.

"To St. Jago be it," said Amyas, "if we can get there: but—God help us!"

And he looked round sadly enough; while no one needed that he should finish his sentence, or explain his "but."

The fore-mast was gone, the main-yard sprung, the rigging hanging in elf-locks, the hull shot through and through in twenty places, the deck strewn with the bodies of nine good men, besides sixteen wounded down below; while the pitiless sun, right above their heads, poured down a flood of fire upon a sea of glass.

And it would have been well if faintness and weariness had been all that was the matter; but now that the excitement was over, the collapse came; and the men sat down listlessly and sulkily by twos and threes upon the deck, starting and wincing when they heard some poor fellow below cry out under the surgeon's knife; or murmuring to each other that all was lost. Drew tried in vain to rouse them, telling them that all depended on rigging a jury-mast forward as soon as possible. They answered only by growls; and at last broke into open reproaches. Even Will Cary's volatile nature, which had kept him up during the fight gave way, when Yeo and the carpenter came aft, and told Amyas in a low voice—

"We are hit somewhere forward, below the waterline, sir. She leaks a terrible deal, and the Lord will not vouchsafe to us to lay our hands on the place, for all our searching."

"What are we to do now, Amyas, in the devil's name?" asked Cary, peevishly.

"What are we to do, in God's name, rather," answered Amyas in a low voice. "Will, Will, what did God make you a gentleman for, but to know better than those poor fickle fellows forward, who blow hot and cold at every change of weather!"

"I wish you'd come forward and speak to them, sir," said Yeo, who had overheard the last words, "or we shall get nought done."

Amyas went forward instantly.

"Now then, my brave lads, what's the matter here, that you are all sitting on your tails like monkeys?"

"Ugh!" grunts one. "Don't you think our day's work has been long enough yet, captain?"

"You don't want us to go in to La Guayra again, sir? There are enough of us thrown away already, I reckon, about that wench there."

"Best sit here, and sink quietly. There's no getting home again, that's plain."

"Why were we brought out here to be killed?"

"For shame, men!" cries Yeo, "murmuring the very minute after the Lord has delivered you from the Egyptians."

Now I do not wish to set Amyas up as better, thank God, than many and many a brave and virtuous captain in her Majesty's service at this very day: but certainly he behaved admirably under that trial. Drake had trained him, as he trained many another excellent officer, to be as stout in discipline and as dogged of purpose, as he himself was: but he had trained him also to feel with and for his men, to make allowances for them, and to keep his temper with them, as he did this day. Amyas's conscience smote him (and his simple and pious soul took the loss of his brother as God's verdict on his conduct), because he had set his own private affection, even his own private revenge, before the safety of his ship's company and the good of his country.

"Ah," said he to himself, as he listened to his men's reproaches, "if I had been thinking, like a loyal soldier, of serving my queen, and crippling the Spaniard, I should have taken that great bark three days ago, and in it the very man I sought!"

So "choking down his old man," as Yeo used to say, he made answer cheerfully—

"Pooh! pooh! brave lads! For shame, for shame! You were lions half-an-hour ago; you are not surely turned sheep already! Why, but yesterday evening you were grumbling because I would not run in and fight those three ships under the batteries of La Guayra, and now you think it too much to have fought them fairly out at sea? Nothing venture, nothing win; and nobody goes birdnesting without a fall at times. If any one wants to be safe in this life, he'd best stay at home and keep his bed; though even there who knows but the roof might fall through on him?"

"Ah, it's all very well for you, captain," said some grumbling younker, with a vague notion that Amyas must be better off than he because he was a gentleman. Amyas's blood rose.

"Yes, sirrah! Do you fancy that I have nothing to lose? I who have adventured in this voyage all I am worth, and more; who, if I fail, must return to beggary and scorn? And if I have ventured rashly, sinfully, if you will, the lives of any of you in my own private quarrel, am I not punished? Have I not lost—?"

His voice trembled and stopped there, but he recovered himself in a moment.

"Pish! I can't stand here chattering. Carpenter! an ax! and help me to cast these spars loose. Get out of my way, there! lumbering the scuppers up like so many moulting fowls! Here, all old friends, lend a hand! *Pelican's* men, stand by your captain! Did we sail round the world for nothing?"

This last appeal struck home, and up leaped half-a-dozen of the old *Pelicans*, and set to work at his side manfully to rig the jury-mast.

"Come along!" cried Cary to the malcontents; "we're raw longshore fellows, but we won't be outdone by any old sea-dog of them all." And setting to work himself, he was soon followed by one and another, till order and work went on well enough.

"And where are we going, when the mast's up?" shouted some saucy hand from behind.

"Where you daren't follow us alone by yourself, so you had better keep us company," replied Yeo.

"I'll tell you where we are going, lads," said Amyas, rising from his work. "Like it or leave it as you will, I have no secrets from my crew. We are going inshore there to find a harbor, and careen the ship."

There was a start and a murmur.

"Inshore! Into the Spaniards' mouths?"

"All in the Inquisition in a week's time."

"Better stay here, and be drowned."

"You're right in that last," shouts Cary. "That's the right death for blind puppies. Look you! I don't know in the least where we are, and I hardly know stem from stern aboard ship; and the captain may be right or wrong—that's nothing to me; but this I know, that I am a soldier, and will obey orders; and where he goes, I go; and whosoever hinders me must walk up my sword to do it."

Amyas pressed Cary's hand, and then—

"And here's my broadside next, men. I'll go nowhere, and do nothing without the advice of Salvation Yeo and Robert Drew; and if any man in the ship knows better than these two, let him up, and we'll give him a hearing. Eh, *Pelicans?*"

There was a grunt of approbation from the *Pelicans;* and Amyas returned to the charge.

"We have five shots between wind and water, and one somewhere below. Can we face a gale of wind in that state, or can we not?"

Silence.

"Can we get home with a leak in our bottom?"

Silence.

"Come along now! Here's the wind again round with the sun, and up to the northwest. Inshore with her."

Sulkily enough, but unable to deny the necessity, the men set to work, and the vessel's head was put toward the land; but when she began to slip through the water, the leak increased so fast that they were kept hard at work at the pumps for the rest of the afternoon.

The current had by this time brought them abreast of the bay of Higuerote. As they ran inward, all eyes were strained greedily to find some opening in the mangrove belt: but none was to be seen for some time. The lead was kept going; and every fresh heave announced shallower water.

"We shall have very shoal work of those mangroves, Yeo," said Amyas; "I doubt whether we shall do aught now, unless we find a river's mouth."

"If the Lord thinks a river good for us, sir, he'll show us one." So on they went, keeping a southeast course, and at last an opening in the mangrove belt was hailed with a cheer from the older hands, though the majority shrugged their shoulders, as men going open-eyed to destruction.

Off the mouth they sent in Drew and Cary with a boat, and watched anxiously for an hour. The boat returned with a good report of two fathoms of water over the bar, impenetrable forests for two miles up, the river sixty yards broad, and no sign of man. The river's banks were soft and sloping mud, fit for careening.

"Safe quarters, sir," said Yeo, privately, "as far as Spaniards go. I hope in God it may be as safe from fevers."

"Beggars must not be choosers," said Amyas. So in they went.

They towed the ship up about half-a-mile to a point where she could not be seen from the seaward; and there moored her to the mangrove-stems. Amyas ordered a boat out, and went up the river himself to reconnoiter. He rowed some three miles, till the right narrowed suddenly, and was all but covered in by the interlacing boughs of mighty trees. There was no sign that man had been there since the making of the world.

He dropped down the stream again, thoughtfully and sadly. How many years ago was it that he had passed this river's mouth? Three days. And yet how much had passed in them! Don Guzman found and lost—Rose found and lost—a great victory gained, and yet lost—perhaps his ship lost—above all, his brother lost.

Lost! O God, how should he find his brother?

Some strange bird out of the woods made mournful answer—"Never, never, never!"

How should he face his mother?

"Never, never, never!" wailed the bird again; and Amyas smiled bitterly, and said "Never!" likewise.

The night mist began to steam and wreath upon the foul beer-colored stream. The loathy floor of liquid mud lay bare beneath the mangrove forest. Upon the endless web of inter-arching roots great purple crabs were crawling up and down. They would have supped with pleasure upon Amyas's corpse; perhaps they might sup on him after all; for a heavy sickening graveyard smell made his heart sink within him, and his stomach heave; and his weary body, and more weary soul, gave themselves up helplessly to the depressing influence of that doleful place. The black bank of the dingy leathern leaves above his head, the endless labyrinth of stems and withes (for every bough had lowered its own living cord, to take fresh hold of the foul soil below); the web of roots, which stretched away inland till it was lost in the shades of evening—all this seemed one horrid complicated trap for him and his; and even where, here and there, he passed the mouth of a lagoon, there was no opening, no relief—nothing but the dark ring of man-groves. Wailing sadly, sad-colored mangrove-hens ran off across the mud into the dreary dark. The hoarse night-raven, hid among the roots, startled the voyagers with a sudden shout, and then all was again silent as a grave. The loathy alligators lounging in the slime lifted their horny eyelids lazily, and leered upon him as he passed with stupid savageness. Lines of tall herons stood dimly in the growing gloom, like white fan-tastic ghosts, watching the passage of the doomed boat. All was foul, sullen, weird as witches' dream. If Amyas had seen a crew of skeletons glide down the stream behind him, with Satan standing at the helm, he would scarcely have been sur-prised. What fitter craft could haunt that Stygian flood?

# THE TERRIBLE SOLOMONS [1]

From "South Sea Tales," BY JACK LONDON

THERE is no gainsaying that the Solomons are a hard-bitten bunch of islands. On the other hand, there are worse places in the world. But to the new chum who has no constitutional understanding of men and life in the rough, the Solomons may indeed prove terrible.

It is true that fever and dysentery are perpetually on the walk-about, that loathsome skin diseases abound, that the air is saturated with a poison that bores into every pore, cut, or abrasion and plants malignant ulcer, and that many strong men who escape dying there return as wrecks to their own countries. It is also true that the natives of the Solomons are a wild lot, with a hearty appetite for human flesh and a fad for collecting human heads. Their highest instinct of sportsmanship is to catch a man with his back turned and to smite him a cunning blow with a tomahawk that severs the spinal column at the base of the brain. It is equally true that on some islands, such as Malaita, the profit and loss account of social intercourse is calculated in homicides. Heads are a medium of exchange, and white heads are extremely valuable. Very often a dozen villages make a jack-pot which they fatten moon by moon, against the time when some brave warrior presents a white man's head, fresh and gory, and claims the pot.

All the foregoing is quite true, and yet there are white men who have lived in the Solomons a score of years and who feel homesick when they go away from them. A man needs only to be careful—and lucky—to live a long time in the Solomons; but he must also be of the right sort. He must have the hall-

[1] Reprinted by courtesy of The Macmillan Company.

mark of the inevitable white man stamped upon his soul. He must be inevitable. He must have a certain grand carelessness of odds, a certain colossal self-satisfaction, and a racial egotism that convinces him that one white is better than a thousand niggers every day in the week, and that on Sunday he is able to clean out two thousand niggers. For such are the things that have made the white man inevitable. Oh, and one other thing —the white man who wishes to be inevitable, must not merely despise the lesser breeds and think a lot of himself; he must also fail to be too long on imagination. He must not understand too well the instincts, customs and mental processes of the blacks, the yellows, and the browns; for it is not in such fashion that the white race has tramped its royal road around the world.

Bertie Arkwright was not inevitable. He was too sensitive, too finely strung, and he possessed too much imagination. The world was too much with him. He projected himself too quiveringly into his environment. Therefore, the last place in the world for him to come was the Solomons. He did not come, expecting to stay. A five-weeks' stop-over between steamers, he decided, would satisfy the call of the primitive he felt thrumming the strings of his being. At least, so he told the lady tourists on the Makembo, though in different terms; and they worshipped him as a hero, for they were lady tourists and they would know only the safety of the steamer's deck as she threaded her way through the Solomons.

There was another man on board, of whom the ladies took no notice. He was a little shriveled wisp of a man, with a withered skin the color of mahogany. His name on the passenger list does not matter, but his other name, Captain Malu, was a name for niggers to conjure with, and to scare naughty pickaninnies to righteousness, from New Hanover to the New Hebrides. He had farmed savages and savagery, and from fever and hardship, the crack of Sniders and the lash of the overseers, had wrested five millions of money in the form of beche-de-mer, sandalwood, pearl-shell and turtle-shell, ivory nuts and copra, grasslands, trading stations, and plantations. Captain

Malu's little finger, which was broken, had more inevitableness in it than Bertie Arkwright's whole carcass. But then, the lady tourists had nothing by which to judge save appearances, and Bertie certainly was a fine-looking man.

Bertie talked with Captain Malu in the smoking-room, confiding to him his intention of seeing life red and bleeding in the Solomons. Captain Malu agreed that the intention was ambitious and honorable. It was not until several days later that he became interested in Bertie, when that young adventurer insisted on showing him an automatic 44-calibre pistol. Bertie explained the mechanism and demonstrated by slipping a loaded magazine up the hollow butt.

"It is so simple," he said. He shot the outer barrel back along the inner one. "That loads it, and cocks it, you see. And then all I have to do is pull the trigger, eight times, as fast as I can quiver my finger. See that safety clutch. That's what I like about it. It is safe. It is positively fool-proof." He slipped out the magazine. "You see how safe it is."

As he held it in his hand, the muzzle came in line with Captain Malu's stomach. Captain Malu's blue eyes looked at it unswervingly.

"Would you mind pointing it in some other direction?" he asked.

"It's perfectly safe," Bertie assured him. "I withdrew the magazine. It's not loaded now, you know."

"A gun is always loaded."

"But this one isn't."

"Turn it away just the same."

Captain Malu's voice was flat and metallic and low, but his eyes never left the muzzle until the line of it was drawn past him and away from him.

"I'll bet a fiver it isn't loaded," Bertie proposed warmly.

The other shook his head.

"Then I'll show you."

Bertie started to put the muzzle to his own temple with the evident intention of pulling the trigger.

"Just a second," Captain Malu said quietly, reaching out his hand. "Let me look at it."

He pointed it seaward and pulled the trigger. A heavy explosion followed, instantaneous with the sharp click of the mechanism that flipped a hot and smoking cartridge sidewise along the deck. Bertie's jaw dropped in amazement.

"I slipped the barrel back once, didn't I?" he explained. "It was silly of me, I must say."

He giggled flabbily, and sat down in a steamer chair. The blood had ebbed from his face, exposing dark circles under his eyes. His hands were trembling and unable to guide the shaking cigarette to his lips. The world was too much with him, and he saw himself with dripping brains prone upon the deck.

"Really," he said, ". . . really."

"It's a pretty weapon," said Captain Malu, returning the automatic to him.

The Commissioner was on board the *Makembo*, returning from Sydney, and by his permission a stop was made at Ugi to land a missionary. And at Ugi lay the ketch *Arla*, Captain Hansen, skipper. Now the *Arla* was one of many vessels owned by Captain Malu, and it was at his suggestion and by his invitation that Bertie went aboard the *Arla* as guest for a four-days' recruiting cruise on the coast of Malaita. Thereafter the *Arla* would drop him at Reminge Plantation (also owned by Captain Malu), where Bertie could remain for a week, and then be sent over to Tulagi, the seat of government, where he would become the Commissioner's guest. Captain Malu was responsible for two other suggestions, which given, he disappears from this narrative. One was to Captain Hansen, the other to Mr. Harriwell, manager of Reminge Plantation. Both suggestions were similar in tenor, namely, to give Mr. Bertram Arkwright an insight into the rawness and redness of life in the Solomons. Also, it is whispered that Captain Malu mentioned that a case of Scotch would be coincidental with any particularly gorgeous insight Mr. Arkwright might receive.

"Yes, Swartz always was too pig-headed. You see, he took four of his boat's crew to Tulagi to be flogged—officially, you know—then started back with them in the whale-boat. It was pretty squally, and the boat capsized just outside. Swartz was the only one drowned. Of course it was an accident."

"Was it? Really?" Bertie asked, only half-interested, staring hard at the black man at the wheel.

Ugi had dropped astern, and the *Arla* was sliding along through a summer sea toward the wooded ranges of Malaita. The helmsman who so attracted Bertie's eyes sported a ten-penny nail, stuck skewerwise through his nose. About his neck was a string of pants buttons. Thrust through holes in his ears were a can-opener, the broken handle of a tooth-brush, a clay pipe, the brass wheel of an alarm clock, and several Winchester rifle cartridges. On his chest, suspended from around his neck hung the half of a china plate. Some forty similarly apparelled blacks lay about the deck, fifteen of which were boat's crew, the remainder being fresh labor recruits.

"Of course it was an accident," spoke up the *Arla's* mate, Jacobs, a slender, dark-eyed man who looked more a professor than a sailor. "Johnny Bedlip nearly had the same kind of accident. He was bringing back several from a flogging, when they capsized him. But he knew how to swim as well as they, and two of them were drowned. He used a boat-stretcher and a revolver. Of course it was an accident."

"Quite common, them accidents," remarked the skipper. "You see that man at the wheel, Mr. Arkwright? He's a man-eater. Six months ago, he and the rest of the boat's crew drowned the then captain of the *Arla*. They did it on deck, sir, right aft there by the mizzen-traveller."

"The deck was in a shocking state," said the mate.

"Do I understand—?" Bertie began.

"Yes, just that," said Captain Hansen. "It was accidental drowning."

"But on deck—?"

"Just so. I don't mind telling you, in confidence, of course, that they used an axe."

"This present crew of yours?"

Captain Hansen nodded.

"The other skipper always was too careless," explained the mate. "He but just turned his back, when they let him have it."

"We haven't any show down here," was the skipper's complaint. "The government protects a nigger against a white every time. You can't shoot first. You've got to give the nigger first shot, or else the government calls it murder and you go to Fiji. That's why there's so many drowning accidents."

Dinner was called, and Bertie and the skipper went below, leaving the mate to watch on deck.

"Keep an eye out for that black devil, Auiki," was the skipper's parting caution. "I haven't liked his looks for several days."

"Right O," said the mate.

Dinner was part way along, and the skipper was in the middle of his story of the cutting out of the *Scottish Chiefs*.

"Yes," he was saying, "she was the finest vessel on the coast. But when she missed stays, and before ever she hit the reef, the canoes started for her. There were five white men, a crew of twenty Santa Cruz boys and Samoans, and only the super-cargo escaped. Besides, there were sixty recruits. They were all kai-kai'd. Kai-kai?—oh, I beg your pardon. I mean they were eaten. Then there was the *James Edwards*, a dandy-rigged—"

But at that moment there was a sharp oath from the mate on deck and a chorus of savage cries. A revolver went off three times, and then was heard a loud splash. Captain Hansen had sprung up the companionway on the instant, and Bertie's eyes had been fascinated by a glimpse of him drawing his revolver as he sprung. Bertie went up more circumspectly, hesitating before he put his head above the companionway slide. But nothing happened. The mate was shaking with excitement, his revolver in his hand. Once he started, and half-jumped around, as if danger threatened his back.

"One of the natives fell overboard," he was saying, in a queer tense voice. "He couldn't swim."

"Who was it?" the skipper demanded.

"Auiki," was the answer.

"But I say, you know, I heard shots," Bertie said, in trembling eagerness, for he scented adventure, and adventure that was happily over with.

The mate whirled upon him, snarling:

"It's a damned lie. There ain't been a shot fired. The nigger fell overboard."

Captain Hansen regarded Bertie with unblinking, lack-lustre eyes.

"I—I thought—" Bertie was beginning.

"Shots? Did you hear any shots, Mr. Jacobs?"

"Not a shot," replied Mr. Jacobs.

The skipper looked at his guest triumphantly, and said:

"Evidently an accident. Let us go down, Mr. Arkwright, and finish dinner."

Bertie slept that night in the captain's cabin, a tiny stateroom off the main-cabin. The for'ard bulkhead was decorated with a stand of rifles. Over the bunk were three more rifles. Under the bunk was a big drawer, which when he pulled it out, he found filled with ammunition dynamite, and several boxes of detonators. He elected to take the settee on the opposite side. Lying conspicuously on the small table, was the *Arla's* log. Bertie did not know that it had been especially prepared for the occasion by Captain Malu, and he read therein how on September 21, two boat's crew had fallen overboard and been drowned. Bertie read between the lines and knew better. He read how the *Arla's* whale-boat had been bushwhacked at Sulu and had lost three men; of how the skipper discovered the cook stewing human flesh on the galley fire—flesh purchased by the boat's crew ashore in Fui; of how an accidental discharge of dynamite, while signalling, had killed another boat's crew; of night attacks; ports fled from between the dawns; attacks by bushmen in mangrove swamps and by fleets of salt-water men in the larger passages. One item that occurred with monotonous frequency was death by dysentery. He noticed with alarm that two white men had so died—guests, like himself, on the *Arla*.

"I say, you know," Bertie said next day to Captain Hansen. "I've been glancing through your log."

The skipper displayed quick vexation that the log had been left lying about.

"And all that dysentery, you know, that's all rot, just like the accidental drownings," Bertie continued. "What does dysentery really stand for?"

The skipper openly admired his guest's acumen, stiffened himself to make indignant denial, then gracefully surrendered.

"You see, it's like this, Mr. Arkwright. These islands have got a bad enough name as it is. It's getting harder every day to sign on white men. Suppose a man is killed. The company has to pay through the nose for another man to take the job. But if the man merely dies of sickness, it's all right. The new chums don't mind disease. What they draw the line at is being murdered. I thought the skipper of the *Arla* had died of dysentery when I took his billet. Then it was too late. I'd signed the contract."

"Besides," said Mr. Jacobs, "there's altogether too many accidental drownings anyway. It don't look right. It's the fault of the government. A white man hasn't a chance to defend himself from the niggers."

"Yes, look at the *Princess* and that Yankee mate," the skipper took up the tale. "She carried five white men besides a government agent. The captain, the agent, and the supercargo were ashore in the two boats. They were killed to the last man. The mate and bosun, with about fifteen of the crew—Samoans and Tongans—were on board. A crowd of niggers came off from the shore. First thing the mate knew, the bosun and the crew were killed in the first rush. The mate grabbed three cartridge-belts and two Winchesters and skinned up to the cross-trees. He was the sole survivor, and you can't blame him for being mad. He pumped one rifle till it got so hot he couldn't hold it, then he pumped the other. The deck was black with niggers. He cleaned them out. He dropped them as they went over the rail, and he dropped them as fast as they picked up their paddles. Then they jumped into the water and started to swim for it, and, being mad, he got half a dozen more. And what did he get for it?"

"Seven years in Fiji," snapped the mate.

"The government said he wasn't justified in shooting after they'd taken to the water," the skipper explained.

"And that's why they die of dysentery nowadays," the mate added.

"Just fancy," said Bertie, as he felt a longing for the cruise to be over.

Later on in the day he interviewed the black who had been pointed out to him as a cannibal. This fellow's name was Sumasai. He had spent three years on a Queensland plantation. He had been to Samoa, and Fiji, and Sydney; and as a boat's crew had been on recruiting schooners through New Britain, New Ireland, New Guinea, and the Admiralties. Also, he was a wag, and he had taken a line on his skipper's conduct. Yes, he had eaten many men. How many? He could not remember the tally. Yes, white men, too; they were very good, unless they were sick. He had once eaten a sick one.

"My word!" he cried, at the recollection. "Me sick plenty along him. My belly walk about too much."

Bertie shuddered, and asked about heads. Yes, Sumasai had several hidden ashore, in good condition, sun-dried, and smoke-cured. One was of the captain of a schooner. It had long whiskers. He would sell it for two quid. Black men's heads he would sell for one quid. He had some pickaninny heads, in poor condition, that he would let go for ten bob.

Five minutes afterward, Bertie found himself sitting on the companionway-slide alongside a black with a horrible skin disease. He sheered off, and on inquiry was told that it was leprosy. He hurried below and washed himself with antiseptic soap. He took many antiseptic washes in the course of the day, for every native on board was afflicted with malignant ulcers of one sort or another.

As the *Arla* drew in to an anchorage in the midst of mangrove swamps, a double row of barbed wire was stretched around above her rail. That looked like business and when Bertie saw the shore canoes alongside, armed with spears, bows and arrows, and Sniders, he wished more earnestly than ever that the cruise was over.

That evening the natives were slow in leaving the ship at sundown. A number of them checked the mate when he ordered them ashore.

"Never mind, I'll fix them," said Captain Hansen, diving below.

When he came back, he showed Bertie a stick of dynamite attached to a fish-hook. Now it happens that a paper-wrapped bottle of chlorodyne with a piece of harmless fuse projecting can fool anybody. It fooled Bertie, and it fooled the natives. When Captain Hansen lighted the fuse and hooked the fish-hook into the tail-end of a native's loin-cloth, that native was smitten with so ardent a desire for the shore that he forgot to shed the loin-cloth. He started for'ard, the fuse sizzling and spluttering at his rear, the natives in his path taking headers over the barbed wire at every jump. Bertie was horror-stricken. So was Captain Hansen. He had forgotten his twenty-five recruits, on each of which he had paid thirty shillings advance. They went over the side along with the shore-dwelling folk and followed by him who trailed the sizzling chlorodyne bottle.

Bertie did not see the bottle go off; but the mate opportunely discharging a stick of real dynamite aft where it would harm nobody, Bertie would have sworn in any admiralty court to a nigger blown to flinders.

The flight of the twenty-five recruits had actually cost the *Arla* forty pounds, and, since they had taken to the bush, there was no hope of recovering them. The skipper and his mate proceeded to drown their sorrow in cold tea. The cold tea was in whiskey bottles, so Bertie did not know it was cold tea they were mopping up. All he knew was that the two men got very drunk and argued eloquently and at length as to whether the exploded nigger should be reported as a case of dysentery or as an accidental drowning. When they snored off to sleep, he was the only white man left, and he kept a perilous watch till dawn, in fear of an attack from shore and an uprising of the crew.

Three more days the *Arla* spent on the coast, and three more nights the skipper and the mate drank overfondly of cold tea, leaving Bertie to keep watch. They knew he could be depended upon, while he was equally certain that if he lived, he would report their drunken conduct to Captain Malu. Then the *Arla* dropped anchor at Reminge Plantation, on Guadalcanar, and Bertie landed on the beach with a sigh of relief and shook hands with the manager. Mr. Harriwell was ready for him.

"Now you mustn't be alarmed if some of our fellows seem downcast," Mr. Harriwell said, having drawn him aside in confidence. "There's been talk of an outbreak, and two or three suspicious signs I'm willing to admit, but personally I think it's all poppycock."

"How—how many blacks have you on the plantation?" Bertie asked, with a sinking heart.

"We're working four hundred just now," replied Mr. Harriwell, cheerfully; "but the three of us, with you, of course, and the skipper and mate of the *Arla*, can handle them all right."

Bertie turned to meet one McTavish, the storekeeper, who scarcely acknowledged the introduction, such was his eagerness to present his resignation.

"It being that I'm a married man, Mr. Harriwell, I can't very well afford to remain on longer. Trouble is working up, as plain as the nose on your face. The niggers are going to break out, and there'll be another Hohono horror here."

"What's a Hohono horror?" Bertie asked, after the storekeeper had been persuaded to remain until the end of the month.

"Oh, he means Hohono Plantation, on Ysabel," said the manager. "The niggers killed the five white men ashore, captured the schooner, killed the captain and mate, and escaped in a body to Malaita. But I always said they were careless on Hohono. They won't catch us napping here. Come along, Mr. Arkwright, and see our view from the veranda."

Bertie was too busy wondering how he could get away to Tulagi to the Commissioner's house, to see much of the view. He was still wondering, when a rifle exploded very near to him behind his back. At the same moment his arm was nearly dislocated, so eagerly did Mr. Harriwell drag him indoors.

"I say, old man, that was a close shave," said the manager, pawing him over to see if he had been hit. "I can't tell you how sorry I am. But it was broad daylight, and I never dreamed."

Bertie was beginning to turn pale.

"They got the other manager that way," McTavish vouchsafed. "And a dashed fine chap he was. Blew his brains out all over the veranda. You noticed that dark stain there between the steps and the door?"

Bertie was ripe for the cocktail which Mr. Harriwell pitched in and compounded for him; but before he could drink it, a man in riding trousers and puttees entered.

"What's the matter now?" the manager asked, after one look at the newcomer's face. "Is the river up again?"

"River be blowed—it's the niggers. Stepped out of the canegrass not a dozen feet away, and whopped at me. It was a Snider, and he shot from the hip. Now what I want to know is where'd he get the Snider? Oh, I beg your pardon. Glad to know you, Mr. Arkwright."

"Mr. Brown is my assistant," explained Mr. Harriwell. "And now let's have that drink."

"But where'd he get that Snider?" Mr. Brown insisted. "I always objected to keeping those guns on the premises."

"They're still there," Mr. Harriwell said, with a show of heat.

Mr. Brown smiled incredulously.

"Come along and see," said the manager.

Bertie joined the procession into the office, where Mr. Harriwell pointed triumphantly at a big packing-case in a dusty corner.

"Well, then, where did the beggar get that Snider?" harped Mr. Brown.

But just then McTavish lifted the packing-case. The manager started, then tore off the lid. The case was empty. They gazed at one another in horrified silence. Harriwell dropped wearily.

Then McTavish cursed.

"What I contended all along—the house-boys are not to be trusted."

"It does look serious," Harriwell admitted, "but we'll come through it all right. What the sanguinary niggers need is a shaking up. Will you gentlemen please bring your rifles to dinner, and will you, Mr. Brown, kindly prepare forty or fifty sticks of dynamite. Make the fuses good and short. We'll give them a lesson. And now, gentlemen, dinner is served."

One thing that Bertie detested was rice and curry, so it happened that he alone partook of an inviting omelet. He had quite finished his plate, when Harriwell helped himself to the omelet. One mouthful he tasted, then spat out vociferously.

"That's the second time," McTavish announced ominously.

Harriwell was still hawking and spitting.

"Second time, what?" Bertie quavered.

"Poison," was the answer. "That cook will be hanged yet."

"That's the way the bookkeeper went out at Cape Marsh," Brown spoke up. "Died horribly. They said on the *Jessie* that they heard him screaming three miles away."

"I'll put the cook in irons," sputtered Harriwell. "Fortunately we discovered it in time."

Bertie sat paralysed. There was no color in his face. He attempted to speak, but only an inarticulate gurgle resulted. All eyed him anxiously.

"Don't say it, don't say it," McTavish cried in a tense voice.

"Yes, I ate it, plenty of it, a whole plateful!" Bertie cried explosively, like a diver suddenly regaining breath.

The awful silence continued half a minute longer, and he read his fate in their eyes.

"Maybe it wasn't poison after all," said Harriwell, dismally.

"Call in the cook," said Brown.

In came the cook, a grinning black boy, nose-spiked and ear-plugged.

"Here, you, Wi-wi, what name that?" Harriwell bellowed, pointing accusingly at the omelet.

Wi-wi was very naturally frightened and embarrassed.

"Him good fella kai-kai," he murmured apologetically.

"Make him eat it," suggested McTavish. "That's a proper test."

Harriwell filled a spoon with the stuff and jumped for the cook, who fled in panic.

"That settles it," was Brown's solemn pronouncement. "He won't eat it."

"Mr. Brown, will you please go and put the irons on him?" Harriwell turned cheerfully to Bertie. "It's all right, old man, the Commissioner will deal with him, and if you die, depend upon it, he will be hanged."

"Don't think the government'll do it," objected McTavish.

"But gentlemen, gentlemen," Bertie cried. "In the meantime think of me."

Harriwell shrugged his shoulders pityingly.

"Sorry, old man, but it's a native poison, and there are no known antidotes for native poisons. Try and compose yourself, and if—"

Two sharp reports of a rifle from without, interrupted the discourse, and Brown, entering, reloaded his rifle and sat down to table.

"The cook's dead," he said. "Fever. A rather sudden attack."

"I was just telling Mr. Arkwright that there are no antidotes for native poisons—"

"Except gin," said Brown.

Harriwell called himself an absent-minded idiot and rushed for the gin bottle.

"Neat, man, neat," he warned Bertie, who gulped down a tumbler two-thirds full of the raw spirits, and coughed and choked from the angry bite of it till the tears ran down his cheeks.

Harriwell took his pulse and temperature, made a show of looking out for him, and doubted that the omelet had been poisoned. Brown and McTavish also doubted; but Bertie discerned an insincere ring in their voices. His appetite had left him, and he took his own pulse stealthily under the table. There was no question but what it was increasing, but he failed to ascribe it to the gin he had taken. McTavish, rifle in hand, went out on the veranda to reconnoitre.

"They're massing up at the cook-house," was his report. "And they've no end of Sniders. My idea is to sneak around on the other side and take them in flank. Strike the first blow, you know. Will you come along, Brown?"

Harriwell ate on steadily, while Bertie discovered that his pulse had leaped up five beats. Nevertheless, he could not help jumping when the rifles began to go off. Above the scattering of Sniders could be heard the pumping of Brown's and McTavish's Winchesters—all against a background of demoniacal screeching and yelling.

"They've got them on the run," Harriwell remarked, as voices and gunshots faded away in the distance.

Scarcely were Brown and McTavish back at the table when the latter reconnoitred.

"They've got dynamite," he said.

"Then let's charge them with dynamite," Harriwell proposed.

Thrusting half a dozen sticks each into their pockets and equipping themselves with lighted cigars, they started for the door. And just then it happened. They blamed McTavish for it afterward, and he admitted that the charge had been a trifle excessive. But at any rate it went off under the house, which lifted up corner-wise and settled back on its foundations. Half the china on the table was shattered, while the eight-day clock stopped. Yelling for vengeance, the three men rushed out into the night, and the bombardment began.

When they returned, there was no Bertie. He had dragged himself away to the office, barricaded himself in, and sunk upon the floor in a gin-soaked nightmare, wherein he died a thousand deaths while the valorous fight went on around him. In the morning, sick and headachy from the gin, he crawled out to find the sun still in the sky and God presumably in heaven, for his hosts were alive and uninjured.

Harriwell pressed him to stay on longer, but Bertie insisted on sailing immediately on the *Arla* for Tulagi, where, until the following steamer day, he stuck close by the Commissioner's house. There were lady tourists on the outgoing steamer, and Bertie was again a hero, while Captain Malu, as usual, passed unnoticed. But Captain Malu sent back from Sydney two cases of the best Scotch whiskey on the market, for he was not able to make up his mind as to whether it was Captain Hansen or Mr. Harriwell who had given Bertie Arkwright the more gorgeous insight into life in the Solomons.

# THE SAILOR'S WIFE

From "An Iceland Fisherman," BY PIERRE LOTI

THE Icelanders were all returning now. Two ships came in the second day, four the next, and twelve during the following week. And all through the country joy returned with them; and there was happiness for the wives and mothers, and junkets in the taverns where the beautiful barmaids of Paimpol served out drink to the fishers.

The *Léopoldine* was among the belated; there were yet another ten expected. They would not be long now; and allowing a week's delay so as not to be disappointed, Gaud waited in happy, passionate joy for Yann, keeping their home bright and tidy for his return. When everything was in good order there was nothing left for her to do; and besides, in her impatience, she could think of nothing else but her husband.

Three more ships appeared; then another five. There were only two lacking now.

"Come, come," they said to her cheerily, "this year the *Léopoldine* and the *Marie-Jeanne* will be the last, to pick up all the brooms fallen overboard from the other craft."

Gaud laughed also. She was more animated and beautiful than ever, in her great joy of expectancy.

But the days succeeded one another without result.

She still dressed up every day, and with a joyful look went down to the harbor to gossip with the other wives. She said that this delay was but natural: was it not the same event every year? These were such safe boats, and had such capital sailors.

But when at home alone, at night, a nervous anxious shiver of apprehension would run through her whole frame.

Was it right to be frightened already? Was there even a

single reason to be so? but she began to tremble at the mere idea of grounds for being afraid.

The 10th of September came. How swiftly the days flew by!

One morning—a true autumn morning, with cold mist falling over the earth in the rising sun—she sat under the porch of the chapel of the shipwrecked mariners, where the widows go to pray; with eyes fixed and glassy, and throbbing temples tightened as by an iron band.

These sad morning mists had begun two days before; and on this particular day Gaud had awakened with a still more bitter uneasiness, caused by the forecast of advancing winter. Why did this day, this hour, this very moment, seem to her more painful than the preceding? Often ships are delayed a fortnight; even a month, for that matter.

But surely there was something different about this particular morning; for she had come to-day for the first time to sit in the porch of this chapel and read the names of the dead sailors, perished in their prime.

### In Memory of
### GAOS YVON
#### Lost at Sea
##### NEAR THE NORDEN-FJORD

Like a great shudder, a gust of wind rose from the sea, and at the same time something fell like rain upon the roof above. It was only the dead leaves, though;—many were blown in at the porch; the old wind-tossed trees of the graveyard were losing their foliage in this rising gale, and winter was marching nearer.

#### Lost at Sea
##### NEAR THE NORDEN-FJORD
In the storm of the 4th and 5th of August, 1880

She read mechanically under the arch of the doorway; her eyes sought to pierce the distance over the sea. That morning it was untraceable under the gray mist, and a dragging drapery of clouds overhung the horizon like a mourning veil.

Another gust of wind, and other leaves danced in whirls. A stronger gust still; as if the western storm which had strewn those dead over the sea wished to deface the very inscriptions which kept their names in memory with the living.

Gaud looked with involuntary persistency at an empty space upon the wall which seemed to yawn expectant. By a terrible impression, she was pursued by the thought of a fresh slab which might soon perhaps be placed there,—with another name which she did not even dare think of in such a spot.

She felt cold, and remained seated on the granite bench, her head reclining against the stone wall.

NEAR THE NORDEN-FJORD

In the storm of the 4th and 5th of August, 1880
At the age of 23 years
*Requiescat in pace!*

Then Iceland loomed up before her, with its little cemetery lighted up from below the sea-line by the midnight sun. Suddenly, in the same empty space on the wall, with horrifying clearness she saw the fresh slab she was thinking of; a clear white one, with a skull and crossbones, and in a flash of foresight a name,—the worshiped name of "Yann Gaos"! Then she suddenly and fearfully drew herself up straight and stiff, with a hoarse wild cry in her throat like a mad creature.

Outside, the gray mist of the dawn fell over the land, and the dead leaves were again blown dancingly into the porch.

Steps on the footpath! Somebody was coming? She rose, and quickly smoothed down her cap and composed her face. Nearer drew the steps. She assumed the air of one who might be there by chance; for above all, she did not wish to appear yet like the widow of a shipwrecked mariner.

It happened to be Fante Floury, the wife of the second mate of the *Léopoldine*. She understood immediately what Gaud was doing there: it was useless to dissemble with her. At first each woman stood speechless before the other. They were angry and almost hated each other for having met holding a like sentiment of apprehension.

"All the men of Tréguier and Saint-Brieuc have been back for a week," said Fante at last, in an unfeeling, muffled, half-irritated voice.

She carried a blessed taper in her hand, to offer up a prayer. Gaud did not wish yet to resort to that extreme resource of despairing wives. Yet silently she entered the chapel behind Fante, and they knelt down together side by side like two sisters.

To the *Star of the Sea* they offered ardent imploring prayers, with their whole soul in them. A sound of sobbing was alone heard, as their rapid tears swiftly fell upon the floor. They rose together, more confident and softened. Fante held up Gaud, who staggered; and taking her in her arms, kissed her.

Wiping their eyes and smoothing their disheveled hair, they brushed off the salt dust from the flag-stones which had soiled their gowns, and went away in opposite directions without another word.

This end of September was like another summer, only a little less lively. The weather was so beautiful that had it not been for the dead leaves which fell upon the roads, one might have thought that June had come back again. Husbands and sweethearts had all returned, and everywhere was the joy of a second springtime of love.

At last, one day, one of the missing ships was signaled. Which one was it?

The groups of speechless and anxious women had rapidly formed on the cliff. Gaud, pale and trembling, was there, by the side of her Yann's father.

"I'm almost sure," said the old fisher, "I'm almost sure it's them. A red rail and a topsail that clews up,—it's very like them, anyhow. What do you make it, Gaud?"

"No, it isn't," he went on, with sudden discouragement:

"we've made a mistake again; the boom isn't the same, and ours has a jigger-sail. Well, well, it isn't our boat this time, it's only the *Marie-Jeanne*. Never mind, my lass, surely they'll not be long now."

But day followed day, and night succeeded night, with uninterrupted serenity.

Gaud continued to dress up every day; like a poor crazed woman, always in fear of being taken for the widow of a shipwrecked sailor, feeling exasperated when others looked furtively and compassionately at her, and glancing aside so that she might not meet those glances which froze her very blood.

She had fallen into the habit of going at the early morning right to the end of the headland, on the high cliffs of Pors-Even; passing behind Yann's old home, so as not to be seen by his mother or little sisters. She went to the extreme point of the Ploubazlanec land, which is outlined in the shape of a reindeer's horn upon the gray waters of the Channel, and sat there all day long at the foot of the lonely cross which rises high above the immense waste of the ocean. There are many of these crosses hereabout; they are set up on the most advanced cliffs of the seabound land, as if to implore mercy, and to calm that restless mysterious power which draws men away, never to give them back, and in preference retains the bravest and noblest.

Around this cross stretches the evergreen waste, strewn with short rushes. At this great height the sea air was very pure; it scarcely retained the briny odor of the weeds, but was perfumed with all the exquisite ripeness of September flowers.

Far away, all the bays and inlets of the coast were firmly outlined, rising one above another; the land of Brittany terminated in jagged edges, which spread out far into the tranquil surface.

Near at hand the reefs were numerous; but out beyond, nothing broke its polished mirror, from which arose a soft caressing ripple, light and intensified from the depths of its many bays. Its horizon seemed so calm, and its depths so soft! The great blue sepulchre of many Gaoses hid its inscrutable mystery; whilst the breezes, faint as human breath, wafted to and fro the perfume of the stunted gorse, which had bloomed again in the latest autumn sun.

At regular hours the sea retreated, and great spaces were left uncovered everywhere, as if the Channel was slowly drying up; then with the same lazy slowness the waters rose again, and continued their everlasting coming without any heed of the dead.

At the foot of the cross Gaud remained, surrounded by these tranquil mysteries, gazing ever before her until the night fell and she could see no more.

September had passed. The sorrowing wife took scarcely any nourishment, and could no longer sleep.

She remained at home now, crouching low with her hands between her knees, her head thrown back and resting against the wall behind. What was the good of getting up or going to bed now? When she was thoroughly exhausted she threw herself, dressed, upon her bed. Otherwise she remained in the same position, chilled and benumbed; in her quiescent state, only her teeth chattered with the cold; she had that continual impression of a band of iron round her brows; her cheeks looked wasted; her mouth was dry, with a feverish taste, and at times a painful hoarse cry rose from her throat and was repeated in spasms, whilst her head beat backwards against the granite wall. Or else she called Yann by his name in a low, tender voice, as if he were quite close to her; whispering words of love to her.

Sometimes she occupied her brain with thoughts of quite insignificant things; for instance, she amused herself by watching the shadow of the china Virgin lengthen slowly over the high woodwork of the bed, as the sun went down. And then the agonized thoughts returned more horribly; and her wailing cry broke out again as she beat her head against the wall.

All the hours of the day passed; and all the hours of evening, and of night; and then the hours of the morning. When she reckoned the time he ought to have been back, she was seized with a still greater terror; she wished to forget all dates and the very names of the days.

Generally, there is some information concerning the wrecks off Iceland; those who return have seen the tragedy from afar, or else have found some wreckage or bodies, or have an indication to guess the rest. But of the *Léopoldine* nothing had been seen, and nothing was known. The *Marie-Jeanne* men—the last to have seen it on the 2d of August—said that she was to have gone on fishing farther towards the north; and beyond that the secret was unfathomable.

Waiting, always waiting, and knowing nothing! When would the time come when she need wait no longer? She did not even know that; and now she almost wished that it might be soon. Oh! if he were dead, let them at least have pity enough to tell her so!

Oh to see her darling, as he was at this very moment,—that is, what was left of him! If only the much-implored Virgin, or some other power, would do her the blessing to show her by second-sight her beloved! either living and working hard to return a rich man, or else as a corpse surrendered by the sea, so that she might at least know a certainty.

Sometimes she was seized with the thought of a ship appearing suddenly upon the horizon: the *Léopoldine* hastening home. Then she would suddenly make an instinctive movement to rise, and rush to look out at the ocean, to see whether it were true.

But she would fall back. Alas! where was this *Léopoldine* now? Where could she be? Out afar, at that awful distance of Iceland,—forsaken, crushed, and lost.

All ended by a never-fading vision appearing to her,—an empty, sea-tossed wreck, slowly and gently rocked by the silent gray and rose-streaked sea; almost with soft mockery, in the midst of the vast calm of deadened waters.

Two o'clock in the morning.

It was at night especially that she kept attentive to approaching footsteps; at the slightest rumor or unaccustomed noise her temples vibrated: by dint of being strained to outward things, they had become fearfully sensitive.

Two o'clock in the morning. On this night as on others, with her hands clasped and her eyes wide open in the dark, she listened to the wind sweeping in never-ending tumult over the heath.

Suddenly a man's footsteps hurried along the path! At this hour who would pass now? She drew herself up, stirred to the very soul, her heart ceasing to beat.

Some one stopped before the door, and came up the small stone steps.

He!—O God!—he! Some one had knocked,—it could be no other than he! She was up now, barefooted; she, so feeble for the last few days, had sprung up as nimbly as a kitten, with her arms outstretched to wind round her darling. Of course the *Léopoldine* had arrived at night, and anchored in Pors-Even Bay, and he had rushed home; she arranged all this in her mind with the swiftness of lightning. She tore the flesh off her fingers in her excitement to draw the bolt, which had stuck.

"Eh?"

She slowly moved backward, as if crushed, her head falling on her bosom. Her beautiful insane dream was over. She could just grasp that it was not her husband, her Yann, and that nothing of him, substantial or spiritual, had passed through the air; she felt plunged again into her deep abyss, to the lowest depths of her terrible despair.

Poor Fantec—for it was he—stammered many excuses: his wife was very ill, and their child was choking in its cot, suddenly attacked with a malignant sore throat; so he had run over to beg for assistance on the road to fetch the doctor from Paimpol.

What did all this matter to her? She had gone mad in her own distress, and could give no thoughts to the troubles of others. Huddled on a bench, she remained before him with fixed glazed eyes, like a dead woman's; without listening to him, or even answering at random or looking at him. What to her was the speech the man was making?

He understood it all, and guessed why the door had been

opened so quickly to him; and feeling pity for the pain he had unwittingly caused, he stammered out an excuse.

"Just so: he never ought to have disturbed her—her in particular."

"I!" ejaculated Gaud quickly, "why should I not be disturbed particularly, Fantec?"

Life had suddenly come back to her; for she did not wish to appear in despair before others. Besides, she pitied him now; she dressed to accompany him, and found the strength to go and see to his little child.

At four o'clock in the morning, when she returned to throw herself on the bed, sleep subdued her, for she was tired out. But that moment of excessive joy had left an impression on her mind, which in spite of all was permanent; she awoke soon with a shudder, rising a little and partially recollecting—she knew not what. News had come to her about her Yann. In the midst of her confusion of ideas, she sought rapidly in her mind what it could be; but there was nothing save Fantec's interruption.

For the second time she fell back into her terrible abyss, nothing changed in her morbid, hopeless waiting.

Yet in that short, hopeful moment, she had felt him so near to her that it was as if his spirit had floated over the sea unto her,—what is called a foretoken (*pressigne*) in Breton land; and she listened still more attentively to the steps outside, trusting that some one might come to her to speak of him.

Just as the day broke, Yann's father entered. He took off his cap, and pushed back his splendid white locks, which were in curls like Yann's, sat down by Gaud's bedside.

His heart ached heavily too; for Yann, his tall, handsome Yann, was his first-born, his favorite and his pride: but he did not despair yet. He comforted Gaud in his own blunt, affectionate way. To begin with, those who had last returned from Iceland spoke of the increasing dense fogs, which might well have delayed the vessel; and then too an idea struck him,—they might possibly have stopped at the distant Faroe Islands on their homeward course, whence letters were so long in traveling. This had happened to him once forty years ago, and his own poor dead and gone mother had had a mass said for his soul. The *Léopoldine* was such a good boat,—next to new,—and her crew were such able-bodied seamen.

Granny Moan stood by them shaking her head: the distress of her granddaughter had almost given her back her own strength and reason. She tidied up the place, glancing from time to time at the faded portrait of Sylvestre, which hung upon the granite wall with its anchor emblems and mourning-wreath of black bead-work. Ever since the sea had robbed her of her own last offspring, she believed no longer in safe returns; she only prayed through fear, bearing Heaven a grudge in the bottom of her heart.

But Gaud listened eagerly to these consoling reasonings; her large sunken eyes looked with deep tenderness out upon this old sire, who so much resembled her beloved one; merely to have him near her was like a hostage against death having taken the younger Gaos; and she felt reassured, nearer to her Yann. Her tears fell softly and silently, and she repeated again her passionate prayers to the *Star of the Sea*.

A delay out at those islands to repair damages was a very likely event. She rose and brushed her hair, and then dressed as if she might fairly expect him. All then was not lost, if a seaman, his own father, did not yet despair. And for a few days she resumed looking out for him again.

Autumn at last arrived,—a late autumn too,—its gloomy evenings making all things appear dark in the old cottage; and all the land looked sombre too.

The very daylight seemed a sort of twilight; immeasurable clouds, passing slowly overhead, darkened the whole country at broad noon. The wind blew constantly with the sound of a great cathedral organ at a distance, but playing profane, despairing dirges; at other times the noise came close to the door, like the howling of wild beasts.

She had grown pale,—aye, blanched,—and bent more than ever; as if old age had already touched her with its featherless wing. Often did she finger the wedding clothes of her Yann, folding them and unfolding them again and again like some maniac,—especially one of his blue woolen jerseys which still had preserved his shape: when she threw it gently on the table, it fell with the shoulders and chest well defined; so she placed it by itself in a shelf of their wardrobe, and left it there, so that it might forever rest unaltered.

Every night the cold mists sank upon the land, as she gazed over the depressing heath through her little window, and watched the thin puffs of white smoke arise from the chimneys of other cottages scattered here and there on all sides. There the husbands had returned, like wandering birds driven home by the frost. Before their blazing hearths the evenings passed, cozy and warm; for the springtime of love had begun again in this land of North Sea fishermen.

Still clinging to the thought of those islands where he might perhaps have lingered, she was buoyed up by a kind hope, and expected him home any day.

But he never returned. One August night, out off gloomy Iceland, mingled with the furious clamor of the sea, his wedding with the sea was performed. It had been his nurse; it had rocked him in his babyhood and had afterwards made him big and strong; then, in his superb manhood, it had taken him back again for itself alone. Profoundest mystery had surrounded this unhallowed union. While it went on, dark curtains hung pall-like over it as if to conceal the ceremony, and the ghoul howled in an awful, deafening voice to stifle his cries. He, thinking of Gaud, his sole, darling wife, had battled with giant strength against this deathly rival, until he at last surrendered, with a deep death-cry like the roar of a dying bull, through a mouth already filled with water; and his arms were stretched apart and stiffened forever.

All those he had invited in days of old were present at his wedding. All except Sylvestre, who had gone to sleep in the enchanted gardens far, far away, at the other side of the earth.

# THE ADVENTURE OF BARNY O'REIRDON

From "Legends and Stories," by SAMUEL LOVER

BARNY O'REIRDON was a fisherman of Kinsale, and a heartier
fellow never hauled a net or cast a line into deep water; indeed,
Barny, independently of being a merry boy among his companions, a lover of good fun and good whisky, was rather
looked up to, by his brother fishermen, as an intelligent fellow,
and few boats brought more fish to market than Barny O'Reirdon's; his opinion on certain points in the craft was considered
law, and in short, in his own little community, Barny was what
was commonly called a leading man. Now, your leading man
is always jealous in an inverse ratio to the sphere of his influence, and the leader of a nation is less incensed at a rival's triumph than the great man of a village. If we pursue this descending scale, what a desperately jealous person the oracle of oyster-
dredgers and cockle-women must be! Such was Barny O'Reirdon.

Seated one night in a public-house, the common resort of
Barny and other marine curiosities, our hero got entangled in
debate with what he called a strange sail—that is to say, a man
he had never met before, and whom he was inclined to treat
rather magisterially upon nautical subjects; at the same time
that the stranger was equally inclined to assume the high hand
over him, till at last the newcomer made a regular outbreak by
exclaiming: "Ah, tare-an-ouns, lave off your balderdash, Mr.
O'Reirdon; by the powdhers o' war it's enough, so it is, to make
a dog bate his father, to hear you goin' an as if you wor Curlum-
berus or Sir Crustyphiz Wran, whin ivery one knows the divil
a farther you iver wor, nor ketchin' crabs or drudgin' oysters."

"Who towld you that, my Watherford Wondher?" rejoined
Barny; "what the dickens do you know about sayfarin', far-

ther nor fishin' for sprats in a bowl wid your grandmother?"

"Oh, baithershin," says the stranger.

"And who made you so bowld with my name?" demanded O'Reirdon.

"No matther for that," says the stranger; "but if you'd like for to know, shure it's your cousin, Molly Mullins, knows me well, and maybe I don't know you and yours as well as the mother that bore you, ay, in troth; and shure I know the very thoughts o' you as well as if I was inside o' you, Barny O'Reirdon."

"By my sowl, thin, you know betther thoughts than your own, Mr. Whippersnapper, if that's the name you go by."

"No, it's not the name I go by; I've as good a name as your own, Mr. O'Reirdon, for want o' a betther, and that's O'Sullivan."

"Throth there's more than there's good o' them," said Barny.

"Good or bad, I'm a cousin o' your own, twice removed by the mother's side."

"And is it the Widda O'Sullivan's boy you'd be that left come Candlemas four years?"

"The same."

"Throth, thin, you might know betther manners to your eldhers, though I'm glad to see you, anyhow, agin; but a little thravelin' puts us beyant ourselves sometimes," said Barny, rather contemptuously.

"Throth, I niver bragged out o' myself yit, and it's what I say, that a man that's only a fishin' aff the land all his life has no business to compare in the regard o' thracthericks wid a man that has sailed to Fingal."

This silenced any further argument on Barny's part. Where Fingal lay was all Greek to him; but, unwilling to admit his ignorance, he covered his retreat with the usual address of his countrymen, and turned the bitterness of debate into the cordial flow of congratulation at seeing his cousin again. . . .

Let us, now, transfer our story to the succeeding morning, when Barny O'Reirdon strolled forth from his cottage. . . .

Barny sauntered about in the sun, at which he often looked up, under the shelter of compressed, bushy brows and long-lashed eyelids, and a shadowing hand across his forehead, to see "what time o' day" it was; and, from the frequency of this action, it was evident the day was hanging heavily with Barny. He retired at last to a sunny nook in a neighboring field, and stretching himself at full length, basked in the sun, and began "to chew the cud of sweet and bitter thought." He first reflected on his own undoubted weight in his little community, but still he could not get over the annoyance of the preceding night, arising from his being silenced by O'Sullivan, "a chap," as he said himself, "that lift the place four years agon a brat iv a boy, and to think of his comin' back and outdoin' his elders, that saw him runnin' about the place, a gassoon, that one could tache a few months before;" 'twas too bad. Barny saw his reputation was in a ticklish position, and began to consider how his disgrace could be retrieved. The very name of Fingal was hateful to him; it was a plague-spot on his peace that festered there incurably. He first thought of leaving Kinsale altogether; but flight implied so much of defeat that he did not long indulge in that notion. No; he *would* stay, "in spite of all the O'Sulli-vans, kith and kin, breed, seed and generation." But at the same time he knew he should never hear the end of that hateful place, Fingal; and if Barny had had the power he would have enacted a penal statute, making it death to name the accursed spot, wherever it was; but not being gifted with such legislative authority, he felt Kinsale was no place for him, if he would not submit to be flouted every hour out of the four-and-twenty, by man, woman, and child, that wished to annoy him. What was to be done? He was in the perplexing situation, to use his own words, "of the cat in the thripe shop," he didn't know which way to choose. At last, after turning himself over in the sun several times, a new idea struck him. Couldn't he go to Fingal himself? and then he'd be equal to that upstart, O'Sullivan. No sooner was the thought engendered than Barny sprang to his feet a new man; his eye brightened, his step became once more elastic, he walked erect, and felt himself to be all over Barny O'Reirdon once more. "Richard was himself again."

But where was Fingal?—there was the rub. That was a profound mystery to Barny, which, until discovered, must hold him in the vile bondage of inferiority. The plain-dealing reader will say, "Couldn't he ask?" No, no; that would never do for Barny; that would be an open admission of ignorance his soul was above; and, consequently, Barny set his brains to work to devise measures of coming at the hidden knowledge by some circuitous route, that would not betray the end he was working for. . . .

But, as the Irish saying is, "to make a long story short," Barny prevailed on Peter Kelly to make an export; but in the nature of the venture they did not agree. Barny had proposed potatoes; Peter said there were enough of them already where he was going, and rejoined: "Praties were so good in themselves there never could be too much o' thim anywhere." But Peter, being a knowledgeable man, and up to all the "saycrets o' the airth, and undherstanding in the the-o-ry and the che-mis-thery," overruled Barny's proposition, and determined upon a cargo of *scalpeens* (which name they gave to pickled mackerel) as a preferable merchandise, quite forgetting that Dublin Bay herrings were a much better and as cheap a commodity, at the command of the Fingalians. But in many similar mistakes the ingenious Mr. Kelly has been paralleled by other speculators. But that is neither here nor there, and it was all one to Barny whether his boat was freighted with potatoes or *scalpeens*, so long as he had the honor and glory of becoming a navigator, and being as good as O'Sullivan.

Accordingly, the boat was laden and all got in readiness for putting to sea, and nothing was now wanting but Barny's orders to haul up the gaff and shake out the jib of his hooker.

But this order Barny refrained to give, and for the first time in his life exhibited a disinclination to leave the shore. One of his fellow-boatmen at last said to him: "Why, thin, Barny O'Reirdon, what the divil is come over you at all at all? What's the maynin' of your loitherin' about here, and the boat ready, and a lovely fine breeze aff o' the land?"

"Oh! never you mind; I believe I know my own business, anyhow; an' it's hard, so it is, if a man can't ordher his own boat to sail when he plazes." . . .

Well, the next day was Friday, and Barny, of course, would not sail any more than any other sailor who could help it, on this unpropitious day. On Saturday, however, he came, running in a great hurry down to the shore, and, jumping aboard, he gave orders to make all sail, and taking the helm of the hooker, he turned her head to the sea, and soon the boat was cleaving the blue waters with a velocity seldom witnessed in so small a craft, and scarcely conceivable to those who have not seen the speed of a Kinsale hooker.

"Why, thin, you tuk the notion mighty suddint, Barny," said the fisherman next in authority to O'Reirdon, as soon as the bustle of getting the boat under way had subsided.

"Well, I hope it's plazin' to you at last," said Barny; "throth, one 'ud think you were never at say before, you wor in such a hurry to be off, as new-fangled a'most as a child with a play-toy."

"Well," said the other of Barny's companions, for there were but two with him in the boat, "I was thinkin' myself as well as Jimmy, that we lost two fine days for nothin', and we'd be there a'most, maybe, now, if we sailed three days agon."

"Don't believe it," said Barny, emphatically. "Now, don't you know yourself that there is some days that the fish won't come near the lines at all, and that we might as well be castin' our nets an the dhry land as in the say, for all we'll catch if we start an an unlooky day; and sure I towld you I was waitin' only till I had it given to me to undherstan' that it was looky to sail, and I go bail we'll be there sooner than if we started three days agon; for, if you don't start, with good look before you, faix, maybe it's never at all to the end o' your thrip you'll come."

"Well, there's no use in talkin' about it now anyhow; but when do you expect to be there?"

"Why, you see we must wait antil I can tell you how the wind is like to hould on, before I can make up my mind to that."

"But you're sure now, Barny, that you're up to the coorse you have to run?"

"See now, lay me alone, and don't be crass-questionin' me—tare-an-ouns, do you think me sitch a bladdherang as for to go to shuperinscribe a thing I wasn't aiquil to?"

"No; I was only goin' to ax you what coorse you wor goin' to steer?"

"You'll find out soon enough when we get there; and so I bid you agin lay me alone—just keep your toe in your pump. Shure I'm here at the helm, and a woight on my mind, and it's fitther for you, Jim, to mind your own business and lay me to mind mine; away wid you, there, and be handy; haul taut that fore-sheet there; we must run close an the wind; be handy, boys; make everything dhraw."

These orders were obeyed, and the hooker soon passed to windward of a ship that left the harbor before her, but could not hold on a wind with the same tenacity as the hooker, whose qualities in this particular render it peculiarly suitable for the purposes to which it is applied—namely, pilot and fishing-boats.

We have said that a ship left the harbor before the hooker had set sail, and it is now fitting to inform the reader that Barny had contrived to ascertain that this ship, then lying in the harbor, was going to the very place Barny wanted to reach. Barny's plan of action was decided upon in a moment; he had now nothing to do but to watch the sailing of the ship and follow in her course. Here was, at once, a new mode of navigation discovered. . . .

For this purpose he went to windward of the ship, and then fell off again, allowing her to pass him, as he did not wish even those on board the ship to suppose he was following in their wake; for Barny, like all people that are quite full of one scheme and fancy everybody is watching them, dreaded lest any one should fathom his motives. All that day Barny held on the same course as his leader, keeping at a respectful distance, however, "for fear 'twould look like dodging her," as he said to himself; but as night closed in, so closed in Barny, with the ship, and kept a sharp lookout that she should not give him the slip in the dark. The next morning dawned, and found the hooker and ship companions still; and thus matters proceeded for four days, during the entire of which time they had not seen land since their first losing sight of it, although the weather was clear.

"By my sowl," thought Barny, "the channel must be mighty wide in these parts, and for the last day or so we've bein' goin' purty free with a flowin' sheet, and I wondher we aren't closin' in wid the shore by this time, or maybe it's farther off than I thought it was." His companions, too, began to question Barny on the subject, but to their queries he presented an impenetrable front of composure, and said, "it was always the best plan to keep a good bowld offin'." In two days more, however, the weather began to be sensibly warmer, and Barny and his companions remarked that it was "goin' to be the finest sayson, God bless it, that ever kem out o' the skies for many a long year; and maybe it's the whate wouldn't be beautiful, and a great plenty of it." It was at the end of a week that the ship which Barny had hitherto kept ahead of him showed symptoms of bearing down upon him, as he thought; and, sure enough, she did; and Barny began to conjecture what the deuce the ship could want with him, and commenced inventing answers to the questions he thought it possible might be put to him in case the ship spoke to him. He was soon put out of suspense by being hailed and ordered to run under her lee, and the captain looking over the quarter, asked Barny where he was going.

"Faith, thin, I'm goin' an my business," said Barny.

"But where?" said the captain.

"Why, sure, an it's no matther where a poor man like me id be goin'," said Barny.

"Only I'm curious to know what the deuce you've been following my ship for the last week?"

"Follyin' your ship! Why, thin, blur an agers, do you think it's follyin' yiz I am?"

"It's very like it," said the captain.

"Why, did two people niver thravel the same road before?"

"I don't say they didn't, but there's a great difference between a ship of seven hundred tons and a hooker."

"Oh, as for that matther," said Barny, "the same high-road sarves a coach-and-four and a low-back car, the thravelin' tinker an' a lord a horseback."

"That's very true," said the captain, "but the cases are not the same, Paddy, and I can't conceive what the devil brings *you* here."

"And who axed you to consayve anything about it?" asked Barny, somewhat sturdily.

"D—n me if I can imagine what you're about, my fine fellow," said the captain, "and my own notion is that you don't know where the devil you're going yourself."

"O *baithershin*," said Barny, with a derisive laugh.

"Why, then, do you object to tell?" said the captain.

"Arrah, sure, captain, an' don't you know that sometimes vessels is bound to sail *saycret ordher!*" said Barny, endeavoring to foil the question by badinage.

There was a universal laugh from the deck of the ship at the idea of a fishing-boat sailing under secret orders—for by this time the whole broadside of the vessel was crowded with grinning mouths and wondering eyes at Barny and his boat. . . .

"Very well," said the captain; "I see there's no use in talking to you, so go to the devil your own way." And away bore the ship, leaving Barny in indignation and his companions in wonder.

"And why wouldn't you tell him?" said they to Barny.

"Why, don't you see," said Barny, whose object was now to blind them, "don't you see, how do I know but maybe he might be goin' to the same place himself, and maybe he has a cargo of *scalpeens* as well as us, and wants to get before us there?"

"Thrue for you, Barny," said they. "Bedad you're right." And, their inquiries being satisfied, the day passed as former ones had done, in pursuing the course of the ship.

In four days more, however, the provisions in the hooker began to fail, and they were obliged to have recourse to the *scalpeens* for sustenance, and Barny then got seriously uneasy at the length of the voyage, and the likely greater length for anything he could see to the contrary; and, urged at last by his own alarms and those of his companions, he was enabled, as the wind was light, to gain on the ship, and when he found himself alongside he demanded a parley with the captain.

The captain, on hearing that the "hardy hooker," as she got christened, was under his lee, came on deck, and, as soon as he appeared, Barny cried out:

"Why, then, blur an agers, captain dear, do you expect to be there soon?"

"Where?" said the captain.

"Oh, you know yourself," said Barny.

"It's well for me I do," said the captain.

"Thrue for you, indeed, your honor," said Barny, in his most insinuating tone; "but whin will you be at the ind o' your voyage, captain, jewel?"

"I daresay in about three months," said the captain.

"Oh, Holy Mother!" ejaculated Barny; "three months! arrah, it's jokin' you are, captain dear, and only want to freken me."

"How should I frighten you?" asked the captain.

"Why, thin, your honor, to tell God's thruth, I heard you were goin' *there*, an' as I wanted to go there too, I thought I couldn't do better nor to folly a knowledgeable gintleman like yourself, and save myself the throuble iv findin' it out."

"And where do you think I *am* going?" said the captain.

"Why, thin," said Barny, "isn't it to Fingal?"

"No," said the captain, " 'tis to *Bengal*."

"Oh, Gog's blakey!" said Barny, "what'll I do now at all at all?"

The captain ordered Barny on deck, as he wished to have some conversation with him on what he, very naturally, considered a most extraordinary adventure. Heaven help the captain! he knew little of Irishmen, or he would not have been so astonished. Barny made his appearance. Puzzling question and more puzzling answer followed in quick succession between the commander and Barny, who, in the midst of his dilemma, stamped about, thumped his head, squeezed his caubeen into all manner of shapes, and vented his despair anathematically:

"Oh, my heavy hathred to you, you tarnal thief iv a long sailor; it's a purty scrape yiv led me into. Begor, I thought it was *Fingal* he said, and now I hear it is *Bingal*. Oh! the divil sweep you for navigation; why did I meddle or make with you at all at all! And my curse light on you, Terry O'Sullivan; why did I iver come across you, you onlooky vagabone, to put sitch thoughts in my head! An' so it's *Bin*gal and not *Fin*gal, you're goin' to, captain?"

"Yes, indeed, Paddy."

"An' might I be bowled to ax, captain, is Bingal much farther nor Fingal?"

"A trifle or so, Paddy."

"Och, thin, millia murther, weirasthru, how'll I iver get there at all at all?" roared out poor Barny.

"By turning about, and getting back the road you've come, as fast as you can."

"Is it back? O Queen iv Heaven! an' how will I iver get back?" said the bewildered Barny.

"Then you don't know your course, it appears?"

"Oh, faix, I knew it iligant, as long as your honor was before me."

"But you don't know your course back?"

"Why, indeed, not to say rightly all out, your honor."

"Can't you steer?" said the captain.

"The divil a betther hand at the tiller in all Kinsale," said Barny, with his usual brag.

"Well, so far so good," said the captain. "And you know the points of the compass—you have a compass, I suppose?"

"A compass!—by my sowl, an' it's not let alone a compass, but a *pair* a compasses I have, that my brother the carpinthir left me for a keepsake whin he wint abroad; but indeed, as for the points o' thim I can't say much, for the childhren spylt thim intirely, rootin' holes in the flure."

"What the plague are you talking about?"

"Wasn't your honor discoorsin' me about the points o' the compasses?"

"Confound your thick head!" said the captain. "Why, what an ignoramus you must be, not to know what a compass is, and you at sea all your life! Do you even know the cardinal points?"

"The cardinal!—faix, an' it's a great respect I have for them, your honor. Sure, aren't they belongin' to the Pope?"

"Confound you, you blockhead!" roared the captain, in a rage; " 'twould take the patience of the Pope and the cardinals, and the cardinal virtues into the bargain, to keep one's temper with you. Do you know the four points of the wind?"

"By my sowl I do, and more."

"Well, never mind more, but let us stick to four. You're sure you know the four points of the wind?"

"Bedad, it would be a quare thing if a sayfarin' man didn't know somethin' about the wind, anyhow. Why, captain dear, you must take me for a nath'ral intirely to suspect me o' the like o' not knowin' all about the wind. Begor, I know as much o' the wind a'most as a pig."

"Indeed, I believe so," laughed out the captain.

"Oh, you may laugh if you plaze; and I see by the same that you don't know about the pig, with all your edication, captain."

"Well, what about the pig?"

"Why, sir, did you never hear a pig can see the wind?"

"I can't say that I did."

"Oh, thin, he does; and for that rayson, who has a right to know more about it?"

"You don't for one, I dare say, Paddy; and maybe you have a pig aboard to give you information."

"Sorra taste, your honor, not as much as a rasher o' bacon; but it's maybe your honor never seen a pig tossin' up his snout, consaited like, and running like mad afore a storm."

"Well, what if I have?"

"Well, sir, that is when they see the wind a-comin'."

"Maybe so, Paddy; but all this knowledge in piggery won't find you your way home. You say you know the four points of the wind—north, south, east, and west."

"Yis, sir."

"How do you know them?—for I must see that you are not likely to make a mistake. How do you know the points?"

"Why, you see, sir, the sun, God bless it, rises in the aist, and sets in the west, which stands to rayson; and when you stand bechuxt the aist and the west, the north is forninst you."

"And when the north is forninst you, as you say, is the east on your right or your left hand?"

"On the right hand, your honor."

"Well, I see you know that much, however. Now," said the captain, "the moment you leave the ship, you must steer a northeast course, and you will make some land near home in about a week, if the wind holds as it is now, and it is likely to do so; but mind me, if you turn out of your course in the smallest degree, you are a lost man."

"Many thanks to your honor."

"And how are you off for provisions?"

"Why, thin, indeed, in the regard o' that same, we are in the hoight o' distress; for exceptin' the scalpeens, sorra a taste passed our lips for these four days."

"Oh, you poor devils!" said the commander, in a tone of sincere commiseration. "I'll order you some provisions on board before you start."

"Long life to your honor!—and *I'd like to drink the health* of so noble a gintleman."

"I understand you, Paddy;—you shall have grog too."

"Musha, the heaven shower blessin's an you, I pray the Virgin Mary and the twelve apostles, Matthew, Mark, Luke, and John, not forgettin' St. Pathrick."

"Thank you, Paddy; but keep all your prayers for yourself, for you need them all to help you home again."

"Oh, never fear, whin the thing is to be done, I'll do it, bedad, wid a heart and a half. And sure, your honor, God is good, an' will mind dissolute craythurs like uz, on the wild oceant as well as ashore."

While some of the ship's crew were putting the captain's benevolent intentions to Barny and his companions into practice, by transferring some provisions to the hooker, the commander entertained himself by further conversation with Barny, who was the greatest original he had ever met. In the course of their colloquy, Barny drove many hard queries at the captain, respecting the wonders of the nautical profession, and at last put the question to him plump.

"Oh, thin, captain dear, and how is it at all at all, that you make your way over the wide says intirely to them furrin parts?"

"You would not understand, Paddy, if I attempted to explain to you."

"Sure enough, indeed, your honor, and I ask your pardon, only I was curious to know, and sure no wonder."

"It requires various branches of knowledge to make a navigator."

"Branches," said Barny, "begor, I think it id take the *whole three o' knowledge* to make it out. And that place you are going to, sir, that *Bing*al (oh, bad luck to it for a *Bing*al, it's the sore *Bing*al to me), is it so far off as you say?"

"Yes, Paddy, half round the world." . . .

"My name's not Paddy, your honor," said Barny; "my name isn't Paddy, sir, but Barny."

"Oh, if it was Solomon, you'll be bare enough when you go home this time; you have not gathered much this trip, Barny."

"Sure, I've been gathering knowledge, anyhow, your honor," said Barny, with a significant look at the captain, and a complimentary tip of his hand to his caubeen, "and God bless you for being so good to me."

"And what's your name besides Barny?" asked the captain.

"O'Reirdon, your honor;—Barny O'Reirdon's my name."

"Well, Barny O'Reirdon, I won't forget your name nor yourself in a hurry, for you are certainly the most original navigator I ever had the honor of being acquainted with."

"Well," said Barny, with a triumphant toss of his head, "I have done out Terry O'Sullivan, at any rate; the divil a half so far he ever was, and that's a comfort. I have muzzled his clack for the rest iv his life, and he won't be comin' over us wid the pride iv his *Fin*gal, while I'm to the fore, that was a'most at *Bin*gal."

"Terry O'Sullivan—who is he?" said the captain.

"Oh, he's a scut iv a chap that's not worth your axin' for—he's not worth your honor's notice—a braggin' poor craythur. Oh, wait till I get home, and the divil a more braggin' they'll hear out of his jaw."

"Indeed, then, Barny, the sooner you turn your face towards home the better," said the captain; "since you will go, there is no need in losing more time."

"Thrue for you, your honor; and sure it's well for me had the luck to meet wid the likes o' your honor, that explained the ins and outs iv it to me, and laid it all down as plain as prent."

"Are you sure you remember my directions?" said the captain.

"Throth, an' I'll niver forget them to the day o' my death, and is bound to pray, more betoken, for you and yours."

"Don't mind praying for me till you get home, Barny; but answer me, how are you to steer when you shall leave me?"

"The *nor-aist coorse,* your honor; that's the coorse agin the world."

"Remember that! never alter that course till you see land; let nothing make you turn out of a north-east course."

"Troth, an' that id be the dirty turn, seein' that it was yourself that ordhered it. Oh, no, I'll depend my life an the *nor-aist coorse;* and God help any one that comes betune me an' it— I'd run him down if he was my father."

"Well, good-by, Barny."

"Good-by, and God bless you, your honor, and send you safe."

"That's a wish you want more for yourself, Barny; never fear for me, but mind yourself well."

"Oh, sure, I'm as good as at home wanst I know the way, barrin' the wind is conthrary; sure, the nor-aist coorse 'ill do the business complate. Good-by, your honor, and long life to you, and more power to your elbow, and a light heart and a heavy purse to you evermore, I pray the Blessed Virgin and all the saints, amin!" and so saying, Barny descended the ship's side, and once more assumed the helm of the "hardy hooker."

The two vessels now separated on their opposite courses. What a contrast their relative situations afforded! Proudly the ship bore away under her lofty and spreading canvas, cleaving the billows before her, manned by an able crew, and under the guidance of experienced officers; the finger of science to point the course of her progress, the faithful chart to warn of the hidden rock and the shoal, the log line and the quadrant to measure her march and prove her position. The poor little hooker cleft not the billows, each wave lifted her on its crest like a sea-bird; but three inexperienced fishermen to manage her; no certain means to guide them over the vast ocean they had to traverse, and the holding of the "fickle wind" the only *chance* of their escape from perishing in the wilderness of waters. By one, the feeling excited is supremely that of man's power; by the other, of his utter helplessness. To the one the expanse of ocean could scarcely be considered "trackless," to the other it was a waste indeed.

Yet the cheer that burst from the ship, at parting, was an-

swered as gayly from the hooker as though the odds had not
been so fearfully against her; and no blither heart beat on board
the ship than that of Barny O'Reirdon.

Happy light-heartedness of my poor countrymen! They
have often need of all their buoyant spirits. How kindly have
they been fortified by Nature against the assaults of adversity;
and if they blindly rush into dangers, they cannot be denied
the possession of gallant hearts to fight their way out of them.

But each hurrah became less audible; by degrees the cheers
dwindled into faintness, and finally were lost in the eddies of
the breeze.

The first feeling of loneliness that poor Barny experienced
was when he could no longer hear the exhilarating sound. The
plash of the surge, as it broke on the bows of his little boat,
was uninterrupted by the kindred sound of human voice; and
as it fell upon his ear it smote upon his heart. But he rallied,
waved his hat, and the silent signal was answered from the ship.

"Well, Barny," said Jemmy, "what was the captain sayin'
to you all the time you wor wid him?"

"Lay me alone," said Barny; "I'll talk to you when I see her
out o' sight, but not a word till thin. I'll look afther him, the
rale gintleman that he is, while there's a topsail o' his ship to
be seen, and thin I'll send my blessin' after him, and pray for
his good fortune wherever he goes, for he's the right sort and
nothin' else." And Barny kept his word, and when his straining eyes could no longer trace a line of the ship, the captain
certainly had the benefit of "a poor man's blessing."

The sense of utter loneliness and desolation had not come
upon Barny until now; but he put his trust in the goodness of
Providence, and in a fervent mental outpouring of prayer resigned himself to the care of his Creator. With an admirable
fortitude, too, he assumed a composure to his companions that
was a stranger to his heart; and we all know how the burden
of anxiety is increased when we have none with whom to sym-
pathize. And this was not all. He had to effect ease and confidence, for Barny not only had no dependence on the firm-

ness of his companions to go through the undertaking before them, but dreaded to betray to them how he had imposed on them in the affair. Barny was equal to all this. He had a stout heart, and was an admirable actor; yet, for the first hour after the ship was out of sight, he could not quite recover himself, and every now and then, unconsciously, he would look back with a wistful eye to the point where last he saw her. Poor Barny had lost his leader.

The night fell, and Barny stuck to the helm as long as nature could sustain want of rest, and then left it in charge of one of his companions, with particular directions how to steer, and ordered if any change in the wind occurred that they should instantly awake him. He could not sleep long, however; the fever of anxiety was upon him, and the morning had not long dawned when he awoke. He had not well rubbed his eyes and looked about him, when he thought he saw a ship in the distance approaching them. As the haze cleared away, she showed distinctly bearing down towards the hooker.

On board the ship the hooker, in such a sea, caused surprise as before, and in about an hour she was so close as to hail and order the hooker to run under her lee.

"The divil a taste," said Barny; "I'll not quit my *nor-aist coorse* for the king of Ingland, nor Bonyparty into the bargain. Bad cess to you, do you think I've nothin' to do but to plaze you?"

Again he was hailed.

"Oh! bad luck to the toe I'll go to you."

Another hail.

"Spake loudher, you'd betther," said Barny, jeeringly, still holding on his course.

A gun was fired ahead of him.

"By my sowl, you spoke loudher that time, sure enough," said Barny.

"Take care, Barny!" cried Jemmy and Peter together. "Blur an' agers, man, we'll be kilt if you don't go to them!"

"Well, and we'll be lost if we turn out iv our *nor-aist coorse,* and that's as broad as it's long. Let them hit iz if they like; sure it 'ud be a pleasanter death nor starvin' at say. I tell you again, I'll turn out o' my *nor-aist coorse* for no man."

A shotted gun was fired. The shot hopped on the water as it passed before the hooker.

"Phew! you missed it, like your mammy's blessin'," said Barny.

"Oh, murther!" said Jemmy, "didn't you see the ball hop aff the wather forninst you? Oh, murther! what 'ud we ha' done if we wor there at all at all?"

"Why, we'd have taken the ball at the hop," said Barny, laughing, "accordin' to the owld sayin'."

Another shot was ineffectually fired.

"I'm thinkin' that's a Connaughtman that's shootin'," [1] said Barny, with a sneer. The allusion was so relished by Jemmy and Peter, that it excited a smile in the midst of their fears from the cannonade.

Again the report of the gun was followed by no damage.

"Augh! never heed them!" said Barny, contemptuously. "It's a barkin' dog that never bites, as the owld saying says;" and the hooker was soon out of reach of further annoyance.

"Now, what a pity it was, to be sure," said Barny, "that I wouldn't go aboard to plaze them. Now, who's right? Ah, lave me alone always, Jemmy. Did you ivir know me wrong yet?"

"Oh, you may hillow now that you're out o' the woods," said Jemmy; "but, accordin' to my idays, it was runnin' a grate rishk to be contrary wid them at all, and they shootin' balls afther us."

"Well, what matther?" said Barny, "since they wor only blind gunners, *an' I knew it*; besides, as I said afore, I won't turn out o' my *nor-aist coorse* for no man."

"That's a new turn you tuk lately," said Peter. "What's the rayson you're runnin' a nor-aist coorse now, an' we never

---

[1] This is an allusion of Barny's to a prevalent saying in Ireland, addressed to a sportsman who returns home unsuccessful. "So you've killed what the Connaughtman shot at."

hear'd iv it afore at all, till afther you quitted the big ship?"

"Why, then, are you sitch an ignoramus all out," said Barny, "as not for to know that in navigation you must lie an a great many different tacks before you can make the port you steer for?"

"Only I think," said Jemmy, "that it's back intirely we're goin' now, and I can't make out the rights o' that at all."

"Why," said Barny, who saw the necessity of mystifying his companions a little, "you see, the captain towld me that I kum around, an' rekimminded me to go th' other way."

"Faix, it's the first I ever heard o' going around by say," said Jemmy.

"Arrah, sure, that's part o' the saycreets o' navigation, and the various branches o' knowledge that is requizit for a navigathor; an' that's what the captain, God bless him, and myself was discoorsin' an aboord; and, like a rale gintleman as he is, 'Barny,' says he; 'Sir,' says I; 'You're come the round,' says he. 'I know that,' says I, 'bekase I like to keep a good bowld offin',' says I, 'in conthrary places.' 'Spoke like a good sayman,' says he. 'That's my prenciples,' says I. 'They're the right sort,' says he. 'But,' says he, '(no offince), I think you were wrong,' says he, 'to pass the short turn in the ladieshoes,' [2] says he. 'I know,' says I, 'you mane beside the threespike headlan'.' 'That's the spot,' says he, 'I see you know it.' 'As well as I know my father,' says I."

"Why, Barny," said Jemmy, interrupting him, "we seen no headlan' at all."

"Whisht, whisht!" said Barny; "bad cess to you, don't thwart me. We passed it in the night, and you couldn't see it. Well, as I was saying, 'I know it as well as I know my father,' says I, 'but I gev the preferince to go the round,' says I. 'You're a good sayman for that same,' says he, 'an' it would be right at any other time than this present,' says he, 'but it's onpossible now, teetotally, on account o' the war,' says he. 'Tare alive,' says I, 'what war?' 'An' didn't you hear of the war?' says he. 'Divil

[2] Some attempt Barny is making at "latitudes."

a word,' says I. 'Why,' says he, 'the naygurs has made war on the king o' Chaynee,' says he, 'bekase he refused them any more tay; an' with that, what did they do,' says he, 'but they put a lumbaago on all the vessels, that sails the round, an' that's the rayson,' says he, 'I carry guns, as you may see; and I'd rekimmind you,' says he, 'to go back, for you're not able for thim, and that's jist the way iv it.' An' now, wasn't it looky that I kem acrass him at all, or maybe we might be cotched by the naygurs, and ate up alive?" . . .

Thus it was that Barny continued most marvelous accounts of the ship and the captain to his companions, and by keeping their attention so engaged prevented their being too inquisitive as to their own immediate concerns, and for two days more Barny and the hooker held on their respective course undeviatingly.

The third day Barny's fears for the continuity of his *nor-aist coorse* were excited, as a large brig hove in sight, and the nearer she approached, the more directly she came athwart Barny's course.

"May the divil sweep you," said Barny; "and will nothin' else sarve you than comin' forninst me that way? Brig, ahoy, there!" shouted Barny, giving the tiller to one of his messmates, and standing at the bow of his boat. "Brig, ahoy, there!—bad luck to you, go 'long out o' my *nor-aist coorse*." The brig, instead of obeying his mandate, hove to, and lay right ahead of the hooker. "Oh, look at this!" shouted Barny, and he stamped on the deck with rage—"look at the blackguards where they're stayin', just a purpose to ruin an unfort'nate man like me. My heavy hathred to you; *quit* this minit, or I'll run down an yez, and if we go to the bottom, we'll hant you for evermore;—go 'long out o' that, I tell you. The curse o' Crummil an you, you stupid vagabones, that won't go out iv a man's *nor-aist coorse!*"

From cursing Barny went to praying as he came closer. "For the tendher marcy o' heavin, lave my way. May the Lord reward you, and get out o' my *nor-aist coorse!* May angels make your bed in heavin, and don't ruinate me thisaway." The brig was immovable, and Barny gave up in despair, having cursed and prayed himself hoarse, and finished with a duet volley of prayers and curses together, apostrophizing the hard case of a man being *"done out of his nor-aist coorse."*

"Ahoy, there!" shouted a voice from the brig, "put down your helm, or you'll be aboard us. I say, let go your jib and foresheet;—what are you about, you lubbers?"

'Twas true that the brig lay so fair in Barny's course that he would have been aboard, but that instantly the maneuver above alluded to was put in practice on board the hooker, as she swept to destruction towards the heavy hull of the brig, and she luffed up into the wind alongside her. A very pale and somewhat emaciated face appeared at the side, and addressed Barny:

"What brings you here?" was the question.

"Throth, thin, and I think I might bether ax what brings *you* here, right in the way o' my *nor-aist coorse.*"

"Where do you come from?"

"From Kinsale; and you didn't come from a bether place, I go bail."

"Where are you bound to?"

"To Fingal."

"Fingal—where's Fingal?"

"Why, thin, ain't you ashamed o' yourself an' not to know where Fingal is?"

"It is not in these seas."

"Oh, that's all you know about it," says Barny.

"You're a small craft to be so far at sea. I suppose you have provisions on board?"

"To be sure we have;—throth, if we hadn't, this id be a bad place to go a beggin'."

"What have you eatable?"

"The finest o' scalpeens."

"What are scalpeens?"

"Why, you're mighty ignorant, intirely," said Barny; "why, scalpeens is pickled mackerel."

"Then you must give us some, for we have been out of everything eatable these three days; and even pickled fish is better than nothing."

It chanced that the brig was a West India trader, which unfavorable winds had delayed much beyond the expected period of time on her voyage, and though her water had not failed, everything eatable had been consumed, and the crew reduced almost to helplessness. In such a strait the arrival of Barny O'Reirdon and his scalpeens was a most providential succor to them, and a lucky chance for Barny, for he got in exchange for his pickled fish a handsome return of rum and sugar, much more than equivalent to their value. Barny lamented much, however, that the brig was not bound for Ireland, that he might practise his own peculiar system of navigation; but as staying with the brig could do no good, he got himself put into his *nor-aist coorse* once more, and plowed away towards home.

The disposal of his cargo was a great godsend to Barny in more ways than one. In the first place, he found the most profitable market he could have had; and, secondly, it enabled him to cover his retreat from the difficulty which still was before him of not getting to Fingal after all his dangers, and consequently being open to discovery and disgrace. All these beneficial results were not thrown away upon one of Barny's readiness to avail himself of every point in his favor; and, accordingly, when they left the brig, Barny said to his companions: "Why, thin, boys, 'pon my conscience, but I'm as proud as a horse wid a wooden leg this minit, that we met them poor unfort'nate craythurs this blessed day, and was enabled to extind our charity to them. Sure, an' it's lost they'd be only for our comin' acrass them, and we, through the blessin' o' God, enabled to do an act of marcy, that is, feedin' the hungry;—and sure every good work we do here is before uz in heavin, and that's a comfort, anyhow. To be sure, now that the scalpeens is sowld, there's no use in goin' to Fingal, and we may jist as well go home."

"Faix, I'm sorry myself," said Jemmy, "for Terry O'Sullivan said it was an iligant place intirely, an' I wanted to see it."

"To the divil with Terry O'Sullivan," said Barny; "how does he know what's an iligant place? What knowledge has he of iligance? I'll go bail, he never was half as far a navigatin' as we;—he wint the short cut, I go bail, and never daar'd for to vinture the round, as I did."

"Bedad we wor a great dale longer, anyhow, than he towld me he was."

"To be sure we wor," said Barny; "he wint skulkin' by the short cut, I tell you; and was afeard to keep a bowld offin' like me. But come, boys, let uz take a dhrop o' that bottle o' sper'ts we got out o' the brig. Begor it's well ye got some bottles iv it; for I wouldn't much like to meddle wid that darlint little kag iv it antil we get home." The rum was put on its trial by Barny and his companions, and in their critical judgment was pronounced quite as good as the captain of the ship had bestowed upon them, but that neither of those specimens of spirit was to be compared to whisky. . . .

Nothing particular occurred for the two succeeding days, during which time Barny most religiously pursued his *nor-aist coorse;* but the third day produced a new and important event. A sail was discovered in the horizon, and in the direction Barny was steering, and a couple of hours made him tolerable certain that the vessel in sight was an American; for though it is needless to say that he was not very conversant in such matters, yet from the frequency of his seeing Americans trading to Ireland, his eye had become sufficiently accustomed to their lofty and tapering spars, and peculiar smartness of rig, to satisfy him that the ship before him was of transatlantic build.

Barny now determined on a maneuver, classing him amongst the first tacticians at securing a good retreat. Moreau's highest fame rests upon his celebrated retrograde movement through the Black Forest. Xenophon's greatest glory is derived from the deliverance of his ten thousand Greeks from impending ruin by his renowned retreat.

Let the ancient and the modern hero "repose under the

shadow of their laurels," as the French have it, while Barny
O'Reirdon's historian, with a pardonable jealousy for the honor
of his country, cuts down a goodly bough of the classic tree,
beneath which our Hibernian hero may enjoy his *"otium cum
dignitate."*

Barny calculated the American was bound for Ireland; and
as she lay *almost* directly in the way of his *nor-aist coorse* as
the West Indian brig, he bore up to and spoke to her.

He was answered by a shrewd Yankee captain.

"Faix, an' it's glad I am to see your honor again," said
Barny. The Yankee had never been to Ireland, and told
Barny so.

"Oh, throth, I couldn't forget a gintleman so easy as that,"
said Barny.

"You're pretty considerably mistaken now, I guess," said
the American.

"Divil a taste," said Barny, with inimitable composure and
pertinacity.

"Well, if you know me so tarnation well, tell me what's my
name?" The Yankee flattered himself he had nailed Barny now.

"Your name, is it?" said Barny, gaining time by repeating
the question, "why, what a fool you are not to know your own
name."

The oddity of the answer posed the American, and Barny
took advantage of the diversion in his favor, and changed the
conversation.

"Bedad, I've been waitin' here these four or five days, ex-
pectin' some of you would be wantin' me."

"Some of us! How do you mean?"

"Sure an' aren't you from Amerikay?"

"Yes;—and what then?"

"Well, I say I was waitin' for some ship or other from
Amerikay, that ud be wantin' me. It's to Ireland you're goin'
I daresay."

"Yes."

"Well, I suppose you'll be wantin' a pilot?" said Barny.

"Yes, when we get inshore, but not yet."

"Oh, I don't want to hurry you," said Barny.

"What port are you a pilot of?"

"Why, indeed, as for the matther o' that," said Barny, "they're all aiqual to me a'most."

"All?" said the American. "Why, I calculate you couldn't pilot a ship into all the ports of Ireland."

"Not all at wanst [once]," said Barny, with a laugh, in which the American could not help joining.

"Well, I say, what ports do you know best?"

"Why, thin, indeed," said Barny, "it would be hard for me to tell; but wherever you want to go, I'm the man that'll do the job for you complate. Where's your honor goin'?"

"I won't tell you that;—but do you tell me what ports you know best?"

"Why, there's Watherford, and there's Youghal, an' Fingal."

"Fingal! Where's that?"

"So you don't know where Fingal is. Oh, I see you're a sthranger, sir;—an' then there's Cork."

"You know Cove, then?"

"Is it the Cove of Cork, why?"

"Yes."

"I was bred an' born there, an' pilots as many ships into Cove as any other two min *out* o' it."

Barny thus sheltered his falsehood under the idiom of his language.

"But what brought you so far out to sea?" asked the captain.

"We wor lyin' out lookin' for ships that wanted pilots, and there kem an the terriblest gale o' wind off the land, an' blew us to say out intirely, an' that's the way iv it, your honor."

"I calculate we got a share of the same gale; 'twas from the nor'east."

"Oh, directly!" said Barny, "faith, you're right enough, 'twas the *nor-aist coorse* we wor an, sure enough; but no matther, now that we've met wid you;—sure we'll have a job home, anyhow."

"Well, get aboard, then," said the American.

"I will in a minit, your honor, whin I jist spake a word to my comrades here."

"Why, sure it's not goin' to turn pilot you are?" said Jemmy, in his simplicity of heart.

"Whisht, you omadhaun!" said Barney, "or I'll cut the tongue out o' you. Now mind me, Pether. You don't undherstan' navigashin and the various branches o' knowledge, an' so all you do is to folly the ship when I get into her, an' I'll show you the way home."

Barny then got aboard the American vessel, and begged of the captain, that as he had been out at sea so long, and had gone through a "power o' hardship intirely," that he would be permitted to go below and turn in to take a sleep; "for, in throth, it's myself and sleep that is sthrayngers for some time," said Barny, "an' if your honor'll be plazed, I'll be thankful if you won't let them disturb me antil I'm wanted, for sure till you see the land there's no use for me in life; an', throth, I want a sleep sorely." His request was granted, and it will not be wondered at that, after so much fatigue of mind and body, he slept profoundly for four-and-twenty hours. He then was called, for land was in sight, and when he came on deck the captain rallied him upon the potency of his somniferous qualities, and "calculated" he had never met any one who could sleep "four-and-twenty hours on a stretch before."

"Oh, sir," said Barny, rubbing his eyes, which were still a little hazy, "whiniver I go to sleep *I pay attintion to it.*"

The land was soon neared, and Barny put in charge of the ship, when he ascertained the first landmark he was acquainted with; but soon as the Head of Kinsale hove in sight, Barny gave a "whoo," and cut a caper that astonished the Yankees, and was quite inexplicable to them, though I flatter myself it is not to those who do Barny the favor of reading his adventures.

"Oh! there you are, my darlint owld head!—an' where's the head like you? Throth, it's little I thought I'd ever set eyes an your good-looking faytures again. But God is good!"

In such half-muttered exclamations did Barny apostrophize each well-known point of his native shore, and when opposite the harbor of Kinsale he spoke the hooker, that was somewhat astern, and ordered Jemmy and Peter to put in there, and tell Molly immediately that he was come back, and would be with her as soon as he could, after piloting the ship into Cove. "But, an your apperl, don't tell Pether Kelly o' the big farm; nor, indeed, don't mintion to man nor mortial about the navigashin we done antil I come home myself and make them sensible of it, bekase, Jemmy and Pether, neither o' yiz is aiqual to it, and doesn't undherstan' the branches o' knowledge requizit for dis-coorsin' o' navigashin."

The hooker put into Kinsale, and Barny sailed the ship into Cove. It was the first ship he had acted the pilot for, and his old luck attended him; no accident befell his charge, and, what was still more extraordinary, he made the American believe he was absolutely the most skilful pilot on the station. So Barny pocketed his pilot's fee, swore the Yankee was a gentleman, for which the republican did not thank him, wished him good-by, and then pushed his way home with what Barny swore was the easiest made money he ever had in his life. So Barny got himself paid for *piloting* the ship that *showed him the way home.* . . .

As for the hitherto triumphant Terry O'Sullivan, from the moment Barny's *Bingal* adventure became known, he was obliged to fly the country, and was never heard of more, while the hero of the hooker became a greater man than before, and never was addressed by any other title afterwards than that of The Commodore.

# THE LAST WHALE

From "The Log of the *Arethusa*,"

BY CAPTAIN WILLIAM HUSSEY MACY

## I

THE passage across the South Pacific Ocean is monotonous and barren of incident. From New Zealand to Cape Horn we had rugged weather and strong winds, for the most part fair for running on our course, at times blowing day after day, with the regularity of trades, again hauling a few points so as to trim for it on the other quarter, and in one or two instances increasing to a gale, so violent as to compel us to heave to for the safety of the ship. As we approached Cape Horn we again encountered the cutting hail squalls which seem almost peculiar to this part of the world, but with the wind aft, we did not mind them so much as when outward bound. Rolling off before the westerly gales with sufficient press of canvas on the ship to keep her well clear of the mountainous seas in chase of her, with everything well secured, and careful men at the wheel, we laughed at the weather now, and wondered at our own progress, as we counted off five, six, or seven degrees of longitude each day, and reckoned how many more days at this rate of sailing ere we should have room to edge away to the northward and begin to steal towards a milder climate. Degrees of longitude are short ones in this latitude, and we seem to be "putting a girdle round about the earth," if not, like Puck, "in forty minutes," yet still at a rate that appears to us marvellous, as we find our clock nearly half an hour behind the sun each day at meridian, and push her ahead to keep her up to our flying rate of progress.

Land ho! most welcome to our eager eyes, rough, barren and uninhabitable though it be, the storm-beaten rock of Diego

Ramirez, for it tells us where we are, better than the whole slateful of figures. "Shake out another reef!" she'll bear it! another day's run, and we can shove her off north-east on the "home side of the land"—the towering seas gather and roll on after us—but keep the canvas on her and she will keep ahead of them—every one of them shoots her on towards "Home, sweet home"—Diego Ramirez fades into the dark squall astern, and if the wind stands where it is, we shall catch Cape Horn asleep. That squall has passed—it is not so heavy as it promised to be— "Give her the mainto'-gallantsail!" We must make the most of the breeze while we have it, for we're homeward bound! The sun rises brightly this morning, and the wind is fresh yet, and canting to the southward— "Never mind! let her slide off two points, east-north-east now!" for we've plenty of sea room —we're in the Atlantic!

We passed to the eastward of the Falklands, and were nearly on the ground where we lost our third mate, when outward-bound. Of course the melancholy circumstance was recalled, and talked over, and the captain mentioned that some twelve years previous, when a mate of the *Colossus*, he had struck a whale in this vicinity, and lost him in consequence of his iron breaking.

"I hope," said he, "to see whales yet in crossing this ground. It bids fair to be a good day to-morrow, and I think we will shorten sail at night and let her jog easy, so as to take a good look along here. One large whale would be all we want to chock us off, and we would go home with flying colors."

The next morning we had hardly got the reefs shaken out, when whales were raised. There were several of them, but they did not appear to run together, but were seen here and there in different directions, and were also irregular in their time of rising and going down.

"These whales have been gallied," said the old man, "and have not got regular yet. Some ship has been whaling here yesterday, I think. But here is one off the lee quarter that I think can be struck, Mr. Grafton. You and Mr. Dunham lower away and go down there and try him, and I will wait a while and take the ship's chance. If you get fast, I'll come down there to you."

Away we went off to leeward, but it soon appeared that his whaleship was too shy for us, and was playing a dodge game with us. In vain we tried to "prick for him"; we spread our chances, and used our best judgment, but all to no purpose. He always rose in some unexpected quarter, and spouting but a few times, was down again before we could get near enough to "stand up." At length he took a start and went off to leeward at a round pace, and led on by our ardor in the chase we pursued it until we were full three miles from the ship, when it became evident that he was moving faster and faster at each rising, and we abandoned the chase, especially as the ship showed no signs of running off, but still lay aback in the same position as when we lowered. We laid round the heads of our boats towards the ship, and pulled to windward, wondering why the old man still kept his luff, when up went the ensign at the peak, and the small signal at the main was run up and down several times in rapid succession.

"Give way hard, boys!" said the mate. "We are wanted in a hurry. The old man must have lowered and struck a whale to windward, and wants help. Perhaps he's stove! spring hard and shoot her up there!"

We put our strength to the oars with a will, the second mate keeping way with us, and, though doing our best, it seemed in our anxiety and impatience, that he did not make any headway. The signal was now and then run up and down again hurriedly, speaking the most urgent language of which it was capable. We saw men on the bearers, apparently trying to clear away the lashings of the spare boat which was turned up overhead, but soon this seemed to be abandoned. We could make out now, as we drew nearer, that the cooper was on the hurricane house, waving with all his might to us and thus stimulated to greater exertion, we toiled away at our oars, the boats jumping into the head sea, and sending the spray all over us. We could hear them hailing us from the ship, long before we could make out the words. We could see them pointing to windward, as if to tell us we were needed there. Up across the stern we held our long and strong stroke, receiving the information as we passed, that the old man had struck a whale off the weather bow, and he had run him into the "sun-glaze," so that they could not see him from the ship, and they thought he must be stoven. He could not be far off, however, as he was not more than a mile from the ship when last seen.

"Give way hard, boys!" said the mate again. "Brace forward, Cooper, and down tacks!" but he was already mustering his small force for this purpose. We "laid back" on our oars, the mates heaving at the stroke oars, and keeping a sharp lookout, not pulling directly at the glare of the sun, but in a direction abaft it so as to look broad off the bow and beam of the boat. Soon the mate's countenance lighted, and he threw her head suddenly off with the steering oar.

"Here they are!" said he, "and not far from us, either! Spring hard, men! They're all on the wreck—two, four, five, six—all safe yet!"

They were, indeed, all safe as yet; but we were none too soon, for they were nearly exhausted, as there was a smart sea on, washing over them, and they had all they could do to keep their positions, the strongest assisting and encouraging the others. My friend Ashton was almost gone when I dragged him into our boat; a few minutes more would have finished him. The whole bottom of their boat was crushed, she had filled and rolled over with them, and they had all clung to the bottom.

"Never mind the boat," said the old man, "she isn't worth picking up. Set a waif for the cooper to tack and stand towards us. Let's get on board, some of us, and get the spare boat out. I think we shall see the whale again if we work up to windward a tack or two."

The ship went about, and soon hove to again close to us. We shot alongside, put the half-drowned men on board, and had hardly done so when the whale came up in the ship's wake, distance less than half a mile. "Shove off!" was the word, and we were after him again with two boats, while the captain with his force were already rousing the third one off the bearers. The second mate got the lead this time and was fast a few minutes after pushing astern of the ship. The whale rounded to, and "showed good play," and we were quickly on hand to let more blood from him. He was already weakened from his wounds, and a few touches of the lance made him our prize. The spare boat was not called into service; but another short tack with the ship, and with shouts of triumph that rang loud and clear over the sea, we hauled alongside our last whale, that was to "chock off" the between decks and fill all our spare casks. Our perils in the attack of these monsters were over, for this voyage. No more hard pulls to windward—no involuntary seabathing —no more tedious "mastheads" to be stood. Well might we shout over this "last but not least" of our hard-earned prizes.

## II

The last whale! How many pleasant recollections are associated with this landmark in the voyage! How many congratulations were exchanged among us, and how many smart things said! Sweethearts and wives are especially remembered, for both married and single are in high feather, and this is emphatically a red-letter day in the *Arethusa's* calendar. The work of cutting goes bravely on, amid a running fire of good-natured remarks and spicy jokes, which, of course, between the regular "natives" bear something of a personal character; for every true knight of the island chivalry in those days had his "ladie-love," whose image, held in fond remembrance, fired his heart and nerved his arm in his perilous encounters with leviathan. Each of our Nantucketers, on occasions like this called to mind some fair face and form, his life-partner, either *in esse* or *in posse;* all had either wives to *main*tain or wives to *ob*tain. The captain himself is not slow to take part in this badinage, for we are cutting the last whale now, and it is a time to waive the little restraints of rank.

"This is a noble whale, and, being the last one, of course, the blubber is uncommonly fat," said he, as he drove his sharp spade into it, and slashed it into convenient pieces with true professional pride; "this is the one that pays for the bridal outfits and town clerk's fees. Let's see, Mr. Grafton, we shall get invitations to three weddings, certain. I don't know but more, but we may count on three."

"Mr. Bunker thinks we needn't count on him," said the mate.

"Nonsense!" returned the old man. "He thinks we Newtowners don't know his cruising-grounds, because the first landfall he means to make is away up North Shore Hill. But he can't throw any dust in my eyes."

"You didn't mean to count me, sir," said Fisher, "for I never have anything to do with the women."

"No, of course not," said the captain. "I'll bet that within forty-eight hours after we all get our new sails bent, I shall meet you, head and head, coming down the fashionable side of Orange Street, with studdingsails out both sides—sweeping common folks like me right off into the gutter."

"Well, I've got sisters, you know, sir," said Fisher with a half-blush. "I must show them round."

"Yes, I know it; but, if the *Fortitude* gets home ahead of us, *one* of your sisters won't want your services."

"That's so," put in the second mate. "You can set a new studdingsail on that boom, Fisher."

"There, you haven't a word to say, Mr. Dunham," replied the captain. "If you were landed there to-day, there would be an invasion of 'Egypt,' and a 'rush to arms' in that quarter of the world that would equal anything in the days of Bonaparte. A-a-ah! my spade!" said he, suddenly changing his tone. "I've struck a ringbolt—no, it isn't—it's something in the blubber—head of an iron—somebody has had a crack at this whale before."

He pulled it out, and wiped it off with a piece of canvas, scraped it lightly with his jackknife, and examined it with an incredulous look.

"Eureka!" he shouted at last, holding up the fragment of the harpoon. "Here's my iron! Who says he isn't my own whale, when he has carried my mark these twelve years!"

It was even as he said. There was little more than the barbed head left, for it must have been long before the wound cicatrized, and the small part of the shank had been reduced to a mere shred of iron from the effects of long attrition and corrosion; but fairly legible on the thick centre-piece of the head were the marks boldly cut with a chisel, S. COL'S. L. B.

"Ship *Colossus's* Larboard Boat," said the old man, triumphantly. "Shouldn't want any more evidence in case of life and death. It's twelve years since I struck that fish—*the first time*, I mean."

The last round of blubber has been "piked off"; the last pot of oil "baled down"; the last pipe stowed that "chocks off betwixt decks," and Old Jeff's immense "plantations" displayed in a triumphant double-shuffle on the main hatches. Now comes the expected and welcome order. "Overboard tryworks!" Crowbars, hammers or whatever else will serve the purpose, are seized, and rapidly the cumbrous pile of greasy bricks and mortar disappears under our vigorous blows, the pots alone being saved for the next voyage; the deck is washed and planed off where it had stood; and the old strainer, shattered by hard service, and half-charred by the fire, travels the same road, overboard. We are all astonished that our ship has such a spacious maindeck; and she herself, by her more buoyant and elastic movement, seems to share in the general joy, at being relieved of this unsightly burden.

Still onward, homeward, she bounds along! down into the south-east trades, where the duty of dressing her up for home begins; where the operations of fitting, rattling down and tarring down furnish ample employment for us all; where outward-bound merchantmen are met, and passed every day, and longitudes compared by chalking them in gigantic figures on boards, like showmen's posters; where the south-east trades haul to north-east, and knock us off into the "bight of Brazil," compelling us to beat off and on for several days, where *cata-marans*, or triangular rafts, fully officered and manned by one Portuguese, come off several miles to sea, to catch fish, and to sell them, too, if a passing ship comes conveniently near; where a big, black steamer, evidently of Yankee build, but wearing the gorgeous Brazilian flag, and showing the name *Bahiana*, passes almost within hail of us. We are favored with a slant of wind at last; Cape St. Augustin is doubled and left astern, the towers of Pernambuco are seen, with ships in the roadstead, and now the coast again trends to the westward, and is soon lost to our view.

"Sail ho!" a whaler, too, right from home! Now for a game, for newspapers, perhaps letters, too, for some of us, for books, for tobacco! She hails us, and gives her name as the *Delta*, of Greenport. No letters for us there; but we get bundles of New York papers, and peruse them, all four pages, from "clew to earring," advertisements and all. They are filled with politics, for this is campaign year (1844), and of course, we are highly competent, after nearly three years' absence, to understand the issues of the hour! Not a word is said about the National Bank, or the Sub-Treasury, or any of the old bones of contention which are familiar to us, everything is Texas or no Texas. Henry Clay's name is prominent, and excites no wonder, for his fame has long been national; but "who is James K. Polk?"

The equator is crossed, and now how we check off the degrees of latitude, day by day, as we run them up in the northeast trades, for we are on the home side of the line! Our rigging is all fitted and tarred down, and a coat of paint from the mastheads down to the water-line, inside and out, works a wonderful change in the appearance of our noble ship. How eagerly we hail the first patches of gulf-weed! and as we plough through immense quantities of it, day after day, and haul great snarls of it on deck, wonder what is the use of it, and what becomes of it all, finally?

We pass Bermuda without the usual heavy squalls characteristic of that locality, but off Hatteras we lie to a couple of days, and ride out a "clear nor'wester," which seems to blow out of the sun and stars, rather than the clouds. Block Island is our first landfall; and, leaving this on our port bow, we shape our course for the Vineyard Sound. It is nearly night when we see a pilot-boat coming for us, and every heart leaps with joy at the thought of soon being at anchor in a home port. Merrily we rouse up the chain cables from their rusty lockers, and tumble the anchors off the bow; our maintopsail is thrown aback, and the pilot-boat shoots up within hail.

"What ship *is* this?" he asks.

"The *Arethusa*, of Nantucket."

"O yes! how d'ye do, Captain Upton? You look deep," says the pilot.

"Full ship," replied the old man, rather proudly. "What's sperm oil worth?"

" 'Bout eighty-five cents. Hain't you got a piece of salt pork to spare, captain?"

"Yes, half a dozen," answers the captain, who, knowing the ropes, has it all prepared beforehand. "Here, pass this meat into the boat."

"Now, hain't you got a few fathoms of second-hand tow-line that you can spare as well as not? You see my peak-halyards, they're about worn out."

"Here it is, waiting for you," says the old man, with a laugh. "It's the most remarkable thing, that a Sound pilot-boat's peak-halyards always *are* about worn out! Here, pass this coil of line into the boat. I suppose you can get us into Oldtown to-night, can't you, pilot?"

"Well, I guess you don't want to go in there, captain. I can get you in to-night as far as Holmes' Hole, anyhow, and if it's fair weather in the morning I'll take you right down to the Bar, and the camels will take you in."

"Ah, yes, the camels; they're a new institution that we've never seen yet. They've been built since we were away. Do they work well?"

"O yes, indeed," says the pilot, "pick the ship right up, cargo and all, and back her into the harbor and drop her alongside the wharf."

"Good," says Captain Upton; "those are the very animals that I want to see."

"I reckon the folks down to Nantucket are getting worried a little about you, captain. They heard from you on Japan, somewhere in the middle of the season, but they didn't hear of your being at the islands in the fall, when we got the reports from the fleet. 'Spose you made a port in some out-of-the-way place?"

"Yes, I made a running cruise of it, and didn't anchor till I made my last port in Sydney; so I've brought my own report from there."

We ran into Holmes' Hole and anchored at nine o'clock among a large fleet of coasting vessels, who had made a harbor for the night like ourselves. Before daylight in the morning we were heaving up again, and, with a fair wind, we ran down for Nantucket Bar with all our bunting flying. Down goes our anchor again in the old berth which we left three years ago, the sails are rolled up to the yards in a hurry, and a boat is lowered to pull the captain ashore. The owner is seen with his horse and the inevitable green box on wheels, waiting on the cliff shore to receive him, and take him to the arms of his family. The boat pulls square in, and lands him on the north beach, and returns to the ship, for an immense black Noah's-ark-looking craft is already seen moving out of the docks in the harbor, which the pilot tells us is "the camels." Several boats soon arrive, with friends and relatives of the Nantucket men. Here is our worthy mate's son in one of them, a stout, well-grown lad and evidently a "chip of the old block"; and here in another boat is an embryo "Cape Horner," a young brother of Obed B., who is already shipped, and is to sail in a fortnight.

"Ah, Obed"; he says, as he hops in over the rail, with hands outstretched, and his nut-brown, young face lighted up with pleasure and excitement, "I'm going in the *Ranger;* and if you hadn't got home just as you did, you wouldn't have seen me for I don't know how many years. Yes, the folks are all well at home, and the camels will have you into the wharf before night. The steamer will be along soon. We've got a new steamboat, too, since you went away. Say, Obed, I got the dollar from Captain Upton's wife this morning. I was the first boy that knew it was the *Arethusa*. One of the men came down out of the old south tower, and told me what signal the ship had set, and I put for the captain's house. I got the dollar, and then I dug for another, for I knew where the mate's wife lived, too; but some other boys had found it out by that time, and I had a tight race for it with Jack Manter, but I was tired then, I had run so far, and Manter got ahead of me, and sung out first, as he rushed into the front entry, but I tumbled right in after him. Mrs. Grafton was scared half to death at first, till she understood what the matter was, and then she laughed and cried both at once, and handed out a dollar, and said we might divide it, if we liked, but it belonged to Jack, for he was a little ahead of me, and I didn't care much, for I'd got one. Some mate's wives don't give but half a dollar," said he, pausing to get breath.

I cannot stop to hear any more, for here is Richards, still outdoor clerk of Messrs. Brooks & Co., and he is the only man likely to have any news for us "off islanders." He is ready with a hearty greeting and handshaking, and is prepared to "infit" us with clothing of any style, price or quality, as soon as we land. He produces a bunch of letters which have been directed to various ships expected to arrive soon, "care of Brooks & Co.," and rapidly shuffles them over. Yes! there is my beloved sister's handwriting, and here is another from my parents. I tear them open with a beating heart; all is well with those nearest and dearest to me. That is enough for the present. I will read the details when more at leisure, and in a few days I will be with them. I shall not write in reply, but, like the ship, I will bring home my own report.

"Here comes the camels round Brant Point!" cries the mate, running with the spyglass to look at the clumsy, floating dock which is creeping slowly at us, without any visible means of propulsion, so far as we can see, for the propellers are under the stern. It looks like nothing in the way of naval architecture that we have ever seen, but might serve as an immense floating battery, to be moored for the defence of a harbor. As it draws nearer, we can see that it is built in two parts, being divided lengthwise. The inside of each section or half is built concave to receive the hull of the ship, and to fit round her sides, and under her bilge and floor, as nearly as possible to its general form. The two parts are connected by several heavy chains, which are secured on the deck of one "camel," passing down through it under the keel of the ship, and up through the other, where they are hove taut with windlasses.

The camels having taken up their position near the ship, the plugs are drawn, allowing them to fill with water and sink. Being now ready to receive the ship, our anchor is hove up, lines streamed, and she is hauled in between them. The connecting chains are then hove taut by the windlasses, and thus the ship is completely docked, her bottom resting fairly on the concave inner surfaces of the camels, and the chains passing under her keel. She is now ready to be raised, and as soon as the steamboat heaves in sight, returning from her regular trip to New Bedford, the steam pumps are set in operation throwing out the water from the camels. The steamer passes within hail, and goes on into the harbor to land her mails and passengers, the captain promising to return at once and hook on to us. Meanwhile the steam-pumps work steadily on, throwing out the water, and the whole fabric is seen gradually to rise, inch by inch, till the water is all out, and the ship is lifted out of the water, the camels themselves being flat and the draft very light. We are just in time for the returning steamboat, hawsers are run to us, she takes us in tow, and after a short struggle to overcome the *vis inertiæ* of the immense arklike contrivance, we move along under good headway. We round Brant Point and steam up nearly to the end of the wharf, when the steamer leaves us, the camels are filled and sink down again, the ship is dropped out from between them, lines run to the pier, and, in a few minutes, she is tied up head and stern alongside her wharf, and ready to discharge her oil. "Hurrah for the camels!" is the sentiment of every man on board, and of nearly every one on shore, too, except the lightermen whose "occupation is gone."

Our old landlord is on hand to furnish us board and lodging at the old rates; Messrs. Brooks & Co. are in the same place, the same business operations are going on now as three years ago, and the same knots of seafaring men, or, at least, their very counterparts, pervade "the store," and pass their time in much the same manner. No one seems to have changed or grown any older. There is nothing new under the sun but the camels and the steamer *Massachusetts*.

Of course, we could not be paid off until the oil was discharged on the wharf, gauged, and filled up, so that our "lays" could be calculated exactly. This detained me several days; for, although I might have drawn money from the owners, or from Brooks & Co., yet I preferred to settle up the whole matter before going home to my friends, rather than to be under the necessity of returning to Nantucket. I, of course, took my place among the veteran whalemen, now. I had earned the right to wear a fine, blue roundabout, and morocco pumps, with long streamers of ribbon, to roll and swagger as becomes the "ancient mariner," and to patronize the green hands who formed the last cargo of the *Lydia Ann*, for that gallant craft is still running as good as new.

# THE CLUB-HAULING OF THE *DIOMEDE*

From "Peter Simple," BY CAPTAIN FREDERICK MARRYAT

WE continued our cruise along the coast, until we had run down into the Bay of Arcason, where we captured two or three vessels, and obliged many more to run on shore. And here we had an instance showing how very important it is that the captain of a man-of-war should be a good sailor, and have his ship in such discipline as to be strictly obeyed by his ship's company. I heard the officers unanimously assert, after the danger was over, that nothing but the presence of mind which was shown by Captain Savage could have saved the ship and her crew. We had chased a convoy of vessels to the bottom of the bay: the wind was very fresh when we hauled off, after running them on shore; and the surf on the beach even at that time was so great, that they were certain to go to pieces before they could be got afloat again. We were obliged to double-reef the topsails as soon as we hauled to the wind, and the weather looked very threatening. In an hour afterwards, the whole sky was covered with one black cloud, which sank so low as nearly to touch our mast-heads, and a tremendous sea, which appeared to have risen up almost by magic, rolled in upon us, setting the vessel on a dead lee shore. As the night closed in, it blew a dreadful gale, and the ship was nearly buried with the press of canvas which she was obliged to carry: for had we sea-room, we should have been lying-to under storm staysails; but we were forced to carry on at all risks, that we might claw off shore. The sea broke over us as we lay in the trough, deluging us with water from the forecastle, aft, to the binnacle; and very often as the ship descended with a plunge, it was with such force that I really thought she would divide in half with the violence of the shock. Double breechings were rove on the guns, and they were further secured with tackles; and strong cleats nailed behind the trunnions; for we heeled over so much when we lurched, that the guns were wholly supported by the breechings and tackles, and had one of them broken loose it must have burst right through the lee side of the ship, and she must have foundered. The captain, first lieutenant, and most of the officers, remained on deck during the whole of the night; and really, what with the howling of the wind, the violence of the rain, the washing of the water about the decks, the working of the chain-pumps, and the creaking and groaning of the timbers, I thought that we must inevitably have been lost; and I said my prayers at least a dozen times during the night, for I felt it impossible to go to bed. I had often wished, out of curiosity, that I might be in a gale of wind; but I little thought it was to have been a scene of this description, or anything half so dreadful. What made it more appalling was, that we were on a lee shore, and the consultations of the captain and officers, and the eagerness with which they looked out for daylight, told us that we had other dangers to encounter besides the storm. At last the morning broke, and the look-out man upon the gangway called out, "Land on the lee beam!" I perceived the master dash his feet against the hammock-rails, as if with vexation, and walk away without saying a word, looking very grave.

"Up there, Mr. Wilson," said the captain to the second lieutenant, "and see how far the land trends forward, and whether you can distinguish the point." The second lieutenant went up the main-rigging, and pointed with his hand to about two points before the beam.

"Do you see two hillocks, inland?"

"Yes, sir," replied the second lieutenant.

"Then it is so," observed the captain to the master, "and if we weather it we shall have more sea-room. Keep her full, and let her go through the water; do you hear, quartermaster?"

"Ay, ay, sir."

"Thus, and no nearer, my man. Ease her with a spoke or two

when she sends; but be careful, or she'll take the wheel out of your hands."

It really was a very awful sight. When the ship was in the trough of the sea, you could distinguish nothing but a waste of tumultuous water; but when she was borne up on the summit of the enormous waves, you then looked down, as it were, upon a low, sandy coast, close to you, and covered with foam and breakers. "She behaves nobly," observed the captain, stepping aft to the binnacle, and looking at the compass; "if the wind does not baffle us, we shall weather." The captain had scarcely time to make the observation, when the sails shivered and flapped like thunder. "Up with the helm; what are you about, quartermaster?"

"The wind has headed us, sir," replied the quartermaster, coolly.

The captain and master remained at the binnacle watching the compass; and when the sails were again full, she had broken off two points, and the point of land was only a little on the lee-bow.

"We must wear her round, Mr. Falcon. Hands, wear ship— ready, oh, ready."

"She has come up again," cried the master, who was at the binnacle.

"Hold fast there a minute. How's her head now?"

"N.N.E., as she was before she broke off, sir."

"Pipe belay," said the captain. "Falcon," continued he, "if she breaks off again we may have no room to wear; indeed, there is so little room now, that I must run the risk. Which cable was ranged last night—the best bower?"

"Yes, sir."

"Jump down, then, and see it double-bitted and stoppered at thirty fathoms. See it well done—our lives may depend upon it."

The ship continued to hold her course good; and we were within half a mile of the point, and fully expected to weather it, when again the wet and heavy sails flapped in the wind, and the ship broke off two points as before. The officers and sea-

men were aghast, for the ship's head was right on to the breakers. "Luff now, all you can, quartermaster," cried the captain.
"Send the men aft directly. My lads, there is no time for words
—I am going to *club-haul* the ship, for there is no room to wear.
The only chance you have of safety is to be cool, watch my eye,
and execute my orders with precision. Away to your stations
for tacking ship. Hands by the best bower anchor. Mr. Wilson,
attend below with the carpenter and his mates, ready to cut
away the cable at the moment that I give the order. Silence
there, fore and aft. Quartermaster, keep her full again for stays.
Mind you ease the helm down when I tell you." About a minute
passed before the captain gave any further orders. The ship had
closed-to within a quarter-mile of the beach, and the waves
curled and topped around us, bearing us down upon the shore,
which presented one continued surface of foam, extending to
within half a cable's length of our position. The captain waved
his hand in silence to the quartermaster at the wheel, and the
helm was put down. The ship turned slowly to the wind, pitching and chopping as the sails were spilling. When she had lost
her way, the captain gave the order, "Let go the anchor. We
will haul all at once, Mr. Falcon," said the captain. Not a word
was spoken; the men went to the fore brace, which had not
been manned; most of them knew, although I did not, that if
the ship's head did not go round the other way, we should be
on shore, and among the breakers, in half a minute. I thought at
the time that the captain had said that he would haul all the
yards at once, there appeared to be doubt or dissent on the
countenance of Mr. Falcon; and I was afterwards told that he
had not agreed with the captain; but he was too good an officer,
and knew that there was no time for discussion, to make any
remark: and the event proved that the captain was right. At
last the ship was head to wind, and the captain gave the signal.
The yards flew round with such a creaking noise, that I thought
the masts had gone over the side, and the next moment the wind
had caught the sails; and the ship, which for a moment or two
had been on an even keel, careened over to her gunwale with

its force. The captain, who stood upon the weather hammock-rails, holding by the main-rigging, ordered the helm a-midships, looked full at the sails, and then at the cable, which grew broad upon the weather-bow, and held the ship from nearing the shore. At last he cried, "Cut away the cable!" A few strokes of the axes were heard, and then the cable flew out of the hawse-hole in a blaze of fire, from the violence of the friction, and disappeared under a huge wave, which struck us on the chess-tree, and deluged us with water fore and aft. But we were now on the other tack, and the ship regained her way, and we had evidently increased our distance from the land.

"My lads," said the captain to the ship's company, "you have behaved well, and I thank you; but I must tell you honestly that we have more difficulties to get through. We have to weather a point of the bay on this tack. Mr. Falcon, splice the main-brace, and call the watch. How's her head, quartermaster?"

"S.W. by S. Southerly, sir."

"Very well; let her go through the water;" and the captain, beckoning to the master to follow him, went down into the cabin. As our immediate danger was over, I went down into the berth to see if I could get anything for breakfast, where I found O'Brien and two or three more.

"By the powers, it was as nate a thing as ever I saw done," observed O'Brien: "the slightest mistake as to time or management, and at this moment the flatfish would have been dubbing at our ugly carcasses. Peter, you're not fond of flatfish, are you, my boy? We may thank Heaven and the captain, I can tell you that, my lads; but now, where's the chart, Robinson? Hand me down the parallel rules and compasses, Peter; they are in the corner of the shelf. Here we are now, a devilish sight too near this infernal point. Who knows how her head is?"

"I do, O'Brien: I heard the quartermaster tell the captain S.W. by S. Southerly."

"Let me see," continued O'Brien, "variation 2¼—leeway—rather too large an allowance of that, I'm afraid; but, however, we'll give her 2½ points; the *Diomede* would blush to make any more, under any circumstances. Here—the compass—now, we'll see;" and O'Brien advanced the parallel rule from the compass to the spot where the ship was placed on the chart. "Bother! you see, it's as much as she'll do to weather the other point now, on this tack, and that's what the captain meant when he told us we had more difficulty. I could have taken my Bible oath that we were clear of everything, if the wind held."

"See what the distance is, O'Brien," said Robinson. It was measured, and proved to be thirteen miles. "Only thirteen miles; and if we do weather, we shall do very well, for the bay is deep beyond. It's a rocky point, you see, just by way of variety. Well, my lads, I've a piece of comfort for you, anyhow. It's not long that you'll be kept in suspense, for by one o'clock this day you'll either be congratulating each other upon your good luck, or you'll be past praying for. Come, put up the chart, for I hate to look at melancholy prospects; and, steward, see what you can find in the way of comfort." Some bread and cheese, with the remains of yesterday's boiled pork, were put on the table, with a bottle of rum, procured at the time they "spliced the main brace," but we were all too anxious to eat much, and one by one returned on deck to see how the weather was, and if the wind at all favored us. On deck the superior officers were in conversation with the captain, who expressed the same fear that O'Brien had in our berth. The men, who knew what they had to expect, were assembled in knots, looking very grave, but at the same time not wanting in confidence. They knew that they could trust to the captain, as far as skill or courage could avail them; and sailors are too sanguine to despair, even at the last moment. As for myself, I felt such admiration for the captain, after what I had witnessed that morning, that, whenever the idea came over me, that in all probability I should be lost in a few hours, I could not help acknowledging how much more serious it was that such a man should be lost to his country. I do not intend to say that it consoled me, but it certainly made me still more regret the chances with which we were threatened.

Before twelve o'clock the rocky point which we so much dreaded was in sight, broad on the lee bow; and if the low sandy coast appeared terrible, how much more did this, even at a distance. The captain eyed it for some minutes in silence, as if in calculation.

"Mr. Falcon," said he, at last, "we must put the mainsail on her."

"She never can bear it, sir."

"She *must* bear it," was the reply. "Send the men aft to the mainsheet. See that careful men attend the bunt-lines."

The mainsail was set, and the effect of it upon the ship was tremendous. She careened over so that her lee channels were under the water; and when pressed by a sea, the lee side of the quarter-deck and gangway were afloat. She now reminded me of a goaded and fiery horse, mad with the stimulus applied; not rising as before, but forcing herself through whole seas, and dividing the waves, which poured in one continual torrent from the forecastle down upon the decks below. Four men were secured to the wheel—the sailors were obliged to cling to prevent being washed away—the ropes were thrown in confusion to leeward—the shot rolled out of the lockers, and every eye was fixed aloft, watching the masts, which were expected every moment to go over the side. A heavy sea struck us on the broadside, and it was some moments before the ship appeared to recover herself; she reeled, trembled, and stopped her way, as if it had stupefied her. The first lieutenant looked at the captain, as if to say, "This will not do." "It is our only chance," answered the captain to the appeal. That the ship went faster through the water, and held a better wind, was certain; but just before we arrived at the point the gale increased in force. "If anything starts we are lost, sir," observed the first lieutenant again.

"I am perfectly well aware of it," replied the captain, in a calm tone; "but, as I said before, and as you must now be aware, it is our only chance. The consequence of any carelessness or neglect in the fitting and securing of the rigging will be felt now; and this danger, if we escape it, ought to remind us how much we have to answer for if we neglect our duty. The lives of a whole ship's company may be sacrificed by the neglect or incompetence of an officer when in harbor. I will pay you the compliment, Falcon, to say, that I feel convinced that the masts of the ship are as secure as knowledge and attention can make them."

The first lieutenant thanked the captain for his good opinion, and hoped that it would not be the last compliment which he paid him.

"I hope not, too; but a few minutes will decide the point."

The ship was now within two cables' lengths of the rocky point; some few of the men I observed to clasp their hands, but most of them were silently taking off their jackets, and kicking off their shoes, that they might not lose a chance of escape provided the ship struck.

" 'Twill be touch and go, indeed, Falcon," observed the captain (for I had clung to the belaying pins, close to them for the last half-hour that the mainsail had been set). "Come aft, you and I must take the helm. We shall want *nerve* there, and only there, now."

The captain and first lieutenant went aft, and took the fore-spokes of the wheel, and O'Brien, at a sign made by the captain, laid hold of the spokes behind him. An old quartermaster kept his station at the fourth. The roaring of the seas on the rocks, with the howling of the wind, were dreadful; but the sight was more dreadful than the noise. For a few minutes I shut my eyes, but anxiety forced me to open them again. As near as I could judge, we were not twenty yards from the rocks, at the time that the ship passed abreast of them. We were in the midst of the foam, which boiled around us; and as the ship was driven nearer to them, and careened with the wave, I thought that our main yard-arm would have touched the rock; and at this moment a gust of wind came on, which laid the ship on her beam-ends, and checked her progress through the water, while the accumulating noise was deafening. A few moments more the ship dragged on, another wave dashed over her and spent itself upon the rocks, while the spray was dashed back from them, and returned upon the decks. The main rock was within ten yards of the counter, when another gust of wind laid us on our beam-ends, the foresail and mainsail split, and were blown clean out of the bolt-ropes—the ship righted, trembling fore and aft. I looked astern:—the rocks were to windward on our quarter, and we were safe. I thought at the time that the ship, relieved of her courses, and again lifting over the waves, was not a bad similitude of the relief felt by us all at that moment; and, like her, we trembled as we panted with the sudden re-action, and felt the removal of the intense anxiety which oppressed our breasts.

The captain resigned the helm, and walked aft to look at the point, which was now broad on the weather-quarter. In a minute or two, he desired Mr. Falcon to get new sails up and bend them, and then went below to his cabin. I am sure it was to thank God for our deliverance: I did most fervently, not only then, but when I went to my hammock at night. We were now comparatively safe—in a few hours completely so; for, strange to say, immediately after we had weathered the rocks, the gale abated, and before morning we had a reef out of the topsails.

# IN NELSON'S TIME [1]

From "Sea Life in Nelson's Time," BY JOHN MASEFIELD

## I

THE punishment most in use in the fleet was flogging on the bare back with the cat-o'-nine-tails. The cat was a short, wooden stick, covered with red baize. The tails were of tough knotted cord, about two feet long. The thieves' cat, with which thieves were flogged, had longer and heavier tails, knotted throughout their length. Flogging was inflicted at the discretion of the captain. It was considered the only punishment likely to be effective with such men as manned the royal ships. It is now pretty certain that it was as useless as it was degrading. Lord Charles Beresford has said that, "in those days we had the cat and no discipline; now we have discipline and no cat." Another skilled observer has said that "it made a bad man worse, and broke a good man's heart." It was perhaps the most cruel and ineffectual punishment ever inflicted. The system was radically bad, for many captains inflicted flogging for all manner of offences, without distinction. The thief was flogged, the drunkard was flogged, the laggard was flogged. The poor, wretched topman who got a ropeyarn into a buntline block was flogged. The very slightest transgression was visited with flogging. Those seamen who had any pride remaining in them went in daily fear of being flogged. Those who had been flogged were generally callous, careless whether they were flogged again, and indifferent to all that might happen to them. It was a terrible weapon in the hands of the officers. In many cases the officers abused the power, by the infliction of excessive punishment for trifling offences. The sailors liked a smart captain.

[1] Reprinted by courtesy of The Macmillan Company.

They liked to be brought up to the mark, and if a captain showed himself a brave man, a good seaman, and a glutton for hard knocks, they would stand any punishment he chose to inflict, knowing that such a one would not be unjust. They hated a slack captain, for a slack captain left them at the mercy of the underlings, and that, they said, was "hell afloat." But worse than anything they hated a tyrant, a man who flogged his whole ship's company for little or no reason, or for the infringement of his own arbitrary rules. Such a man, who kept his crew in an agony of fear, hardly knowing whether to kill themselves or their tyrant, was dreaded by all. He was not uncommon in the service until the conclusion of the Great War. It was his kind who drove so many of our men into the American navy. It was his kind who did so much to cause the mutinies at the Nore and Spithead, the loss of the *Hermione* frigate, and (to some extent) the losses we sustained in the American War. Lastly, it was his kind who caused so many men to desert, in defiance of the stern laws against desertion. That kind of captain was the terror of the fleet. We do not know what percentage of captains gave the lash unmercifully. Jack Nastyface tells us that of the nine ships of the line he sailed aboard only two had humane commanders. These two received services of plate from the sailors under their command at the paying-off of their ships; the other seven, we are to presume, ranged from the severe to the brutal.

After all, the cat was not essential to discipline. This was proved time and time again while it was most in use. There were, of course, stubborn, brutal, and mutinous sailors. A fleet so manned could not lack such men. When such men were brought before Lord Nelson, he would say: "Send them to Collingwood. He will tame them, if no one else can." Lord Collingwood was the man who swore, by the god of war, that his men should salute a reefer's coat, even when it were merely hung to dry. Yet he didn't tame his men by cutting their backs into strips. He would have his whole ship's company in perfect order, working like machines, with absolute, unquestioning fidelity. But he seldom flogged more than one man a month, and punished really serious offences, such as drunkenness, inciting to mutiny, and theft, with six, nine, or at most a dozen, lashes. His system tamed the hardest cases in the fleet—good men, whom Lord St. Vincent would have flogged to death, or sent to the yard-arm. In conclusion we may quote one of those who saw the last days of flogging: "My firm conviction is that the bad man was very little the better; the good man very much the worse. The good man felt the disgrace, and was branded for life. His self-esteem was permanently maimed, and he rarely held up his head or did his best again." Such was the effect of the favourite punishment in the time of the consulship of Plancus.

Those who transgressed the rules of the ship or of the service during the day were put upon the report of the master-at-arms. The names were submitted by that officer to the first lieutenant, who passed them to the captain every forenoon. Drunkards and mutinous subjects generally passed a night in irons under the half-deck, in the care of an armed marine, before coming up for sentence. Every forenoon, at about half-past ten, those who were on the report went below for their smartest clothes, in the hope that a neat appearance might mollify the captain. Those who were in irons got their messmates to bring them their clothes. At six bells, or eleven o'clock in the forenoon, the captain came on deck, with a paper bearing the names of all delinquents. He bade the lieutenant turn the hands aft to witness punishment. The lieutenant sent a midshipman to the boatswain's mates, and the order was piped and shouted. The marines fell in upon the poop, with their muskets and side-arms. The junior officers gathered to windward under the break of the poop. The captain and lieutenants stood on the weather quarter-deck. The ship's company fell in anyhow, on the booms, boats, and lee-side of the ship, directly forward of the main-mast. The doctor and purser fell in to leeward, under the break of the poop, with the boatswain's mates in a little gang in front of them. The captain's first order was "rig the gratings." The carpenter and carpenter's mates at once dragged aft two of the wooden gratings which covered the hatches. One of these was placed flat upon the deck. The other was placed upright, and secured in that position against the ship's side or poop railings. When the gratings had been reported rigged the captain called forward the first offender on his list, and told him that he had transgressed the rules of the service, knowing the penalty. He asked the man if he had anything to say in extenuation. If he had nothing to say the order was "Strip." The man flung off his shirt, and advanced bare-shouldered to the gratings, and extended his arms upon the upright. The captain then gave the order "Seize him up." The quartermasters advanced, with lengths of spun-yarn, with which they tied the man's hands to the grating. They then reported "Seized up, sir." At this point the captain produced a copy of the Articles of War, and read that Article which the offender had infringed. As he read he took off his hat, to show his respect for the King's commandments. Every man present did the same. While the Article was being read one of the boatswain's mates undid a red baize bag, and produced the red-handled cat, with which he was to execute punishment. At the order "Do your duty," he advanced to the man at the grating, drew the cat tails through his fingers, flung his arm back, and commenced to flog, with his full strength, at the full sweep of his arm. He was generally a powerful seaman, and he knew very well that any sign of favouritism would infallibly cause his disrating, if it did not subject him to the same torture. Some seamen could take a dozen, or, as they expressed it, "get a red checked shirt at the gangway," without crying aloud. But the force of each blow was such that the recipient had the breath knocked clean out of him, "with an involuntary Ugh." One blow was sufficient to take off the skin, and to draw blood wherever the knots fell. Six blows were enough to make the back perfectly raw. Twelve blows cut deeply into it, and left it a horrible red slough, sickening to look upon. Yet three dozen was a common punishment. Six dozen lashes were counted as nothing. Three hundred lashes were very frequently given.

Before a severe punishment the sufferer's messmates used to bring him their tots of grog, saved up from supper the night before, so that he might at least begin his torture in blessed stupefaction. After a severe punishment they took the poor mangled body down to the sick-bay, and left it there in the care of the surgeon. A body that had been severely lashed looked something like raw veal. It generally healed up, but for weeks after the punishment the sufferer's life was a misery to him, for reasons which may be read in the proper place, but which need not be quoted here.

It may interest some people to know what the punishment felt like. A ruffian has left it on record that it was "nothing but an O, and a few O my Gods, and then you can put on your shirt." It was more than that. A very hardy fellow may have found a dozen or so comparatively easy to bear. But when the lashes ran into the scores it became a different matter. We will quote a poor soldier who was flogged in 1832 with a cat precisely similar to that used in the King's fleet.

"I felt an astounding sensation between the shoulders, under my neck, which went to my toe-nails in one direction, and my finger-nails in another, and stung me to the heart, as if a knife had gone through my body. . . . He came on a second time a few inches lower, and then I thought the former stroke was sweet and agreeable compared with that one. . . . I felt my flesh quiver in every nerve, from the scalp of my head to my toe-nails. The time between strokes seemed so long as to be agonising, and yet the next came too soon. . . . The pain in my lungs was more severe, I thought, than on my back. I felt as if I would burst in the internal parts of my body. . . . I put my tongue between my teeth, held it there, and bit it almost in two pieces. What with the blood from my tongue, and my lips, which I had also bitten, and the blood from my lungs, or some other internal part, ruptured by the writhing agony, I was almost choked, and became black in the face. . . . Only fifty had been inflicted, and the time since they began was like a long period of life; I felt as if I had lived all the time of my real life in pain and torture, and that the time when existence had pleasure in it was a dream, long, long gone by."

Another man, who saw a good deal of flogging in his time, has told us that, after the infliction of two dozen lashes, "the lacerated back looks inhuman; it resembles roasted meat burnt nearly black before a scorching fire." The later blows were not laid on less heartily than the first. The striker cleaned the tails of the cat after each blow, so that they should not clog together with flesh and blood, and thus deaden the effect. A fresh boatswain's mate was put on to flog after each two dozen. Some captains boasted of having left-handed boatswain's mates, who could "cross the cuts" made by the right-handed men.

For striking "an admiral, a commodore, captain, or lieutenant," or "for attempting to escape," no matter what provocation may have been given, the most lenient punishment inflicted was flogging through the fleet. The man was put into the ship's longboat, and lashed by his wrists to a capstan bar. Stockings were inserted between the wrists and the lashing "to prevent him from tearing the flesh off in his agonies." The other boats of the ship were lowered, and each ship in the harbour sent a boat manned with marines to attend the punishment. The master-at-arms and the ship's surgeon accompanied the victim. Before the boat cast off from the ship the captain read the sentence from the gangway. A boatswain's mate then came down the ladder, and inflicted a certain number of lashes on the man. The boat then rowed away from the ship, to the sound of the half-minute bell, the oars keeping time to the drummer, who beat the rogue's march beside the victim. The attendant boats followed, in a doleful procession, rowing slowly to the same music. On coming to the next ship the ceremony was repeated, after which the poor man was cast off and covered with a blanket, and allowed to compose himself. He received a portion of his torture near each ship in the port, "until the sentence was completed." If he fainted he was plied with wine or rum, or, in some cases, taken back to the sick-bay of his ship to recover. In the latter case he stayed till his back had healed, when he was again led out to receive the rest of the sentence. "After he has been alongside of several ships," says Jack Nastyface, who often saw these punishments, "his back resembles so much putrefied liver." Those who lived through the whole of the punishment were washed with brine, cured, and sent back to their duty. But the punishment was so terrible that very few lived through it all. Joshua Davis tells us of a corpse being brought alongside, with the head hanging down and the bones laid bare from the neck to the waist. There were still fifty lashes due to the man, so they were given to the corpse, at the captain's order. Those who died during the infliction of the punishment were rowed ashore, and buried in the mud below the tidemark, without religious rites. Those who survived such fearful ordeals were broken men when they came out of the sick-bay. They lived but a little while afterwards, in a nervous and pitiful condition, suffering acutely in many ways. It is said that those who were flogged through the fleet were offered the alternative of the gallows.

A man caught thieving was generally set to run the gauntlet. The members of the ship's crew formed into a double line right round the main or spar deck. Each man armed himself with three tarry rope yarns, which he twisted up into what was called a knittle or nettle, knotted at the end, and about three feet long. The thief was stripped to the waist, and brought to one end of the line. The master-at-arms stood in front of him, with a drawn sword pointing to his breast. Two ship's corporals stood close behind him, with drawn swords pointing to his back. If he went too quickly or too slowly the sword points pricked him. When he was placed in position at the end of a line a boatswain's mate gave him a dozen lashes with the thieves' cat. He was then slowly walked (or dragged on a grating) through the double line of men, who flogged him with their nettles as he walked past them. When he arrived at the end of a line a boatswain's mate gave him another taste of the thieves' cat, and either started him down another line or turned him back by the way he had come. It was very cruel punishment, for it flayed the whole of the upper part of a man's body, not omitting his head. After running the gauntlet the man went into hospital, to be rubbed with brine and healed. He was then sent back to his duty, "without a stain upon his character." He had purged his offence. It was never again mentioned by his shipmates.

Those who contradicted an officer—or appeared to contradict him, by answering back, however respectfully—were punished by gagging. The lieutenants had no power to flog, but they had power to inflict minor punishments. Gagging was one of those they inflicted on their own initiative. The offender was brought to the rigging, or to the bitts, with his hands tied behind him. An iron marline spike was placed across his mouth, between his teeth, like a bit. The ends were fitted with spunyarn, which was passed round the head, and knotted there to keep the iron in position. With this heavy piece of iron in his mouth the man had to stand till his mouth was bloody, or till the officer relented. If a man displeased an officer at any time he was often punished on the spot, by a boatswain's mate. The officer would call a boatswain's mate and say: "Start that man." The boatswain's mate at once produced a hard knotted cord, called a starter, with which he beat the man unmercifully about the head and shoulders, till the officer bade him to desist. The sailors found the starting even harder to bear than the cat, for it generally fell upon their arms as they raised them to protect their heads. It was very severe punishment, and frequently caused such swollen and bruised arms that the sailors could not bear to wear their jackets. It was inflicted with very little cause. Whenever an order was given the boatswain's mates drew out their colts or starters and thrashed the men to their duty with indiscriminating cruelty. It was not lawful punishment, being wholly unauthorised by regulation. But there was no appeal;

the sailors had to grin and bear it. After 1811 it was very strictly suppressed.

The boatswain, master-at-arms, and ship's corporals, with their rattans, or supplejacks, were every whit as ready to thrash the seamen as the boatswain's mates. They, too, carried colts, or starters, made of 3-inch rope, so unlaid that the strands made three knotted tails. With these they beat the seamen for any slight, or fancied slight, until their arms were tired. The sergeant of marines was similarly provided, but his attentions were confined to his own department. He had no power over the bluejackets, except in fifth and sixth rates. Besides all these petty tyrants there were the lesser bullies, the midshipmen, who took delight in torturing the seamen in many ways.

The old-fashioned punishments of ducking from the yard-arm, and keel-hauling, were not practised in our fleet. They had fallen out of use during the eighteenth century, though the French still practised them. Captain Glascock saw a Frenchman keel-hauled early in the last century. Instead of them, there were other punishments, such as a disciplinarian could invent on the spot. Spitting on the decks was discouraged by fastening buckets round the offender's neck, and causing the man to walk the lower deck, as a sort of peripatetic cuspidor. Minor offences were punished by stoppage of grog, or of some part of it; by the infliction of dirty or harassing duty; or by riding a man on a gun with his feet tied together beneath the piece.

Capital offences were expiated at the yard-arm. The man was taken to the cathead, a yellow flag was flown at the masthead, a gun was fired, and all the bad characters of the ship manned the yard-rope, and ran the victim up to the end of the yard.

## II

At the first sight of a suspicious ship, all hands were called, and the drummer of the marines beat to quarters. The roll to quarters was short, quick, and determined, being the tune of the song "Hearts of Oak." Directly the drumming ceased the sailors sprang to their tasks. They knew their posts, and the work allotted to them. The ship was cleared quickly and quietly, each man of the hundreds aboard going at once to his place to fit it for battle. The carpenter with his mates, and a number of allotted assistants, repaired aft to the officers' cabins, to unship the wooden bulkheads. The light wooden screens were easily knocked from their grooves, and hurried down into the hold. The captain's furniture, generally no more than a table, settee, and a few chairs, was handed down to the same place, and secured by a rope or two. If the ship had to be cleared in a hurry these things were tossed overboard. The French seem to have left them standing, trusting to fortune to keep the splinters from doing any hurt. Men from each mess went to the lower-deck, to the berth, to clear away the crockery, kit-bags, sea chests, etc., and to run them down out of the way into the wings. The topmen securely "stopped" the top-sail sheets, rove preventer-lifts, slung their lower-yards with chain, prepared their muskets, swivel-guns, pistols and hand-grenades, and got up a few coils of rope and some spare blocks ready for emergencies. If it were dark, or likely to be dark before the fight had been brought to a conclusion, the pursuer issued "pursuer's glims," in heavy battle lanterns, one of which was secured to the ship's side by each gun. As the lanterns were liable to be shaken from their places by the concussion of the firing they were secured very tightly. They gave little light; but by the help of the moon, if any shone, and by instinct, and the knowledge of what was to be done, the sailors managed very well. Few actions were fought in the dark, as the risk was too great. It was always well to have a good look at the enemy before engaging.

The hammocks, which ran all around the upper or spar deck, made a good protection to the men engaged upon the gangways. Before going into action, a number of hammocks were taken from the nettings and lashed to the lower rigging, over the dead-eyes and lanyards. A few hammocks were sometimes whipped into the tops, to protect the topmast-rigging in the same way. Strong rope nettings were hung over the upper-deck under the masts, to catch any wreck or men falling from above. Some buckets of water were sent aloft and poured over the sails. Sometimes the engine was rigged, and placed upon the poop, so that the hose played upon the courses. The booms and boats were liberally drenched. The buckets hanging on the quarter-deck were filled, and fire hoses were laid along each deck. Buckets of water were placed in the chains and head. The pumps were rigged in case the ship started to leak. Wet swabs were laid by all the hatchways, ready for use. A bucket of fresh water, a tub of salt water, and a swab, were placed behind each gun, for the refreshment of the men, and in case of fire. Wet sand was sprinkled over every deck, to make the planking moist, so as to lessen the risk of fire, and to give surety to the footing of the men. The match tubs were half filled with water. Wet canvas cloths were rolled along the orlop to the mouths of the magazines. Wet frieze screens were then nailed round the magazine hatches, so that no spark could possibly penetrate to them. Wetted blankets were hung round each hatchway.

While the appointed men were doing these things, the captains of the guns went to the gunner's storerooms to get their cartouche boxes, or square leather cases, filled with the powder tubes or quills, for insertion in the touch-holes of the guns. They also received the flinted gun-locks with which to fire the guns. The men told off to the cannon cast their guns loose from their lashings, struck their ports open, cleared away the side-tackles, preventer-tackles, and breechings, took out the tompions, cast off the leaden aprons, made ready the crows and handspikes, and laid the sponge ready for use. They got the cheeses of wads ready, and placed "garlands," or rope-rings containing round shot, between the guns. Those of the gun's crews who were told off as boarders put a couple of loaded pistols, and a ship's cutlass in their belts. The gun-captains hung up their powder horns, full of priming powder, above their pieces, and struck their priming-irons into their belts ready for use. The powder-boys brought up their "salt-boxes" full of cartridges for the first broadsides. The marines, or at any rate some of their number, fell in upon the poop quarter-deck and forecastle, with their muskets and side-arms. They were expected to shoot the enemy's topmen, and to pick off the musketeers and the sail-trimmers on the poop and quarter-deck of the opposing ship. Some of their number helped to work the heavy carronades of the upper after-batteries. The drummers and fifers of the company, who were generally little fellows, younger than the ship's boys, were employed to keep them supplied with powder and ball-cartridge.

Any animals below decks were generally hoisted up and slung overboard, so that the pens in which they lived might be demolished. Hen-coops generally went over the side in the same way. If they were stowed in the boats on the booms, they were allowed to remain. We read of a cock which was liberated by a round shot in time to cheer the ship's company by crowing from the stump of a mast. If there were pigs in the manger, which was a very powerful barricade, little likely to be destroyed, they were suffered to stay there.

It took but a few minutes to clear a ship for action. The guns were cast loose, the lumber cleared away, yards slung, sheets stopped, and the galley-fire extinguished in much less time than a landsman would think possible. As soon as the men had taken their places the lieutenants walked round the gun-decks, to see that all was ready, at the same time giving orders that the guns should be loaded and run out. All this work was done silently: there was no singing out or loud talking. Down below the gun-decks the gunner was busy in his magazines, handing out cartridges to the powder-boys, who put them in the wooden or leathern cases, and carried them to the guns. His mates were kept employed filling fresh cartridges to replace those discharged. The surgeon, with his assistants, prepared the cockpit for the wounded, making ready a number of tourniquets and pledgets for first intentions. A number of tourniquets were distributed about the gun-decks for use by the men who carried down the wounded. As a final preparation, the ship's hatches were tripped up, so that the men could not run below to the security of the orlop-deck. The small fore and after hatches were left standing, to allow the powder-boys and messengers to pass down. They were, however, guarded by marines, who had orders to allow no one save powder-boys and midshipmen to go down by them. Those hatches which led from the gun-deck to the orlop were guarded by midshipmen with pistols, who had orders to shoot any man trying to escape his duty. To prevent anyone from trying to impose upon these hatchway sentries, it was the rule that all powder-boys going for powder should display their cartridge cases as they reached the ladder. The gunner, also, had orders to refuse to give powder to any-one without a proper case.

When all was ready the lieutenant, and sometimes the cap-tain, made the tour of the decks to cheer the men, and to give their final orders. At the same time the carpenter and his mates took up their stations on the orlop-deck and in the hold, with their shot plugs ready for immediate insertion.

Many of the sailors delighted in battle, not because they were fond of fighting, but because discipline was relaxed during the fight, and, in spite of the extra duty, for a day or two after-wards; and because a victory meant prize-money and a jolly time in port. A fight broke the monotony of a cruise. It made the officers rather more humane in their treatment. Lastly, it was exciting in itself. It was, however, less popular among the men than among the officers. If an officer was badly hurt he got promotion and half pay. If a man was maimed he had nothing but Greenwich Hospital to look for. If he could not get into the hospital he was free to starve, saying with Goldsmith's sailor, that those who got both legs shot off, and a consequent pension, were born with golden spoons in their mouths. Never-theless, they always went into action cheerily. Their motto was "The hotter the war the sooner the peace," and they knew that they would not be discharged till peace had been declared. Even those who were stationed in the waist or midship guns were merry as they went to quarters. "The very idea of going

into action" was "a source of joy to them." They were as brave
as they were careless. A hot engagement was meat and drink
to them. The thought of a general action kept them from their
beds.

It was their custom, when going into action, to strip to the
waist. They took their black silk handkerchiefs, and bound
them very tightly round their heads over their ears, so that the
roar of the guns might not deafen them for life. It was remarked
that men going into action always wore a sullen frown, however merry they were in their talk. Before the firing began they
used to settle among themselves what amount of prize-money
they would win, and how they would spend it. They also made
their wills, not in writing, but verbally: "If they get me, Jack,
you can have my kit. Tom, you can have my trousers to buy
you a mourning ring," etc., always merrily, as though the prospect of death was very remote. They would also whisper to
each other, as they came down to the enemy, as to her strength,
size, and appearance, guessing her nationality, length of absence
from home, etc., from the cut and shape of her masts and sails,
and the colour of the bunt patches in her top-sails.

It is not known how a gun-deck looked during the heat of an
engagement; for those who saw most of the fighting have left
us but a poor account of their experiences. We may take Smollett's word for it, that it was "a most infernal scene of slaughter,
fire, smoke and uproar." We can imagine fifteen or sixteen
cannon in a row, all thundering and recoiling and flashing fire;
on the other side of the ship a similar row, nearly certain to be
thundering and flashing fire, if the action were general, instead
of a duel between ships. Up above, immediately overhead, not
more than a foot from one's hat crown, was a similar double
row of cannon, with heavy carriages which banged and leaped
at each recoil. Up above those, perhaps, if the ship were a first
or second rate, was yet another gun-deck, with its thundering
great guns and banging gun-trucks. And above that, as a sort
of pendant, was the upper battery of carronades, making a terrible roaring at each shot; and marines firing their muskets, and

topmen firing their swivels, and blocks and spars and heavy ropes coming down from aloft with a clatter. And every now and again, if not every minute, the awful ear-splitting crash, "like the smashing of a door with crowbars," as a shot struck home, and sent the splinters scattering. Then, continually, the peculiar hissing and screaming of the passing round shot made a lighter music, "like the tearing of sails," to the bass of the cannon. One heard, too, the yells of perhaps five or six hundred men, as they tugged at the tackling, or hove the guns round with the handspikes. Then there were wounded men screaming, and port-lids coming down with a bang, and perhaps a gun bursting, or thudding clean out of its carriage, as a shot struck a trunnion; and every now and then a horrible noise, as a ball exploded a cartridge on the deck.

So much for the racket. The noise was the clearest impression one could gather. One could see little enough when once the firing had begun. A large ship, fighting only one broadside at a time, burned from 500 to 1,100 lbs. of powder every minute, according to the heat of the battle and the distance of the target. It was black powder, and the decks were black with smoke after the first broadside, if they were engaging to windward, for the smoke blew back at the ports, and poured up the hatches like the reek of factory chimneys. In the murk and stench one might see the flash from the spouting touch-holes, as the "huff" leaped out, to burn a hole in the beams above. One could mark the little light of the slow matches at those guns where the flints of the locks had broken. One could see a sailor's face in the glow, as he blew at the red end to clear away the ashes.

The least pleasant part of a ship of war in action was the waist or midship part, near the main rigging. It was the custom in these sea engagements to converge a broad-side fire upon some central point in the opposing ship's side. The men stationed in the waist or main battery always suffered more in proportion than the men at the after or forward guns. That part of a ship's lower-deck between the fore and after hatchways, was known as "the slaughter-house," on account of the

massacre which generally took place at that part. In the midst
of the fury and confusion, with the ship shaking like a tautened
rope from the concussion, and the blood "flowing like bilge
water," there was yet a certain order and human purpose. The
lieutenants walked to and fro about the batteries, regulating
the fire, and keeping the men to their guns. The powder-boys
skipped here and there on their errands for powder. The half-
dozen men told off for cockpit duty came and went with the
wounded, or paused at the gun-ports to heave a dead or dying
man overboard, "with no other ceremony than shoving him
through the port." Now and then some men left their guns and
ran on deck to do any sail-trimming which might be necessary.
Others broke away to bring up shot from the hold. If the ship
carried any women or sailors' wives they, too, were employed
about the deck in carrying water or powder. The master-at-
arms went his rounds slowly, passing from deck to deck, asking
for complaints, and noting how things were going. He had to
make a note of the losses at the guns, of the expenditure of
powder, and of the shot-holes between wind and water. His
visits were godsends to the men working below the gun-deck
in the magazines. The work there was mechanical, not feverish,
like the work of the men at the guns. They had time to think,
and found the situation "not one of danger, but most wounding
to the feelings, and trying to the patience." One of the gunner's
crew of H.M.S. *Goliah*, a 74-gun ship engaged at the battle of
St. Vincent, has told us that—

"I was stationed in the after-magazine serving powder from
the screen, and could see nothing; but I could feel every shot
that struck the *Goliah:* and the cries and groans of the wounded
were most distressing, as there was only the thickness of the
blankets of the screen between me and them. Busy as I was, the
time hung upon me with a dreary weight. Not a soul spoke to
me but the master-at-arms, as he went his rounds to inquire if
all was safe. No sick person ever longed more for his physician
than I for the voice of the master-at-arms. I would, if I had had
my choice, have been on the deck; there I would have seen

what was passing, and the time would not have hung so heavy."

If, during the engagement, the ships came grinding together, with a crash which knocked the lower-deck ports in, the matter was settled by boarding. The two or three men of each gun's crew who were told off as boarders were then "called away." They dropped their gun-tackles, drew their cutlasses and pistols, and skipped up on deck, into the enemy's rigging, and down on to her decks, to carry her by hand-to-hand fighting. More generally the action was determined by superior gunnery. The ship which lost her rudder or her foremast, or caught fire either aloft or below, was the one to strike. If one of the combatants became unmanageable her opponent took up a position on her bow or quarter, and raked her into submission, at a safe distance. When a ship struck, a boat was sent to take possession of her. Her officers were sent aboard the captor as the guests of the ward-room and cabin. The men were hunted down into the hold under a guard of marines. If they showed signs of rising, or if they were too numerous for safety, they were put in irons. In extreme cases they were battened down below, with cannon, loaded with grape, pointing down the hatchways at them.

We quote part of the account of a boy who fought in one of the hottest of our frigate actions. The action belongs to a period half-a-dozen years after that of Trafalgar, but, nevertheless, as the author says, "it will reveal the horrors of war, and show at what a fearful price a victory is won or lost."

"The whole scene grew indescribably confused and horrible. I was busily supplying my gun with powder, when I saw blood suddenly fly from the arm of a man stationed at our gun. I saw nothing strike him; the effect alone was visible: . . . the third lieutenant tied his handkerchief round the wounded arm, and sent the groaning wretch below to the surgeon. The cries of the wounded rang through all parts of the ship . . . those more fortunate men who were killed outright were immediately thrown overboard. . . . Two of the boys stationed on the quarter-deck were killed. A man, who saw one of them killed, afterwards told me that his powder caught fire and burnt the flesh almost off his face. In this pitiable situation, the agonised boy lifted up both hands, as if imploring relief, when a passing shot instantly cut him in two. . . . A man named Aldrich had one of his hands cut off by a shot, and almost at the same moment he received another shot, which tore open his bowels in a terrible manner. As he fell, two or three men caught him in their arms and, as he could not live, threw him overboard. . . . Our men kept cheering with all their might. I cheered with them, though I confess I scarcely knew for what. Certainly there was nothing very inspiriting in the aspect of things where I was stationed. Not only had we several boys and men killed and wounded, but several of the guns were disabled. The one I belonged to had a piece of the muzzle knocked out. . . . The brave boatswain, who came from the sick-bay to the din of battle, was fastening a stopper on a backstay, which had been shot away, when his head was smashed to pieces by a cannonball; another man, going to complete the unfinished task, was also struck down. . . . A fellow named John, who for some petty offence had been sent on board as a punishment, was carried past me wounded. I distinctly heard the large blood drops fall pat, pat, pat on the deck. Even a poor goat kept by the officers for her milk, did not escape the general carnage; her hind legs were shot off, and poor Nan was thrown overboard. Such was the terrible scene, amid which we kept on our shouting and firing. I felt pretty much as I suppose everyone does at such a time. We all appeared cheerful, but I know that many a serious thought ran through my mind. . . . I thought a great deal of the other world . . . but being without any particular knowledge of religious truth I satisfied myself by repeating again and again the Lord's Prayer."

The poor little boy was barely fourteen years old.

After an action a supply of vinegar was heated for the sprinkling of the ship, to drive away the smell of blood from decks and beams. The last of the dead were thrown overboard, the wounded were made as comfortable as the circumstance allowed, and as many men as could be spared were sent on deck to knot and splice the rigging. Before the repairs were begun the cannon were secured, and a gill of rum served out to every man and boy. Then the heaviest work of the action began. "It is after the action the disagreeable part commences." There was then no excitement to support the worker. The tired men had to turn to with a will, to unbend sails and bend new ones, to send up new spars, or new yards, to reeve new running-rigging, and set up new stays and shrouds. "For days they have no remission of their toil, repairing the rigging and other parts injured in the action." The work of a prize-crew, in charge of a prize, was especially arduous, for they were generally a mere handful of men, barely sufficient to sail the vessel, let alone to repair her. A prize-crew were sometimes too busy to clean the prize's decks. The *Chesapeake* came into Halifax six days after her capture by the *Shannon* with her decks still horrible with blood, and with human fingers sticking in her sides, "as though they had been thrust through from without." In any case a ship which had been in a hot engagement needed to be cleansed in every part with vinegar, and disinfected with brimstone, before the shambles smell was removed from her.

The sailors were often inconvenienced indirectly during a hot engagement by the destruction of the hammocks. The hammock nettings stopped a great number of cannon balls, and the gangways were frequently littered with hammocks thrown out by the shot, torn in pieces, or shot clean through. As a 32 lb. round shot made a very big hole in a purser's blanket, and as the sailors paid for their own bedding, this was a real hardship. However, "everything is a joke at sea." The thought of prize-money atoned for the discomfort.

# THE CAPTURE OF THE GREAT WHITE WHALE

### From "Moby Dick," BY HERMAN MELVILLE

THAT night, in the mid-watch, when the old man—as was his wont at intervals—stepped forth from the scuttle in which he leaned, and went to his pivothole, he suddenly thrust out his face fiercely, snuffing up the sea air as a sagacious ship's dog will, in drawing nigh to some barbarous isle. He declared that a whale must be near. Soon that peculiar odor, sometimes to a great distance given forth by the living sperm whale, was palpable to all the watch; nor was any mariner surprised when, after inspecting the compass, and then the dogvane, and then ascertaining the precise bearing of the odor as nearly as possible, Ahab rapidly ordered the ship's course to be slightly altered, and the sail to be shortened.

The acute policy dictating these movements was sufficiently vindicated at daybreak, by the sight of a long sleek on the sea directly and lengthwise ahead, smooth as oil, and resembling in the pleated watery wrinkles bordering it, the polished metallic-like marks of some swift tide-rip, at the mouth of a deep, rapid stream.

"Man the mast-heads! Call all hands!"

Thundering with the butts of three clubbed handspikes on the forecastle deck, Daggoo roused the sleepers with such judgment claps that they seemed to exhale from the scuttle, so instantaneously did they appear with their clothes in their hands.

"What d'ye see?" cried Ahab, flattening his face to the sky.

"Nothing, nothing, sir!" was the sound hailing down in reply.

"T'gallant sails!—stunsails! alow and aloft, and on both sides!"

All sail being set, he now cast loose the life-line, reserved for swaying him to the main royal-mast head; and in a few moments they were hoisting him thither, when, while but two-thirds of the way aloft, and while peering ahead through the horizontal vacancy between the main-top-sail and top-gallant-sail, he raised a gull-like cry in the air, "There she blows!—there she blows! A hump like a snow-hill! It is Moby Dick!"

Fired by the cry which seemed simultaneously taken up by the three look-outs, the men on deck rushed to the rigging to behold the famous whale they had so long been pursuing. Ahab had now gained his final perch, some feet above the other look-outs, Tashtego standing just beneath him on the cap of the top-gallant-mast, so that the Indian's head was almost on a level with Ahab's heel. From this height the whale was now seen some mile or so ahead, at every roll of the sea revealing his high sparkling hump, and regularly jetting his silent spout into the air. To the credulous mariners it seemed the same silent spout they had so long ago beheld in the moonlit Atlantic and Indian Oceans.

"And did none of ye see it before?" cried Ahab, hailing the perched men all around him.

"I saw him almost that same instant, sir, that Captain Ahab did, and I cried out," said Tashtego.

"Not the same instant; not the same—no, the doubloon is mine, Fate reserved the doubloon for me. I only; none of ye could have raised the White Whale first. There she blows! there she blows!—there she blows! There again—there again!" he cried, in long-drawn, lingering, methodic tones, attuned to the gradual prolongings of the whale's visible jets. "He's going to sound! In stunsails! Down top-gallant-sails! Stand by three boats. Mr. Starbuck, remember, stay on board, and keep the ship. Helm there! Luff, luff a point! So; steady, man, steady! There go flukes! No, no; only black water! All ready the boats there? Stand by, stand by! Lower me, Mr. Starbuck; lower,

lower,—quick, quicker!" and he slid through the air to the deck.

"He is heading straight to leeward, sir," cried Stubb, "right away from us; cannot have seen the ship yet."

"Be dumb, man! Stand by the braces! Hard down them helm!—brace up! Shiver her!—shiver her! So; well that! Boats, boats!"

Soon all the boats but Starbuck's were dropped; all the boat-sails set—all the paddles plying; with rippling swiftness, shooting to leeward; and Ahab heading the onset. A pale, death-glimmer lit up Fedallah's sunken eyes; a hideous motion gnawed his mouth.

Like noiseless nautilus shells, their light prows sped through the sea; but only slowly they neared the foe. As they neared him, the ocean grew still more smooth; seemed drawing a carpet over its waves; seemed a noon-meadow, so serenely it spread. At length the breathless hunter came so nigh his seemingly unsuspecting prey, that his entire dazzling hump was distinctly visible, sliding along the sea as if an isolated thing, and continually set in a revolving ring of finest, fleecy, greenish foam. He saw the vast, involved wrinkles of the slightly projecting head beyond. Before it, far out on the soft Turkish-rugged waters, went the glistening white shadow from his broad, milky forehead, a musical rippling playfully accompanying the shade; and behind, the blue waters interchangeably flowed over into the moving valley of his steady wake; and on either hand bright bubbles arose and danced by his side. But these were broken again by the light toes of hundreds of gay fowl softly feathering the sea, alternate with their fitful flight; and like to some flag-staff rising from the painted hull of an argosy, the tall but shattered pole of a recent lance projected from the white whale's back; and at intervals one of the cloud of soft-toed fowls hovering, and to and fro skimming like a canopy over the fish, silently perched and rocked on this pole, the long tail feathers streaming like pennons.

A gentle joyousness—a mighty mildness of repose in swiftness, invested the gliding whale. Not the white bull Jupiter swimming away with ravished Europa clinging to his graceful horns; his lovely, leering eyes sideways intent upon the maid; with smooth bewitching fleetness, rippling straight for the nuptial bower in Crete; not Jove, not that great majesty Supreme! did surpass the glorified White Whale as he so divinely swam.

On each soft side—coincident with the parted swell, that but once leaving him, then flowed so wide away—on each bright side, the whale shed off enticings. No wonder there had been some among the hunters who namelessly transported and allured by all this serenity, had ventured to assail it; but had fatally found that quietude but the vesture of tornadoes. Yet calm, enticing calm, oh, whale! thou glidest on, to all who for the first time eye thee, no matter how many in that same way thou may'st have bejuggled and destroyed before.

And thus, through the serene tranquillities of the tropical sea, among waves whose hand-clappings were suspended by exceeding rapture, Moby Dick moved on, still withholding from sight the full terrors of his submerged trunk, entirely hiding the wrenched hideousness of his jaw. But soon the fore part of him slowly rose from the water; for an instant his whole marbleized body formed a high arch, like Virginia's Natural Bridge, and warningly waving his bannered flukes in the air, the grand god revealed himself, sounded, and went out of sight. Hoveringly, halted, and dipping on the wing, the white sea-fowls longingly lingered over the agitated pool that he left.

With oars apeak, and paddles down, the sheets of their sails adrift, the three boats now stilly floated, awaiting Moby Dick's reappearance.

"An hour," said Ahab, standing rooted in his boat's stern; and he gazed beyond the whale's place, toward the dim blue spaces and wide wooing vacancies to leeward. It was only an instant; for again his eyes seemed whirling round in his head as he swept the watery circle. The breeze now freshened; the sea began to swell.

"The birds!—the birds!" cried Tashtego.

In long Indian file, as when herons take wing, the white birds were now all flying towards Ahab's boat; and when within a few yards began fluttering over the water there, wheeling round and round, with joyous, expectant cries. Their vision was keener than man's; Ahab could discover no sign in the sea. But suddenly as he peered down and down into its depths, he profoundly saw a white living spot no bigger than a white weasel, with wonderful celerity uprising, and magnifying as it rose, till it turned, and then there were plainly revealed two long crooked rows of white, glistening teeth, floating up from the undiscoverable bottom. It was Moby Dick's open mouth and scrolled jaw; his vast, shadowed bulk still half blending with the blue of the sea. The glittering mouth yawned beneath the boat like an open-doored marble tomb; and giving one sidelong sweep with his steering oar, Ahab whirled the craft aside from this tremendous apparition. Then, calling upon Fedallah to change places with him, went forward to the bows, and seizing Perth's harpoon, commanded his crew to grasp their oars and stand by to stern.

Now, by reason of this timely spinning round the boat upon its axis, its bow, by anticipation, was made to face the whale's head while yet under water. But as if perceiving this stratagem, Moby Dick, with that malicious intelligence ascribed to him, sidelingly transplanted himself, as it were, in an instant, shooting his pleated head lengthwise beneath the boat.

Through and through; through every plank and each rib, it thrilled for an instant, the whale obliquely lying on his back, in the manner of a biting shark, slowly and feelingly taking its bows full within his mouth, so that the long, narrow, scrolled lower jaw curled high up into the open air, and one of the teeth caught in a row-lock. The bluish pearl-white of the inside of the jaw was within six inches of Ahab's head, and reached higher than that. In this attitude the White Whale now shook the slight cedar as a mildly cruel cat her mouse. With unastonished eyes Fedallah gazed, and crossed his arms; but the tiger-yellow crew were tumbling over each other's heads to gain the uttermost stern.

And now, while both elastic gunwales were springing in and out, as the whale dallied with the doomed craft in this devilish way; and from his body being submerged beneath the boat, he could not be darted at from the bows, for the bows were almost inside of him, as it were; and while the other boats involuntarily paused, as before a quick crisis impossible to withstand, then it was that monomaniac Ahab, furious with this tantalizing vicinity of his foe, which placed him all alive and helpless in the very jaws he hated; frenzied with all this, he seized the long bone with his naked hands, and wildly strove to wrench it from its gripe. As now he thus vainly strove, the jaw slipped from him; the frail gunwales bent in, collapsed, and snapped, as both jaws, like an enormous shears, sliding further aft, bit the craft completely in twain, and locked themselves fast again in the sea, midway between the two floating wrecks. These floated aside, the broken ends drooping, the crew at the stern-wreck clinging to the gunwales, and striving to hold fast to the oars to lash them across.

At that preluding moment, ere the boat was yet snapped, Ahab, the first to perceive the whale's intent, by the crafty upraising of his head, a movement that loosed his hold for the time; at that moment his hand had made one final effort to push the boat out of the bite. But only slipping further into the whale's mouth, and tilting over sideways as it slipped, the boat had shaken off his hold on the jaw; spilled him out of it, as he leaned to the push; and so he fell flat-faced upon the sea.

Rippingly withdrawing from his prey, Moby Dick now lay at a little distance, vertically thrusting his oblong white head up and down in the billows; and at the same time slowly revolving his whole spindled body; so that when his vast wrinkled forehead rose—some twenty or more feet out of the water— the now rising swells, with all their confident waves, dazzlingly broke against it; vindictively tossing their shivered spray still higher into the air.[1] So, in a gale, the but half baffled Channel billows only recoil from the base of the Eddy-stone, triumphantly to overleap its summit with their scud.

But soon resuming his horizontal attitude, Moby Dick swam swiftly round and round the wrecked crew; sideways churning the water in his vengeful wake, as if lashing himself up to still another and more deadly assault. The sight of the splintered boat seemed to madden him, as the blood of grapes and mulberries cast before Antiochus's elephants in the book of Maccabees. Meanwhile Ahab half smothered in the foam of the whale's insolent tail, and too much of a cripple to swim,—though he could still keep afloat, even in the heart of such a whirlpool as that; helpless Ahab's head was seen, like a tossed bubble which the least chance shock might burst. From the boat's fragmentary stern, Fedallah incuriously and mildly eyed him; the clinging crew, at the other drifting end, could not succor him; more than enough was it to look to themselves. For so revolvingly appalling was the White Whale's aspect, and so planetarily swift the ever-contracting circles he made, that he seemed horizontally swooping upon them. And though the other boats unharmed, still hovered hard by; still they dared not pull into the eddy to strike, lest that should be the signal for the instant destruction of the jeopardized castaways, Ahab and all; nor in that case could they themselves hope to escape. With straining eyes, then, they remained on the outer edge of the direful zone, whose centre had now become the old man's head.

Meantime, from the beginning all this had been descried from the ship's mast heads; and squaring her yards, she had borne down upon the scene; and was now so nigh, that Ahab in the water hailed her:—"Sail on the"—but that moment a breaking sea dashed on him from Moby Dick, and whelmed him for the

[1] This motion is peculiar to the sperm whale. It receives its designation (pitchpoling) from its being likened to that preliminary up-and-down poise of the whale-lance, in the exercise called pitchpoling previously described. By this motion the whale must best and most comprehensively view whatever objects may be encircling him.

time. But struggling out of it again, and chancing to rise on a towering crest, he shouted,—"Sail on the whale!—Drive him off!"

The *Pequod's* prows were pointed; and breaking up the charmed circle, she effectually parted the whale from his victim. As he suddenly swam off, the boats flew to the rescue.

Dragged into Stubb's boat with blood-shot, blinded eyes, the white brine caking in his wrinkles; the long tension of Ahab's bodily strength did crack, and helplessly he yielded to his body's doom: for a long time, lying all crushed in the bottom of Stubb's boat, like one trodden under foot of herds of elephants. Far inland, nameless wails came from him, as desolate sounds from out ravines.

But this intensity of his physical prostration did but so much the more abbreviate it. In an instant's compass, great hearts sometimes condense to one deep pang, the sum total of those shallow pains kindly diffused through feebler men's whole lives. And so, such hearts, though summary in each one suffering; still, if the gods decree it, in their life-time aggregate a whole age of woe, wholly made up of instantaneous intensities; for even in their pointless centres, those noble natures contain the entire circumferences of inferior souls.

"The harpoon," said Ahab, half way rising, and draggingly leaning on one bended arm—"is it safe!"

"Aye, sir, for it was not darted; this is it," said Stubb, showing it.

"Lay it before me;—any missing men!"

"One, two, three, four, five;—there were five oars, sir, and here are five men."

"That's good.—Help me, man; I wish to stand. So, so, I see him! there! there! going to leeward still; what a leaping spout! —Hands off from me! The eternal sap runs up in Ahab's bones again! Set the sail; out oars; the helm!"

It is often the case that when a boat is stove, its crew, being picked up by another boat, help to work that second boat; and the chase is thus continued with what is called double-banked oars. It was thus now. But the added power of the boat did not equal the added power of the whale, for he seemed to have treble-banked his every fin; swimming with a velocity which plainly showed, that if now, under these circumstances, pushed on, the chase would prove an indefinitely prolonged, if not a hopeless one; nor could any crew endure for so long a period, such an unintermitted, intense straining at the oar; a thing barely tolerable only in some one brief vicissitude. The ship itself, then, as it sometimes happens, offered the most promising intermediate means of overtaking the chase. Accordingly, the boats now made for her, and were soon swayed up to their cranes—the two parts of the wrecked boat having been previously secured by her—and then hoisting everything to her side, and stacking her canvas high up, and sideways outstretching it with stun-sails, like the double-jointed wings of an albatross; the *Pequod* bore down in the leeward wake of Moby Dick. At the well known, methodic intervals, the whale's glittering spout was regularly announced from the manned mast-heads; and when he would be reported as just gone down, Ahab would take the time, and then pacing the deck, binnacle-watch in hand, so soon as the last second of the allotted hour expired, his voice was heard.—"Whose is the doubloon now? D'ye see him?" and if the reply was, No, sir! straightway he commanded them to lift him to his perch. In this way the day wore on; Ahab, now aloft and motionless; anon, unrestingly pacing the planks.

As he was thus walking, uttering no sound, except to hail the men aloft, or to bid them hoist a sail still higher, or to spread one to a still greater breadth—thus to and fro pacing, beneath his slouched hat, at every turn he passed his own wrecked boat, which had been dropped upon the quarter-deck, and lay there reversed; broken bow to shattered stern. At last he paused before it; and as in an already over-clouded sky fresh troops of clouds will sometimes sail across, so over the old man's face there now stole some such added gloom as this.

Stubb saw him pause; and perhaps intending, not vainly, though, to evince his own unabated fortitude, and thus keep up a valiant place in his Captain's mind, he advanced, and eyeing the wreck exclaimed—"The thistle the ass refused; it pricked his mouth too keenly, sir; ha! ha!"

"What soulless thing is this that laughs before a wreck? Man, man! did I not know thee brave as fearless fire (and as mechanical) I could swear thou wert a poltroon. Groan nor laugh should be heard before a wreck."

"Aye, sir," said Starbuck drawing near, " 'tis a solemn sight; an omen, and an ill one."

"Omen? omen?—the dictionary! If the gods think to speak outright to man, they will honorably speak outright; not shake their heads, and give an old wives' darkling hint.—Begone! Ye two are the opposite poles of one thing; Starbuck is Stubb reversed, and Stubb is Starbuck; and ye two are all mankind; and Ahab stands alone among the millions of the peopled earth, nor gods nor men his neighbors! Cold, cold—I shiver!—How now? Aloft there! D'ye see him? Sing out for every spout, though he spout ten times a second!"

The day was nearly done; only the hem of his golden robe was rustling. Soon, it was almost dark, but the look-out men still remained unset.

"Can't see the spout now, sir;—too dark"—cried a voice from the air.

"How heading when last seen?"

"As before, sir,—straight to leeward."

"Good! he will travel slower now 'tis night. Down royals and top-gallant stun-sails, Mr. Starbuck. We must not run over him before morning; he's making a passage now, and may heave-to a while. Helm there! keep her full before the wind!—Aloft! come down!—Mr. Stubb, send a fresh hand to the foremast head, and see it manned till morning."—Then advancing towards the doubloon in the main-mast—"Men, this gold is mine, for I earned it; but I shall let it abide here till the White Whale is dead; and then, whosoever of ye first raises him, upon the day he shall be killed, this gold is that man's; and if on that day I shall again raise him, then, ten times its sum shall be divided among all of ye! Away now!—the deck is thine, sir."

And so saying, he placed himself half way within the scuttle, and slouching his hat, stood there till dawn, except when at intervals rousing himself to see how the night wore on.

### SECOND DAY

At day-break, the three mast-heads were punctually manned afresh.

"D'ye see him?" cried Ahab, after allowing a little space for the light to spread.

"See nothing, sir."

"Turn up all hands and make sail! he travels faster than I thought for;—the top-gallant sails!—aye, they should have been kept on her all night. But no matter—'tis but resting for the rush."

Here be it said, that this pertinacious pursuit of one particular whale, continued through day into night, and through night into day, is a thing by no means unprecedented in the South Sea fishery. For such is the wonderful skill, prescience of experience, and invincible confidence acquired by some great natural geniuses among the Nantucket commanders; that from the simple observation of a whale when last descried, they will, under certain given circumstances, pretty accurately foretell both the direction in which he will continue to swim for a time, while out of sight, as well as his probable rate of progression during that period. And, in these cases, somewhat as a pilot, when about losing sight of a coast, whose general trending he well knows, and which he desires shortly to return to again, but at some further point; like as this pilot stands by his compass, and takes the precise bearing of the cape at present visible, in order the more certainly to hit aright the remote, unseen headland, eventually to be visited: so does the fisherman, at his compass, with the whale; for after being chased, and diligently marked, through several hours of daylight, then, when night obscures the fish, the creature's future wake through the darkness is almost as established to the sagacious mind of the hunter, as the pilot's coast is to him. So that to this hunter's wondrous skill, the proverbial evanescence of a thing writ in water, a wake, is to all desired purposes well-nigh as reliable as the stead-fast land. And as the mighty iron Leviathan of the modern rail-way is so familiarly known in its every pace, that, with watches in their hands, men time his rate, as doctors that of a baby's pulse; and lightly say of it, the up train or the down train will reach such or such a spot, at such or such an hour; even so, almost, there are occasions when these Nantucketers time that other Leviathan of the deep, according to the observed humor of his speed; and say to themselves, so many hours hence this whale will have gone two hundred miles, will have about reached this or that degree of latitude or longitude. But to render this acuteness at all successful in the end, the wind and the sea must be the whaleman's allies, for of what present avail to the becalmed or windbound mariner is the skill that assures him he is exactly ninety-three leagues and a quarter from his port? Inferable from these statements, are many collateral sub-tile matters touching the chase of whales.

The ship tore on; leaving such a furrow in the sea as when a cannon-ball, missent, becomes a ploughshare and turns up the level field.

"By salt and hemp!" cried Stubb, "but this swift motion of the deck creeps up one's legs and tingles at the heart. This ship and I are two brave fellows!—Ha! ha! Some one take me up, and launch me, spine-wise, on the sea,—for by live-oaks! my spine's a keel. Ha, ha! we go the gait that leaves no dust behind!"

"There she blows—she blows!—she blows!—right ahead!" was now the mast-head cry.

"Aye, aye!" cried Stubb, "I knew it—ye can't escape—blow on and split your spout, O whale! the mad fiend himself is after ye! blow your trump—blister your lungs!—Ahab will dam off your blood, as a miller shuts his water-gate upon the stream!"

And Stubb did but speak out for well-nigh all that crew. The frenzies of the chase had by this time worked them bubblingly up, like old wine worked anew. Whatever pale fears and forebodings some of them might have felt before; these were not only now kept out of sight through the growing awe of Ahab, but they were broken up, and on all sides routed, as timid prairie hares that scatter before the bounding bison. The hand of Fate had snatched all their souls; and by the stirring perils of the previous day; the rack of the past night's suspense; the fixed, unfearing, blind, reckless way in which their wild craft went plunging towards its flying mark; by all these things, their hearts were bowled along. The wind that made great bellies of their sails, and rushed the vessel on by arms invisible as irresistible; this seemed the symbol of that unseen agency which so enslaved them to the race.

They were one man, not thirty. For as the one ship that held them all; though it was put together of all contrasting things—oak, and maple, and pine wood; iron, and pitch, and hemp—yet all these ran into each other in the one concrete hull, which shot on its way, both balanced and directed by the long central keel; even so, all the individualities of the crew, this man's valor, that man's fear; guilt and guiltiness, all varieties were welded into oneness, and were all directed to that fatal goal which Ahab their one lord and keel did point to.

The rigging lived. The mast-heads, like the tops of tall palms, were outspreadingly tufted with arms and legs. Clinging to a spar with one hand, some reached forth the other with impatient wavings; others, shading their eyes from the vivid sunlight, sat far out on the rocking yards; all the spars in full bearing of mortals, ready and ripe for their fate. Ah! how they still strove through that infinite blueness to seek out the thing that might destroy them!

"Why sing ye not out for him, if ye see him?" cried Ahab, when, after the lapse of some minutes since the first cry, no more had been heard. "Sway me up, men; ye have been deceived; not Moby Dick casts one odd jet that way, and then disappears."

It was even so; in their headlong eagerness, the men had mistaken some other thing for the whale-spout, as the event itself soon proved; for hardly had Ahab reached his perch; hardly was the rope belayed to its pin on deck, when he struck the keynote to an orchestra, that made the air vibrate as with the combined discharge of rifles. The triumphant halloo of thirty buckskin lungs was heard, as—much nearer to the ship than the place of the imaginary jet, less than a mile ahead—Moby Dick bodily burst into view! For not by any calm and indolent spoutings! not by the peaceable gush of that mystic fountain in his head, did the White Whale now reveal his vicinity; but by the far more wondrous phenomenon of breaching. Rising with his utmost velocity from the furthest depths, the Sperm Whale thus booms his entire bulk into the pure element of air, and piling up a mountain of dazzling foam, shows his place to the distance of seven miles and more. In those moments, the torn, enraged waves he shakes off, seem his mane; in some cases, this breaching is his act of defiance.

"There she breaches! there she breaches!" was the cry, as in his immeasurable bravadoes the White Whale tossed himself salmon-like to Heaven. So suddenly seen in the blue plain of the sea, and relieved against the still bluer margin of the sky, the spray that he raised, for the moment, intolerably glittered and glared like a glacier; and stood there gradually fading and fading away from its first sparkling intensity, to the dim mistiness of an advancing shower in a vale.

"Aye, breach your last to the sun, Moby Dick!" cried Ahab, "thy hour and thy harpoon are at hand!—Down! down all of ye, but one man at the fore. The boats!—stand by!"

Unmindful of the tedious rope-ladders of the shrouds, the men, like shooting stars, slid to the deck, by the isolated back-stays and halyards; while Ahab, less dartingly, but still rapidly was dropped from his perch.

"Lower away," he cried, so soon as he had reached his boat—a spare one, rigged the afternoon previous. "Mr. Starbuck, the ship is thine—keep away from the boats, but keep near them. Lower, all!"

As if to strike a quick terror into them, by this time being the first assailant himself, Moby Dick had turned, and was now coming for the three crews. Ahab's boat was central; and cheering his men, he told them he would take the whale head-and-head,—that is, pull straight up to his forehead,—a not uncommon thing; for when within a certain limit, such a course excludes the coming onset from the whale's sidelong vision. But ere that close limit was gained, and while yet all three boats were plain as the ship's three masts to his eye; the White Whale churning himself into furious speed, almost in an instant as it were, rushing among the boats with open jaws, and a lashing tail, offered appalling battle on every side; and heedless of the irons darted at him from every boat, seemed only intent on annihilating each separate plank of which those boats were made. But skillfully manoeuvred, incessantly wheeling like trained charges in the field; the boats for a while eluded him; though, at times, but by a plank's breadth; while all the time, Ahab's unearthly slogan tore every other cry but his to shreds.

But at last in his untraceable evolutions, the White Whale so crossed and recrossed, and in a thousand ways entangled the clack of the three lines now fast to him, that they foreshortened, and, of themselves, warped the devoted boats towards the planted irons in him; though now for a moment the whale drew aside a little, as if to rally for a more tremendous charge. Seizing that opportunity, Ahab first paid out more line: and then was rapidly hauling and jerking in upon it again—hoping that way to disencumber it of some snarls—when lo!—a sight more savage than the embattled teeth of sharks!

Caught and twisted—corkscrewed in the mazes of the line, loose harpoons and lances, with all their bristling barbs and points, came flashing and dripping up to the chocks in the bows of Ahab's boat. Only one thing could be done. Seizing the boat-knife, he critically reached within—through—and then, without—the rays of steel; dragged in the line beyond, passed it inboard, to the bowsman, and then, twice sundering the rope near the chocks—dropped the intercepted fagot of steel into the sea; and was all fast again. That instant, the White Whale made a sudden rush among the remaining tangles of the other lines; by so doing, irresistibly dragged the more involved boats of Stubb and Flask towards his flukes; dashed them together like two rolling husks on a surf-beaten beach, and then, diving down into the sea, disappeared in a boiling maelstrom, in which, for a space, the odorous cedar chips of the wrecks danced round and round, like grated nutmeg in a swiftly stirred bowl of punch.

While the two crews were yet circling in the waters, reaching out after the revolving line-tubs, oars, and other floating furniture, while aslope little Flask bobbed up and down like an empty vial, twitching his legs upwards to escape the dreaded jaws of sharks; and Stubb was lustily singing out for some one to ladle him up; and while the old man's line—now parting—admitted of his pulling into the creamy pool to rescue whom he could;—in that wild simultaneousness of a thousand concreted perils,—Ahab's yet unstricken boat seemed drawn up towards Heaven by invisible wires,—as, arrow-like, shooting perpendicularly from the sea, the White Whale dashed his broad forehead against its bottom, and sent it, turning over and over, into the air; till it fell again—gunwale downwards—and Ahab and his men struggled out from under it, like seals from a sea-side cave.

The first uprising momentum of the whale—modifying its direction as he struck the surface—involuntarily launched him along it, to a little distance from the centre of the destruction he had made; and with his back to it, he now lay for a moment slowly feeling with his flukes from side to side; and whenever a stray oar, bit of plank, the least chip or crumb of the boats touched his skin, his tail swiftly drew back, and came sideways smiting the sea. But soon, as if satisfied that his work for that time was done, he pushed his pleated forehead through the ocean, and trailing after him the intertangled lines, continued his leeward way at a traveller's methodic pace.

As before, the attentive ship having descried the whole fight, again came bearing down to the rescue, and dropping a boat, picked up the floating mariners, tubs, oars, and whatever else could be caught at, and safely landed them on her decks. Some sprained shoulders, wrists, and ankles; livid contusions; wrenched harpoons and lances; inextricable intricacies of rope; shattered oars and planks; all these were there; but no fatal or even serious ill seemed to have befallen any one. As with Fedallah the day before, so Ahab was now found grimly clinging to his boat's broken half, which afforded a comparatively easy float; nor did it so exhaust him as the previous day's mishap.

But when he was helped to the deck, all eyes were fastened upon him; as instead of standing by himself he still half-hung upon the shoulder of Starbuck, who had thus far been the foremost to assist him. His ivory leg had been snapped off, leaving but one short sharp splinter.

"Aye, aye, Starbuck, 'tis sweet to lean sometimes, be the leaner who he will; and would old Ahab had leaned oftener than he has."

"The ferrule has not stood, sir," said the carpenter, now coming up; "I put good work into that leg."

"But no bones broken, sir, I hope," said Stubb with true concern.

"Aye! and all splintered to pieces, Stubb!—d'ye see it.— But even with a broken bone, old Ahab is untouched; and I account no living bone of mine one jot more me, than this dead one that's lost. Nor white whale, nor man, nor fiend, can so much as graze old Ahab in his own proper and inaccessible being. Can any lead touch yonder floor, any mast scrape yonder roof?—Aloft there! which way?"

"Dead to leeward, sir."

"Up helm, then; pile on the sail again, ship keepers! down the rest of the spare boats and rig them—Mr. Starbuck away, and muster the boat's crews."

"Let me first help thee towards the bulwarks, sir."

"Oh, oh, oh! how this splinter gores me now! Accursed fate! that the unconquerable captain in the soul should have such a craven mate!"

"Sir?"

"My body, man, not thee. Give me something for a cane—there, that shivered lance will do. Muster the men. Surely I have not seen him yet. By heaven it cannot be!—missing?—quick! call them all."

The old man's hinted thought was true. Upon mustering the company, the Parsee was not there.

"The Parsee!" cried Stubb—"he must have been caught in—"

"The black vomit wrench thee!—run all of ye above, alow, cabin, forecastle—find him—not gone—not gone!"

But quickly they returned to him with the tidings that the Parsee was nowhere to be found.

"Aye, sir," said Stubb—"caught among the tangles of your line—I thought I saw him dragging under."

"*My* line! *my* line? Gone?—gone? What means that little word?—What death-knell rings in it, that old Ahab shakes as if he were the belfry. The harpoon, too!—toss over the litter there,—d'ye see it?—the forged iron, men, the white whale's—no, no, no,—blistered fool! this hand did dart it!—'tis in the fish!—Aloft there! Keep him nailed—Quick!—all hands to the rigging of the boats—collect the oars—harpooners! the irons, the irons! hoist the royals higher—a pull on all the sheets! helm there! steady, steady for your life! I'll ten-times girdle the unmeasured globe; yea and dive straight through it, but I'll slay him yet!"

"Great God! but for one single instant show thyself," cried Starbuck; "never, never wilt thou capture him, old man—In Jesus' name no more of this, that's worse than devil's madness. Two days chased; twice stove to splinters; thy very leg once more snatched from under thee; thy evil shadow gone—all good angels mobbing thee with warnings:—what more wouldst thou have?—Shall we keep chasing this murderous fish till he swamps the last man? Shall we be dragged by him to the bottom of the sea? Shall we be towed by him to the infernal world? Oh, oh,—impiety and blasphemy to hunt him more!"

"Starbuck, of late I've felt strangely moved to thee; ever since that hour we both saw—thou know'st what, in one another's eyes. But in this matter of the whale, be the front of thy face to me as the palm of this hand—a lipless, unfeatured blank. Ahab is for ever Ahab, man. This whole act's immutably decreed. 'Twas rehearsed by thee and me a billion years before this ocean rolled. Fool! I am the Fates' lieutenant; I act under orders. Look thou, underling! that thou obeyest mine.—Stand round me, men. Ye see an old man cut down to the stump; leaning on a shivered lance; propped up on a lonely foot. 'Tis Ahab—his body's part; but Ahab's soul's a centipede, that moves upon a hundred legs. I feel strained, half-stranded, as ropes that tow dismasted frigates in a gale; and I may look so. But ere I break, ye'll hear me crack; and till ye hear *that*, know that Ahab's hawser tows his purpose yet. Believe ye, men, in the things called omens? Then laugh aloud, and cry encore! For ere they drown, drowning things will twice rise to the surface; then rise again, to sink for evermore. So with Moby Dick —two days he's floated—to-morrow will be the third. Aye, men, he'll rise once more,—but only to spout his last! D'ye feel brave, men, brave?"

"As fearless fire," cried Stubb.

"And as mechanical," muttered Ahab. Then as the men went forward, he muttered on:—"The things called omens! And yesterday I talked the same to Starbuck there, concerning my broken boat. Oh! how valiantly I seek to drive out of others' hearts what's clinched so fast in mine!—The Parsee—the Parsee!—gone, gone? and he was to go before:—but still was to be seen again ere I could perish— How's that?—There's a riddle now might baffle all the lawyers backed by the ghosts of the whole line of judges:—like a hawk's beak it pecks my brain. *I'll, I'll* solve it, though!"

When dusk descended, the whale was still in sight to leeward.

So once more the sail was shortened, and everything passed nearly as on the previous night; only, the sound of hammers, and the hum of the grindstone was heard till nearly daylight, as the men toiled by lanterns in the complete and careful rigging of the spare boats and sharpening their fresh weapons for the morrow. Meantime, of the broken keel of Ahab's wrecked craft the carpenter made him another leg; while still as on the night before, slouched Ahab stood fixed within his scuttle; his hid, heliotrope glance anticipatingly gone backward on its dial; sat due eastward for the earliest sun.

### THIRD DAY

The morning of the third day dawned fair and fresh, and once more the solitary night-man at the fore-mast-head was relieved by crowds of the daylight lookouts, who dotted every mast and almost every spar.

"D'ye see him?" cried Ahab; but the whale was not yet in sight.

"In his infallible wake, though; but follow that wake, that's all. Helm there; steady, as thou goest, and hast been going. What a lovely day again! were it a new-made world, and made for a summer-house to the angels, and this morning the first of its throwing open to them, a fairer day could not dawn upon that world. Here's food for thought, had Ahab time to think; but Ahab never thinks; he only feels, feels, feels; *that's* tingling enough for mortal man! to think's audacity. God only has that right and privilege. Thinking is, or ought to be, a coolness and a calmness; and our poor hearts throb, and our poor brains beat too much for that. And yet, I've sometimes thought my brain was very calm—frozen calm, this old skull cracks so, like a glass in which the contents turned to ice, and shiver it. And still this hair is growing now; this moment growing, and the heat must breed it; but no, it's like that sort of common grass that will grow anywhere, between the earthly clefts of Greenland ice or in Vesuvius lava. How the wild winds blow; they whip about me as the torn shreds of split sails lash the tossed ship they cling to. A vile wind that has no doubt blown ere this through prison corridors and cells, and wards of hospitals, and ventilated them, and now comes blowing hither as innocent as fleeces. Out upon it!—it's tainted. Were I the wind, I'd blow no more on such a wicked, miserable world. I'd crawl somewhere to a cave, and slink there. And yet, 'tis a noble and heroic thing, the wind! who ever conquered it? In every fight it has the last and bitterest blow. Run tilting at it, and you but run through it. Ha! a coward wind that strikes stark naked men, but will not stand to receive a single blow. Even Ahab is a braver thing—a nobler thing than *that*. Would now the wind but had a body; but all the things that most exasperate and outrage mortal man, all these things are bodiless, but only bodiless as objects, not as agents. There's a most special, a most cunning, oh, a most malicious difference! And yet, I say again, and swear it now, that there's something all glorious and gracious in the wind. These warm Trade Winds, at least, that in the clear heavens blow straight on, in strong and steadfast, vigorous mildness; and veer not from their mark, however the baser currents of the sea may turn and tack, and mightiest Mississippis of the land swift and swerve about, uncertain where to go at last. And by the eternal Poles! these same Trades that so directly blow my good ship on; these Trades, or something like them—something so unchangeable, and full as strong, blow my keeled soul along! To it! Aloft there! What d'ye see?"

"Nothing, sir."

"Nothing! and noon at hand! The doubloon goes a-begging! See the sun! Aye, aye, it must be so. I've oversailed him. How, got the start? Aye, he's chasing *me* now; not I, *him*—that's bad; I might have known it, too. Fool! the lines—the harpoons he's towing. Aye, aye, I have run him by last night. About! about! Come down, all of ye, but the regular lookouts! Man the braces!"

Steering as she had done, the wind had been somewhat on the *Pequod's* quarter, so that now being pointed in the reverse direction, the braced ship sailed hard upon the breeze as she rechurned the cream in her own white wake.

"Against the wind he now steers for the open jaw," mur-

mured Starbuck to himself, as he coiled the new-hauled main-
brace upon the rail. "God keep us, but already my bones feel
damp within me, and from the inside wet my flesh. I misdoubt
me that I disobey my God in obeying him!"

"Stand by to sway me up!" cried Ahab, advancing to the
hempen basket. "We should meet him soon."

"Aye, aye, sir," and straightway Starbuck did Ahab's bidding, and once more Ahab swung on high.

A whole hour now passed; gold-beaten out to ages. Time
itself now held long breaths with keen suspense. But at last,
some three points off the weather bow, Ahab descried the spout
again, and instantly from the three mast-heads three shrieks
went up as if the tongues of fire had voiced it.

"Forehead to forehead I meet thee, this third time, Moby
Dick! On deck there!—brace sharper up; crowd her into the
wind's eye. He's too far off to lower yet, Mr. Starbuck. The
sails shake! Stand over that helmsman with a top-maul! So, so;
he travels fast, and I must down. But let me have one more good
round look aloft here at the sea; there's time for that. An old,
old sight, and yet somehow so young; aye, and not changed a
wink since I first saw it, a boy, from the sand-hills of Nantucket! The same!—the same!—the same to Noah as to me.
There's a soft shower to leeward. Such lovely leewardings!
They must lead somewhere—to something else than common
land, more palmy than the palms. Leeward! the white whale
goes that way; look to windward, then; the better if the bitterer
quarter. But good bye, good bye, old mast-head! What's this?
—green? aye, tiny mosses in these warped cracks. No such
green weather stains on Ahab's head! There's the difference
now between man's old age and matter's. But aye, old mast, we
both grow old together; sound in our hulls, though, are we not
my ship? Aye, minus a leg, that's all. By heaven this dead wood
has the better of my live flesh every way. I can't compare with
it; and I've known some ships made of dead trees outlast the
lives of men made of the most vital stuff of vital fathers. What's
that he said? he should still go before me, my pilot; and yet to

be seen again? But where? Will I have eyes at the bottom of
the sea, supposing I descend those endless stairs? and all night
I've been sailing from him, wherever he did sink to. Aye, aye,
like many more thou told'st direful truth as touching thyself,
O Parsee; but, Ahab, there thy shot fell short. Good bye, mast-
head—keep a good eye upon the whale, the while I'm gone.
We'll talk to-morrow, nay, to-night, when the white whale
lies down there, tied by head and tail."

He gave the word! and still gazing round him, was steadily
lowered through the cloven blue air to the deck.

In due time the boats were lowered; but as standing in his
shallop's stern, Ahab just hovered upon the point of the descent,
he waved to the mate,—who held one of the tackle-ropes on
deck—and bade him pause.

"Starbuck!"

"Sir?"

"For the third time my soul's ship starts upon this voyage,
Starbuck."

"Aye, sir, thou wilt have it so."

"Some ships sail from their ports, and ever afterwards are
missing, Starbuck!"

"Truth, sir: saddest truth."

"Some men die at ebb tide; some at low water; some at the
full of the flood;—and I feel now like a billow that's all one
crested comb, Starbuck. I am old;—shake hands with me, man."

Their hands met; their eyes fastened; Starbuck's tears the
glue.

"Oh, my captain, my captain!—noble heart—go not—go
not!—see, it's a brave man that weeps; how great the agony of
the persuasion then!"

"Lower away!"—cried Ahab, tossing the mate's arm from
him. "Stand by the crew!"

In an instant the boat was pulling round close under the
stern.

"The sharks! the sharks!" cried a voice from the low cabin-
window there; "O master, my master, come back!"

But Ahab heard nothing; for his own voice was high-lifted then; and the boat leaped on.

Yet the voice spake true; for scarce had he pushed from the ship, when numbers of sharks, seemingly rising from out the dark waters beneath the hull, maliciously snapped at the blades of the oars, every time they dipped in the water; and in this way accompanied the boat with their bites. It is a thing not uncommonly happening to the whale-boats in those swarming seas; the sharks at times apparently following them in the same prescient way that vultures hover over the banners of marching regiments in the east. But these were the first sharks that had been observed by the *Pequod* since the White Whale had been first descried; and whether it was that Ahab's crew were all such tiger-yellow barbarians, and therefore their flesh more musky to the senses of the sharks—a matter sometimes well known to affect them, however it was, they seemed to follow that one boat without molesting the others.

"Heart of wrought steel!" murmured Starbuck, gazing over the side and following with his eyes the receding boat—"canst thou yet ring boldly to that sight?—lowering thy keel among ravening sharks, and followed by them, open-mouthed to the chase; and this the critical third day?—For when three days flow together in one continuous intense pursuit; be sure the first is the morning, the second the noon, and the third the evening and the end of that thing—be that end what it may. Oh! my God! what is this that shoots through me, and leaves me so deadly calm, yet expectant,—fixed at the top of a shudder! Future things swim before me, as in empty outlines and skeletons; all the past is somehow grown dim. Mary, girl! thou fadest in pale glories behind me; boy! I seem to see but thy eyes grown wondrous blue. Strangest problems of life seem clearing; but clouds sweep between—Is my journey's end coming? My legs feel faint; like his who has footed it all day. Feel thy heart,—beats it yet?—Stir thyself, Starbuck!—stave it off— move, move! speak aloud!—Mast-head there. See ye my boy's hand on the hill?—Crazed;—aloft there!—keep thy keenest

eye upon the boats:—mark well the whale!—Ho! again!—
drive off that hawk! see! he pecks—he tears the vane"—pointing to the red flag flying at the main-truck—"Ha! he soars away
with it!—Where's the old man now? see'st thou that sight, oh
Ahab!—shudder, shudder!"

The boats had not gone very far, when by a signal from the
mast-heads—a downward pointed arm, Ahab knew that the
whale had sounded; but intending to be near him at the next
rising, he held on his way a little sideways from the vessel; the
becharmed crew maintaining the profoundest silence, as the
head-beat waves hammered and hammered against the opposing
bow.

"Drive, drive in your nails, oh ye waves! to their uttermost
heads drive them in! ye but strike a thing without a lid; and no
coffin and no hearse can be mine:—and hemp only can kill me!
Ha! ha!"

Suddenly the waters around them slowly swelled in broad
circles; then quickly upheaved, as if sideways sliding from a
submerged berg of ice, swiftly rising to the surface. A low rumbling sound was heard; a subterraneous hum; and then all held
their breaths; as bedraggled with trailing ropes, and harpoons,
and lances, a vast form shot lengthwise, but obliquely from the
sea. Shrouded in a thin drooping veil of mist, it hovered for a
moment in the rainbowed air; and then fell swamping back into
the deep. Crushed thirty feet upwards, the waters flashed for
an instant like heaps of fountains, then brokenly sank in a
shower of flakes, leaving the circling surface creamed like new
milk round the marble trunk of the whale.

"Give way!" cried Ahab to the oarsmen, and the boats darted
forward to the attack; but maddened by yesterday's fresh irons
that corroded in him, Moby Dick seemed combinedly possessed by all the angels that fell from heaven. The wide tiers
of welded tendons overspreading his broad white forehead, beneath the transparent skin, looked knitted together; as head on,
he came churning his tail among the boats; and once more
flailed them apart; spilling out the irons and lances from the

two mates' boats, and dashing in one side of the upper part of their bows, but leaving Ahab's almost without a scar.

While Daggoo and Queequeg were stopping the strained planks; and as the whale swimming out from them, turned, and showed one entire flank as he shot by them again; at that moment a quick cry went up. Lashed round and round to the fish's back; pinioned in the turns upon turns in which, during the past night, the whale had reeled the involutions of the lines around him, the half torn body of the Parsee was seen; his sable raiment frayed to shreds; his distended eyes turned full upon old Ahab.

The harpoon dropped from his hand.

"Befooled, befooled!"—drawing in a long lean breath— "Aye, Parsee! I see thee again.—Aye, and thou goest before; and this, *this* then is the hearse that thou didst promise. But I hold thee to the last letter of thy word. Where is the second hearse? Away, mates, to the ship! those boats are useless now; repair them if ye can in time, and return to me; if not, Ahab is enough to die—Down, men! the first thing that but offers to jump from this boat I stand in, that thing I harpoon. Ye are not other men, but my arms and my legs; and so obey me.—Where's the whale? gone down again?"

But he looked too nigh the boat; for as if bent upon escaping with the corpse he bore, and as if the particular place of the last encounter had been but a stage in his leeward voyage, Moby Dick was now again steadily swimming forward; and had almost passed the ship,—which thus far had been sailing in the contrary direction to him, though for the present her headway had been stopped. He seemed swimming with his utmost velocity, and now only intent upon pursuing his own straight path in the sea.

"Oh! Ahab," cried Starbuck, "not too late is it, even now, the third day, to desist. See! Moby Dick seeks thee not. It is thou, thou, that madly seekest him!"

Setting sail to the rising wind, the lonely boat was swiftly impelled to leeward, by both oars and canvas. And at last when

Ahab was sliding by the vessel, so near as plainly to distinguish Starbuck's face as he leaned over the rail, he hailed him to turn the vessel about, and follow him, not too swiftly, at a judicious interval. Glancing upwards, he saw Tashtego, Queequeg, and Daggoo, eagerly mounting to the three mast-heads; while the oarsmen were rocking in the two staved boats which had but just been hoisted to the side, and were busily at work in repairing them. One after the other, through the portholes, as he sped, he also caught flying glimpses of Stubb and Flack, busying themselves on deck among bundles of new irons and lances. As he saw all this; as he heard the hammers in the broken boats; far other hammers seemed driving a nail into his heart. But he rallied. And now marking that the vane or flag was gone from the main-mast-head, he shouted to Tashtego, who had just gained that perch, to descend again for another flag, and a hammer and nails, and so nail it to the mast.

Whether fagged by the three days' running chase, and the resistance to his swimming in the knotted hamper he bore; or whether it was some latent deceitfulness and malice in him: whichever was true, the White Whale's way now began to abate, as it seemed, from the boat so rapidly nearing him once more; though indeed the whale's last start had not been so long a one as before. And still as Ahab glided over the waves the unpitying sharks accompanied him; and so pertinaciously stuck to the boat; and so continually bit at the plying oars, that the blades became jagged and crunched, and left small splinters in the sea, at almost every dip.

"Heed them not! those teeth but give new rowlocks to your oars. Pull on! 'tis the better rest, the shark's jaw than the yielding water."

"But at every bite, sir, the thin blades grow smaller and smaller!"

"They will last long enough! pull on!—But who can tell" —he muttered—"whether these sharks swim to feast on the whale or on Ahab?—But pull on! Aye, all alive, now—we near him. The helm! take the helm; let me pass,"—and so saying, two of the oarsmen helped him forward to the bows of the still flying boat.

At length as the craft was cast to one side, and ran ranging along with the White Whale's flank, he seemed strangely oblivious of its advance—as the whale sometimes will—and Ahab was fairly within the smoky mountain mist, which, thrown off from the whale's spout, curled round his great, Monadnock rump; he was even thus close to him; when, with body arched back, and both arms lengthwise high-lifted to the poise, he darted his fierce iron, and his far fiercer curse into the hated whale. As both steel and curse sank to the socket, as if sucked into a morass, Moby Dick sideways writhed; spasmodically rolled his nigh flank against the bow, and, without staving a hole in it, so suddenly canted the boat over, that had it not been for the elevated part of the gunwale to which he then clung, Ahab would once more have been tossed into the sea. As it was, three of the oarsmen—who foreknew not the precise instant of the dart, and were therefore unprepared for its effects—these were flung out; but so fell, that, in an instant two of them clutched the gunwale again, and rising to its level on a combining wave, hurled themselves bodily inboard again; the third man helplessly dropping astern, but still afloat and swimming.

Almost simultaneously, with a mighty volition of ungraduated, instantaneous swiftness, the White Whale darted through the weltering sea. But when Ahab cried out to the steersman to take new turns with the line, and hold it so; and commanded the crew to turn round on their seats, and tow the boat up to the mark; the moment the treacherous line felt that double strain and tug, it snapped in the empty air!

"What breaks in me? Some sinew cracks!—'tis whole again; oars! oars! Burst in upon him!"

Hearing the tremendous rush of the sea-crashing boat, the whale wheeled round to present his blank forehead at bay; but in that evolution, catching sight of the nearing black hull of the ship; seemingly seeing in it the source of all his persecutions; bethinking it—it may be—a larger and nobler foe; of a sudden, he bore down upon its advancing prow, smiting his jaws amid fiery showers of foam.

Ahab staggered; his hand smote his forehead. "I grow blind; hands! stretch out before me that I may yet grope my way. Is't night?"

"The whale! The ship!" cried the cringing oarsmen.

"Oars! oars! Slope downwards to thy depths, O sea, that ere it be forever too late, Ahab may slide this last, last time upon his mark! I see: the ship! the ship! Dash on, my men! Will ye not save my ship?"

But as the oarsmen violently forced their boat through the sledge-hammering seas, the before whale-smitten bow-ends of two planks burst through, and in an instant almost, the temporarily disabled boat lay nearly level with the waves; its half-wading, splashing crew, trying hard to stop the gap and bale out the pouring water.

Meantime, for that one beholding instant, Tashtego's mast-head hammer remained suspended in his hand; and the red flag, half-wrapping him as with a plaid, then streamed itself straight out from him, as his own forward-flowing heart; while Starbuck and Stubb, standing upon the bowsprit beneath, caught sight of the down-coming monster just as soon as he.

"The whale, the whale! Up helm, up helm! Oh, all ye sweet powers of air, now hug me close! Let not Starbuck die, if die he must, in a woman's fainting fit. Up helm, I say—ye fools, the jaw! the jaw! Is this the end of all my bursting prayers? all my life-long fidelities? Oh, Ahab, Ahab, lo, thy work. Steady! helmsman, steady. Nay, nay! Up helm again! He turns to meet us! Oh, his unappeasable brow drives on towards one, whose duty tells him he cannot depart. My God, stand by me now!"

"Stand not by me, but stand under me, whoever you are that will now help Stubb; for Stubb, too, sticks here. I grin at thee, thou grinning whale! Who ever helped Stubb, or kept Stubb awake, but Stubb's own unwinking eye? And now poor Stubb goes to bed upon a mattress that is all too soft; would it were stuffed with brushwood! I grin at thee, thou grinning whale!

Look ye, sun, moon, and stars! I call ye assassins of as good a fellow as ever spouted up his ghost. For all that, I would yet ring glasses with ye, would ye but hand the cup! Oh, oh! oh, oh! thou grinning whale, but there'll be plenty of gulping soon! Why fly ye not, O Ahab! For me, off shoes and jacket to it; let Stubb die in his drawers! A most mouldy and over-salted death, though;—cherries! cherries! cherries! Oh, Flask, for one red cherry ere we die!"

"Cherries? I only wish that we were where they grow. Oh, Stubb, I hope my poor mother's drawn my part-pay ere this; if not, few coppers will now come to her, for the voyage is up."

From the ship's bows, nearly all the seamen now hung inactive; hammers, bits of plank, lances, and harpoons, mechanically retained in their hands, just as they had darted from their various employments; all their enchanted eyes intent upon the whale, which from side to side strangely vibrating his predestinating head, sent a broad band of overspreading semicircular foam before him as he rushed. Retribution, swift vengeance, eternal malice were in his whole aspect, and spite of all that mortal man could do, the solid white buttress of his forehead smote the ship's starboard bow, till men and timbers reeled. Some fell flat upon their faces. Like dislodged trucks, the heads of the harpooners aloft shook on their bull-like necks. Through the breach, they heard the waters pour, as mountain torrents down a flume.

"The ship! The hearse!—the second hearse!" cried Ahab from the boat; "its wood could only be American!"

Diving beneath the settling ship, the whale ran quivering along its keel; but turning under water, swiftly shot to the surface again, far off the other bow, but within a few yards of Ahab's boat, where, for a time, he lay quiescent.

"I turn my body from the sun. What ho, Tashtego! let me hear thy hammer. Oh! ye three unsurrendered spires of mine; thou uncracked keel; and only god-bullied hull; thou firm deck, and haughty helm, and Pole-pointed prow,—death-glorious ship! must ye then perish, and without me? Am I cut off from the last fond pride of meanest shipwrecked captains? Oh, lonely death on lonely life! Oh, now I feel my topmost greatness lies in my topmost grief. Ho, ho! from all your furthest bounds, pour ye now in, ye bold billows of my whole foregone life, and top this one piled comber of my death! Towards thee I roll, thou all-destroying but unconquering whale; to the last I grapple with thee; from hell's heart I stab at thee; for hate's sake I spit my last breath at thee. Sink all coffins and all hearses to one common pool! and since neither can be mine, let me then tow to pieces, while still chasing thee, though tied to thee, thou damned whale! *Thus*, I give up the spear!"

The harpoon was darted; the stricken whale flew forward; with igniting velocity the line ran through the groove;—ran foul. Ahab stooped to clear it; he did clear it! but the flying turn caught him round the neck, and voicelessly as Turkish mutes bowstring their victim, he was shot out of the boat, ere the crew knew he was gone. Next instant, the heavy eye-splice in the rope's final end flew out of the stark-empty tub, knocked down an oarsmen, and smiting the sea, disappeared in its depths.

For an instant, the tranced boat's crew stood still; then turned. "The ship! Great God, where is the ship?" Soon they through dim, bewildering mediums saw her sidelong fading phantom, as in the gaseous *Fata Morgana;* only the uppermost masts out of water; while fixed by infatuation, or fidelity, or fate, to their once lofty perches, the pagan harpooners still maintained their sinking lookouts on the sea. And now, concentric circles seized the lone boat itself, and all its crew, and each floating oar, and every lance-pole, and spinning, animate and inanimate, all round and round in one vortex, carried the smallest chip of the *Pequod* out of sight.

But as the last whelmings intermixingly poured themselves over the sunken head of the Indian at the main-mast, leaving a few inches of the erect spar yet visible, together with long streaming yards of the flag, which calmly undulated, with ironical coincidings, over the destroying billows they almost touched;—at that instant, a red arm and a hammer hovered backwardly uplifted in the open air, in the act of nailing the flag faster and yet faster to the subsiding spar. A sky-hawk that tauntingly had followed the main-truck downwards from its natural home among the stars, pecking at the flag, and incommoding Tashtego there; this bird now chanced to intercept its broad fluttering wing between the hammer and the wood; and simultaneously feeling that ethereal thrill, the submerged savage beneath, in his death-gasp, kept his hammer frozen there; and so the bird of heaven, with arch-angelic shrieks, and his imperial beak thrust upwards, and his whole captive form folded in the flag of Ahab, went down with his ship, which, like Satan, would not sink to hell till she had dragged a living part of heaven along with her, and helmeted herself with it.

Now small fowls flew screaming over the yet yawning gulf; a sullen white surf beat against its steep sides; then all collapsed, and the great shroud of the sea rolled on as it rolled five thousand years ago.

# TAMANGO

From "Carmen and Other Stories," BY PROSPER MÉRIMÉE

CAPTAIN LEDOUX was a born sailor. Starting at the bottom, he had worked his way up to the rank of assistant quartermaster. Then, in the battle of Trafalgar, his left hand was wounded and had to be amputated, and he was given an honorable discharge. But the peaceful life of a land-lubber soon grew so tiresome that, when he had a chance to go to sea as second lieutenant on a privateer, he did not hesitate a moment. With his share of the loot from the corsair's prizes, he bought books on navigation and studied them assiduously. Finally, he became captain of a pirate lugger, with a crew of sixty bold men and three guns.

Then came peace with England, and Captain Ledoux was greatly downcast; for he had made a small fortune out of the war and he had counted on increasing it. It was still easy enough for him to get a ship to command—he had a reputation for courage and resourcefulness—but he had to go into the merchant service. When, however, the slave trade was made illegal, he came into his own again. It was a risky business, for it meant eluding both the French and the English officials. Captain Ledoux was just the man for the "ebony" dealers. (Slave traders called themselves by that name.)

Now most men who have started out as simple sailors suffer from a kind of ingrained hatred of the new—a love of the habitual and the familiar which they cannot lose when they reach positions of command. But not Captain Ledoux. It was he who first used metal tanks for fresh water on his ship. The handcuffs and chains, which all slavers must have, he had specially made and painted to prevent rust. And he was famous among the traders for the ship which he designed himself and had built according to his own directions. She was called the *Hope*. Swift, narrow and long like a man-o'-war, she could carry a large number of slaves. Their quarters between decks were just forty inches high. For, said Captain Ledoux, any ordinary black could sit up comfortably in that space, and as for standing—they would get plenty of that when they reached their destination.

The slaves had to sit in two parallel lines, their backs against the sides of the ship. The space between their feet served as a gangway in any other slave ship. But Ledoux conceived the idea of using this empty space by making other slaves sit at right angles to their fellows. Thus he could carry almost a dozen more than any other ship of the same size. If necessary, he could have squeezed in a few more, but he was not unreasonable. He allowed that each black ought to have an area of five by two feet in which to stretch out during the six-week voyage. As an excuse for his generosity, he maintained that blacks were human beings after all.

The *Hope* sailed from Nantes on a Friday—a date which the superstitious afterward remembered. The customs inspectors did not discover aboard her the six big boxes containing chains, handcuffs and the irons which, for some obscure reason, were called "bonds of justice." Nor were they surprised by the *Hope's* large supply of fresh water, although she was supposed to be headed only for Senegambia to take on wood and ebony. It would be a short trip, but they may have thought the water was a cautious provision in case the ship was becalmed.

Well, the *Hope* sailed on a Friday, thoroughly provisioned and equipped. At first Ledoux feared the masts might not be stout enough, but in time the vessel lived up to his hopes entirely. They had a first-rate trip, and soon anchored at Joal on the African coast, a place that the English were not guarding at that moment. The native traders immediately came aboard.

Ledoux had arrived at the right time. Tamango, a notorious warrior and slave dealer, had just reached the coast with a herd of blacks which he was selling off cheaply with the confidence of a man who believes his supply will always equal the demand.

Captain Ledoux came ashore a little way up the river and

called on Tamango. He was sitting in a straw hut, which had been hastily put up, with his two wives, some petty traders and the slave drivers. Tamango had felt obliged to put on some clothes to receive the white captain. The old blue uniform he wore had once belonged to a corporal, but on each shoulder were two gold epaulets, both hooked over the same button and hanging down, one behind, the other in front. The tunic was too small for him and, since he wore no shirt, a wide strip of black skin stretched between the white facings of the tunic and the canvas trousers. It looked like a belt. A heavy cavalry sword hung from a string at his side, and a fine double-barreled English rifle completed his outfit.

Captain Ledoux stared at him in silence. And Tamango, believing that he had made a great impression on the captain, drew himself up like a grenadier being inspected by a strange general. Ledoux examined him critically, then turned to his chief officer and remarked, "There's a piece of brawn that would fetch a thousand crowns if we could only land him safe and sound at Martinique."

With a sailor who had a smattering of the Yolof language as interpreter, they exchanged greetings and sat down. A basket full of bottles of brandy was brought, and they began to drink. Ledoux gave Tamango a handsome copper powder flask with a portrait of Napoleon embossed on it. Tamango accepted it with the customary show of gratitude and suggested that they go and sit in the shade, with the brandy bottle, and inspect the slaves he had for sale.

They filed past in a long line, drooping from fear and weariness. Each one bore on his shoulders a huge wooden fork more than two yards long, the two prongs of which were fastened at the back of the neck with a wooden bar. Whenever they walked, the slave driver carried on his shoulder the handle of the yoke of the first slave who, in turn, bore the yoke-handle of the man behind him. The second carried the handle of the third and so on down the line. When a halt was made, the leader drove the sharp end of his handle into the ground, and the whole column came to a standstill. Naturally, no one could escape with the heavy six-foot yoke around his neck.

The captain shrugged his shoulders as the slaves filed past. They were weaklings, he said; the females were too old or too young; the black race was degenerating.

"It was different in the old days," he complained. "Then all the women were five foot six, and four men could easily have worked a frigate's capstan and raised the sheet anchor."

Nevertheless he critically picked out a few, choosing the strong and good-looking for which he was willing to pay the usual price; on the remainder he demanded a considerable reduction. But Tamango knew his own mind; he insisted that his wares were valuable, and spoke of the scarcity of men and the dangers of the traffic. He ended by quoting the very lowest price he could possibly accept for the slaves the white captain still had room for on board.

Ledoux stared at him in amazement and indignation when he heard Tamango's proposal interpreted. The captain got up, swearing like a trooper, apparently with the intention of putting an end there and then to all bargaining with a man so unreasonable. But Tamango, after some difficulty, persuaded him to sit down. Another bottle was opened and the discussion renewed. Now it was the black man's turn to call the white captain's views outrageous and extravagant.

They talked and haggled as bottle after bottle was emptied; but the liquor was having quite a different effect on the two contracting parties. The more the Frenchman drank the less became his offers, and the more Tamango drank the less he insisted on his demands. So, when the case of brandy was finished, it was found they had come to terms. In exchange for the hundred and sixty slaves, Tamango accepted a quantity of worthless cotton, powder, gun-flints, three casks of brandy, and fifty rusty rifles. Immediately the slaves were handed over to the French sailors, who lost no time in putting on iron chains and handcuffs in place of the wooden yokes—a striking demonstration of the superiority of European civilization.

There were still about thirty slaves—children, old men, or infirm women. But there was no more room on board. Tamango, not knowing what to do with this refuse, offered to sell them to the captain at the rate of a bottle of brandy a head. The offer was a tempting one. Ledoux remembered a performance of the *Sicilian Vespers*, at Nantes, at which he had noticed that a considerable number of sturdy and well-furnished people had managed to push their way into the pit which was already full, and ultimately find seats, thanks to the compressibility of human bodies. He agreed to take the twenty slimmest of the thirty slaves. Tamango then offered to dispose of the ten remaining for a glass of brandy a head. The fact that children go half-price and take up half-room in railway carriages crossed the captain's mind. So he accepted three children, but said he would not take one more. Tamango, seeing himself left still with seven slaves on his hands, seized his rifle and took aim at the nearest woman. She was the mother of three children.

"Buy her," he said to the white man, "or I'll fire. Half a glass of brandy, or she dies."

"But what the deuce am I to do with her?" asked Ledoux.

Tamango fired, and the slave fell down dead.

"Now for another!" cried Tamango, taking aim at a decrepit old man. "A glass of brandy, or—"

The bullet went off at random, for one of his wives had suddenly seized his arm. She had happened to recognize in the old man whom her husband was about to kill a *guiriot*, or magician, who had prophesied that she would be queen.

Tamango, excited by all the brandy he had consumed, lost control of himself when he found himself thwarted. He struck his wife roughly with the butt end of his gun, and turned toward the captain.

"Take her," he said; "I'll make you a present of this woman."

"I shall be able to find room for you," said Ledoux, as he took her by the hand, and he smiled when he saw how beautiful she was.

The interpreter—a charitable man—asked Tamango for the

remaining six slaves in exchange for a cardboard snuffbox. He took off their yokes and told them to go where they liked. They hurried away in different directions, at a loss to know how to reach their homes, two hundred leagues from the coast.

In the meantime the captain had said goodbye to Tamango and was hard at work getting his cargo on board. He did not think it safe to remain longer in the river, for fear of the English cruisers which might return at any moment. So he made up his mind to set sail on the morrow. Tamango could not do anything but lie down on the grass in the shade, and sleep away the effects of the brandy.

When he woke up the vessel was already under sail, and moving down the river. Tamango, still very dizzy from the effects of his recent debauch, called for his wife Ayché. He was reminded that she had been unfortunate enough to displease him, and that he had made a present of her to the white captain who had taken her away on board with him. Half stupefied at this news, Tamango clasped his head in his hands; then, seizing his gun, he rushed away by the most direct route toward a little creek about half a mile from the sea. He knew the river made several detours before it reached the sea, and, by means of a small boat which ought to be there, he hoped to overtake the brig, delayed by the winding river. He was right; he leaped into the boat and just managed to reach the slave ship in time.

Ledoux was surprised to see him; still more so to learn that he wanted his wife back.

"You gave her to me," he said, "and I have no intention of giving you back your present." And he turned and left him.

But the black insisted, said he would give back some of the goods he had received in exchange for the slaves. The captain laughed, and told him that Ayché was a fine woman and that he intended to keep her. Poor Tamango burst into a torrent of tears, and groaned and cried like a man being tortured by a surgeon. He flung himself about the deck calling for his darling Ayché, and dashed his head against the planks as though he were trying to commit suicide. The captain, quite unmoved, pointed to the shore, and suggested that it was time for him to go. But Tamango held to his point. He went to the length of offering his golden epaulettes, his sword, his rifle. All in vain.

Meantime the lieutenant of the *Hope* suggested to the captain, "Why not take this lusty brute in place of the three slaves who died during the night; he is worth more than they."

Ledoux looked at him. Yes. He was worth at least a thousand crowns. Besides, this journey, which promised to be exceptionally remunerative, would probably be his last; his fortune would be made, and he would give up the slave trade. If so, what did it matter what sort of a reputation he left behind on the coast of Guinea? There was not a soul in sight on the shore, and the black chieftain was entirely at his mercy. It would only be a matter of disarming him, for it would hardly be safe to lay hands on him while he still had arms in his possession. So Ledoux asked him for his gun, as if he wished to examine it to see whether it was really worth exchanging for the beautiful Negress. While he was scrutinizing it, he took care to jerk the charge out. The lieutenant succeeded in obtaining his sword, and Tamango stood disarmed. Two sturdy sailors sprang on him, brought him to the ground, and tried to bind him. But the black man struggled heroically as soon as he recovered from the surprise. By sheer strength he sprang to his feet, and with one blow he felled the man who held him by the neck. Leaving half his coat in the hands of the other sailor, he dashed furiously toward the lieutenant to regain his sword, and received a cut on the head which, without going deep, made a large wound. He fell a second time, and the sailors soon bound him hand and foot. He yelled with rage and struggled and writhed like a wild boar caught in a net; after a while, seeing that all resistance was useless, he shut his eyes and remained absolutely motionless. Had it not been for his heavy and hurried breathing, one might have thought him dead.

"Bless my soul!" exclaimed the captain, "won't these slaves he sold to us chuckle when they see him a slave like them! They will begin to think there must be such a thing as Providence."

Meanwhile poor Tamango was bleeding fast. The charitable interpreter, who, the day before, had saved the lives of the six slaves, came to bind up his wound and speak a few words of sympathy with him. Tamango remained as motionless as a corpse. Two sailors carried him like a package down to his allotted place in the 'tween decks. For two days he refused to touch anything to eat or drink, and he scarcely opened his eyes. His companions in captivity, once his prisoners, had watched him brought into their midst with terror-stricken amazement. So great was the awe with which his mere presence still inspired them that not one of them dared jeer at the misery of the man who was the cause of all their suffering.

Sailing rapidly before a strong land breeze, the vessel was soon out of sight of the coast of Africa. The captain's mind, no longer haunted with visions of English cruisers, began to dwell on the prospective fortune he hoped to reap in the colonies toward which he was sailing. His cargo of "ebony" was in good health. There were no contagious diseases. Only twelve Negroes had died of suffocation, and they were the weakest—a mere trifle. But in order to preserve his human cargo as much as possible from the effects of the passage, he had them brought up on deck once a day. Three successive batches of these unhappy slaves came up to inhale, for one hour each batch, the stock of fresh air which was to last through the twenty-four hours. A portion of the crew mounted guard, armed to the teeth for fear of insurrection; but they took care that the slaves were never entirely freed from their shackles. Sometimes a sailor who could play the violin would treat them to some music, and it was curious to watch all those black faces gazing up at the fiddler, gradually losing their look of abject despair, and then breaking forth into loud laughter—clapping their hands too, as much as their chains would allow them. Exercise being essential to health, one of Captain Ledoux's salutary regulations was that all the slaves should be made to dance, just as horses are made to prance when embarked on a long journey.

"Come along, my boys, dance and amuse yourselves!" the

captain would shout in a voice of thunder, cracking his heavy slave-whip. In less than no time the poor blacks were leaping and dancing.

For some time Tamango's wound kept him below the hatches. But at length he appeared on deck; at first he stood in the midst of the crowd of cringing slaves, holding his proud head very high, and his sad but untroubled eyes gazed over the wide expanse of ocean which surrounded the ship; then he lay down, or rather threw himself down on deck, without even troubling to shift his chains into a less awkward position. Ledoux was sitting behind him on the quarterdeck, smoking his pipe at ease. Near him stood Ayché, holding in her hand a tray of liquors which she was ready to pour out for him. Instead of shackles she wore a pretty blue cotton dress and dainty morocco shoes, which clearly showed that she occupied a position of honor in the captain's domestic circle. One of the black men who loathed Tamango pointed her out to him. As soon as he caught sight of her he cried out, and, springing up impetuously, reached the quarterdeck before the sailors on guard could prevent such a flagrant breach of naval discipline.

"Ayché!" he shouted at the top of his voice—and Ayché shrieked as he added, "do you imagine that there is no MAMA JUMBO in the land of the white man?"

The sailors rushed to his side with uplifted clubs, but he calmly folded his arms and walked slowly back to his place, while Ayché burst into a flood of tears, and seemed appalled at his mysterious question.

The interpreter explained what the awful Mama Jumbo was, the very mention of which had roused such terror.

"It is the bogey of the black men," he said. "When a husband is afraid his wife is going to behave as some wives do, as well in France as Africa, he threatens her with Mama Jumbo. I have seen Mama Jumbo with my own eyes, and I understand the trick; but the poor blacks . . . they are so unsophisticated they do not understand anything. Picture to yourself a group of women dancing in an evening—having a *folgar*, as they call it in their dialect—near a thick and somber grove. Suddenly weird music is heard. Not a soul is to be seen, for all the musicians are hidden among the trees. The sounds of the reed flutes, wooden drums, *balafos*, and guitars made of the half of a gourd make a melody calculated to produce the devil himself. No sooner do the women hear the music than they begin to tremble and would run away if their husbands would let them; they know too well what is going to happen. Suddenly a huge white figure as tall as our top-gallant-mast comes stalking out of the wood, with a head as big as a pumpkin, eyes like hawse-holes, and a mouth like the devil's, full of fire. It moves slowly, very slowly, and does not come more than half a cable's length away from the grove. The women shriek and yell like costermongers. It is 'Mama Jumbo.' And then their husbands tell them to confess their sins, for if they do not speak the Mama Jumbo is there to gobble them up alive. Some of the women are foolish enough to acknowledge everything, and their husbands proceed to give them a sound thrashing."

"But what is the white figure, this Mama Jumbo?" asked the captain.

"Why, it's only some Merry Andrew, muffled up in a white sheet, holding up on the end of a stick a hollow gourd, with a lighted candle inside, that serves as a head. It is nothing worse than that, for it does not require much ingenuity to deceive these poor blacks. But, when all's said and done, it's not such a bad invention, this Mama Jumbo of theirs; I wish my wife believed in it."

"If my wife knows nothing of Mistress Jumbo," said Ledoux, "she has met with Master Stick, and she knows well enough what the result would be if she played any pranks with me. We are not a long-suffering family, we Ledoux, and though I have only one fist left, it can still use a rope's-end to some purpose. As to that joker who started the subject of Mama Jumbo, tell him to keep still, and that if he frightens this little woman again I'll have him flogged till his skin changes from black to the color of an underdone beefsteak."

The captain led Ayché down to his room and tried to comfort her, but neither his caresses nor his blows (there was a limit even to the captain's patience) succeeded in pacifying her. Her tears flowed in torrents. Ledoux went up on deck in a bad humor and vented his feelings on the officer on duty concerning the first thing that came uppermost.

During the night, when nearly everyone on board was sound asleep and the men on watch were listening to a low, sad, monotonous chant, which seemed to come from the 'tween decks, they heard the shrill, piercing shriek of a woman. Then they heard Ledoux's fierce voice swearing and threatening, and the sound of his heavy whip echoed through the whole vessel. Then the noise ceased, and all was silent. On the morrow Tamango came on deck, his face disfigured, but still as proud and undaunted as ever.

As soon as Ayché caught sight of him she rushed from the quarter-deck, where she had been sitting by the side of the captain, and fell on her knees before Tamango, exclaiming in a frenzy of despair—

"Forgive me, Tamango, forgive me!"

Tamango looked steadily into her eyes for a minute, and then, seeing that the interpreter was not within earshot, he said "A file!" and, turning his back upon her, lay down on the deck. The captain chid her savagely, even struck her once or twice, and enjoined her never again to speak to her ex-husband. But he had not the least inkling of the meaning of the few words they had exchanged, and he did not ask any questions about them.

Tamango, meanwhile, locked up with the other slaves, continually exhorted them to make one great effort to regain their liberty. He spoke to them of the small number of the white men, and called their attention to the increasing carelessness of their guards; and, without going into details, he promised them that he would find some way of leading them back to their country. He boasted of his knowledge of the occult sciences, for which the black races have great veneration, and declared that any who refused to assist in the attempt would incur the wrath of the devil. All these harangues were delivered in the dialect of the Peules, which was known to most of the slaves, but which the interpreter did not understand. Such was the credit of the dreaded orator, and so inveterate was their habit of obeying him, that his eloquence worked wonders, and he was begged to fix a day for their emancipation long before he had even had time to work out all his plans. So he told the conspirators vaguely that the time was not yet come, and that the devil, who appeared to him at night, had not yet given the word; but he bade them hold themselves in readiness for the first signal. In the meantime he did not lose any opportunity of testing the vigilance of the crew. One day he saw a sailor leaning over the side of the vessel watching a shoal of flying-fish which were following the ship. Tamango took the rifle which had been left standing against the gunwale, and began to handle it, mimicking grotesquely the exercises he had seen the sailors do. The rifle was immediately taken from him, but he had learnt that it was possible to touch a weapon without at once arousing suspicion. When the time came for him to use one in earnest, woe betide the man who tried then to wrest it from him!

One morning Ayché threw him a biscuit, making at the same time a sign which he alone understood. The biscuit contained a small file, and on that tool hung the success of the plot. Tamango took good care not to let his companions see the file; but, when night had fallen, he began to utter unintelligible sounds, accompanied by weird gestures. Gradually he became more and more excited, and the mutterings increased to loud groans. As they listened to the varied intonations of his voice, the slaves felt convinced that he was engaged in an animated conversation with an unseen person. They were all terrified, not doubting that the devil was at that moment in their midst. Tamango put the finishing touch to the scene by exclaiming joyfully—

"Comrades! the spirit which I have conjured has at length

fulfilled his promises, and I hold in my hand the talisman which is to save us. Now you only need to summon up a little courage, and you are free men."

Those near him were allowed to feel the file, and not one of them was sharp enough to suspect that the whole thing was a gross imposture.

At length, after many days of expectation, the great day of liberty and vengeance dawned. The conspirators had been sworn to secrecy by a solemn oath, and the arrangements had been settled after much deliberation. The strongest among those who happened to go on deck at the same time as Tamango were to seize the arms of their guards, some of the others were to go to the captain's room to fetch the arms which were kept there. Those who had succeeded in filing through their handcuffs were to lead the way; but in spite of several nights' persistent toil, the majority of the slaves were still unable to take any active part in the attack. So three lusty Negroes were singled out to slay the man who kept in his pocket the keys of the manacles, and to return at once and unfetter their companions.

That day Captain Ledoux seemed in the best of tempers. Contrary to his usual habits he pardoned a cabin boy who had incurred a flogging. He congratulated the officer of the watch on his seamanship, told the crew he was pleased with their work and promised to give them all a bonus at Martinique, which they would reach very soon. All the sailors at once began to amuse themselves by making plans as to how they would use the bonus. Their thoughts were of brandy and of the swart women of Martinique, when Tamango and his fellow-conspirators were brought up on deck.

They had been careful to file their handcuffs in such a way that nothing was noticeable, but at the same time so that they could break them open easily. Furthermore, they rattled their chains so much that morning, that they seemed to be twice as heavily laden as usual. When they had had time to drink in the air, they all joined hands and began to dance, whilst Tamango intoned his tribal war song which he always used before going

to battle. After they had danced for some time, Tamango, as if
tired out, stretched himself at full length near a sailor who was
leaning back at his ease against the ship's bulwarks; all the others
followed his example, so that every one of the guards was
singled out by the several Negroes.

As soon as he had managed to remove his handcuffs quietly,
Tamango gave a tremendous shout, which was the signal, seized
the sailor near him violently by the legs, threw him head over
heels, and, planting his foot on his stomach, wrenched the gun
away from him and shot the officer of the watch. Simultaneously every other sailor on deck was seized, disarmed, and
forthwith strangled. From all sides came sounds of the struggle.
The boatswain's mate, who had the keys of the handcuffs, was
one of the first victims. In a moment the deck was swarming
with a crowd of Negroes. Those who could not find arms
seized the bars of the capstan or the oars of the gig. The fate
of the white men was already sealed; a few sailors made a show
of resistance on the quarter-deck, but they lacked weapons
and resolution. Ledoux, however, was still alive, and had not
lost any of his courage.

Seeing that Tamango was the soul of the revolt, he hoped
that if he could kill him, short work might be made of his ac-
complices. So he sprang forward, sword in hand, calling to him
at the top of his voice. Tamango lost no time in rushing to the
encounter. The two commanders met in one of the gangways—
one of those narrow passages leading aft from the quarter-deck.
Tamango, holding his gun by the barrel, and using it as a club,
was the first to strike. The white man dexterously avoided the
blow; the butt end of the musket, falling violently on the planks,
was smashed, and the weapon was dashed out of Tamango's
hand. He stood defenceless, and Ledoux advanced with a
diabolical grin. But before he had time to make use of his sword,
Tamango, as agile as the panthers of his native country, sprang
into his adversary's arms and seized the hand which held the
sword. The one strained to hold the sword, the other to wrench
it from him. During this desperate struggle both stumbled, but

the black man fell undermost. Without a moment's hesitation Tamango hugged his adversary with all his strength, and bit his neck with such vehemence that the blood spurted out as it does under the teeth of a lion. The sword slipped from the weakened hand of the captain. Tamango seized it, sprang up, and, his mouth streaming with blood, yelled his triumph as he stabbed his dying enemy through and through.

The victory was complete. The few remaining sailors entreated the Negroes to have pity on them, but all, even the interpreter who had never done them any harm, were mercilessly massacred. The lieutenant fell fighting heroically. He had withdrawn aft, behind one of those small cannons which turn on a pivot, and are loaded with grapeshot. With his left hand he worked the gun and with his right he used the sword so dexterously that he attracted a crowd of Negroes round him. Then he fired the gun into their midst and paved a way with dead and dying. The next moment he was torn to pieces.

When the body of the last white man had been hacked to pieces and thrown overboard the Negroes began to feel that their thirst for vengeance was satiated, and they gazed up at the ship's sails which were swollen by the fresh breeze, and seemed still to obey their oppressors and to carry the conquerors in spite of their triumph to the land of slavery.

"All our labor is lost!" they murmured in their despair. "Will the great fetish of the white men lead us back to our homes now that we have shed the blood of so many of his worshippers?"

Someone suggested that Tamango might be able to make the fetish obey. So they all began to shout for Tamango.

He was in no hurry to hear them. They found him standing in the fore cabin, one hand resting on the captain's bloody sword, the other stretched out to his wife Ayché, who was on her knees kissing it. But the joy of victory could not obliterate a strange look of anxiety which was visible in every line of his face. Less fatuous than the rest, he was better able to understand the difficulties of the situation.

At last he came up on deck, affecting a serenity which he did not feel. Urged by a hundred confused voices to change the course of the vessel, he stalked slowly toward the helm as if to postpone for a while the moment which would determine both for himself and for the others the extent of his power.

Not even the dullest Negro on board had failed to notice the influence exercised on the movements of the ship by a certain wheel and the box fixed in front of it; but the whole mechanism was a profound mystery to them. Tamango examined the compass for some time, moving his lips as if he were reading the characters which were printed on it; then he put his hand to his head and assumed the pensive look of a man doing mental arithmetic. All the Negroes stood round him, their mouths wide open, their eyes one stare, anxiously taking note of his slightest movement. At length, with that mixture of fear and confidence which ignorance inspires, he gave the guiding wheel a tremendous turn.

Like a noble steed which rears when some impudent rider drives in his spurs, the good ship *Hope* plunged into the waves at this unwonted handling, as if she felt insulted and wished to sink together with her stupid pilot. The sails being now entirely at cross purposes with the helm, the ship heeled over so suddenly that it looked as if she were bound to founder. Her long yards soused into the sea; many of the Negroes stumbled and some fell overboard. However, the ship righted herself and stood proudly against the swell, as if to make one last effort to avoid destruction. But there came a sudden gust of wind, and, with a deafening crash, the two masts fell, snapped a few feet above the deck, which was strewn with wreckage and covered with a tangled network of ropes. The terrified Negroes fled below the hatchway howling with fear, but as there was nothing left to catch the breeze, the vessel remained steady and merely rocked to and fro on the billows.

Presently the more daring amongst them came up again and began clearing away the wreckage which encumbered the deck. Tamango remained motionless, leaning on the binnacle, his face buried in his folded arms. Ayché, who was beside him, did not dare to speak. One by one the Negroes approached him; they began to murmur, and soon a torrent of insults and abuse was let loose upon him.

"Traitor! impostor!" they cried, "you are the cause of our ills: you sold us to the white men, you persuaded us to rebel, you boasted your wisdom, you promised to take us back to our homes. We trusted you, fools that we were! and now we have narrowly escaped destruction because you have offended the white man's fetish."

Tamango raised his head proudly, and the Negroes who stood round him slunk back. He picked up two guns, beckoned to his wife to follow him, and strode through the group of men, who made way for him. He went to the bow of the vessel, where he constructed a kind of barricade of planks and barrels; behind this intrenchment he fixed the two muskets in such a way that the bayonets were menacingly prominent. There he sat down and they left him alone.

Some of the Negroes were in tears; others raised their hands to the sky, and called on their own and the white man's fetishes; others knelt down by the compass and wondered at its ceaseless movements, entreating it to take them to their homes again; the remainder lay on the deck in a state of abject despair. Amongst these wretches were women and children shrieking from sheer terror, and a score of wounded men imploring the relief which no one dreamt of bringing them.

All of a sudden a Negro appeared on deck, his face beaming with joy. He came to tell them that he had discovered where the white men stored their brandy; and his excitement and general demeanor clearly showed that he had already helped himself to some. This piece of news silenced for a while the cries of the distracted slaves. They rushed down to the steward's room and gorged the liquor. In about an hour's time they were all dancing and roaring on deck, giving vent to the excesses of brutish drunkenness. The noise of their singing and dancing mingled with the groans and sobs of the wounded. Night fell, and still the orgy continued.

Next morning, when they woke, despair again possessed them. During the night a great number of the wounded had died. The vessel was surrounded by floating corpses, and clouds were lowering over the heavy sea. They held a conference. Several experts in the art of magic, who had not dared speak of their knowledge before for fear of Tamango, now offered their services, and several potent incantations were tried. The failure of each attempt increased their despondency till at length they appealed to Tamango, who was still behind his barricade. After all, he was the wisest of them, and he alone could extricate them from the desperate condition into which he had brought them. An old man approached him with overtures of peace, and begged him to give them his advice. But Tamango, as inexorable as Coriolanus, turned a deaf ear to his entreaties. During the night, in the midst of the tumult, he had fetched a supply of biscuit and salt meat. To all appearance he had no intention of leaving the solitude of his retreat.

There was still plenty of brandy left. That at all events, helped them to forget the sea, slavery and the approach of death. They went to sleep, and in their dreams saw Africa with its forests of gum trees, its thatched huts, and its baobabs, whose foliage shaded whole villages. The orgy of the day before was renewed, and continued for some time. They did nothing but howl and weep and tear their hair, or drink and sleep. Several died of drinking, others jumped into the sea or stabbed themselves.

One morning Tamango left his fort and advanced to the stump of the mainmast.

"Slaves!" he shouted, "the Spirit has appeared to me in a dream and revealed to me the means of helping you to return to your homes. You deserve to be abandoned to your fates, but I pity the women and children who are crying. I pardon you. Listen!"

All the Negroes bowed their heads submissively, and gathered round him.

"Only the white men," continued Tamango, "know the

mystic formulas which guide these massive wooden houses; but we can steer without difficulty those small boats, which are like our own" (he pointed to the sloop and the other ship's boats). "Let us fill them with provisions, set out in them, and row in the direction of the wind. My Master and yours will make it blow in the direction of our homes."

They took his word for it. No plan could have been more reckless. Without any knowledge of the compass, ignorant as to their whereabouts, they could not do anything but row at random. His belief was that by rowing straight ahead they were certain to come, sooner or later, to a land inhabited by black men; for he had heard his mother say that white men lived in their ships, and that black men possessed the earth.

Soon afterward everything was ready to be embarked, but only the sloop and one small boat were found to be serviceable. It was impossible to find room for the eighty Negroes who were still alive, so the sick and wounded had to be abandoned. The majority of them begged to be slain rather than be left.

After endless difficulties the two boats were got under way, so heavily laden that they might at any moment be swamped in such a choppy sea. Tamango and Ayché were in the sloop, which was soon left behind by the other boat—a mere cockboat, and far less overcharged. The wailing of the poor wretches who had been left behind on board the brig was still audible when a big wave suddenly caught the sloop athwart and swamped her. In less than a minute she had disappeared. The smaller boat saw the catastrophe, and immediately the oars were plied with redoubled energy, for fear of having to pick up those who were shipwrecked. Nearly all who were in the sloop were drowned. Only a dozen or so managed to reach the vessel again; amongst whom were Tamango and Ayché. When the sun set they could see the other boat far away on the horizon. No one knows what became of it.

Why should I weary the reader with a revolting description of the tortures of famine? About a score of human beings, crowded together, now tossed about on a stormy sea, now scorched by the fierce heat of the sun, fought daily for what scanty remains of food there were—every scrap of biscuit entailing a fight. . . . The weaker died, not because the stronger killed him, but because he chose to let him expire. After a few days only two were still alive on board the good brig *Hope*—Ayché and Tamango.

One night the sea was rough, the wind blew high, and the darkness was so intense that one end of the ship could not be seen from the other. Ayché lay on a mattress in the captain's room and Tamango sat at her feet. They had not spoken a word for many hours.

"Tamango," murmured Ayché at length, "it is I who have brought all this suffering upon you."

"I do not suffer," he answered quickly, and threw the half-biscuit, which he still had left, on the mattress beside her.

"Keep it yourself," she said gently, returning the biscuit. "I am no longer hungry. Besides, why eat? Is not mine hour come?"

Tamango got up without answering and staggered to the deck, where he sat down against the stump of the mast. His head lolled on his breast, and he began to whistle his tribal war song. Suddenly a loud cry reached his ear in spite of the noise of the tempest; a light flashed; other shouts followed, and a huge black ship glided swiftly past the brig—so close that Tamango could see her yards pass over his head. He only saw two faces in the light of a lantern which hung from a mast. They shouted again; then their vessel, swept along by the storm, disappeared into the darkness. Doubtless the men on watch had caught sight of the disabled hulk, but the violence of the tempest had prevented their tacking. The next moment Tamango saw the flash of a cannon and heard the report; then another flash, but no report; then he saw nothing more. On the morrow not a sail was visible on the horizon. Tamango threw himself down on his mattress and closed his eyes. His wife Ayché had died that night.

I do not know how long it was before an English frigate, the

*Bellona*, sighted a dismasted vessel, to all appearances abandoned by her crew. They sent a sloop alongside and found a Negress dead and a Negro by her side, so haggard and so thin that he looked like a skeleton. He was unconscious, but there was still a breath left in him. The doctor took charge of him and did all he could for him, so that when they reached Kingston, Tamango had regained his health. He was asked to give an account of his adventures, and he told them all he could remember. The Jamaica planters suggested that he should be hung as a rebel, but the governor was a kind-hearted man and took an interest in the Negro, whose crime was, after all, justifiable, since he had but acted in self-defense; and, besides, the men he had murdered were only Frenchmen. He was treated in the same way as the slaves who are found on board a captured slave trader. They set him at liberty—that is to say they made him work for the Government. And he earned three-pence a day besides his keep. One day the colonel of the 75th caught sight of this splendid specimen of a man, and made him a drummer in his regimental band. Tamango learnt a little English, but hardly ever spoke. To make up for that he was always drinking rum or tafia. He died in the hospital of congestion of the lungs.

# THE BATTLE FOR SEVASTOPOL [1]

From "Red Star." BY EUGENE PETROV

THE destroyer *Tashkent* was to run the blockade, reach Sevastopol, unload ammunition, take on board women, children and wounded men. Then, running the blockade again, the ship was to return to its base.

On June 26, the long, narrow, bluish-colored ship sailed from the mainland. Worse weather for running a blockade would be difficult to imagine. The sun was blazing in the clearest of skies; the sea was perfectly smooth, polished to a glassy sheen. It was murderous. I heard someone on the bridge say: "They will attack from the direction of the sun." But everything was quiet for a long time after that. Nothing disturbed the dazzling calm of the blue waters and the blue sky.

The *Tashkent* looked very strange. A year ago, if anyone had told the sailors—who love their elegant ships as a horseman loves his mount—that they would sail on such a vessel, they would have scoffed at the idea. Decks, passages and cabins were crammed with cases and sacks—as if this were not the destroyer *Tashkent*, the finest, swiftest ship of the Black Sea Fleet, but some heavy plodding cargo boat. Passengers on a warship! Could there be anything stranger!

But the Russian people have long since stopped wondering at the oddities of war. The sailors knew that the cases and sacks were needed by the defenders of Sevastopol, that the passengers they were carrying were Red Army men intended to relieve somewhat the desperate position of these heroic defenders.

The men immediately made themselves at home on deck. The sailors watched the Red Army men—Siberians who had never before seen the sea—hastily roll machine guns fore and aft,

[1] Courtesy of Helen Black.

place sub-machine guns along the deck and station themselves so as to be able to shoot in all directions.

"Look at these eagles we are carrying," they said. And at once the sailors and the Red Army men struck up a friendship.

At 4 P. M. the bugle sounded the alarm. A German scout plane appeared in the sky. The bell rang thinly and incessantly, as if someone were pulling a fine copper wire through one's heart. Anti-aircraft guns rattled. The scout plane vanished in the skies. Now hundreds of eyes, aided by field-glasses, range-finders and stereoscopic sights scanned the sky and sea still more intently. In dead silence the ship sped forward to the inevitable encounter.

Fighting began an hour later. We expected an attack by torpedo carriers, but instead came long-range Heinkel bombers. There were thirteen of them. They attacked in turn from the direction of the sun, and when directly over the ship they dropped large caliber bombs. It seemed to me they did it with a kind of leisurely slowness.

Now the success of the cruise, the fate of the ship and the destinies of the men on board were in the hands of one man. The commander of the *Tashkent*, Captain Vasili Yaroshenko, a man of medium stature, broad chested, swarthy, with a jet black mustache, did not leave the bridge. Without any fuss he paced the bridge from right to left, squinting his eyes upward. Then arriving at a decision in some split fraction of a second, he suddenly shouted in a hoarse, overstrained voice: "Helm to port!"

"Aye, helm to port!" repeated the steersman.

From the very moment the battle began, the tall, blue-eyed steersman performed his tasks with especial smartness. Quickly he spun the wheel, sending a shudder throughout the ship's hull. Then a second—which according to vulgar novels must appear an eternity—passed. A muddy white fountain of water and splinters rose to right and left, to fore and aft, of our ship.

"Explosion off leeboard!" reported the signalman.

"Fine," said the commander.

The battle lasted three hours almost without a break. While some Heinkels took turns in bombing the ship, others left for fresh loads of bombs. We longed for darkness as a man in the desert longs for a gulp of water.

On the bridge, Commander Yaroshenko paced tirelessly from right to left, squinting into the sky. Hundreds of eyes followed him. To us he seemed superhuman. Once when he passed me during an interval between two explosions, this superhuman suddenly winked his jet-black eye, showed his white teeth and shouted:

"Like hell they'll get us! I'll cheat them yet!"

He used even stronger language, but not everything a man says at sea during a battle can be printed.

In all, the Germans dropped about forty heavy bombs—one every four minutes. Their aim was very good, for at least ten bombs fell exactly on the spot where we would have been if Commander Yaroshenko had not made a timely maneuver.

At dusk, as the moon rose, the last bomb dropped far off lee-board. Ten or fifteen minutes before that we had watched with pleasure one Heinkel crash into the sea after the setting sun, in a huge cloud of pink smoke.

Night fell; a huge moon floated in the sky. The bombing ceased, the suspense persisted. We were approaching Sevastopol. The dark outline of our ship stood out sharply against the track of the moon. Approximately off Balaclava the signalman shouted:

"Torpedo boats off starboard!"

At night one does not see a torpedo and cannot evade it. We waited, but there was no explosion. Evidently the torpedo missed its mark. The *Tashkent* forged ahead at full speed. No more torpedo boats were to be seen. Probably they fell behind.

Then we saw in the moonlight the patch of rocky land about which the whole Soviet country still thinks with pride and compassion. I know how small the Sevastopol sector of the front was, but my heart missed a beat when I saw it from the sea—it was so very small.

When we moored at the pier and the ship's engines stopped, we heard at once the heavy rumble of incessant cannonading. The Sevastopol cannonade of June, 1942! Commander Yaroshenko did not leave the bridge. In fact, the battle still continued. This was but another stage. We had docked our ship where before the war no one would have dared to take a vessel such as the *Tashkent*, and no captain in the world would have dared to dock.

We must debark men and cargo, take on wounded men and women and children. And this was to be done at such a speed as to enable us to leave while it was still dark.

The commander knew that the Germans would lie in wait for us in the morning, that planes were already being prepared, that bombs were being placed in bomb-racks. Not so bad if these were Heinkels, but what if dive-bombers came?

The commander knew that whatever course he might steer from Sevastopol he would be spotted. An encounter would be unavoidable, and the Germans would do their utmost to destroy us on our way back.

I saw the commander standing on the bridge watching the loading. In the moonlight his face was tense. What was he thinking about as he watched the lightly wounded supporting each other up the gangway, the gravely wounded carried on stretchers, mothers clasping sleeping children to their breasts? The loading went on almost in silence. Everyone spoke in a low voice.

The ship was unloaded and loaded again within two hours. The commander took two thousand people on board. Everyone coming on deck looked up at the bridge, where the commander paced back and forth.

Vasili Yaroshenko knew well what the sinking of a ship at sea is like. He had been in command of a small ship that was sunk by a direct bomb hit. Defending his ship to the last, he was himself gravely wounded. The ship went to the bottom, but Yaroshenko saved the crew. There were no passengers that time.

Now he had passengers—women, children, wounded men.
Now he must save the ship or go to the bottom with her.
At two in the morning the *Tashkent* sailed from Sevastopol.

*The Tashkent reached the mainland safely, but
Eugene Petrov was killed in the line of duty before he
was able to record its return voyage.*

# A DESCENT INTO THE MAELSTRÖM

From "Prose Tales," BY EDGAR ALLAN POE

The ways of God in Nature, as in Providence, are not as *our* ways;
nor are the models that we frame in any way commensurate to the
vastness, profundity, and unsearchableness of His works *which have a
depth in them greater than the well of Democritus.*

JOSEPH GLANVILL.

WE had now reached the summit of the loftiest crag. For some
minutes the old man seemed too much exhausted to speak.

"Not long ago," said he at length, "and I could have guided
you on this route as well as the youngest of my sons; but, about
three years past, there happened to me an event such as never
happened before to mortal man—or, at least, such as no man
ever survived to tell of—and the six hours of deadly terror
which I then endured have broken me up body and soul. You
suppose me a *very* old man—but I am not. It took less than a
single day to change these hairs from a jetty black to white, to
weaken my limbs, and to unstring my nerves, so that I tremble
at the least exertion, and am frightened at a shadow. Do you
know I can scarcely look over this little cliff without getting
giddy?"

The "little cliff," upon whose edge he had so carelessly
thrown himself down to rest that the weightier portion of his
body hung over it, while he was only kept from falling by the
tenure of his elbow on its extreme and slippery edge—this "little
cliff" arose, a sheer unobstructed precipice of black shining
rock, some fifteen or sixteen hundred feet from the world of
crags beneath us. Nothing would have tempted me to be within
half a dozen yards of its brink. In truth so deeply was I excited
by the perilous position of my companion, that I fell at full
length upon the ground, clung to the shrubs around me, and

dared not even glance upward at the sky—while I struggled in vain to divest myself of the idea that the very foundations of the mountain were in danger from the fury of the winds. It was long before I could reason myself into sufficient courage to sit up and look out into the distance.

"You must get over these fancies," said the guide, "for I have brought you here that you might have the best possible view of the scene of that event I mentioned—and to tell you the whole story with the spot just under your eye."

"We are now," he continued, in that particularising manner which distinguished him—"we are now close upon the Norwegian coast—in the sixty-eighth degree of latitude—in the great province of Nordland—and in the dreary district of Lofoden. The mountain upon whose top we sit is Helseggen, the Cloudy. Now raise yourself up a little higher—hold on to the grass if you feel giddy—so—and look out, beyond the belt of vapour beneath us, into the sea."

I looked dizzily, and beheld a wide expanse of ocean, whose waters wore so inky a hue as to bring at once to my mind the Nubian geographer's account of the *Mare Tenebrarum*. A panorama more deplorably desolate no human imagination can conceive. To the right and left, as far as the eye could reach, there lay outstretched, like ramparts of the world, lines of horridly black and beetling cliff, whose character of gloom was but the more forcibly illustrated by the surf which reared high up against it its white and ghastly crest, howling and shrieking for ever. Just opposite the promontory upon whose apex we were placed, and at a distance of some five or six miles out at sea, there was visible a small, bleak-looking island; or, more properly, its position was discernible through the wilderness of surge in which it was enveloped. About two miles nearer the land, arose another of smaller size, hideously craggy and barren, and encompassed at various intervals by a cluster of dark rocks.

The appearance of the ocean, in the space between the more distant island and the shore, had something very unusual about

it. Although, at the time, so strong a gale was blowing landward that a brig in the remote offing lay to under a double-reefed trysail, and constantly plunged her whole hull out of sight, still there was here nothing like a regular swell, but only a short, quick, angry cross dashing of water in every direction—as well in the teeth of the wind as otherwise. Of foam there was little except in the immediate vicinity of the rocks.

"The island in the distance," resumed the old man, "is called by the Norwegians Vurrgh. The one midway is Moskoe. That a mile to the northward is Ambaaren. Yonder are Islesen, Hotholm, Keildhelm, Suarven, and Buckholm. Further off—between Moskoe and Vurrgh—are Otterholm, Flimen, Sandflesen, and Stockholm. These are the true names of the places—but why it has been thought necessary to name them at all, is more than either you or I can understand. Do you hear anything? Do you see any change in the water?"

We had now been about ten minutes upon the top of Helseggen, to which we had ascended from the interior of Lofoden, so that we had caught no glimpse of the sea until it had burst upon us from the summit. As the old man spoke, I became aware of a loud and gradually increasing sound, like the moaning of a vast herd of buffaloes upon an American prairie; and at the same moment I perceived that what seamen term the *chopping* character of the ocean beneath us, was rapidly changing into a current which set to the eastward. Even while I gazed, this current acquired a monstrous velocity. Each moment added to its speed—to its headlong impetuosity. In five minutes the whole sea as far as Vurrgh, was lashed into ungovernable fury; but it was between Moskoe and the coast that the main uproar held its sway. Here the vast bed of the waters seamed and scarred into a thousand conflicting channels, burst suddenly into frenzied convulsion—heaving, boiling, hissing—gyrating in gigantic and innumerable vortices, and all whirling and plunging on to the eastward with a rapidity which water never elsewhere assumes, except in precipitous descents.

In a few minutes more, there came over the scene another radical alteration. The general surface grew somewhat more smooth, and the whirlpools, one by one, disappeared, while prodigious streaks of foam became apparent where none had been seen before. These streaks, at length, spreading out to a great distance, and entering into combination, took unto themselves the gyratory motion of the subsided vortices, and seemed to form the germ of another more vast. Suddenly—very suddenly—this assumed a distinct and definite existence, in a circle of more than a mile in diameter. The edge of the whirl was represented by a broad belt of gleaming spray; but no particle of this slipped into the mouth of the terrific funnel, whose interior, as far as the eye could fathom it, was a smooth, shining, and jet-black wall of water, inclined to the horizon at an angle of some forty-five degrees, speeding dizzily round and round with a swaying and sweltering motion, and sending forth to the winds an appalling voice, half shriek, half roar, such as not even the mighty cataract of Niagara ever lifts up in its agony to Heaven.

The mountain trembled to its very base, and the rock rocked. I threw myself upon my face, and clung to the scant herbage in an excess of nervous agitation.

"This," said I at length, to the old man—"this *can* be nothing else than the great whirlpool of the Maelström."

"So it is sometimes termed," said he. "We Norwegians call it the Moskoe-ström, from the island of Moskoe in the midway."

The ordinary account of this vortex had by no means prepared me for what I saw. That of Jonas Ramus, which is perhaps the most circumstantial of any, cannot impart the faintest conception either of the magnificence, or of the horror of the scene—or of the wild bewildering sense of *the novel* which confounds the beholder. I am not sure from what point of view the writer in question surveyed it, nor at what time; but it could neither have been from the summit of Helseggen, nor during a storm. There are some passages of his description, neverthe-

less, which may be quoted for their details, although their effect is exceedingly feeble in conveying an impression of the spectacle.

"Between Lofoden and Moskoe," he says, "the depth of the water is between thirty-six and forty fathoms; but on the other side, toward Ver (Vurrgh) this depth decreases so as not to afford a convenient passage for a vessel, without the risk of splitting on the rocks, which happens even in the calmest weather. When it is flood, the stream runs up the country between Lofoden and Moskoe with a boisterous rapidity; but the roar of its impetuous ebb to the sea is scarce equalled by the loudest and most dreadful cataracts; the noise being heard several leagues off, and the vortices or pits are of such an extent and depth, that if a ship comes within its attraction, it is inevitably absorbed and carried down to the bottom, and there beat to pieces against the rocks; and when the water relaxes, the fragments thereof are thrown up again. But these intervals of tranquillity are only at the turn of the ebb and flood, and in calm weather, and last but a quarter of an hour, its violence gradually returning. When the stream is most boisterous, and its fury heightened by a storm, it is dangerous to come within a Norway mile of it. Boats, yachts, and ships have been carried away by not guarding against it before they were carried within its reach. It likewise happens frequently, that whales come too near the stream, and are overpowered by its violence; and then it is impossible to describe their howlings and bellowings in their fruitless struggles to disengage themselves. A bear once, attempting to swim from Lofoden to Moskoe, was caught by the stream and borne down, while he roared terribly, so as to be heard on shore. Large stocks of firs and pine trees, after being absorbed by the current, rise again broken and torn to such a degree as if bristles grew upon them. This plainly shows the bottom to consist of craggy rocks, among which they are whirled to and fro. This stream is regulated by the flux and reflux of the sea—it being constantly high and low water every six hours. In the year 1645, early in the morning of Sexagesima

Sunday, it raged with such noise and impetuosity that the very stones of the houses on the coast fell to the ground."

In regard to the depth of the water, I could not see how this could have been ascertained at all in the immediate vicinity of the vortex. The "forty fathoms" must have reference only to portions of the channel close upon the shore either of Moskoe or Lofoden. The depth in the centre of the Moskoe-ström must be unmeasurably greater; and no better proof of this fact is necessary than can be obtained from even the sidelong glance into the abyss of the whirl which may be had from the highest crag of Helseggen. Looking down from this pinnacle upon the howling Phlegethon below, I could not help smiling at the simplicity with which the honest Jonas Ramus records, as a matter difficult of belief, the anecdotes of the whales and the bears, for it appeared to me, in fact, a self-evident thing, that the largest ships of the line in existence, coming within the influence of that deadly attraction, could resist it as little as a feather the hurricane, and must disappear bodily and at once.

The attempts to account for the phenomenon—some of which, I remember, seemed to me sufficiently plausible in perusal—now wore a very different and unsatisfactory aspect. The idea generally received is that this, as well as three smaller vortices among the Ferroe Islands, "have no other cause than the collision of waves rising and falling, at flux and reflux, against a ridge of rocks and shelves, which confines the water so that it precipitates itself like a cataract; and thus the higher the flood rises, the deeper must the fall be, and the natural result of all is a whirlpool or vortex, the prodigious suction of which is sufficiently known by lesser experiments."—These are the words of the *Encyclopædia Britannica*. Kircher and others imagine that in the centre of the channel of the Maelström is an abyss penetrating the globe, and issuing in some very remote part—the Gulf of Bothnia being somewhat decidedly named in one instance. This opinion, idle in itself, was the one to which, as I gazed, my imagination most readily assented; and, mentioning it to the guide, I was rather surprised to hear him say that, although it was the view almost universally entertained of the subject by the Norwegians, it nevertheless was not his own. As to the former nation he confessed his inability to comprehend it; and here I agreed with him—for, however conclusive on paper, it becomes altogether unintelligible, and even absurd, amid the thunder of the abyss.

"You have had a good look at the whirl now," said the old man, "and if you creep round this crag, so as to get in its lee, and deaden the roar of the water, I will tell you a story that will convince you I ought to know something of the Moskoe-ström."

I placed myself as desired, and he proceeded.

"Myself and my two brothers once owned a schooner-rigged smack of about seventy tons burthen, with which we were in the habit of fishing among the islands beyond Moskoe, nearly to Vurrgh. In all violent eddies at sea there is good fishing, at proper opportunities, if one has only the courage to attempt it: but among the whole of the Lofoden coastmen, we three were the only ones who made a regular business of going out to the islands, as I tell you. The usual grounds are a great way lower down to the southward. There fish can be got at all hours, without much risk, and therefore these places are preferred. The choice spots over here among the rocks, however, not only yield the finest variety, but in far greater abundance; so that we often got in a single day, what the more timid of the craft could not scrape together in a week. In fact, we made it a matter of desperate speculation—the risk of life standing instead of labour, and courage answering for capital.

"We kept the smack in a cove about five miles higher up the coast than this; and it was our practice, in fine weather, to take advantage of the fifteen minutes' slack to push across the main channel of the Moskoe-ström, far above the pool, and then drop down upon anchorage somewhere near Otterholm, or Sand-flesen, where the eddies are not so violent as elsewhere. Here we used to remain until nearly time for slack-water again, when we weighed and made for home. We never set out upon this

expedition without a steady side wind for going and coming—
one that we felt sure would not fail us before our return—and
we seldom made a miscalculation upon this point. Twice, during six years, we were forced to stay all night at anchor on
account of a dead calm, which is a rare thing indeed just about
here; and once we had to remain on the grounds nearly a week,
starving to death, owing to a gale which blew up shortly after
our arrival, and made the channel too boisterous to be thought
of. Upon this occasion we should have been driven out to sea
in spite of everything (for the whirlpools threw us round and
round so violently, that, at length, we fouled our anchor and
dragged it) if it had not been that we drifted into one of the
innumerable cross currents—here to-day and gone to-morrow
—which drove us under the lee of Flimen, where, by good
luck, we brought up.

"I could not tell you the twentieth part of the difficulties we
encountered 'on the ground'—it is a bad spot to be in, even in
good weather—but we make shift always to run the gauntlet of
the Moskoe-ström itself without accident: although at times my
heart has been in my mouth when we happened to be a minute
or so behind or before the slack. The wind sometimes was not
as strong as we thought it at starting, and then we made rather
less way than we could wish, while the current rendered the
smack unmanageable. My eldest brother had a son eighteen
years old, and I had two stout boys of my own. These would
have been of great assistance at such times, in using the sweeps
as well as afterward in fishing—but, somehow, although we ran
the risk ourselves, we had not the heart to let the young ones
get into the danger—for, after all said and done, it *was* a horrible danger, and that is the truth.

"It is now within a few days of three years since what I am
going to tell you occurred. It was on the tenth of July, 18—,
a day which the people of this part of the world will never forget—for it was one in which blew the most terrible hurricane
that ever came out of the heavens. And yet all the morning, and
indeed until late in the afternoon, there was a gentle and steady

breeze from the south-west, while the sun shone brightly, so that the oldest seaman among us could not have foreseen what was to follow.

"The three of us—my two brothers and myself—had crossed over to the islands about two o'clock p. m., and soon nearly loaded the smack with fine fish, which, we all remarked, were more plenty that day than we had ever known them. It was just seven, *by my watch*, when we weighed and started for home, so as to make the worst of the Ström at slack water, which we knew would be at eight.

"We set out with a fresh wind on our starboard quarter, and for some time spanked along at a great rate, never dreaming of danger, for indeed we saw not the slightest reason to apprehend it. All at once we were taken aback by a breeze from over Helseggen. This was most unusual—something that had never happened to us before—and I began to feel a little uneasy, without exactly knowing why. We put the boat on the wind, but could make no headway at all for the eddies, and I was upon the point of proposing to return to the anchorage, when, looking astern, we saw the whole horizon covered with a singular copper-coloured cloud that rose with the most amazing velocity.

"In the meantime the breeze that had headed us off fell away and we were dead becalmed, drifting about in every direction. This state of things, however, did not last long enough to give us time to think about it. In less than a minute the storm was upon us—in less than two the sky was entirely overcast—and what with this and the driving spray, it became suddenly so dark that we could not see each other in the smack.

"Such a hurricane as then blew it is folly to attempt describing. The oldest seaman in Norway never experienced anything like it. We had let our sails go by the run before it cleverly took us; but, at the first puff, both our masts went by the board as if they had been sawed off—the mainmast taking with it my youngest brother, who had lashed himself to it for safety.

"Our boat was the lightest feather of a thing that ever sat

upon water. It had a complete flush deck, with only a small hatch near the bow, and this hatch it had always been our custom to batten down when about to cross the Ström, by way of precaution against the chopping seas. But for this circumstance we should have foundered at once—for we lay entirely buried for some moments. How my elder brother escaped destruction I cannot say, for I never had an opportunity of ascertaining. For my part, as soon as I had let the foresail run, I threw myself flat on deck, with my feet against the narrow gunwale of the bow, and with my hands grasping a ring-bolt near the foot of the foremast. It was mere instinct that prompted me to do this—which was undoubtedly the very best thing I could have done—for I was too much flurried to think.

"For some moments we were completely deluged, as I say, and all this time I held my breath, and clung to the bolt. When I could stand it no longer I raised myself upon my knees, still keeping hold with my hands, and thus got my head clear. Presently our little boat gave herself a shake, just as a dog does in coming out of the water, and thus rid herself, in some measure, of the seas. I was now trying to get the better of the stupor that had come over me, and to collect my senses so as to see what was to be done, when I felt somebody grasp my arm. It was my elder brother, and my heart leaped for joy, for I had made sure that he was overboard—but the next moment all this joy was turned into horror—for he put his mouth close to my ear, and screamed out the word '*Moskoe-ström!*'

"No one ever will know what my feelings were at that moment. I shook from head to foot as if I had had the most violent fit of the ague. I knew what he meant by that one word well enough—I knew what he wished to make me understand. With the wind that now drove us on, we were bound for the whirl of the Ström, and nothing could save us!

"You perceive that in crossing the Ström *channel*, we always went a long way up above the whirl, even in the calmest weather, and then had to wait and watch carefully for the slack —but now we were driving right upon the pool itself, and in such a hurricane as this! 'To be sure,' I thought, 'we shall get there just about the slack—there is some little hope in that'—but in the next moment I cursed myself for being so great a fool as to dream of hope at all. I knew very well that we were doomed, had we been ten times a ninety-gun ship.

"By this time the first fury of the tempest had spent itself, or perhaps we did not feel it so much, as we scudded before it, but at all events the seas, which at first had been kept down by the wind, and lay flat and frothing, now got up into absolute mountains. A singular change, too, had come over the heavens. Around in every direction it was still as black as pitch, but nearly overhead there burst out, all at once, a circular rift of clear sky—as clear as I ever saw—and of a deep bright blue—and through it there blazed forth the full moon with a lustre that I never before knew her to wear. She lit up everything about us with the greatest distinctness—but, oh God, what a scene it was to light up.

"I now made one or two attempts to speak to my brother—but in some manner which I could not understand, the din had so increased that I could not make him hear a single word, although I screamed at the top of my voice in his ear. Presently he shook his head, looking as pale as death, and held up one of his fingers, as if to say '*listen!*'

"At first I could not make out what he meant—but soon a hideous thought flashed upon me. I dragged my watch from its fob. It was not going. I glanced at its face by the moonlight, and then burst into tears as I flung it far away into the ocean. *It had run down at seven o'clock! We were behind the time of the slack, and the whirl of the Ström was in full fury!*

"When a boat is well built, properly trimmed, and not deep laden, the waves in a strong gale, when she is going large, seem always to slip from beneath her—which appears strange to a landsman—and this is what is called *riding*, in sea phrase.

"Well, so far we had ridden the swells very cleverly; but presently a gigantic sea happened to take us right under the counter, and bore us with it as it rose—up—up—as if into the sky. I would not have believed that any wave could rise so high. And then down we came with a sweep, a slide, and a plunge that made me feel sick and dizzy, as if I was falling from some lofty mountain-top in a dream. But while we were up I had thrown a quick glance around—and that one glance was all-sufficient. I saw our exact position in an instant. The Moskoe-ström whirlpool was about a quarter of a mile dead ahead—but no more like the every-day Moskoe-ström than the whirl, as you now see it, is like a mill-race. If I had not known where we were, and what we had to expect, I should not have recognised the place at all. As it was, I involuntarily closed my eyes in horror. The lids clenched themselves together as if in a spasm.

"It could not have been more than two minutes afterwards until we suddenly felt the waves subside, and were enveloped in foam. The boat made a sharp half turn to larboard, and then shot off in its new direction like a thunderbolt. At the same moment the roaring noise of the water was completely drowned in a kind of shrill shriek—such a sound as you might imagine given out by the water-pipes of many thousand steam-vessels letting off their steam all together. We were now in the belt of surf that always surrounds the whirl; and I thought, of course, that another moment would plunge us into the abyss, down which we could only see indistinctly on account of the amazing velocity with which we were borne along. The boat did not seem to sink into the water at all, but to skim like an air-bubble upon the surface of the surge. Her starboard side was next the whirl, and on the larboard arose the world of ocean we had left. It stood like a huge writhing wall between us and the horizon.

"It may appear strange, but now, when we were in the very jaws of the gulf, I felt more composed than when we were only approaching it. Having made up my mind to hope no more, I got rid of a great deal of that terror which unmanned me at first. I suppose it was despair that strung my nerves.

"It may look like boasting—but what I tell you is truth—I

began to reflect how magnificent a thing it was to die in such a manner, and how foolish it was in me to think of so paltry a consideration as my own individual life, in view of so wonderful a manifestation of God's power. I do believe that I blushed with shame when this idea crossed my mind. After a little while I became possessed with the keenest curiosity about the whirl itself. I positively felt a *wish* to explore its depths, even at the sacrifice I was going to make; and my principal grief was that I should never be able to tell my old companions on shore about the mysteries I should see. These, no doubt, were singular fancies to occupy a man's mind in such extremity— and I have often thought since, that the revolutions of the boat around the pool might have rendered me a little light-headed.

"There was another circumstance which tended to restore my self-possession; and this was the cessation of the wind, which could not reach us in our present situation—for, as you saw for yourself, the belt of the surf is considerably lower than the general bed of the ocean, and this latter now towered above us, a high, black, mountainous ridge. If you have never been at sea in a heavy gale, you can form no idea of the confusion of mind occasioned by the wind and spray together. They blind, deafen, and strangle you, and take away all power of action or reflection. But we were now, in a great measure, rid of these annoyances—just as death-condemned felons in prison are allowed petty indulgences, forbidden them while their doom is yet uncertain.

"How often we made the circuit of the belt it is impossible to say. We careered round and round for perhaps an hour, flying rather than floating, getting gradually more and more into the middle of the surge, and then nearer and nearer to its horrible inner edge. All this time I had never let go of the ring-bolt. My brother was at the stern, holding on to a small empty water-cask which had been securely lashed under the coop of the counter, and was the only thing on deck that had not been swept overboard when the gale first took us. As we approached the brink of the pit he let go his hold upon this, and made for the ring, from which, in the agony of his terror, he endeavoured to force my hands, as it was not large enough to afford us both a secure grasp. I never felt deeper grief than when I saw him attempt this act—although I knew he was a madman when he did it—a raving maniac through sheer fright. I did not care, however, to contest the point with him. I knew it could make no difference whether either of us held on at all; so I let him have the bolt, and went astern to the cask. This there was no great difficulty in doing; for the smack flew round steadily enough, and upon an even keel—only swaying to and fro with the immense sweeps and swelters of the whirl. Scarcely had I secured myself in my new position, when we gave a wild lurch to starboard, and rushed headlong into the abyss. I muttered a hurried prayer to God, and thought all was over.

"As I felt the sickening sweep of the descent, I had instinctively tightened my hold upon the barrel, and closed my eyes. For some seconds I dared not open them—while I expected instant destruction, and wondered that I was not already in my death-struggles with the water. But moment after moment elapsed. I still lived. The sense of falling had ceased; and the motion of the vessel seemed much as it had been before, while in the belt of foam, with the exception that she now lay more along. I took courage and looked once again upon the scene.

"Never shall I forget the sensation of awe, horror, and admiration with which I gazed about me. The boat appeared to be hanging, as if by magic, midway down, upon the interior surface of a funnel vast in circumference, prodigious in depth, and whose perfectly smooth sides might have been mistaken for ebony, but for the bewildering rapidity with which they spun around, and for the gleaming and ghastly radiance they shot forth, as the rays of the full moon, from that circular rift amid the clouds which I have already described, streamed in a flood of golden glory along the black walls, and far away down into the inmost recesses of the abyss.

"At first I was too much confused to observe anything accurately. The general burst of terrific grandeur was all that I beheld. When I recovered myself a little, however, my gaze fell instinctively downward. In this direction I was able to obtain an unobstructed view, from the manner in which the smack hung on the inclined surface of the pool. She was quite upon an even keel—that is to say, her deck lay in a plane parallel with that of the water—but this latter sloped at an angle of more than forty-five degrees, so that we seemed to be lying upon our beam ends. I could not help observing, nevertheless, that I had scarcely more difficulty in maintaining my hold and footing in this situation, than if we had been upon a dead level; and this, I suppose, was owing to the speed at which we revolved.

"The rays of the moon seemed to search the very bottom of the profound gulf: but still I could make out nothing distinctly on account of a thick mist in which everything there was enveloped, and over which there hung a magnificent rainbow, like that narrow and tottering bridge which Mussulmans say is the only pathway between Time and Eternity. This mist, or spray, was no doubt occasioned by the clashing of the great walls of the funnel, as they all met together at the bottom—but the yell that went up to the heavens from out of that mist I dare not attempt to describe.

"Our first slide into the abyss itself, from the belt of foam above, had carried us to a great distance down the slope; but our further descent was by no means proportionate. Round and round we swept—not with any uniform movement—but in dizzying swings and jerks, that sent us sometimes only a few hundred yards—sometimes nearly the complete circuit of the whirl. Our progress downward, at each revolution, was slow, but very perceptible.

"Looking about me upon the wide waste of liquid ebony on which we were thus borne, I perceived that our boat was not the only object in the embrace of the whirl. Both above and below us were visible fragments of vessels, large masses of building-timber and trunks of trees, with many smaller articles, such as pieces of house furniture, broken boxes, barrels and

staves. I have already described the unnatural curiosity which
had taken the place of my original terrors. It appeared to grow
upon me as I drew nearer and nearer to my dreadful doom. I
now began to watch, with a strange interest, the numerous
things that floated in our company. I *must* have been delirious,
for I even sought *amusement* in speculating upon the relative
velocities of their several descents toward the foam below.
'This fir-tree,' I found myself at one time saying, 'will certainly
be the next thing that takes the awful plunge and disappears,'
—and then I was disappointed to find that the wreck of a Dutch
merchant ship overtook it and went down before. At length,
after making several guesses of this nature, and being deceived
in all—this fact—the fact of my invariable miscalculation, set
me upon a train of reflection that made my limbs again tremble,
and my heart beat heavily once more.

"It was not a new terror that thus affected me, but the dawn
of a more exciting *hope*. This hope arose partly from memory,
and partly from present observation. I called to mind the great
variety of buoyant matter that strewed the coast of Lofoden,
having been absorbed and then thrown forth by the Moskoe-
ström. By far the greater number of the articles were shattered
in the most extraordinary way—so chafed and roughened as
to have the appearance of being stuck full of splinters—but
then I distinctly recollected that there were *some* of them
which were not disfigured at all. Now I could not account for
this difference except by supposing that the roughened fragments were the only ones which had been *completely absorbed*
—that the others had entered the whirl at so late a period of the
tide, or, from some reason, had descended so slowly after entering, that they did not reach the bottom before the turn of the
flood came, or of the ebb, as the case might be. I conceived it
possible, in either instance, that they might thus be whirled up
again to the level of the ocean, without undergoing the fate
of those which had been drawn in more early or absorbed more
rapidly. I made, also, three important observations. The first
was, that as a general rule, the larger the bodies were, the more

rapid their descent—the second, that, between two masses of
equal extent, the one spherical, and the other *of any other
shape*, the superiority in speed of descent was with the sphere
—the third, that, between two masses of equal size, the one
cylindrical, and the other of any other shape, the cylinder was
absorbed the more slowly. Since my escape, I have had several
conversations on this subject with an old school-master of the
district; and it was from him that I learned the use of the words
'cylinder' and 'sphere.' He explained to me—although I have
forgotten the explanation—how what I observed was, in fact,
the natural consequence of the forms of the floating fragments
—and showed me how it happened that a cylinder, swimming
in a vortex, offered more resistance to its suction, and was
drawn in with greater difficulty than an equally bulky body,
of any form whatever.[1]

"There was one startling circumstance which went a great
way in enforcing these observations, and rendering me anxious
to turn them to account, and this was that, at every revolution,
we passed something like a barrel, or else the yard or the mast
of a vessel, while many of these things, which had been on our
level when I first opened my eyes upon the wonders of the
whirlpool, were now high up above us, and seemed to have
moved but little from their original station.

"I no longer hesitated what to do. I resolved to lash myself
securely to the water-cask upon which I now held, to cut it
loose from the counter, and to throw myself with it into the
water. I attracted my brother's attention by signs, pointed to
the floating barrels that came near us, and did everything in my
power to make him understand what I was about to do. I
thought at length that he comprehended my design—but,
whether this was the case or not, he shook his head despairingly,
and refused to move from his station by the ring-bolt. It was
impossible to reach him; the emergency admitted of no delay;
and so, with a bitter struggle, I resigned him to his fate, fastened

[1] See Archimedes, "*De Incidentibus in Fluido*," lib. 2.

myself to the cask by means of the lashings which secured it to the counter, and precipitated myself with it into the sea, without another moment's hesitation.

"The result was precisely what I hoped it might be. As it is myself who now tell you this tale—as you see that I *did* escape —and as you are already in possession of the mode in which this escape was effected, and must therefore anticipate all that I have farther to say—I will bring my story quickly to conclusion. It might have been an hour, or thereabouts, after my quitting the smack, when, having descended to a vast distance beneath me, it made three or four wild gyrations in rapid succession and, bearing my loved brother with it, plunged headlong, at once and for ever, into the chaos of foam below. The barrel to which I was attached sunk very little further than half the distance between the bottom of the gulf and the spot at which I leaped overboard, before a great change took place in the character of the whirlpool. The slope of the sides of the vast funnel became momently less and less steep. The gyrations of the whirl grew, gradually, less and less violent. By degrees, the froth and the rainbow disappeared, and the bottom of the gulf seemed slowly to uprise. The sky was clear, the winds had gone down, and the full moon was setting radiantly in the west, when I found myself on the surface of the ocean, in full view of the shores of Lofoden, and above the spot where the pool of the Moskoe-ström *had been*. It was the hour of the slack—but the sea still heaved in mountainous waves from the effects of the hurricane. I was borne violently into the channel of the Ström, and in a few minutes, was hurried down the coast into the "grounds" of the fishermen. A boat picked me up—exhausted from fatigue—and (now that the danger was removed) speechless from the memory of its horror. Those who drew me on board were my old mates and daily companions—but they knew me no more than they would have known a traveller from the spirit-land. My hair, which had been raven black the day before, was as white as you see it now. They say too that the whole expression of my countenance had changed. I told them my story—they did not believe it. I now tell it to *you*— and I can scarcely expect you to put more faith in it than did the merry fishermen of Lofoden."

# THE *REVENGE*

BY Sir Walter Raleigh, with introduction and final note
BY James Anthony Froude

In August, 1591, Lord Thomas Howard, with six English line-of-battle ships, six victuallers, and two or three pinnaces, was lying at anchor under the Island of Florez. Light in ballast and short of water, with half his men disabled by sickness, Howard was unable to pursue the aggressive purpose on which he had been sent out. Several of the ships' crews were on shore; the ships themselves "all pestered and rommaging," with everything out of order. In this condition they were surprised by a Spanish fleet consisting of fifty-three men-of-war. Eleven out of the twelve English ships obeyed the signal of the admiral, to cut or weigh their anchors, and escape as they might. The twelfth, the *Revenge*, was unable for the moment to follow. Of her crew of 190, ninety were sick on shore, and, from the position of the ship, there was some delay and difficulty in getting them on board. The *Revenge* was commanded by Sir Richard Grenville, of Bideford, a man well known in the Spanish seas, and the terror of the Spanish sailors; so fierce he was said to be, that mythic stories passed from lip to lip about him, and, like Earl Talbot or Cœur de Lion, the nurses at the Azores frightened children with the sound of his name. "He was of great revenues, of his own inheritance," they said, "but of unquiet mind, and greatly affected to wars"; and from his uncontrollable propensities for blood-eating, he had volunteered his services to the Queen; "of so hard a complexion was he, that I (John Huighen von Linschoten, who is our authority here, and who was with the Spanish fleet after the action) have been told by divers credible persons who stood and beheld him, that he would carouse three or four glasses of wine, and take the glasses between his teeth and crush them in pieces and swallow them down." Such Grenville was to the Spaniard. To the English he was a goodly and gallant gentleman, who had never turned his back upon an enemy, and was remarkable in that remarkable time for his constancy and daring. In this surprise at Florez he was in no haste to fly. He first saw all his sick on board and stowed away on the ballast; and then, with no more than 100 men left him to fight and work the ship, he deliberately weighed, uncertain, as it seemed at first, what he intended to do. The Spanish fleet were by this time on his weather bow, and he was persuaded (we here take his cousin Raleigh's beautiful narrative, and follow it in Raleigh's words) "to cut his mainsail and cast about, and trust to the sailing of the ship":—

"But Sir Richard utterly refused to turn from the enemy, alledging that he would rather choose to die than to dishonour himself, his country, and her Majesty's ship, persuading his company that he would pass through their two squadrons in spite of them, and enforce those of Seville to give him way: which he performed upon diverse of the foremost, who, as the mariners term it, sprang their luff, and fell under the lee of the *Revenge*. But the other course had been the better, and might right well have been answered in so great an impossibility of prevailing: notwithstanding, out of the greatness of his mind, he could not be persuaded.

"The wind was light; the *San Philip*, a huge 'high-carged ship' of 1500 tons, came up to winward of him, and, taking the wind out of his sails, ran aboard him.

"After the *Revenge* was entangled with the *San Philip*, four others boarded her, two on her larboard and two on her starboard. The fight thus beginning at three o'clock in the afternoon continued very terrible all that evening. But the great *San Philip*, having received the lower tier of the *Revenge*, shifted herself with all diligence from her sides, utterly misliking her first entertainment. The Spanish ships were filled with soldiers, in some 200, besides the mariners, in some 500, in others 800. In ours there were none at all, besides the mariners, but the servants of the commander and some few voluntary gentlemen only. After many enterchanged vollies of great ordnance and small shot, the Spaniards deliberated to enter the *Revenge*, and made divers attempts, hoping to force her by the multitude of their armed soldiers and musketeers; but were still repulsed again and again, and at all times beaten back into their own ship or into the sea. In the beginning of the fight the *George Noble*, of London, having received some shot through her by the Armadas, fell under the lee of the *Revenge*, and asked Sir Richard what he would command him; but being one of the victuallers, and of small force, Sir Richard bade him save himself, and leave him to his fortune."

This last was a little touch of gallantry, which we should be glad to remember with the honour due to the brave English sailor who commanded the *George Noble;* but his name has passed away, and his action is an *In Memoriam*, on which time has effaced the writing. All that August night the fight continued, the stars rolling over in their sad majesty, but unseen through the sulphurous clouds which hung over the scene. Ship after ship of the Spaniards came on upon the *Revenge*, so that never less than two mighty galleons were at her side and aboard her, washing up like waves upon a rock, and falling foiled and shattered back amidst the roar of the artillery. Before morning fifteen several Armadas had assailed her, and all in vain; some had been sunk at her side, and the rest, "so ill approving of their entertainment, that at break of day they were far more willing to hearken to a composition, than hastily to make more assaults or entries." "But as the day increased," says Raleigh, "so our men decreased; and as the light grew more and more, by so much the more grew our discomfort, for none appeared in sight but enemies, save one small ship called the *Pilgrim*, commanded by Jacob Whiddon, who hovered all night to see the success, but in the morning, bearing with the *Revenge*, was hunted like a hare among many ravenous hounds —but escaped."

"All the powder in the *Revenge* was now spent, all her pikes

were broken, forty out of her hundred men killed, and a great
number of the rest wounded. Sir Richard, though badly hurt
early in the battle, never forsook the deck till an hour before
midnight; and was then shot through the body while his wounds
were being dressed, and again in the head. His surgeon was
killed while attending on him; the masts were lying over the
side, the rigging cut or broken, the upper works all shot in
pieces, and the ship herself, unable to move, was settling slowly
in the sea; the vast fleet of Spaniards lying round her in a ring,
like dogs round a dying lion, and wary of approaching him in
his last agony. Sir Richard, seeing that it was past hope, having
fought for fifteen hours, and 'having by estimation eight hundred shot of great artillery through him,' 'commanded the
master gunner, whom he knew to be a most resolute man, to
split and sink the ship, that thereby nothing might remain of
glory or victory to the Spaniards; seeing in so many hours they
were not able to take her, having had above fifteen hours' time,
above ten thousand men, and fifty-three men-of-war to perform it withal; and persuaded the company, or as many as he
could induce, to yield themselves unto God and to the mercy
of none else; but as they had, like valiant resolute men, repulsed
so many enemies, they should not now shorten the honour of
their nation by prolonging their own lives for a few hours or
a few days.'

"The gunner and a few others consented. But such δαιμονίη
ἀρετή [1] was more than could be expected of ordinary seamen.
They had dared do all which did become men, and they were
not more than men. Two Spanish ships had gone down, above
1500 of their crew were killed, and the Spanish admiral could
not induce any one of the rest of his fleet to board the *Revenge*
again, 'doubting lest Sir Richard would have blown up himself
and them, knowing his dangerous disposition.' Sir Richard lying disabled below, the captain, 'finding the Spaniards as ready
to entertain a composition as they could be to offer it,' gained
over the majority of the surviving company; and the remainder

[1] Superhuman courage.

then drawing back from the master gunner, they all, without further consulting their dying commander, surrendered on honourable terms. If unequal to the English in action, the Spaniards were at least as courteous in victory. It is due to them to say, that the conditions were faithfully observed, and 'the ship being marvellous unsavourie,' Alonzo de Baçan, the Spanish admiral, sent his boat to bring Sir Richard on board his own vessel.

"Sir Richard, whose life was fast ebbing away, replied that 'he might do with his body what he list, for that he esteemed it not'; and as he was carried out of the ship he swooned, and reviving again, desired the company to pray for him.

"The admiral used him with all humanity, 'commending his valour and worthiness, being unto them a rare spectacle, and a resolution seldom approved.' The officers of the fleet, too, John Higgins tells us, crowded round to look at him; and a new fight had almost broken out between the Biscayans and the 'Portugals,' each claiming the honour of having boarded the *Revenge*.

"In a few hours Sir Richard, feeling his end approaching, showed not any sign of faintness, but spake these words in Spanish, and said, 'Here die I, Richard Grenville, with a joyful and quiet mind, for that I have ended my life as a true soldier ought to do that hath fought for his country, queen, religion, and honour. Whereby my soul most joyfully departeth out of this body, and shall always leave behind it an everlasting fame of a valiant and true soldier that hath done his duty as he was bound to do.' When he had finished these or other such like words, he gave up the ghost with great and stout courage, and no man could perceive any sign of heaviness in him."

Such was the fight at Florez, in that August of 1591; without its equal in such of the annals of mankind as the thing which we call history has preserved to us; scarcely equalled by the most glorious fate which the imagination of Barrère could invent for the *Vengeur*.[2] Nor did the matter end without a sequel

[2] The gallant antagonist of the *Brunswick* in the "Glorious First of June," 1794.

awful as itself. Sea battles have been often followed by storms, and without a miracle; but with a miracle, as the Spaniards and the English alike believed, or without one, as we moderns would prefer believing, "there ensued on this action a tempest so terrible as was never seen or heard the like before." A fleet of merchantmen joined the Armada immediately after the battle, forming in all 140 sail; and of these 140, only 32 ever saw Spanish harbour. The rest foundered, or were lost on the Azores. The men-of-war had been so shattered by shot as to be unable to carry sail; and the *Revenge* herself, disdaining to survive her commander, or as if to complete his own last baffled purpose, like Samson, buried herself and her two hundred prize crew under the rocks of St. Michael's.

And the stately Spanish men to their flagship bore him then,
Where they laid him by the mast, old Sir Richard caught at last,
And they praised him to his face with their courtly foreign grace;
But he rose upon their decks, and he cried:
"I have fought for Queen and Faith like a valiant man and true;
I have only done my duty as a man is bound to do:
With a joyful spirit I, Sir Richard Grenville, die!"
And he fell upon their decks and he died.—Tennyson.

# THE MERCHANTMAN AND THE PIRATE

From "Hard Cash," BY CHARLES READE

NORTH Latitude 23½, Longitude East 113; the time March of this same year; the wind southerly; the port Whampoa in the Canton River. Ships at anchor reared their tall masts here and there; and the broad stream was enlivened and colored by junks and boats of all sizes and vivid hues, propelled on the screw principle by a great scull at the stern, with projecting handles for the crew to work; and at times a gorgeous mandarin boat, with two great glaring eyes set in the bows, came flying, rowed with forty paddles by an armed crew, whose shields hung on the gunwale and flashed fire in the sunbeams; the mandarin, in conical and buttoned hat, sitting on the top of his cabin calmly smoking Paradise, alias opium, while his gong boomed and his boat flew fourteen miles an hour, and all things scuttled out of his celestial way. And there, looking majestically down on all these water ants, the huge *Agra*, cynosure of so many loving eyes and loving hearts in England, lay at her moorings; homeward bound.

Her tea not being yet on board, the ship's hull floated high as a castle, and to the subtle, intellectual, doll-faced, bolus-eyed people, that sculled to and fro, busy as bees, though looking forked mushrooms, she sounded like a vast musical shell: for a lusty harmony of many mellow voices vibrated in her great cavities, and made the air ring cheerily around her. The vocalists were the Cyclops, to judge by the tremendous thumps that kept clean time to their sturdy tune. Yet it was but human labor, so heavy and so knowing, that it had called in music to help. It was the third mate and his gang completing his floor to receive the coming tea chests. Yesterday he had stowed his dunnage, many hundred bundles of light flexible canes from

Sumatra and Malacca; on these he had laid tons of rough salt-petre, in 200 lb. gunny-bags: and was now mashing it to music, bags and all. His gang of fifteen, naked to the waist, stood in line, with huge wooden beetles, called commanders, and lifted them high and brought them down on the nitre in cadence with true nautical power and unison. . . .

When the saltpetre was well mashed, they rolled ton water-butts on it, till the floor was like a billiard table. A fleet of chop boats then began to arrive, so many per day, with the tea chests. Mr. Grey proceeded to lay the first tier on his salt-petre floor, and then built the chests, tier upon tier, beginning at the sides, and leaving in the middle a lane somewhat nar-rower than a tea chest. Then he applied a screw jack to the chests on both sides, and so enlarged his central aperture, and forced the remaining tea chests in; and behold the enormous cargo packed as tight as ever shopkeeper packed a box—19,806 chests, 60 half chests, 50 quarter chests.

While Mr. Grey was contemplating his work with singular satisfaction, a small boat from Canton came alongside, and Mr. Tickell, midshipman, ran up the side, skipped on the quarter-deck, saluted it first, and then the first mate; and gave him a line from the captain, desiring him to take the ship down to Second Bar—for her water—at the turn of the tide.

Two hours after receipt of this order the ship swung to the ebb. Instantly Mr. Sharpe unmoored, and the *Agra* began her famous voyage, with her head at right angles to her course; for the wind being foul, all Sharpe could do was to set his topsails, driver, and jib, and keep her in the tide way, and clear of the numerous craft, by backing or filling as the case required; which he did with considerable dexterity, making the sails steer the helm for the nonce: he crossed the Bar at sunset, and brought to with the best bower anchor in five fathoms and a half. Here they began to take in their water, and on the fifth day the six-oared gig was ordered up to Canton for the captain. The next afternoon he passed the ship in her, going down the river, to Lin Tin, to board the Chinese admiral for his

chop, or permission to leave China. All night the *Agra* showed
three lights at her mizzen peak for him, and kept a sharp lookout. But he did not come: he was having a very serious talk with
the Chinese admiral; at daybreak, however, the gig was reported in sight: Sharpe told one of the midshipmen to call the
boatswain and man the side. Soon the gig ran alongside; two
of the ship's boys jumped like monkeys over the bulwarks,
lighting, one on the main channels, the other on the midship
port, and put the side ropes assiduously in the captain's hands;
he bestowed a slight paternal smile on them, the first the imps
had ever received from an officer, and went lightly up the
sides. The moment his foot touched the deck, the boatswain
gave a frightful shrill whistle; the men at the sides uncovered,
the captain saluted the quarter-deck, and all the officers saluted
him, which he returned, and stepping for a moment to the
weather side of his deck, gave the loud command, "All hands
heave anchor." He then directed Mr. Sharpe to get what sail
he could on the ship, the wind being now westerly, and dived
into his cabin.

The boatswain piped three shrill pipes, and "All hands up
anchor" and thrice repeated forward, followed by private ad-
monitions, "Rouse and bitt!" "Show a leg!" etc., and up tumbled the crew with "homeward bound" written on their tanned
faces.

(Pipe.) "Up all hammocks!"

In ten minutes the ninety and odd hammocks were all stowed
neatly in the netting, and covered with a snowy hammock
cloth; and the hands were active, unbitting the cable, shipping
the capstan bars, etc.

"All ready below, sir," cried a voice.

"Man the bars," returned Mr. Sharpe from the quarter-deck.
"Play up, fifer. Heave away!"

Out broke the merry fife with a rhythmical tune, and tramp,
tramp, tramp went a hundred and twenty feet round and
round, and, with brawny chests pressed tight against the capstan bars, sixty fine fellows walked the ship up to her anchor,

drowning the fife at intervals with their sturdy song, as pat
to their feet as an echo:

> Heave with a will ye jolly boys,
> Heave around:
> We're off from Chainee, jolly boys,
> Homeward bound.

"Short stay apeak, sir," roars the boatswain from forward.
"Unship the bars. Way aloft. Loose sails. Let fall!"
The ship being now over her anchor, and the topsails set,
the capstan bars were shipped again, the men all heaved with
a will, the messenger grinned, the anchor was torn out of China
with a mighty heave, and then run up with a luff tackle and
secured; the ship's head cast to port:
"Up with a jib! man the topsail halyards! all hands make
sail!" Round she came slow and majestically; the sails filled,
and the good ship bore away for England.
She made the Bogue forts in three or four tacks, and there
she had to come to again for another chop, China being a place
as hard to get into as Heaven, and to get out of as—Chancery.
At three P. M. she was at Macao, and hove to four miles from
the land, to take in her passengers.
A gun was fired from the forecastle. No boats came off.
Sharpe began to fret: for the wind, though light, had now got
to the N.W., and they were wasting it. After a while the captain came on deck, and ordered all the carronades to be scaled.
The eight heavy reports bellowed the great ship's impatience
across the water, and out pulled two boats with the passengers. While they were coming, Dodd sent and ordered the gunner to load the carronades with shot, and secure and apron
them. . . .
The *Agra* had already shown great sailing qualities: the log
was hove at sundown and gave eleven knots; so that with a
good breeze abaft few fore-and-aft-rigged pirates could overhaul her. And this wind carried her swiftly past one nest of
them at all events; the Ladrone Isles. At nine P. M. all the lights

were ordered out. Mrs. Beresford had brought a novel on board, and refused to comply; the master-at-arms insisted; she threatened him with the vengeance of the Company, the premier, and the nobility and gentry of the British realm. The master-at-arms, finding he had no chance in argument, doused the glim—pitiable resource of a weak disputant—then basely fled the rhetorical consequences.

The northerly breeze died out, and light variable winds baffed the ship. It was the 6th April ere she passed the Macclesfield Bank in latitude 16. And now they sailed for many days out of sight of land; Dodd's chest expanded: his main anxiety at this part of the voyage lay in the state cabin; of all the perils of the sea none shakes a sailor like fire. He set a watch day and night on that spoiled child.

On the 1st of May they passed the great Nantuna, and got among the Bornese and Malay Islands: at which the captain's glass began to sweep the horizon again: and night and day at the dizzy foretop-gallant-masthead he perched an eye.

They crossed the line in longitude 107, with a slight breeze, but soon fell into the Doldrums. A dead calm, and nothing to do but kill time. . . .

After lying a week like a dead log on the calm but heaving waters came a few light puffs in the upper air and inflated the topsails only: the ship crawled southward, the crew whistling for wind.

At last, one afternoon, it began to rain, and after the rain came a gale from the eastward. The watchful skipper saw it purple the water to windward, and ordered the topsails to be reefed and the lee ports closed. This last order seemed an excess of precaution; but Dodd was not yet thoroughly acquainted with his ship's qualities: and the hard cash round his neck made him cautious. The lee ports were closed, all but one, and that was lowered. Mr. Grey was working a problem in his cabin, and wanted a little light and a little air, so he just dropped his port; but, not to deviate from the spirit of his captain's instructions, he fastened a tackle to it; that he might have mechanical force to close it with should the ship lie over.

Down came the gale with a whoo, and made all crack. The ship lay over pretty much, and the sea poured in at Mr. Grey's port. He applied his purchase to close it. But though his tackle gave him the force of a dozen hands, he might as well have tried to move a mountain: on the contrary, the tremendous sea rushed in and burst the port wide open. Grey, after a vain struggle with its might, shrieked for help; down tumbled the nearest hands, and hauled on the tackle in vain. Destruction was rushing on the ship, and on them first. But meantime the captain, with a shrewd guess at the general nature of the danger he could not see, had roared out, "Slack the main sheet!" The ship righted, and the port came flying to, and terror-stricken men breathed hard, up to their waists in water and floating boxes. Grey barred the unlucky port, and went aft, drenched in body, and wrecked in mind, to report his own fault. He found the captain looking grim as death. He told him, almost crying, what he had done, and how he had miscalculated the power of the water.

Dodd looked and saw his distress. "Let it be a lesson, sir," said he, sternly. "How many ships have been lost by this in fair weather, and not a man saved to tell how the craft was fooled away?"

"Captain, bid me fling myself over the side, and I'll do it."

"Humph! I'm afraid I can't afford to lose a good officer for a fault he—will—never—repeat."

It blew hard all night and till twelve the next day. The *Agra* showed her weak point: she rolled abominably. A dirty night came on. At eight bells Mr. Grey touched by Dodd's clemency, and brimful of zeal, reported a light in Mrs. Beresford's cabin. It had been put out as usual by the master-at-arms; but the refractory one had relighted it.

"Go and take it away," said Dodd.

Soon screams were heard from the cabin. "Oh! mercy! mercy! I will not be drowned in the dark."

Dodd, who had kept clear of her so long, went down and tried to reassure her.

"Oh, the tempest! the tempest!" she cried. "AND TO BE DROWNED IN THE DARK!"

"Tempest? It is blowing half a gale of wind; that is all."

"Half a gale! Ah, that is the way you always talk to us ladies. Oh, pray give me my light, and send me a clergyman!"

Dodd took pity, and let her have her light, with a midshipman to watch it. He even made her a hypocritical promise that, should there be one grain of danger, he would lie to; but said he must not make a foul wind of a fair one for a few lurches. The *Agra* broke plenty of glass and crockery though with her fair wind and her lee lurches.

Wind down at noon next day, and a dead calm.

At two P. M. the weather cleared; the sun came out high in heaven's centre; and a balmy breeze from the west.

At six twenty-five, the grand orb set calm and red, and the sea was gorgeous with miles and miles of great ruby dimples: it was the first glowing smile of southern latitude. The night stole on so soft, so clear, so balmy, all were loth to close their eyes on it: the passengers lingered long on deck, watching the Great Bear dip, and the Southern Cross rise, and overhead a whole heaven of glorious stars most of us have never seen, and never shall see in this world. No belching smoke obscured, no plunging paddles deafened; all was musical; the soft air sighing among the sails; the phosphorescent water bubbling from the ship's bows; the murmurs from little knots of men on deck subdued by the great calm: home seemed near, all danger far; Peace ruled the sea, the sky, the heart: the ship, making a track of white fire on the deep, glided gently yet swiftly homeward, urged by snowy sails piled up like alabaster towers against a violet sky, out of which looked a thousand eyes of holy tranquil fire. So melted the sweet night away.

Now carmine streaks tinged the eastern sky at the water's edge: and that water blushed; now the streaks turned orange, and the waves below them sparkled. Thence splashes of living gold flew and settled on the ship's white sails, the deck, and the faces; and with no more prologue, being so near the line, up came majestically a huge, fiery, golden sun, and set the sea flaming liquid topaz.

Instantly the lookout at the foretop-gallant-masthead hailed the deck below.

"STRANGE SAIL! RIGHT AHEAD!"

The strange sail was reported to Captain Dodd, then dressing in his cabin. He came soon after on deck and hailed the lookout: "Which way is she standing?"

"Can't say, sir. Can't see her move any."

Dodd ordered the boatswain to pipe to breakfast; and taking his deck glass went lightly up to the foretop-gallant-mast-crosstrees. Thence, through the light haze of a glorious morning, he espied a long low schooner, lateen-rigged, lying close under Point Leat, a small island about nine miles distant on the weather bow; and nearly in the *Agra's* course then approaching the Straits of Gaspar, 4 Latitude S.

"She is hove to," said Dodd, very gravely.

At eight o'clock, the stranger lay about two miles to windward; and still hove to.

By this time all eyes were turned upon her, and half a dozen glasses. Exerybody, except the captain, delivered an opinion. She was a Greek lying to for water: she was a Malay coming north with canes, and short of hands: she was a pirate watching the Straits.

The captain leaned silent and sombre with his arms on the bulwarks, and watched the suspected craft.

Mr. Fullalove joined the group, and levelled a powerful glass, of his own construction. His inspection was long and minute, and, while the glass was at his eye, Sharpe asked him half in a whisper, could he make out anything?

"Wal," said he, "the varmint looks considerably snaky." Then, without moving his glass, he let drop a word at a time, as if the facts were trickling into his telescope at the lens, and out at the sight. "One—two—four—seven, false ports."

There was a momentary murmur among the officers all round. But British sailors are undemonstrative: Colonel Kenealy, strolling the deck with a cigar, saw they were watching another ship with maritime curiosity, and making comments; but he discerned no particular emotion nor anxiety in what they said, nor in the grave low tones they said it in. Perhaps a brother seaman would though.

The next observation that trickled out of Fullalove's tube was this: "I judge there are too few hands on deck, and too many—white—eyeballs—glittering at the portholes."

"Confound it!" muttered Bayliss, uneasily; "how can you see that?"

Fullalove replied only by quietly handing his glass to Dodd. The captain, thus appealed to, glued his eye to the tube.

"Well, sir; see the false ports, and the white eyebrows?" asked Sharpe, ironically.

"I see this is the best glass I ever looked through," said Dodd doggedly, without interrupting his inspection.

"I think he is a Malay pirate," said Mr. Grey.

Sharpe took him up very quickly, and, indeed, angrily: "Nonsense! And if he is, he won't venture on a craft of this size."

"Says the whale to the swordfish," suggested Fullalove, with a little guttural laugh.

The captain, with the American glass to his eye, turned half round to the man at the wheel: "Starboard!"

"Starboard it is."

"Steer South South East."

"Ay, ay, sir." And the ship's course was thus altered two points.

This order lowered Dodd fifty per cent in Mr. Sharpe's estimation. He held his tongue as long as he could: but at last his surprise and dissatisfaction burst out of him, "Won't that bring him out on us?"

"Very likely, sir," replied Dodd.

"Begging your pardon, captain, would it not be wiser to keep our course, and show the blackguard we don't fear him?"

"When we *do?* Sharpe, he has made up his mind an hour ago whether to lie still, or bite; my changing my course two points won't change his mind; but it may make him declare it; and *I* must know what he does intend, before I run the ship into the narrows ahead."

"Oh, I see," said Sharpe, half convinced.

The alteration in the *Agra's* course produced no movement on the part of the mysterious schooner. She lay to under the land still, and with only a few hands on deck, while the *Agra* edged away from her and entered the straits between Long Island and Point Leat, leaving the schooner about two miles and a half distant to the N.W.

Ah! The stranger's deck swarms black with men.

His sham ports fell as if by magic, his guns grinned through the gaps like black teeth; his huge foresail rose and filled, and out he came in chase.

The breeze was a kiss from Heaven, the sky a vaulted sapphire, the sea a million dimples of liquid, lucid gold. . . .

The way the pirate dropped the mask, showed his black teeth, and bore up in chase, was terrible: so dilates and bounds the sudden tiger on his unwary prey. There were stout hearts among the officers of the peaceful *Agra;* but danger in a new form shakes the brave; and this was their first pirate: their dismay broke out in ejaculations not loud but deep. . . .

"Sharpe," said Dodd, in a tone that conveyed no suspicion of the newcomer, "set the royals, and flying jib.—Port!"

"Port it is," cried the man at the helm.

"Steer due South!" And, with these words in his mouth, Dodd dived to the gun deck.

By this time elastic Sharpe had recovered the first shock; and the order to crowd sail on the ship galled his pride and his manhood; he muttered, indignantly, "The white feather!" This eased his mind, and he obeyed orders briskly as ever. While he and his hands were setting every rag the ship could carry on that tack, the other officers, having unluckily no orders to execute, stood gloomy and helpless, with their eyes glued, by a sort of sombre fascination, on that coming fate. . . .

Realize the situation, and the strange incongruity between the senses and the mind in these poor fellows! The day had ripened its beauty; beneath a purple heaven shone, sparkled, and laughed a blue sea, in whose waves the tropical sun seemed to have fused his beams; and beneath that fair, sinless, peaceful sky, wafted by a balmy breeze over those smiling, transparent, golden waves, a bloodthirsty Pirate bore down on them with a crew of human tigers; and a lady babble babble babble babble babble babble babbled in their quivering ears.

But now the captain came bustling on deck, eyed the loftier sails, saw they were drawing well, appointed four midshipmen in a staff to convey his orders; gave Bayliss charge of the carronades, Grey of the cutlasses, and directed Mr. Tickell to break the bad news gently to Mrs. Beresford, and to take her below to the orlop deck; ordered the purser to serve out beef, biscuit, and grog to all hands, saying, "Men can't work on an empty stomach: and fighting is hard work;" then beckoned the officers to come round him. "Gentlemen," said he, confidentially, "in crowding sail on this ship I had no hope of escaping that fellow on this tack, but I was, and am, most anxious to gain the open sea, where I can square my yards and run for it, if I see a chance. At present I shall carry on till he comes up within range: and then, to keep the Company's canvas from being shot to rags, I shall shorten sail; and to save ship and cargo and all our lives, I shall fight while a plank of her swims.

Better to be killed in hot blood than walk the plank in cold."

The officers cheered faintly: the captain's dogged resolution stirred up theirs. . . .

"Shorten sail to the taupsles and jib, get the colors ready on the halyards, and then send the men aft. . . ."

Sail was no sooner shortened, and the crew ranged, than the captain came briskly on deck, saluted, jumped on a carronade, and stood erect. He was not the man to show the crew his forebodings.

(Pipe.) "Silence fore and aft."

"My men, the schooner coming up on our weather quarter is a Portuguese pirate. His character is known; he scuttles all the ships he boards, dishonors the women, and murders the crew. We cracked on to get out of the narrows, and now we have shortened sail to fight this blackguard, and teach him not to molest a British ship. I promise, in the Company's name, twenty pounds prize money to every man before the mast if we beat him off or out-manœuvre him; thirty if we sink him; and forty if we tow him astern into a friendly port. Eight guns are clear below, three on the weather side, five on the lee; for, if he knows his business, he will come up on the lee quarter: if he doesn't, that is no fault of yours nor mine. The muskets are all loaded, the cutlasses ground like razors—"

"Hurrah!"

"We have got women to defend—"

"Hurrah!"

"A good ship under our feet, the God of justice overhead, British hearts in our bosoms, and British colors flying—run 'em up!—over our heads." (The ship's colors flew up to the fore, and the Union Jack to the mizzen peak.) "Now lads, I mean to fight this ship while a plank of her" (stamping on the deck) "swims beneath my foot and—WHAT DO YOU SAY?"

The reply was a fierce "hurrah!" from a hundred throats, so loud, so deep, so full of volume, it made the ship vibrate, and rang in the creeping-on pirate's ears. Fierce, but cunning, he saw mischief in those shortened sails, and that Union Jack, the terror of his tribe, rising to a British cheer; he lowered his mainsail, and crawled up on the weather quarter. Arrived within a cable's length, he double reefed his foresail to reduce his rate of sailing nearly to that of the ship; and the next moment a tongue of flame, and then a gash of smoke, issued from his lee bow, and the ball flew screaming like a seagull over the *Agra's* mizzen top. He then put his helm up, and fired his other bow-chaser, and sent the shot hissing and skipping on the water past the ship. This prologue made the novices wince. Bayliss wanted to reply with a carronade; but Dodd forbade him sternly, saying, "If we keep him aloof we are done for."

The pirate drew nearer, and fired both guns in succession, hulled the *Agra* amidships, and sent an eighteen pound ball through her foresail. Most of the faces were pale on the quarter-deck; it was very trying to be shot at, and hit, and make no return. The next double discharge sent one shot smash through the stern cabin window, and splintered the bulwark with another, wounding a seaman slightly.

"LIE DOWN FORWARD!" shouted Dodd, through his trumpet. "Bayliss, give him a shot."

The carronade was fired with a tremendous report, but no visible effect. The pirate crept nearer, steering in and out like a snake to avoid the carronades, and firing those two heavy guns alternately into the devoted ship. He hulled the *Agra* now nearly every shot.

The two available carronades replied noisily, and jumped as usual; they sent one thirty-two pound shot clean through the schooner's deck and side; but that was literally all they did worth speaking of.

"Curse them!" cried Dodd; "load them with grape! They are not to be trusted with ball. And all my eighteen-pounders dumb! The coward won't come alongside and give them a chance."

At the next discharge the pirate chipped the mizzen mast,

and knocked a sailor into dead pieces on the forecastle. Dodd put his helm down ere the smoke cleared, and got three carronades to bear, heavily laden with grape. Several pirates fell, dead or wounded, on the crowded deck, and some holes appeared in the foresail; this one interchange was quite in favor of the ship.

But the lesson made the enemy more cautious; he crept nearer, but steered so adroitly, now right astern, now on the quarter, that the ship could seldom bring more than one carronade to bear, while he raked her fore and aft with grape and ball.

In this alarming situation, Dodd kept as many of the men below as possible; but, for all he could do four were killed and seven wounded.

Fullalove's word came too true: it was the swordfish and the whale: it was a fight of hammer and anvil; one hit, the other made a noise. Cautious and cruel, the pirate hung on the poor hulking creature's quarters and raked her at point blank distance. He made her pass a bitter time. And her captain! To see the splintering hull, the parting shrouds, the shivered gear, and hear the shrieks and groans of his wounded; and he unable to reply in kind! The sweat of agony poured down his face. Oh, if he could but reach the open sea, and square his yards, and make a long chase of it; perhaps fall in with aid. Wincing under each heavy blow, he crept doggedly, patiently on, towards that one visible hope.

At last, when the ship was cloven with shot, and peppered with grape, the channel opened: in five minutes more he could put her dead before the wind.

No. The pirate, on whose side luck had been from the first, got half a broadside to bear at long musket shot, killed a midshipman by Dodd's side, cut away two of the *Agra's* mizzen shrouds, wounded the gaff, and cut the jib stay; down fell the powerful sail into the water, and dragged across the ship's forefoot, stopping her way to the open sea she panted for; the mates groaned; the crew cheered stoutly, as British tars do in any great disaster; the pirates yelled with ferocious triumph, like the devils they looked.

But most human events, even calamities, have two sides. The *Agra* being brought almost to a standstill, the pirate forged ahead against his will, and the combat took a new and terrible form. The elephant gun popped, and the rifle cracked, in the *Agra's* mizzen top, and the man at the pirate's helm jumped into the air and fell dead: both Theorists claimed him. Then the three carronades peppered him hotly; and he hurled an iron shower back with fatal effect. Then at last the long 18-pounders on the gun-deck got a word in. The old Niler was not the man to miss a vessel alongside in a quiet sea; he sent two round shot clean through him; the third splintered his bulwark, and swept across his deck.

"His masts! fire at his masts!" roared Dodd to Monk, through his trumpet; he then got the jib clear, and made what sail he could without taking all the hands from the guns.

This kept the vessels nearly alongside a few minutes, and the fight was hot as fire. The pirate now for the first time hoisted his flag. It was black as ink. His crew yelled as it rose: the Britons, instead of quailing, cheered with fierce derision: the pirate's wild crew of yellow Malays, black chinless Papuans, and bronzed Portuguese, served their side guns, 12-pounders, well and with ferocious cries; the white Britons, drunk with battle now, naked to the waist, grimed with powder, and spotted like leopards with blood, their own and their mates', replied with loud undaunted cheers, and deadly hail of grape from the quarter-deck; while the master gunner and his mates loading with a rapidity the mixed races opposed could not rival, hulled the schooner well between wind and water, and then fired chain shot at her masts, as ordered, and began to play the mischief with her shrouds and rigging. Meantime, Fullalove and Kenealy, aided by Vespasian, who loaded, were quietly butchering the pirate crew two a minute, and hoped to settle the question they were fighting for; smooth-bore *v.* rifle: but unluckily neither fired once without killing; so "there was nothing proven."

The pirate, bold as he was, got sick of fair fighting first; he hoisted his mainsail and drew rapidly ahead, with a slight bearing to windward, and dismounted a carronade and stove in the ship's quarter-boat, by way of a parting kick.

The men hurled a contemptuous cheer after him; they thought they had beaten him off. But Dodd knew better. He was but retiring a little way to make a more deadly attack than ever: he would soon wear, and cross the *Agra's* defenceless bows, to rake her fore and aft at pistol-shot distance; or grapple, and board the enfeebled ship two hundred strong.

Dodd flew to the helm, and with his own hands put it hard aweather, to give the deck guns one more chance, the last, of sinking or disabling the *Destroyer.* As the ship obeyed, and a deck gun bellowed below him, he saw a vessel running out from Long Island, and coming swiftly up on his lee quarter.

It was a schooner. Was she coming to his aid?

Horror! A black flag floated from her foremast head.

While Dodd's eyes were staring almost out of his head at this death blow to hope, Monk fired again; and just then a pale face came close to Dodd's, and a solemn voice whispered in his ear: "Our ammunition is nearly done!"

Dodd seized Sharpe's hand convulsively, and pointed to the pirate's consort coming up to finish them; and said, with the calm of a brave man's despair, "Cutlasses! and die hard!"

At that moment the master gunner fired his last gun. It sent a chain shot on board the retiring pirate, took off a Portuguese head and spun it clean into the sea ever so far to windward, and cut the schooner's foremast so nearly through that it trembled and nodded, and presently snapped with a loud crack, and came down like a broken tree, with the yard and sail; the latter overlapping the deck and burying itself, black flag and all, in the sea; and there, in one moment, lay the *Destroyer* buffeting and wriggling—like a heron on the water with its long wing broken—an utter cripple.

The victorious crew raised a stunning cheer.

"Silence!" roared Dodd, with his trumpet. "All hands make sail!"

He set his courses, bent a new jib, and stood out to windward close hauled, in hopes to make a good offing, and then put his ship dead before the wind, which was now rising to a stiff breeze. In doing this he crossed the crippled pirate's bows, within eighty yards; and sore was the temptation to rake him; but his ammunition being short, and his danger being imminent from the other pirate, he had the self-command to resist the great temptation.

He hailed the mizzen top: "Can you two hinder them from firing that gun?"

"I rather think we can," said Fullalove, "eh, colonel?" and tapped his long rifle.

The ship no sooner crossed the schooner's bows than a Malay ran forward with a linstock. Pop went the colonel's ready carbine, and the Malay fell over dead, and the linstock flew out of his hand. A tall Portuguese, with a movement of rage, snatched it up, and darted to the gun; the Yankee rifle cracked, but a moment too late. Bang! went the pirate's bow-chaser, and crashed into the *Agra's* side, and passed nearly through her.

"Ye missed him! Ye missed him!" cried the rival theorist, joyfully. He was mistaken: the smoke cleared, and there was the pirate captain leaning wounded against the mainmast with a Yankee bullet in his shoulder, and his crew uttering yells of dismay and vengeance. They jumped, and raged, and brandished their knives and made horrid gesticulations of revenge; and the white eyeballs of the Malays and Papuans glittered fiendishly; and the wounded captain raised his sound arm and had a signal hoisted to his consort, and she bore up in chase, and jamming her fore lateen flat as a board, lay far nearer the wind than the *Agra* could, and sailed three feet to her two besides. On this superiority being made clear, the situation of the merchant vessel, though not so utterly desperate as before Monk fired his lucky shot, became pitiable enough. If she ran before the wind, the fresh pirate would cut her off: if she lay to windward, she might postpone the inevitable and fatal collision with a foe as strong as that she had only escaped by a rare piece of luck; but this would give the crippled pirate time to refit and unite to destroy her. Add to this the failing ammunition, and the thinned crew!

Dodd cast his eyes all around the horizon for help.

The sea was blank.

The bright sun was hidden now; drops of rain fell, and the wind was beginning to sing; and the sea to rise a little.

"Gentlemen," said he, "let us kneel down and pray for wisdom, in this sore strait."

He and his officers kneeled on the quarter-deck. When they rose, Dodd stood rapt about a minute; his great thoughtful eye saw no more the enemy, the sea, nor anything external; it was turned inward. His officers looked at him in silence.

"Sharpe," said he, at last, "there *must* be a way out of them with such a breeze as this is now; if we could but see it."

"Ay, *if*," groaned Sharpe.

Dodd mused again.

"About ship!" said he, softly, like an absent man.

"Ay, ay, sir!"

"Steer due north!" said he, still like one whose mind was elsewhere.

While the ship was coming about, he gave minute orders to the mates and the gunner, to ensure co-operation in the delicate and dangerous manœuvres that were sure to be on hand.

The wind was W.N.W.: he was standing north: one pirate lay on his lee beam stopping a leak between wind and water, and hacking the deck clear of his broken masts and yards. The other fresh, and thirsting for the easy prey, came up to weather on him and hang on his quarter, pirate fashion.

When they were distant about a cable's length, the fresh pirate, to meet the ship's change of tactics, changed his own, luffed up, and gave the ship a broadside, well aimed but not destructive, the guns being loaded with ball.

Dodd, instead of replying immediately, put his helm hard up and ran under the pirate's stern, while he was jammed up in the wind, and with his five eighteen-pounders raked him fore and aft, then paying off, gave him three carronades crammed with grape and canister; the almost simultaneous discharge of eight guns made the ship tremble, and enveloped her in thick smoke; loud shrieks and groans were heard from the schooner; the smoke cleared; the pirate's mainsail hung on deck, his jib-boom was cut off like a carrot and the sail struggling; his foresail looked lace, lanes of dead and wounded lay still or writhing on his deck and his lee scuppers ran blood into the sea. Dodd squared his yards and bore away.

The ship rushed down the wind, leaving the schooner staggered and all abroad. But not for long; the pirate wore and fired his bow chasers at the now flying *Agra*, split one of the carronades in two, and killed a Lascar, and made a hole in the foresail; this done, he hoisted his mainsail again in a trice, sent his wounded below, flung his dead overboard, to the horror of their foes, and came after the flying ship, yawing and firing his bow chasers. The ship was silent. She had no shot to throw away. Not only did she take these blows like a coward, but all signs of life disappeared on her, except two men at the wheel, and the captain on the main gangway.

Dodd had ordered the crew out of the rigging, armed them with cutlasses, and laid them flat on the forecastle. He also compelled Kenealy and Fullalove to come down out of harm's way, no wiser on the smooth-bore question than they went up.

The great patient ship ran environed by her foes; one destroyer right in her course, another in her wake, following her with yells of vengeance, and pounding away at her—but no reply.

Suddenly the yells of the pirates on both sides ceased, and there was a moment of dead silence on the sea.

Yet nothing fresh had happened.

Yes, this had happened: the pirates to windward, and the pirates to leeward, of the *Agra*, had found out, at one and the same moment, that the merchant captain they had lashed, and bullied, and tortured, was a patient but tremendous man. It was not only to rake the fresh schooner he had put his ship before the wind, but also by a double, daring, master-stroke to hurl his monster ship bodily on the other. Without a foresail she could never get out of his way. Her crew had stopped the leak, and cut away and unshipped the broken foremast, and were stepping a new one, when they saw the huge ship bearing down in full sail. Nothing easier than to slip out of her way could they get the foresail to draw; but the time was short, the deadly intention manifest, the coming destruction swift. After that solemn silence came a storm of cries and curses, as their seamen went to work to fit the yard and raise the sail; while their fighting men seized their matchlocks and trained the guns. They were well commanded by an heroic able villain. Astern the consort thundered; but the *Agra's* response was a dead silence more awful than broadsides.

For then was seen with what majesty the enduring Anglo-Saxon fights.

One of the indomitable race on the gangway, one at the foremast, two at the wheel, conned and steered the great ship down on a hundred matchlocks, and a grinning broadside, just as they would have conned and steered her into a British harbor.

"Starboard!" said Dodd, in a deep calm voice, with a motion of his hand.

"Starboard it is."

The pirate wriggled ahead a little. The man forward made a silent signal to Dodd.

"Port!" said Dodd, quietly.

"Port it is."

But at this critical moment the pirate astern sent a mischievous shot, and knocked one of the men to atoms at the helm.

Dodd waved his hand without a word, and another man rose from the deck, and took his place in silence, and laid his unshaking hand on the wheel stained with that man's warm blood whose place he took.

The high ship was now scarce sixty yards distant: *she seemed to know:* she reared her lofty figurehead with great awful shoots into the air.

But now the panting pirates got their new foresail hoisted with a joyful shout: it drew, the schooner gathered way, and their furious consort close on the *Agra's* heels just then scourged her deck with grape.

"Port!" said Dodd, calmly.

"Port it is."

The giant prow darted at the escaping pirate. That acre of coming canvas took the wind out of the swift schooner's foresail; it flapped: oh, then she was doomed! . . . CRASH! the Indiaman's cut-water in thick smoke beat in the schooner's broadside: down went her masts to leeward like fishing-rods whipping the water; there was a horrible shrieking yell; wild forms leaped off on the *Agra*, and were hacked to pieces almost ere they reached the deck—a surge, a chasm in the ear, filled with an instant rush of engulfing waves, a long, awful, grating, grinding noise, never to be forgotten in this world, all along under the ship's keel—and the fearful majestic monster passed on over the blank she had made, with a pale crew standing silent and awestruck on her deck; a cluster of wild heads and staring eyeballs bobbing like corks in her foaming wake, sole relic of the blotted-out *Destroyer;* and a wounded man staggering on the gangway, with hands uplifted and staring eyes.

# THE DERELICT *NEPTUNE* [1]

From "Spun Yarn," BY MORGAN ROBERTSON

ACROSS the Atlantic Ocean from the Gulf of Guinea to Cape St. Roque moves a great body of water—the Main Equatorial Current—which can be considered a motive power, or mainspring, of the whole Atlantic current system, as it obtains its motion directly from the ever-acting push of the tradewinds. At Cape St. Roque this broad current splits into two parts, one turning north, the other south. The northern part contracts, increases its speed, and, passing up the northern coast of South America as the Guiana Current, enters through the Caribbean Sea into the Gulf of Mexico, where it circles around to the northward; then, colored a deep blue from the fine river silt of the Mississippi, and heated from its long surface exposure under a tropical sun to an average temperature of eighty degrees, it emerges into the Florida Channel as the Gulf Stream.

From here it travels northeast, following the trend of the coast line, until, off Cape Hatteras, it splits into three divisions, one of which, the westernmost, keeps on to lose its warmth and life in Baffin's Bay. Another impinges on the Hebrides, and is no more recognizable as a current; and the third, the eastern and largest part of the divided stream, makes a wide sweep to the east and south, enclosing the Azores and the deadwater called the Sargasso Sea, then, as the African Current, runs down the coast until, just below the Canary Isles, it merges into the Lesser Equatorial Current, which, parallel to the parent stream, and separated from it by a narrow band of backwater, travels west and filters through the West Indies, making puzzling combinations with the tides, and finally bearing so heavily on the young Gulf Stream as to give to it the sharp turn to the northward through the Florida Channel.

[1] Reprinted by courtesy of Harper & Brothers.

In the South Atlantic, the portion of the Main Equatorial Current split off by Cape St. Roque and directed south leaves the coast at Cape Frio, and at the latitude of the River Plate assumes a due easterly direction, crossing the ocean as the Southern Connecting Current. At the Cape of Good Hope it meets the cold, northeasterly Cape Horn Current, and with it passes up the coast of Africa to join the Equatorial Current at the starting-point in the Gulf of Guinea, the whole constituting a circulatory system of ocean rivers, of speed value varying from eighteen to ninety miles a day.

On a bright morning in November, 1894, a curious-looking craft floated into the branch current which, skirting Cuba, flows westward through the Bahama Channel. A man standing on the highest of two points enclosing a small bay near Cape Maisi, after a critical examination through a telescope, disappeared from the rocks, and in a few moments a light boat, of the model used by whalers, emerged from the mouth of the bay, containing this man and another. In the boat also was a coil of rope.

The one who had inspected the craft from the rocks was a tall young fellow, dressed in flannel shirt and trousers, the latter held in place by a cartridge-belt, such as is used by the American cowboy. To this was hung a heavy revolver. On his head was a broad-brimmed cork helmet, much soiled, and resembling in shape the Mexican sombrero. Beneath this headgear was a mass of brown hair, which showed a non-acquaintance with barbers for, perhaps, months, and under this hair a sun-tanned face, lighted by serious gray eyes. The most noticeable feature of this face was the extreme arching of the eyebrows—a never-failing index of the highest form of courage. It was a face that would please. The face of the other was equally pleasing in its way. It was red, round, and jolly, with twinkling eyes, the whole borrowing a certain dignity from closely cut white hair and mustaches. The man was about fifty, dressed and armed like the other.

"What do you want of pistols, Boston?" he said to the

younger man. "One might think this an old-fashioned, piratical cutting out."

"Oh, I don't know, Doc. It's best to have them. That hulk may be full of Spaniards, and the whole thing nothing but a trick to draw us out. But she looks like a derelict. I don't see how she got into this channel, unless she drifted up past Cape Maisi from the southward, having come in with the Guiana Current. It's all rocks and shoals to the eastward."

The boat, under the impulse of their oars, soon passed the fringing reef and came in sight of the strange craft, which lay about a mile east and half a mile off shore. "You see," resumed the younger man, called Boston, "there's a back-water inside Point Mulas, and if she gets into it she may come ashore right here."

"Where we can loot her. Nice business for a respectable practitioner like me to be engaged in! Doctor Bryce, of Havana, consorting with Fenians from Canada, exiled German socialists, Cuban horse-thieves who would be hung in a week if they went to Texas, and a long-legged sailor man who calls himself a retired naval officer, but who looks like a pirate; and all shouting for *Cuba Libre! Cuba Libre!* It's plunder you want."

"But none of us ever manufactured dynamite," answered Boston, with a grin. "How long did they have you in Moro Castle, Doc?"

"Eight months," snapped the doctor, his face clouding. "Eight months in that rathole, with the loss of my property and practice—all for devotion to science. I was on the brink of the most important and beneficent discovery in explosives the world ever dreamed of. Yes, sir, 'twould have made me famous and stopped all warfare."

"The captain told me this morning that he'd heard from Marti," said Boston, after an interval. "Good news, he said, but that's all I learned. Maybe it's from Gomez. If he'll only take hold again we can chase the Spanish off the island now. Then we'll put some of your stuff under Moro and lift it off the earth."

In a short time, details of the craft ahead, hitherto hidden by distance, began to show. There was no sign of life aboard; her spars were gone, with the exception of the foremast, broken at the hounds, and she seemed to be of about a thousand tons burden, colored a mixed brown and dingy gray, which, as they drew near, was shown as the action of iron rust on black and lead-colored paint. Here and there were outlines of painted ports. Under the stump of a shattered bowsprit projected from between bluff bows a weather-worn figurehead, representing the god of the sea. Above on the bows were wooden-stocked anchors stowed inboard, and aft on the quarters were iron davits with blocks intact—but no falls. In a few of the dead-eyes in the channels could be seen frayed rope-yarns, rotten with age, and, with the stump of the foremast, the wooden stocks of the anchors, and the teak-wood rail, of a bleached gray color. On the round stern, as they pulled under it, they spelled, in raised letters, flecked here and there with discolored gilt, the name "Neptune, of London." Unkempt and forsaken, she had come in from the mysterious sea to tell her story.

They climbed the channels, fastened the painter, and peered over the rail. There was no one in sight, and they sprang down, finding themselves on a deck that was soft and spongy with time and weather.

"She's an old tub," said Boston, scanning the gray fabric fore and aft; "one of the first iron ships built, I should think. They housed the crew under the t'gallant forecastle. See the doors forward, there? And she has a full-decked cabin—that's old style. Hatches are all battened down, but I doubt if this tarpaulin holds water." He stepped on the main hatch, brought his weight on the ball of one foot, and turned around. The canvas crumbled to threads, showing the wood beneath. "Let's go below. If there were any Spaniards here they'd have shown themselves before this."

The cabin doors were latched but not locked, and they opened them.

"Hold on," said the doctor, "this cabin may have been closed for years, and generated poisonous gases. Open that upper door, Boston."

Boston ran up the shaky poop ladder and opened the companion-way above, which let a stream of the fresh morning air and sunshine into the cabin, then, after a moment or two, descended and joined the other, who had entered from the main-deck. They were in an ordinary ship's cabin, surrounded by staterooms, and with the usual swinging lamp and tray; but the table, chairs, and floor were covered with fine dust.

"Where the deuce do you get so much dust at sea?" coughed the doctor.

"Nobody knows, Doc. Let's hunt for the manifest and the articles. This must have been the skipper's room." They entered the largest stateroom, and Boston opened an old-fashioned desk. Among the discolored documents it contained, he found one and handed it to the doctor. "Articles," he said; "look at it." Soon he took out another. "I've got it. Now we'll find what she has in her hold, and if it's worth bothering about."

"Great Scott!" exclaimed the doctor; "this paper is dated 1844, fifty years ago." Boston looked over his shoulder.

"That's so; she signed her crew at Boston, too. Where has she been all this time? Let's see this one."

The manifest was short, and stated that her cargo was 3,000 barrels of lime, 8,000 kids of tallow, and 2,500 carboys of acid, 1,700 of which were sulphuric, the rest of nitric acid. "That cargo won't be much good to us, Doc. I'd hoped to find something we could use. Let's find the log-book, and see what happened to her." Boston rummaged what seemed to be the first-mate's room. "Plenty of duds here," he said; "but they're ready to fall to pieces. Here's the log."

He returned with the book, and, seated at the dusty table, they turned the yellow leaves. "First departure, Highland Light, March 10, 1844," read Boston. "We'll look in the remarks column."

Nothing but the ordinary incidents of a voyage were found until they reached the date June 1st, where entry was made of the ship being "caught aback" and dismasted off the Cape of Good Hope in a sudden gale. Then followed daily "remarks" of the southeasterly drift of the ship, the extreme cold (which, with the continuance of the bad weather, prevented saving the wreck for jury-masts), and the fact that no sails were sighted.

June 6th told of her being locked in soft, slushy ice, and still being pressed southward by the never-ending gale; June 10th said that the ice was hard, and at June 15th was the terrible entry: "Fire in the hold!"

On June 16th was entered this: "Kept hatches battened down and stopped all air-holes, but the deck is too hot to stand on, and getting hotter. Crew insist on lowering the boats and pulling them northward over the ice to open water in hopes of being picked up. Good-bye." In the position columns of this date the latitude was given as 62 degrees 44 minutes S. and the longitude as 30 degrees 50 minutes E. There were no more entries.

"What tragedy does this tell of?" said the doctor. "They left this ship in the ice fifty years ago. Who can tell if they were saved?"

"Who indeed?" said Boston. "The mate hadn't much hope. He said 'Good-bye.' But one thing is certain; we are the first to board her since. I take it she stayed down there in the ice until she drifted around the Pole, and thawed out where she could catch the Cape Horn Current, which took her up to the Hope. Then she came up with the South African Current till she got into the Equatorial drift, then west, and up with the Guiana Current into the Caribbean Sea to the southward of us, and this morning the flood-tide brought her through. It isn't a question of winds; they're too variable. It's currents, though it may have taken her years to get here. But the surprising part of it is that she hasn't been boarded. Let's look in the hold and see what the fire has done."

When they boarded the hulk, the sky, with the exception of a filmy haze overhanging the eastern end of the island, was clear. Now, as they emerged from the cabin, this haze had solidified and was coming—one of the black and vicious squalls of the West India seas.

"No man can tell what wind there is in them," remarked Boston, as he viewed it. "But it's pretty close to the water, and dropping rain. Hold on, there, Doc. Stay aboard. We couldn't pull ashore in the teeth of it." The doctor had made a spasmodic leap to the rail. "If the chains were shackled on, we might drop one of the hooks and hold her; but it's two hours' work for a full crew."

"But we're likely to be blown away, aren't we?" asked the doctor.

"Not far. I don't think it'll last long. We'll make the boat fast astern and get out of the wet." They did so, and entered the cabin. Soon the squall, coming with a shock like that of a solid blow, struck the hulk broadside to and careened her. From the cabin door they watched the nearly horizontal rain as it swished across the deck, and listened to the screaming of the wind, which prevented all conversation. Silently they waited— one hour—two hours—then Boston said: "This is getting serious. It's no squall. If it wasn't so late in the season I'd call it a hurricane. I'm going on deck."

He climbed the companionway stairs to the poop, and shut the scuttle behind him—for the rain was flooding the cabin— then looked around. The shore and horizon were hidden by a dense wall of gray, which seemed not a hundred feet distant. From to windward this wall was detaching great waves or sheets of almost solid water, which bombarded the ship in successive blows, to be then lost in the gray whirl to leeward. Overhead was the same dismal hue, marked by hurrying masses of darker cloud, and below was a sea of froth, white and flat; for no waves could raise their heads in that wind. Drenched to the skin, he tried the wheel and found it free in its movements. In front of it was a substantial binnacle, and within a compass, which, though sluggish, as from a well-worn pivot, was practically in good condition. "Blowing us about nor'west by west," he muttered, as he looked at it—"straight up the coast. It's better than the beach in this weather, but may land us in Havana." He examined the boat. It was full of water, and tailing to windward, held by its painter. Making sure that this was fast, he went down.

"Doc," he said, as he squeezed the water from his limp cork helmet and flattened it on the table, "have you any objections to being rescued by some craft going into Havana?"

"I have—decided objections."

"So have I; but this wind is blowing us there—sideways. Now, such a blow as this, at this time of year, will last three days at least, and I've an idea that it'll haul gradually to the south, and west towards the end of it. Where'll we be then? Either piled up on one of the Bahama keys or interviewed by the Spaniards. Now I've been thinking of a scheme on deck. We can't get back to camp for a while—that's settled. This iron hull is worth something, and if we can take it into an American port we can claim salvage. Key West is the nearest, but Fernandina is the surest. We've got a stump of a foremast and a rudder and a compass. If we can get some kind of sail up forward and bring her 'fore the wind, we can steer any course within thirty degrees of the wind line."

"But I can't steer. And how long will this voyage take? What will we eat?"

"Yes, you can steer—good enough. And, of course, it depends on food, and water, too. We'd better catch some of this that's going to waste."

In what had been the steward's storeroom they found a harness-cask with bones and dry rust in the bottom. "It's salt meat, I suppose," said the doctor, "reduced to its elements." With the handles of their pistols they carefully hammered down the rusty hoops over the shrunken staves, which were well preserved by the brine they had once held, and taking the cask on deck, cleaned it thoroughly under the scuppers—or drain-holes—of the poop, and let it stand under the stream of water to swell and sweeten itself.

"If we find more casks we'll catch some more," said Boston;

"but that will last us two weeks. Now we'll hunt for her stores. I've eaten salt-horse twenty years old, but I can't vouch for what we may find here." They examined all the rooms adjacent to the cabin, but found nothing.

"Where's the lazarette in this kind of a ship?" asked Boston. "The cabin runs right aft to the stern. It must be below us." He found that the carpet was not tacked to the floor, and, raising the after end, discovered a hatch, or trap-door, which he lifted. Below, when their eyes were accustomed to the darkness, they saw boxes and barrels—all covered with the same fine dust which filled the cabin.

"Don't go down there, yet, Boston," said the doctor. "It may be full of carbonic acid gas. She's been afire, you know. Wait." He tore a strip from some bedding in one of the rooms, and, lighting one end by means of a flint and steel which he carried, lowered the smouldering rag until it rested on the pile below. It did not go out.

"Safe enough, Boston," he remarked. "But you go down; you're younger."

Boston smiled and sprang down on the pile, from which he passed up a box. "Looks like tinned stuff, Doc. Open it, and I'll look over here."

The doctor smashed the box with his foot, and found, as the other had thought, that it contained cylindrical cans; but the labels were faded with age. Opening one with his jack-knife, he tasted the contents. It was a mixture of meat and a fluid, called by sailors "soup-and-bully," and as fresh and sweet as though canned the day before.

"We're all right, Boston," he called down the hatch. "Here's as good a dish as I've tasted for months. Ready cooked, too."

Boston soon appeared. "There are some beef or pork barrels over in the wing," he said, "and plenty of this canned stuff. I don't know what good the salt meat is. The barrels seem tight, but we won't need to broach one for a while. There's a bag of coffee—gone to dust, and some hard bread that isn't fit to eat; but this'll do." He picked up the open can.

"Boston," said the doctor, "if those barrels contain meat, we'll find it cooked—boiled in its own brine, like this."

"Isn't it strange," said Boston, as he tasted the contents of the can, "that this stuff should keep so long?"

"Not at all. It was cooked thoroughly by the heat, and then frozen. If your barrels haven't burst from the expansion of the brine under the heat or cold, you'll find the meat just as good."

"But rather salty, if I'm a judge of salt-horse. Now, where's the sail-locker? We want a sail on that fore-mast. It must be forward."

In the forecastle they found sailor's chests and clothing in all stages of ruin, but none of the spare sails that ships carry. In the boatswain's locker, in one corner of the forecastle, however, they found some iron-strapped blocks in fairly good condition, which Boston noted. Then they opened the main-hatch, and discovered a mixed pile of boxes, some showing protruding necks of large bottles, or carboys, others nothing but the circular opening. Here and there in the tangled heap were sections of canvas sails—rolled and unrolled, but all yellow and worthless. They closed the hatch and returned to the cabin, where they could converse.

"They stowed their spare canvas in the 'tween-deck on top of the cargo," said Boston; "and the carboys—"

"And the carboys burst from the heat and ruined the sails," broke in the doctor. "But another question is, what became of that acid?"

"If it's not in the 'tween-deck yet, it must be in the hold—leaked through the hatches."

"I hope it hasn't reached the iron in the hull, Boston, my boy. It takes a long time for cold acids to act on iron after the first oxidation, but in fifty years mixed nitric and sulphuric will do lots of work."

"No fear, Doc; it had done its work when you were in your cradle. What'll we do for canvas? We must get this craft before the wind. How'll the carpet do?" Boston lifted the edge, and tried the fabric in his fingers. "It'll go," he said; "we'll double it. I'll hunt for a palm-and-needle and some twine." These articles he found in the mate's room. "The twine's no better than yarn," said he, "but we'll use four parts."

Together they doubled the carpet diagonally, and with long stitches joined the edges. Then Boston sewed into each corner a thimble—an iron ring—and they had a triangular sail of about twelve feet hoist. "It hasn't been exposed to the action of the air like the ropes in the locker forward," said Boston, as he arose and took off the palm; "and perhaps it'll last till she pays off. Then we can steer. You get the big pulley-blocks from the locker, Doc, and I'll get the rope from the boat. It's lucky I thought to bring it; I expected to lift things out of the hold with it."

At the risk of his life Boston obtained the coil from the boat, while the doctor brought the blocks. Then, together, they rove off a tackle. With the handles of their pistols they knocked bunk-boards to pieces and saved the nails; then Boston climbed the foremast, as a painter climbs a steeple—by nailing successive billets of wood above his head for steps. Next he hauled up and secured the tackle to the forward side of the mast, with which they pulled up the upper corner of their sail, after lashing the lower corners to the windlass and fife-rail.

It stood the pressure, and the hulk paid slowly off and gathered headway. Boston took the wheel and steadied her at northwest by west—dead before the wind—while the doctor, at his request, brought the open can of soup and lubricated the wheel-screw with the only substitute for oil at their command; for the screw worked hard with the rust of fifty years.

Their improvised sail, pressed steadily on but one side, had held together, but now, with the first flap as the gale caught it from another direction, appeared a rent; with the next flap the rag went to pieces.

"Let her go!" sang out Boston gleefully; "we can steer now. Come here, Doc, and learn to steer."

The doctor came; and when he left that wheel, three days later, he had learned. For the wind had blown a continuous gale the whole of this time, which, with the ugly sea raised as the ship left the lee of the land, necessitated the presence of both men at the helm. Only occasionally was there a lull during which one of them could rush below and return with a can of soup. During one of these lulls Boston had examined the boat, towing half out of water, and concluded that a short painter was best with a water-logged boat, had reinforced it with a few turns of his rope from forward. In the three days they had sighted no craft except such as their own—helpless—hove-to or scudding.

Boston had judged rightly in regard to the wind. It had hauled slowly to the southward, allowing him to make the course he wished—through the Bahama and up the Florida Channel with the wind over the stern. During the day he could guide himself by landmarks, but at night, with a darkened binnacle, he could only steer blindly on with the wind at his back. The storm centre, at first to the south of Cuba, had made a wide circle, concentric with the curving course of the ship, and when the latter had reached the upper end of the Florida Channel, had spurted ahead and whirled out to sea across her bows. It was then that the undiminished gale, blowing nearly west, had caused Boston, in despair, to throw the wheel down and bring the ship into the trough of the sea—to drift. Then the two wet, exhausted, hollow-eyed men slept the sleep that none but sailors and soldiers know; and when they awakened, twelve hours later, stiff and sore, it was to look out on a calm, starlit evening, with an eastern moon silvering the surface of the long, northbound rollers, and showing in sharp relief a dark horizon, on which there was no sign of land or sail.

They satisfied their hunger; then Boston, with a rusty iron pot from the galley, to which he fastened the end of his rope, dipped up some of the water from over the side. It was warm to the touch, and, aware that they were in the Gulf Stream, they crawled under the musty bedding in the cabin berths and slept through the night. In the morning there was no promise of the easterly wind that Boston hoped would come to blow them to port, and they secured their boat—reeving off davit-tackles, and with the plug out, pulling it up, one end at a time, while the water drained out through the hole in the bottom.

"Now, Boston," said the doctor, "here we are, as you say, on the outer edge of the Gulf Stream, drifting out into the broad Atlantic at the rate of four miles an hour. We've got to make the best of it until something comes along; so you hunt through that store-room and see what else there is to eat, and I'll examine the cargo. I want to know where that acid went."

They opened all the hatches, and while Boston descended to the lazarette, the doctor, with his trousers rolled up, climbed down the notched steps in a stanchion. In a short time he came up with a yellow substance in his hand, which he washed thoroughly with fresh water in Boston's improvised draw-bucket, and placed in the sun to dry. Then he returned to the 'tween-deck. After a while, Boston, rummaging the lazarette, heard him calling through the bulkhead, and joined him.

"Look here, Boston," said the doctor; "I've cleared away the muck over this hatch. It's 'corked,' as you sailormen call it. Help me get it up."

They dug the compacted oakum from the seams with their knives, and by iron rings in each corner, now eaten with rust to almost the thinness of wire, they lifted the hatch. Below was a filthy-looking layer of whitish substance, protruding from which were charred, half-burned staves. First they repeated the experiment with the smouldering rag, and finding that it burned, as before, they descended. The whitish substance was hard enough to bear their weight, and they looked around. Overhead, hung to the under side of the deck and extending the length of the hold, were wooden tanks, charred, and in some places burned through.

"She must have been built for a passenger or troop ship," said Boston. "Those tanks would water a regiment."

"Boston," answered the doctor, irrelevantly, "will you climb up and bring down an oar from the boat? Carry it down—don't throw it, my boy." Boston obliged him, and the doctor, picking his way forward, then aft, struck each tank with the oar. "Empty—all of them," he said.

He dug out with his knife a piece of the whitish substance under foot, and examined it closely in the light from the hatch.

"Boston," he said, impressively, "this ship was loaded with lime, tallow, and acids—acids above, lime and tallow down here. This stuff is neither; it is lime soap. And, moreover, it has not been touched by acids." The doctor's ruddy face was ashen.

"Well?" asked Boston.

"Lime soap is formed by the cauticizing action of lime on tallow in the presence of water and heat. It is easy to understand this fire. One of those tanks leaked and dribbled down on the cargo, attacking the lime—which was stowed underneath, as all these staves we see on top are from tallow-kids. The heat generated by the slaking lime set fire to the barrels in contact, which in turn set fire to others, and they burned until the air was exhausted, and then went out. See, they are but partly consumed. There was intense heat in this hold, and expansion of the water in all the tanks. Are tanks at sea filled to the top?"

"Chock full, and a cap screwed down on the upper end of the pipes."

"As I thought. The expanding water burst every tank in the hold, and the cargo was deluged with water, which attacked every lime barrel in the bottom layer, at least. Result—the bursting of those barrels from the ebullition of slaking lime, the melting of the tallow—which could not burn long in the closed-up-space—and the mixing of it in the interstices of the lime barrels with water and lime—a boiling hot mess. What happens under such conditions?"

"Give it up," said Boston, laconically.

"Lime soap is formed, which rises, and the water beneath is in time all taken up by the lime."

"But what of it?" interrupted the other.

"Wait. I see that this hold and the 'tween-deck are lined with wood. Is that customary in iron ships?"

"Not now. It used to be a notion that an iron skin damaged the cargo; so the first iron ships were ceiled with wood."

"Are there any drains in the 'tween-deck to let water out, in case it gets into that deck from above—a sea, for instance?"

"Yes, always; three or four scupper-holes each side amidships. They lead the water into the bilges, where the pumps can reach it."

"I found up there," continued the doctor, "a large piece of wood, badly charred by acid for half its length, charred to a lesser degree for the rest. It was oval in cross section, and the larger end was charred most."

"Scupper plug. I suppose they plugged the 'tween-deck scuppers to keep any water they might ship out of the bilges and away from the lime."

"Yes, and those plugs remained in place for days, if not weeks or months, after the carboys burst, as indicated by the greater charring of the larger end of the plug. I burrowed under the debris, and found the hole which that plug fitted. It was worked loose, or knocked out of the hole by some internal movement of the broken carboys, perhaps. At any rate, it came out, after remaining in place long enough for the acids to become thoroughly mixed and for the hull to cool down. She was in the ice, remember. Boston, the mixed acid went down that hole, or others like it. Where is it now?"

"I suppose," said Boston, thoughtfully, "that it soaked up into the hold, through the skin."

"Exactly. The skin is calked with oakum, is it not?" Boston nodded.

"That oakum would contract with the charring action, as did the oakum in the hatch, and every drop of that acid—ten thousand gallons, as I have figured—has filtered up into the hold, with the exception of what remained between the frames under the skin. Have you ever studied organic chemistry?"

"Slightly."

"Then you can follow me. When tallow is saponified there is formed, from the palmitin, stearin, and olein contained, with the cauticizing agent—in this case, lime—a soap. But there are two ends to every equation, and at the bottom of this immense soap vat, held in solution by the water, which would afterwards be taken up by the surplus lime, was the other end of this equation; and as the yield from tallow of this other product is about thirty per cent., and as we start with eight thousand fifty-pound kids—four hundred thousand pounds—all of which has disappeared, we know that, sticking to the skin and sides of the barrels down here, is—or was once—one hundred and twenty thousand pounds, or sixty tons, of the other end of the equation —glycerine!"

"Do you mean, Doc," asked Boston, with a startled look, "that—"

"I mean," said the doctor, emphatically, "that the first thing the acids—mixed in the 'tween-deck to just about the right proportions, mind you—would attack, on oozing through the skin, would be this glycerine; and the certain product of this union under intense cold—this hull was frozen in the ice, remember—would be nitro-glycerine; and, as the yield of the explosive is two hundred and twenty per cent. of the glycerine, we can be morally sure that in the bottom of this hold, each minute globule of it held firmly in a hard matrix of sulphate or nitrate of calcium—which would be formed next when the acids met the hydrates and carbonates of lime—is over one hundred and thirty tons of nitro-glycerine, all the more explosive from not being washed of free acids. Come up on deck. I'll show you something else."

Limp and nerveless, Boston followed the doctor. This question was beyond his seamanship.

The doctor brought the yellow substance—now well dried. "I found plenty of this in the 'tween-deck," he said; "and I should judge they used it to pack between the carboy boxes. It was once cotton-batting. It is now, since I have washed it, a very good sample of gun-cotton. Get me a hammer—crowbar —something hard."

Boston brought a marline-spike from the locker, and the

doctor, tearing off a small piece of the substance and placing it on the iron barrel of a gipsy-winch, gave it a hard blow with the marline spike, which was nearly torn from his hand by the explosion that followed.

"We have in the 'tween-deck," said the doctor, as he turned, "about twice as many pounds of this stuff as they used to pack the carboys with; and, like the nitro-glycerine, is the more easily exploded from the impurities and free acids. I washed this for safe handling. Boston, we are adrift on a floating bomb that would pulverize the rock of Gibraltar!"

"But, doctor," asked Boston, as he leaned against the rail for support, "wouldn't there be evolution of heat from the action of the acids on the lime—enough to explode the nitro-glycerine just formed?"

"The best proof that it did not explode is the fact that this hull still floats. The action was too slow, and it was very cold down there. But I can't yet account for the acids left in the bilges. What have they been doing all these fifty years?"

Boston found a sounding-rod in the locker, which he scraped bright with his knife, then, unlaying a strand of the rope for a line, sounded the pump-well. The rod came up dry, but with a slight discoloration on the lower end, which Boston showed to the doctor.

"The acids have expended themselves on the iron frames and plates. How thick are they?"

"Plates, about five-eighths of an inch; frames, like railroad iron."

"This hull is a shell! We won't get much salvage. Get up some kind of distress signal, Boston." Somehow the doctor was now the master-spirit.

A flag was nailed to the mast, union down, to be blown to pieces with the first breeze; then another, and another, until the flag locker was exhausted. Next they hung out, piece after piece, all they could spare of the rotten bedding, until that too was exhausted. Then they found, in a locker of their boat, a flag of Free Cuba, which they decided not to waste, but to hang out only when a sail appeared.

But no sail appeared, and the craft, buffeted by gales and seas, drifted eastward, while the days became weeks, and the weeks became months. Twice she entered the Sargasso Sea—the graveyard of derelicts—to be blown out by friendly gales and resume her travels. Occasional rains replenished the stock of fresh water, but the food they found at first, with the exception of some cans of fruit, was all that came to light; for the salt meat was leathery, and crumbled to a salty dust on exposure to the air. After a while their stomachs revolted at the diet of cold soup, and they ate only when hunger compelled them.

At first they had stood watch-and-watch, but the lonely horror of the long night vigils in the constant apprehension of instant death had affected them alike, and they gave it up, sleeping and watching together. They had taken care of their boat and provisioned it, ready to lower and pull into the track of any craft that might approach. But it was four months from the beginning of this strange voyage when the two men, gaunt and hungry—with ruined digestions and shattered nerves—saw, with joy which may be imagined, the first land and the first sail that gladdened their eyes after the storm in the Florida Channel.

A fierce gale from the southwest had been driving them, broadside on, in the trough of the sea, for the whole of the preceding day and night; and the land they now saw appeared to them a dark, ragged line of blue, early in the morning. Boston could only surmise that it was the coast of Portugal or Spain. The sail—which lay between them and the land, about three miles to leeward—proved to be the try-sail of a black craft, hove-to, with bows nearly towards them.

Boston climbed the foremast with their only flag and secured it; then, from the high poop-deck, they watched the other craft, plunging and wallowing in the immense Atlantic combers, often raising her forefoot into plain view, again descending with a dive that hid the whole forward half in a white cloud of spume.

"If she was a steamer I'd call her a cruiser," said Boston; "one of England's black ones, with a storm-sail on her military mainmast. She has a ram bow, and—yes, sponsons and guns. That's what she is, with her funnels and bridge carried away."

"Isn't she right in our track, Boston?" asked the doctor, excitedly. "Hadn't she better get out of our way?"

"She's got steam up—a full head; see the escape-jet? She isn't helpless. If she don't launch a boat, we'll take to ours and board her."

The distance lessened rapidly—the cruiser plunging up and down in the same spot, the derelict heaving to leeward in great, swinging leaps, as the successive seas caught her, each one leaving her half a length farther on. Soon they could make out the figures of men.

"Take us off," screamed the doctor, waving his arms, "and get out of our way!"

"We'll clear her," said Boston; "see, she's started her engine."

As they drifted down on the weather-side of the cruiser they shouted repeatedly words of supplication and warning. They were answered by a solid shot from a secondary gun, which flew over their heads. At the same time, the ensign of Spain was run up on the flagstaff.

"They're Spanish, Boston. They're firing on us. Into that boat with you! If a shot hits our cargo, we won't know what struck us."

They sprang into the boat, which luckily hung on the lee side, and cleared the falls—fastened and coiled in the bow and stern. Often during their long voyage they had rehearsed the launching of the boat in a seaway—an operation requiring quick and concerted action.

"Ready, Doc?" sang out Boston. "One, two, three—let go!" The falls overhauled with a whir, and the falling boat, striking an uprising sea with a smack, sank with it. When it raised they unhooked the tackle blocks, and pushed off with the oars just as a second shot hummed over their heads.

"Pull, Boston; pull hard—straight to windward!" cried the doctor.

The tight whaleboat shipped no water, and though they were pulling in the teeth of a furious gale, the hulk was drifting away from them, so, in a short time, they were separated from their late home by a full quarter-mile of angry sea. The cruiser had forged ahead in plain view, and, as they looked, took in the try-sail.

"She's going to wear," said Boston. "See, she's paying off."

"I don't know what 'wearing' means, Boston," panted the doctor, "but I know the Spanish nature. She's going to ram that hundred and thirty tons of nitro. Don't stop. Pull away. Hold on, there; hold on, you fools!" he shouted. "That's a torpedo; keep away from her!"

Forgetting his own injunction to "pull away," the doctor stood up, waving his oar frantically, and Boston assisted. But if their shouts and gestures were understood aboard the cruiser, they were ignored. She slowly turned in a wide curve and headed straight for the *Neptune* which had drifted to leeward of her.

What was in the minds of the officers on that cruiser's deck will never be known. Cruisers of all nations hold roving commissions in regard to derelicts, and it is fitting and proper for one of them to gently prod a "vagrant of the sea" with the steel prow and send her below to trouble no more. But it may be that the sight of the Cuban flag, floating defiantly in the gale, had something to do with the full speed at which the Spanish ship approached. When but half a length separated the two craft, a heavy sea lifted the bow of the cruiser high in air; then it sank, and the sharp steel ram came down like a butcher's cleaver on the side of the derelict.

A great semicircular wall of red shut out the gray of the sea and sky to leeward, and for an instant the horrified men in the boat saw—as people see by a lightning flash—dark lines radiating from the centre of this red wall, and near this centre poised on end in mid-air, with deck and sponsons still intact, a bowless, bottomless remnant of the cruiser. Then, and before the remnant sank into the vortex beneath, the spectacle went out in the darkness of unconsciousness; for a report, as of concentrated thunder, struck them down. A great wave had left the crater-like depression in the sea, which threw the boat on end, and with the inward rush of surrounding water rose a mighty gray cone, which then subsided to a hollow, while another wave followed the first. Again and again this gray pillar rose and fell, each subsidence marked by the sending forth of a wave. And long before these concentric waves had lost themselves in the battle with the storm-driven combers from the ocean, the half-filled boat, with her unconscious passengers, had drifted over the spot where lay the shattered remnant, which, with the splintered fragments of wood and iron strewn on the surface and bottom of the sea for a mile around, and the lessening cloud of dust in the air, was all that was left of the derelict *Neptune* and one of the finest cruisers in the Spanish navy.

A few days later, two exhausted, half-starved men pulled a whaleboat up to the steps of the wharf at Cadiz, where they told some lies and sold their boat. Six months after, these two men, sitting at a camp-fire of the Cuban army, read from a discolored newspaper, brought ashore with the last supplies, the following:

"By cable to the 'Herald.'

"CADIZ, March 13, 1895.—Anxiety for the safety of the *Reina Regente* has grown rapidly to-day, and this evening it is feared, generally, that she went down with her four hundred and twenty souls in the storm which swept the southern coast on Sunday night and Monday morning. Despatches from Gibraltar say that pieces of a boat and several semaphore flags belonging to the cruiser came ashore at Ceuta and Tarifa this afternoon."

# A STORM AND A RESCUE

From "The Wreck of the *Grosvenor*," BY W. CLARK RUSSELL

ALL that night it blew terribly hard, and raised as wild and raging a sea as ever I remember hearing or seeing described. During my watch—that is, from midnight until four o'clock— the wind veered a couple of points, but had gone back again only to blow harder; just as though it had stepped out of its way a trifle to catch extra breath.

I was quite worn out by the time my turn came to go below; and though the vessel was groaning like a live creature in its death agonies, and the seas thumping against her with such shocks as kept me thinking that she was striking hard ground, I fell asleep as soon as my head touched the pillow, and never moved until routed out by Duckling four hours afterward.

All this time the gale had not bated a jot of its violence, and the ship labored so heavily that I had the utmost difficulty in getting out of the cuddy on to the poop. When I say that the decks fore and aft were streaming wet, I convey no notion of the truth: the main-deck was simply *afloat*, and every time the ship rolled, the water on her deck rushed in a wave against the bulwarks and shot high in the air, to mingle sometimes with fresh and heavy inroads of the sea, both falling back upon the deck with the boom of a gun.

I had already ascertained from Duckling that the well had been sounded and the ship found dry; and therefore, since we were tight below, it mattered little what water was shipped above, as the hatches were securely battened down fore and aft, and the mast-coats unwrung. But still she labored under the serious disadvantage of being overloaded; and the result was, her fore parts were being incessantly swept by seas which at times completely hid her forecastle in spray.

361

Shortly after breakfast, Captain Coxon sent me forward to dispatch a couple of hands on to the jib-boom to snug the inner jib, which looked to be rather shakily stowed. I managed to dodge the water on the main-deck by waiting until it rolled to the starboard scuppers and then cutting ahead as fast as I could; but just as I got upon the forecastle, I was saluted by a green sea which carried me off my legs, and would have swept me down on the main-deck had I not held on stoutly with both hands to one of the fore-shrouds. The water nearly drowned me, and kept me sneezing and coughing for ten minutes afterward. But it did me no further mischief; for I was incased in good oilskins and sou'-wester, which kept me as dry as a bone inside.

Two ordinary seamen got upon the jib-boom, and I bade them keep a good hold, for the ship sometimes danced her figurehead under water and buried her sprit-sail-yard; and when she sunk her stern, her flying jib-boom stood up like the mizzenmast. I waited until this job of snugging the sail was finished, and then made haste to get off the forecastle, where the seas flew so continuously and heavily that had I not kept a sharp lookout, I should several times have been knocked overboard.

Partly out of curiosity and partly with a wish to hearten the men, I looked into the forecastle before going aft. There were sliding-doors let into the entrance on either side the windlass, but one of them was kept half open to admit air, the forescuttle above being closed. The darkness here was made visible by an oil lamp,—in shape resembling a tin coffee-pot with a wick in the spout,—which burned black and smokily. The deck was up to my ankles in water, which gurgled over the pile of swabs that lay at the open entrance. It took my eye some moments to distinguish objects in the gloom; and then by degrees the strange interior was revealed. A number of hammocks were swung against the upper deck and around the forecastle were two rows of bunks, one atop the other. Here and there were sea-chests lashed to the deck; and these, with the huge windlass, a range of chain cable, lengths of rope, odds and ends of pots and dishes, with here a pair of breeches hanging from a hammock, and there a row of oilskins swinging from a beam,—pretty well made up all the furniture that met my eye.

The whole of the crew were below. Some of the men lay smoking in their bunks, others in their hammocks with their boots over the edge; one was patching a coat, another greasing his boots; others were seated in a group talking; while under the lamp were a couple of men playing at cards upon a chest, three or four watching and holding on by the hammocks over their heads.

A man, lying in his bunk with his face toward me, started up and sent his legs, incased in blanket trousers and brown woolen stockings, flying out.

"Here's Mr. Royle, mates!" he called out. "Let's ask him the name of the port the captain means to touch at for proper food, for we aren't goin' to wait much longer."

"Don't ask me any questions of that kind, my lads," I replied promptly, seeing a general movement of heads in the bunks and hammocks. "I'd give you proper victuals if I had the ordering of them; and I have spoken to Captain Coxon about you, and I am sure he will see this matter put to rights."

I had difficulty in making my voice heard, for the striking of the seas against the ship's bows filled the place with an overwhelming volume of sound; and the hollow, deafening thunder was increased by the uproar of the ship's straining timbers.

"Who the devil thinks," said a voice from a hammock, "that we're going to let ourselves be grinded as we was last night without proper wittles to support us? I'd rather have signed articles for a coal-barge, with drowned rats to eat from Gravesend to Whitstable, than shipped in this here cursed vessel, where the bread's just fit to make savages retch!"

I had not bargained for this, but had merely meant to address them cheerily, with a few words of approval of the smart way in which they had worked the ship in the night. Seeing that my presence would do no good, I turned about and left the forecastle, hearing, as I came away, one of the Dutchmen cry out:—

"Look here, Mister Rile, vill you be pleashed to ssay when we are to hov' something to eat?—for by Gott! ve vill kill te dom pigs in the long-boat if the skipper don't mindt—so look out!"

As ill-luck would have it, Captain Coxon was at the break of the poop, and saw me come out of the forecastle. He waited until he had got me alongside of him, when he asked me what I was doing among the men.

"I looked in to give them a good word for the work they did last night," I answered.

"And who asked you to give them a good word, as you call it?"

"I have never had to wait for orders to encourage a crew."

"Mind what you are about, sir!" he exclaimed, in a voice tremulous with rage. "I see through your game, and I'll put a stopper upon it that you won't like."

"What game, sir? Let me have your meaning."

"An infernal mutinous game!" he roared. "Don't talk to me, sir! I know you! I've had my eye upon you! You'll play false if you can, and are trying to smother up your d—d rebel meanings with genteel airs! Get away, sir!" he bellowed, stamping his foot. "Get away aft! You're a lumping useless incumbrance! But by thunder! I'll give you two for every one you try to give me! So stand by!"

And apparently half mad with his rage, he staggered away in the very direction in which he had told me to go, and stood near the wheel, glaring upon me with a white face, which looked indescribably malevolent in the fur cap and ear-protectors that ornamented it.

I was terribly vexed by this rudeness, which I was powerless to resist, and regretted my indiscretion in entering the forecastle after the politic resolutions I had formed. However, Captain Coxon's ferocity was nothing new to me; truly I believed he was not quite right in his mind, and expected, as in former cases, that he would come round a bit by-and-by when his insane temper had passed. Still his insinuations were highly dangerous, not to speak of their offensiveness. It was no joke to be charged, even by a madman, with striving to arouse the crew to mutiny. Nevertheless I tried to console myself as best I could by reflecting that he could not prove his charges; that I need only to endure his insolence for a few weeks, and that there was always a law to vindicate me and punish him, should his evil temper betray him into any acts of cruelty against me.

The gale, at times the severest that I was ever in, lasted three days; during which the ship drove something like eighty miles to the northwest. The sea on the afternoon of the third day was appalling: had the ship attempted to run, she would have been pooped and smothered in a minute; but lying close, she rode fairly well, though there were moments when I held my breath as she sunk in a hollow like a coal-mine, filled with the astounding noise of boiling water,—really believing that the immense waves which came hurtling towards us with solid, sharp, transparent ridges, out of which the wind tore lumps of water and flung them through the rigging of the ship, must overwhelm the vessel before she could rise to it.

The fury of the tempest and the violence of the sea, which the boldest could not contemplate without feeling that the ship was every moment in more or less peril, kept the crew subdued; and they eat as best they could the provisions, without complaint. However, it needed nothing less than a storm to keep them quiet: for on the second day a sea extinguished the galley fire, and until the gale abated no cooking could be done; so that the men had to put up with cold water and biscuit. Hence all hands were thrown upon the ship's bread for two days; and the badness of it, therefore, was made even more apparent than heretofore, when its wormy moldiness was in some degree qualified by the nauseousness of bad salt pork and beef and the sickly flavor of damaged tea.

As I had anticipated, the captain came round a little a few hours after his insulting attack upon me. I think his temper frightened him when it had reference to me. Like others of his breed, he was a bit of a cur at the bottom. My character was a trifle beyond him; and he was ignorant enough to hate and fear what he could not understand. Be this as it may, he made some rough attempts at a rude kind of politeness when I went below to get some grog, and condescended to say that when I had been to sea as long as he, I would know that the most ungrateful rascals in the world were sailors; that every crew he had sailed with had always taken care to invent some grievance to growl over: either the provisions were bad, or the work too heavy, or the ship unseaworthy; and that long ago he had made up his mind never to pay attention to their complaints, since no sooner would one wrong be redressed than another would be coined and shoved under his nose.

I took this opportunity of assuring him that I had never willingly listened to the complaints of the men, and that I was always annoyed when they spoke to me about the provisions, as I had nothing whatever to do with that matter; and that so far from my wishing to stir up the men into rebellion, my conduct had been uniformly influenced by the desire to conciliate them and represent their conditions as very tolerable, so as to repress any tendency to disaffection which they might foment among themselves.

To this he made no reply, and soon we parted; but all the next day he was sullen again, and never addressed me save to give an order.

On the evening of the third day the gale broke; the glass had risen since the morning; but until the first dog-watch the wind did not bate one iota of its violence, and the horizon still retained its stormy and threatening aspect. The clouds then broke in the west, and the setting sun shone forth with deep crimson light upon the wilderness of mountainous waters. The wind fell quickly, then went round to the west and blew freshly; but there was a remarkable softness and sweetness in the feel and taste of it.

A couple of reefs were at once shaken out of the main-topsail, and a sail made. By midnight the heavy sea had subsided into a deep, long, rolling swell, still (strangely enough) coming from the south; but the fresh westerly wind held the ship steady, and for the first time for nearly a hundred hours we were able to move about the decks with comparative comfort. Early the next morning the watch were set to wash down and clear up the decks; and when I left my cabin at eight o'clock, I found the weather bright and warm, with a blue sky shining among heavy, white, April-looking clouds, and the ship making seven knots under all plain sail. The decks were dry and comfortable, and the ship had a habitable and civilized look, by reason of the row of clothes hung by the seamen to dry on the forecastle.

It was half past nine o'clock, and I was standing near the taffrail looking at a shoal of porpoises playing some hundreds of feet astern, when the man who was steering asked me to look in the direction to which he pointed—that was, a little to the right of the bowsprit—and say if there was anything to be seen there; for he had caught sight of something black upon the horizon twice, but could not detect it now.

I turned my eyes toward the quarter of the sea indicated, but could discern nothing whatever; and telling him that what he had seen was probably a wave, which, standing higher than his fellows, will sometimes show black a long distance off, walked to the fore part of the poop.

The breeze still held good; and the vessel was slipping easily through the water, though the southerly swell made her roll and at times shook the wind out of the sails. The skipper had gone to lie down,—being pretty well exhausted, I daresay; for he had kept the deck for the greater part of three nights running. Duckling was also below. Most of my watch were on the forecastle, sitting or lying in the sun, which shone very warm upon the decks; the hens under the long-boat were chattering briskly, and the cocks crowing, and the pigs grunting, with the comfort of the warmth.

Suddenly, as the ship rose, I distinctly beheld something black out away upon the horizon, showing just under the foot of the foresail. It vanished instantly; but I was not satisfied, and went for the glass which lay upon the brackets just under the companion. I then told the man who was steering to keep her away a couple of points for a few moments; and resting the glass against the mizzen-royal backstay, pointed it toward the place where I had seen the black object.

For some moments nothing but sea or sky filled the field of the glass as the ship rose and fell; but all at once there leaped into this field the hull of a ship, deep as her main-chains in the water, which came and went before my eye as the long seas lifted or dropped in the foreground. I managed to keep her sufficiently long in view to perceive that she was totally dismasted.

"It's a wreck," said I, turning to the man: "let her come to again and luff a point. There may be living creatures aboard of her."

Knowing what sort of man Captain Coxon was, I do not think that I should have had the hardihood to luff the ship a point out of her course had it involved the bracing of the yards; for the songs of the men would certainly have brought him on deck, and I might have provoked some ugly insolence. But the ship was going free, and would head more westerly without occasioning further change than slightly slackening the weather-braces of the upper yards. This I did quietly; and the dismantled hull was brought right dead on end with our flying jib-boom. The men now caught sight of her, and began to stare and point; but did not sing out, as they saw by the telescope in my hand that I perceived her. The breeze unhappily began to slacken somewhat, owing perhaps to the gathering heat of the sun; our pace fell off: and a full hour passed before we brought the wreck near enough to see her permanently,—for up to this she had been constantly vanishing under the rise of the swell. She was now about two miles off, and I took a long and steady look at her through the telescope. It was a black hull with painted ports. The deck was flush fore and aft, and there was a good-sized house just before where the mainmast should have been. This house was uninjured, though the galley was split up, and to starboard stood up in splinters like the stump of a tree struck by lightning. No boats could be seen aboard of her. Her jib-boom was gone, and so were all three masts,— clean cut off at the deck, as though a hand-saw had done it; but the mizzenmast was alongside, held by the shrouds and backstays, and the port main and fore shrouds streamed like serpents from her chains into the water. I reckoned at once that she must be loaded with timber, for she never could keep afloat at that depth with any other kind of cargo in her.

She made a most mournful and piteous object in the sunlight, sluggishly rolling to the swell which ran in transparent volumes over her sides and foamed around the deck-house. Once when her stern rose, I read the name *Cecilia* in broad white letters.

I was gazing intently, in the effort to witness some indication of living thing on board, when, to my mingled consternation and horror, I witnessed an arm projecting through the window of the deck-house and frantically waving what resembled a white handkerchief. As none of the men called out, I judged the signal was not perceptible to the naked eye; and in my excitement I shouted, "There's a living man on board of her, my lads!" dropped the glass, and ran aft to call the captain.

I met him coming up the companion ladder. The first thing he said was, "You're out of your course," and looked up at the sails.

"There's a wreck yonder," I cried, pointing eagerly, "with a man on board signaling to us."

"Get me the glass," he said sulkily; and I picked it up and handed it to him.

He looked at the wreck for some moments; and addressing the man at the wheel, exclaimed, making a movement with his hand, "Keep her away! Where in the devil are you steering to?"

"Good heaven!" I ejaculated: "there's a man on board— there may be others!"

"Damnation!" he exclaimed between his teeth: "what do you mean by interfering with me? Keep her away!" he roared out.

During this time we had drawn sufficiently near to the wreck to enable the sharper-sighted among the hands to remark the signal, and they were calling out that there was somebody flying a handkerchief aboard the hull.

"Captain Coxon," said I, with as firm a voice as I could command,—for I was nearly in as great a rage as he, and rendered insensible to all consequences by his inhumanity,—"if you bear away and leave that man yonder to sink with that wreck when he can be saved with very little trouble, you will become as much a murderer as any ruffian who stabs a man asleep."

When I had said this, Coxon turned black in the face with passion. His eyes protruded, his hands and fingers worked as though he were under some electrical process, and I saw for the first time in my life a sight I had always laughed at as a bit of impossible novelist description,—a mouth foaming with rage. He rushed aft, just over Duckling's cabin, and stamped with all his might.

"Now," thought I, "they may try to murder me!" And without a word I pulled off my coat, seized a belaying-pin, and stood ready; resolved that happen what might, I would give the first man who should lay his fingers on me something to remember me by while he had breath in his body.

The men, not quite understanding what was happening, but seeing that a "row" was taking place, came to the forecastle and advanced by degrees along the main-deck. Among them I noticed the cook, muttering to one or the other who stood near.

Mr. Duckling, awakened by the violent clattering over his head, came running up the companion-way with a bewildered, sleepy look in his face. The captain grasped him by the arm, and pointing to me, cried out with an oath that "that villain was breeding a mutiny on board, and he believed wanted to murder him and Duckling."

I at once answered, "Nothing of the kind! There is a man miserably perishing on board that sinking wreck, Mr. Duckling, and he ought to be saved. My lads!" I cried, addressing the men on the main-deck, "is there a sailor among you all who would have the heart to leave that man yonder without an effort to rescue him?"

"No, sir!" shouted one of them. "We'll save the man; and if the skipper refuses, we'll make him!"

"Luff!" I called to the man at the wheel.

"Luff at your peril!" screamed the skipper.

"Aft here, some hands," I cried, "and lay the mainyard aback. Let go the port main-braces!"

The captain came running toward me.

"By the living God!" I cried in a fury, grasping the heavy brass belaying-pin, "if you come within a foot of me, Captain Coxon, I'll dash your brains out!"

My attitude, my enraged face and menacing gesture, produced the desired effect. He stopped dead, turned a ghastly white, and looked round at Duckling.

"What do you mean by this (etc.) conduct, you (etc.) mutinous scoundrels?" roared Duckling, with a volley of foul language.

"Give him one for himself if he says too much, Mr. Royle!" sung out some hoarse voice on the main-deck; "we'll back yer!" And then came cries of "They're a cursed pair o' murderers!" "Who run the smack down?" "Who lets men drown?" "Who starves honest men?" This last exclamation was followed by a roar.

The whole of the crew were now on deck, having been aroused by our voices. Some of them were looking on with a grin, others with an expression of fierce curiosity. It was at once understood that I was making a stand against the captain and chief mate; and a single glance at them assured me that by one word I could set the whole of them on fire to do my bidding, even to shedding blood.

In the meantime, the man at the wheel had luffed until the

weather leeches were flat and the ship scarcely moving. And at this moment, that the skipper might know their meaning, a couple of hands jumped aft and let go the weather main-braces. I took care to keep my eyes on Coxon and the mate, fully prepared for any attack that one or both might make on me. Duckling eyed me furiously but in silence, evidently baffled by my resolute air and the position of the men. Then he said something to the captain, who looked exhausted and white and haggard with his useless passion. They walked over to the lee side of the poop; and after a short conference, the captain to my surprise went below, and Duckling came forward.

"There's no objection," he said, "to your saving the man's life, if you want. Lower away the starboard quarter-boat,—and you go along in her," he added to me, uttering the last words in such a thick voice that I thought he was choking.

"Come along, some of you!" I cried out, hastily putting on my coat; and in less than a minute I was in the boat with the rudder and thole-pins shipped, and four hands ready to out oars as soon as we touched the water.

Duckling began to fumble at one end of the boat's falls.

"Don't let him lower away!" roared out one of the men in the boat. "He'll let us go with a run. He'd like to see us drowned!"

Duckling fell back, scowling with fury; and shoving his head over as the boat sunk quietly into the water, he discharged a volley of execrations at us, saying that he would shoot some of us, if he swung for it, before he was done, and especially applying a heap of abusive terms to me.

The fellow pulling the bow oar laughed in his face; and another shouted out, "We'll teach you to say your prayers yet, you ugly old sinner!"

We got away from the ship's side cleverly, and in a short time were rowing fast for the wreck. The excitement under which I labored made me reckless of the issue of this adventure. The sight of the lonely man upon the wreck, coupled with the unmanly, brutal intention of Coxon to leave him to his fate, had goaded me into a state of mind infuriate enough to have done and dared anything to *compel* Coxon to save him. He might call it mutiny, but I called it humanity; and I was prepared to stand or fall by my theory. The hate the crew had for their captain and chief mate was quite strong enough to guarantee me against any foul play on the part of Coxon; otherwise I might have prepared myself to see the ship fill and stand away, and leave us alone on the sea with the wreck. One of the men in the boat suggested this; but another immediately answered, "They'd pitch the skipper overboard if he gave such an order, and glad o' the chance. There's no love for 'em among us, I can tell you; and by ——! there'll be bloody work done aboard the *Grosvenor* if things aren't mended soon, as you'll see."

They all four pulled at their oars savagely as these words were spoken; and I never saw such sullen and ferocious expressions on men's faces as came into theirs, as they fixed their eyes as with one accord upon the ship.

*She*, deep as she was, looked a beautiful model on the mighty surface of the water, rolling with marvelous grace to the swell, the strength and volume of which made me feel my littleness and weakness as it lifted the small boat with irresistible power. There was wind enough to keep her sails full upon her graceful, slender masts, and the brass-work upon her deck flashed brilliantly as she rolled from side to side.

Strange contrast, to look from her to the broken and desolate picture ahead! My eyes were riveted upon it now with new and intense emotion, for by this time I could discern that the person who was waving to us was a female,—woman or girl I could not yet make out,—and that her hair was like a veil of gold behind her swaying arm.

"It's a woman!" I cried in my excitement; "it's no man at all. Pull smartly, my lads! pull smartly, for God's sake!"

The men gave way stoutly, and the swell favoring us, we were soon close to the wreck. The girl, as I now perceived she was, waved her handkerchief wildly as we approached; but my attention was occupied in considering how we could best board the wreck without injury to the boat. She lay broadside to us, with her stern on our right, and was not only rolling heavily with wallowing, squelching movements, but was swirling the heavy mizzenmast that lay alongside through the water each time she went over to starboard; so that it was necessary to approach her with the greatest caution to prevent our boat from being stove in. Another element of danger was the great flood of water which she took in over her shattered bulwarks, first on this side, then on that, discharging the torrent again into the sea as she rolled. This water came from her like a cataract, and in a second would fill and sink the boat, unless extreme care were taken to keep clear of it.

I waved my hat to the poor girl, to let her know that we saw her and had come to save her, and steered the boat right around the wreck, that I might observe the most practical point for boarding her.

She appeared to be a vessel of about seven hundred tons. The falling of her masts had crushed her port bulwarks level with the deck, and part of her starboard bulwarks was also smashed to pieces. Her wheel was gone, and the heavy seas that had swept her deck had carried away capstans, binnacle, hatchway gratings, pumps—everything, in short, but the deck-house and the remnants of the galley. I particularly noticed a strong iron boat's-davit twisted up like a corkscrew. She was full of water, and lay as deep as her main-chains; but her bows stood high, and her fore-chains were out of the sea. It was miraculous to see her keep afloat as the long swell rolled over her in a cruel, foaming succession of waves.

Though these plain details impressed themselves upon my memory, I did not seem to notice anything, in the anxiety that possessed me to rescue the lonely creature in the deck-house. It would have been impossible to keep a footing upon the main-deck without a life-line or something to hold on by; and seeing this, and forming my resolutions rapidly, I ordered the man in the bow of the boat to throw in his oar and exchange places with me, and head the boat for the starboard port-chains. As we approached I stood up with one foot planted on the gunwale ready to spring; the broken shrouds were streaming aft and alongside, so that if I missed the jump and fell into the water there was plenty of stuff to catch hold of.

"Gently—'vast rowing—ready to back astern smartly!" I cried as we approached. I waited a moment: the hull rolled toward us, and the succeeding swell threw up our boat; the deck, though all aslant, was on a line with my feet. I sprung with all my strength, and got well upon the deck, but fell heavily as I reached it. However, I was up again in a moment, and ran forward out of the water.

Here was a heap of gear—stay-sail, and jib-halyards, and other ropes, some of the ends swarming overboard. I hauled in one of these ends, but found I could not clear the raffle; but looking round, I perceived a couple of coils of line—spare stun'-sail tacks or halyards I took them to be—lying close against the foot of the bowsprit. I immediately seized the end of one of these coils, and flung it into the boat, telling them to drop clear of the wreck astern; and when they found they had backed as far as the length of the line permitted, I bent on the end of the other coil, and paid that out until the boat was some fathoms astern. I then made my end fast, and sung out to one of the men to get on board by the starboard mizzen-chains, and to bring the end of the line with him. After waiting a few minutes, the boat being hidden, I saw the fellow come scrambling over the side with a red face, his clothes and hair streaming, he having fallen overboard. He shook himself like a dog, and crawled with the line, on his hands and knees, a short distance forward, then hauled the line taut and made it fast.

"Tell them to bring the boat round here," I cried, "and lay off on their oars until we are ready. And you get hold of this line and work yourself up to me."

Saying which, I advanced along the deck, clinging tightly with both hands. It very providentially happened that the door of the deck-house faced the forecastle within a few feet of where the remains of the galley stood. There would be, there-

fore, less risk in opening it than had it faced beamwise: for the
water, as it broke against the sides of the house, disparted clear
of the fore and after parts; that is, the great bulk of it ran clear,
though of course a foot's depth of it at least surged against the
door.

I called out to the girl to open the door quickly, as it slid
in grooves like a panel, and was not to be stirred from the outside. The poor creature appeared mad; and I repeated my request three times without inducing her to leave the window.
Then, not believing that she understood me, I cried out, "Are
you English?"

"Yes," she replied. "For God's sake, save us!"

"I cannot get you through that window," I exclaimed.
"Rouse yourself and open that door, and I will save you."

She now seemed to comprehend, and drew in her head. By
this time the man out of the boat had succeeded in sliding along
the rope to where I stood, though the poor devil was nearly
drowned on the road; for when about half-way, the hull took
in a lump of swell which swept him right off his legs, and he
was swung hard a-starboard, holding on for his life. However,
he recovered himself smartly when the water was gone, and
came along hand over fist, snorting and cursing in wonderful
style.

Meanwhile, though I kept a firm hold of the life-line, I took
care to stand where the inroads of water were not heavy, waiting impatiently for the door to open. It shook in the grooves,
tried by a feeble hand; then a desperate effort was made, and
it slid a couple of inches.

"That will do!" I shouted. "Now then, my lad, catch hold
of me with one hand, and the line with the other."

The fellow took a firm grip of my monkey-jacket, and I
made for the door. The water washed up to my knees, but I
soon inserted my fingers in the crevice of the door and thrust
it open.

The house was a single compartment, though I had expected
to find it divided into two. In the centre was a table that traveled

on stanchions from the roof to the deck. On either side were a couple of bunks. The girl stood near the door. In a bunk to the left of the door lay an old man with white hair. Prostrate on his back, on the deck, with his arms stretched against his ears, was the corpse of a man, well dressed; and in a bunk on the right sat a sailor, who, when he saw me, yelled out and snapped his fingers, making horrible grimaces.

Such, in brief, was the *coup d'œil* of that weird interior as it met my eyes.

I seized the girl by the arm.

"You first," said I. "Come; there is no time to be lost."

But she shrunk back, pressing against the door with her hand to prevent me from pulling her, crying in a husky voice, and looking at the old man with the white hair, "My father first! my father first!"

"You shall all be saved, but you must obey me. Quickly now!" I exclaimed passionately; for a heavy sea at that moment flooded the ship, and a rush of water swamped the house through the open door and washed the corpse on the deck up into a corner.

Grasping her firmly, I lifted her off her feet, and went staggering to the life-rope, slinging her light body over my shoulder as I went. Assisted by my man, I gained the bow of the wreck, and hailing the boat, ordered it alongside.

"One of you," cried I, "stand ready to receive this lady when I give the signal."

I then told the man who was with me to jump into the fore-chains, which he instantly did. The wreck lurched heavily to port. "Stand by, my lads!" I shouted. Over she came again, with the water swooping along the main-deck. The boat rose high, and the fore-chains were submerged to the height of the man's knees. "Now!" I called, and lifted the girl over. She was seized by the man in the chains, and pushed toward the boat; the fellow standing in the bow of the boat caught her, and at the same moment down sunk the boat, and the wreck rolled wearily over. But the girl was safe.

"Hurrah, my lad!" I sung out. "Up with you,—there are others remaining;" and I went sprawling along the line to the deck-house, there to encounter another rush of water, which washed as high as my thighs, and fetched me such a thump in the stomach that I thought I must have died of suffocation.

I was glad to find that the old man had got out of his bunk, and was standing at the door.

"Is my poor girl safe, sir?" he exclaimed, with the same huskiness of voice that had grated so unpleasantly in the girl's tone.

"Quite safe; come along."

"Thanks be to Almighty God!" he ejaculated, and burst into tears.

I seized hold of his thin cold hands, but shifted my fingers to catch him by the coat collar, so as to exert more power over him; and handed him along the deck, telling my companion to lay hold of the seaman and fetch him away smartly. We managed to escape the water, for the poor old gentleman bestirred himself very nimbly, and I helped him over the fore-chains; and when the boat rose, tumbled him into her without ceremony. I saw the daughter leap toward him and clasp him in her arms; but I was soon again scrambling on to the deck, having heard cries from my man, accompanied with several loud curses, mingled with dreadful yells.

"He's bitten me, sir!" cried my companion, hauling himself away from the deck-house. "He's roaring mad."

"It can't be helped," I answered. "We must get him out."

He saw me pushing along the life-line, plucked up heart, and went with myself through a sousing sea to the door. I caught a glimpse of a white face glaring at me from the interior: in a second a figure shot out, fled with incredible speed toward the bow, and leaped into the sea just where our boat lay.

"They'll pick him up," I exclaimed. "Stop a second;" and I entered the house and stooped over the figure of the man on the deck.

I was not familiar with death, and yet I knew it was here. I cannot describe the signs in his face; but such as they were, they told me the truth. I noticed a ring upon his finger, and that his clothes were good. His hair was black, and his features well shaped, though his face had a half-convulsed expression, as if something frightful had appeared to him, and he had died of the sight of it.

"This wreck must be his coffin," I said. "He is a corpse. We can do no more."

We scrambled for the last time along the life-line and got into the fore-chains; but to our consternation, saw the boat rowing away from the wreck. However, the fit of rage and terror that possessed me lasted but a moment or two; for I now saw they were giving chase to the madman, who was swimming steadily away. Two of the men rowed, and the third hung over the bows, ready to grasp the miserable wretch. The *Grosvenor* stood steady, about a mile off, with her mainyards backed; and just as the fellow over the boat's bows caught hold of the swimmer's hair, the ensign was run up on board the ship and dipped three times.

"Bring him along!" I shouted. "They'll be off without us if we don't bear a hand."

They nearly capsized the boat as they dragged the lunatic, streaming like a drowned rat, out of the water; and one of the sailors tumbled him over on his back, and knelt upon him, while he took some turns with the boat's painter round his body, arms and legs. The boat then came alongside; and watching our opportunity, we jumped into her and shoved off.

I had now leisure to examine the persons whom we had saved.

They—father and daughter, as I judged them by the girl's exclamation on the wreck—sat in the stern-sheets, their hands locked. The old man seemed nearly insensible; leaning backward with his chin on his breast and his eyes partially closed. I feared he was dying; but could do no good until we reached the *Grosvenor*, as we had no spirits in the boat.

The girl appeared to be about twenty years of age; very fair, her hair of golden straw color, which hung wet and streaky down her back and over her shoulders, though a portion of it was held by a comb. She was deadly pale, and her lips blue; and in her fine eyes was such a look of mingled horror and rapture as she cast them around her,—first glancing at me, then at the wreck, then at the *Grosvenor*,—that the memory of it will last me to my death. Her dress, of some dark material, was soaked with salt water up to her hips, and she shivered and moaned incessantly, though the sun beat so warmly upon us that the thwarts were hot to the hand.

The mad sailor lay at the bottom of the boat, looking straight into the sky. He was a horrid-looking object, with his streaming hair, pasty features, and red beard, his naked shanks and feet protruding through his soaking, clinging trousers, which figured his shin-bones as though they clothed a skeleton. Now and again he would give himself a wild twirl and yelp out fiercely; but he was well-nigh spent with his swim, and on the whole was quiet enough.

I said to the girl, "How long have you been in this dreadful position?"

"Since yesterday morning," she answered, in a choking voice painful to hear, and gulping after each word. "We have not had a drop of water to drink since the night before last. He is mad with thirst, for he drank the water on the deck;" and she pointed to the man in the bottom of the boat.

"My God!" I cried to the men, "do you hear her? They have not drunk water for two days! For the love of God, give way!"

They bent their backs to the oars, and the boat foamed over the long swell. The wind was astern and helped us. I did not speak again to the poor girl; for it was cruel to make her talk, when the words lacerated her throat as though they were pieces of burning iron.

After twenty minutes, which seemed as many hours, we reached the vessel. The crew pressing round the gangway cheered when they saw we had brought people from the wreck. Duckling and the skipper watched us grimly from the poop.

"Now then, my lads," I cried, "up with this lady first. Some of you on deck get water ready, as these people are dying of thirst."

In a few minutes, both the girl and the old man were handed over the gangway. I cut the boat's painter adrift from the ring-bolt so that we could ship the madman without loosening his bonds, and he was hoisted up like a bale of goods. Then four of us got out of the boat, leaving one to drop her under the davits and hook on the falls.

At this moment a horrible scene took place.

The old man, tottering on the arms of two seamen, was being led into the cuddy, followed by the girl, who walked unaided. The madman, in the grasp of the big sailor named Johnson, stood near the gangway; and as I scrambled on deck, one of the men was holding a pannikin full of water to his face. The poor wretch was shrinking away from it, with his eyes half out of their sockets; but suddenly tearing his arm with a violent effort from the rope that bound him, he seized the pannikin and bit clean through the *tin;* after which, throwing back his head, he swallowed the whole draught, dashed the pannikin down, his face turned black and he fell dead on the deck.

The big sailor sprung aside with an oath, forced from him by his terror; and from every looker-on there broke a groan. They all shrunk away and stood staring with blanched faces. Such a piteous sight as it was, lying doubled up, with the rope pinioning the miserable limbs, the teeth locked, and the right arm uptossed!

"Aft here and get the quarter-boat hoisted up!" shouted Duckling, advancing on the poop; and seeing the man dead on the deck, he added, "Get a tarpaulin and cover him up, and let him lie on the fore-hatch."

"Shall I tell the steward to serve out grog to the men who went with me?" I asked him.

He stared at me contemptuously, and walked away without answering.

# IN GOOD KING GEORGE'S TIME

From "Roderick Random," BY TOBIAS SMOLLETT

## I

I NOW saw no resource but the army or navy, between which I hesitated so long, that I found myself reduced to a starving condition. My spirit began to accommodate itself to my beggarly fate, and I became so mean as to go down towards Wapping, with an intention to inquire for an old schoolfellow, who, I understood, had got the command of a small coasting vessel, then in the river, and implore his assistance. But my destiny prevented this abject piece of behaviour; for, as I crossed Tower Wharf, a squat tawny fellow, with a hanger by his side, and a cudgel in his hand, came up to me, calling, "Yo, ho! brother, you must come along with me." As I did not like his appearance, instead of answering his salutation, I quickened my pace, in hope of ridding myself of his company; upon which he whistled aloud, and immediately another sailor appeared before me, who laid hold of me by the collar, and began to drag me along. Not being of a humour to relish such treatment, I disengaged myself of the assailant, and with one blow of my cudgel, laid him motionless on the ground; and perceiving myself surrounded in a trice, by ten or a dozen more, exerted myself with such dexterity and success, that some of my opponents were fain to attack me with drawn cutlasses; and, after an obstinate engagement, in which I received a large wound on my head, and another on my left cheek, I was disarmed, taken prisoner, and carried on board a pressing tender, where, after being pinioned like a malefactor, I was thrust down into the hold among a parcel of miserable wretches, the sight of whom well-nigh distracted me. As the commanding officer had not humanity enough to order my wounds to be dressed, and I could not use my own hands, I desired one of my fellow-captives, who was unfettered, to take a handkerchief out of my pocket, and tie it round my head to stop the bleeding. He pulled out my handkerchief, 'tis true; but, instead of applying it to the use for which I designed it, went to the grating of the hatchway, and with astonishing composure, sold it before my face to a bum-boat woman [1] then on board, for a quart of gin, with which he treated my companions, regardless of my circumstances and intreaties.

I complained bitterly of this robbery to the midshipman on deck, telling him at the same time, that unless my hurts were dressed, I should bleed to death. But compassion was a weakness of which no man could justly accuse this person, who, squirting a mouthful of dissolved tobacco upon me through the gratings, told me, "I was a mutinous dog, and that I might die and be d——d." Finding there was no other remedy, I appealed to patience, and laid up this usage in my memory, to be recalled at a fitter season. In the meantime, loss of blood, vexation, and want of food, contributed, with the noisome stench of the place, to throw me into a swoon; out of which I was recovered by a tweak of the nose, administered by the tar who stood sentinel over us, who at the same time regaled me with a draught of flip, and comforted me with the hopes of being put on board the *Thunder* next day, where I should be freed of my handcuffs, and cured of my wounds by the doctor. I no sooner heard him name the *Thunder*, than I asked if he had belonged to that ship long? and he giving me to understand, he had belonged to her five years, I inquired if he knew Lieutenant Bowling? "Know Lieutenant Bowling?" said he,—"odds my life! and that I do! and a good seaman he is, as ever stepp'd upon forecastle,—and a brave fellow as ever crack'd biscuit;—none of your Guinea pigs,—nor your fresh-water, wishy-washy, fair-weather fowls. Many a taut gale of wind has honest Tom

---

[1] A bum-boat woman is one who sells bread, cheese, greens, liquor, and fresh provisions to the sailors, in a small boat that lies alongside the ship.

Bowling and I weathered together. Here's his health with all
my heart, wherever he is, aloft or alow—in heaven or in hell—
all's one for that—he needs not be ashamed to show himself."
I was so much affected with this eulogium, that I could not
refrain from telling him that I was Lieutenant Bowling's kins-
man; in consequence of which connexion he expressed an inclination to serve me, and, when he was relieved, brought some
cold boiled beef in a platter, and biscuit, on which we supped
plentifully, and afterwards drank another can of flip together.
While we were thus engaged, he recounted a great many exploits of my uncle, who, I found, was very much beloved by
the ship's company, and pitied for the misfortune that had
happened to him in Hispaniola, which I was very glad to be
informed was not so great as I imagined; for Captain Oakum
had recovered of his wounds, and actually at that time commanded the ship. Having, by accident, in my pocket, my uncle's
letter, written from Port Louis, I gave it to my benefactor,
whose name was Jack Rattlin, for his perusal; but honest Jack
told me frankly he could not read, and desired to know the
contents; which I immediately communicated. When he heard
that part of it in which he says he had writ to his landlord in
Deal, he cried, "Body o' me! that was old Ben Block—he was
dead before the letter came to hand. Ey, ey, had Ben been alive,
Lieutenant Bowling would have had no occasion to skulk so
long. Honest Ben was the first man that taught him to hand,
reef, and steer.—Well, well, we must all die, that's certain,—
we must all come to port sooner or later—at sea, or on shore;
we must be fast moored one day; death's like the best bower
anchor, as the saying is, it will bring us all up."
I could not but signify my approbation of the justness of
Jack's reflections; and inquired into the occasion of the quarrel
between Captain Oakum and my uncle; which he explained in
this manner: "Captain Oakum, to be sure, is a good man enough,
—besides he's my commander;—but what's that to me?—I do
my duty, and value no man's anger of a rope's end.—Now the
report goes, as how he's a lord or baron knight's brother,

whereby, d'ye see me, he carries a strait arm, and keeps aloof from his officers, thof, may hap, they may be as good men in the main as he. Now we lying at anchor in Tuberoon Bay, Lieutenant Bowling had the middle watch, and as he always kept a good look out, he made, d'ye see, three lights in the offing, whereby he ran down to the great cabin for orders, and found the captain asleep; whereupon he waked him, which put him in a main high passion, and he swore woundily at the lieutenant, and called him a lousy Scotch s—— of a w—— (for I being then sentinel in the steerage, heard all), and swab, and lubber, whereby the lieutenant returned the salute, and they jawed together, fore and aft, a good spell, till at last the captain turned out, and laying hold of a rattan, came athwart Mr. Bowling's quarter; whereby he told the captain, that, if he was not his commander, he would heave him over board, and demanded satisfaction ashore; whereby, in the morning watch, the captain went ashore in the pinnace, and afterwards the lieutenant carried the cutter ashore; and so they, leaving their boats' crews on their oars, went away together; and so, d'ye see, in less than a quarter of an hour we heard firing, whereby we made for the place, and found the captain lying wounded on the beach, and so brought him on board to the doctor, who cured him in less than six weeks. But the lieutenant clapp'd on all the sail he could bear, and had got far enow ahead before we knew anything of the matter; so that we could never after get sight of him, for which we were not sorry, because the captain was mainly wroth, and would certainly have done him a mischief; —for he afterwards caused him to be run on the ship's books, whereby he lost all his pay, and if he should be taken, would be tried as a deserter."

This account of the captain's behaviour gave me no advantageous idea of his character; and I could not help lamenting my own fate, that had subjected me to such a commander. However, making a virtue of necessity, I put a good face on the matter, and next day was, with the other pressed men, put on board of the *Thunder*, lying at the Nore. When we came alongside, the mate who guarded us thither ordered my handcuffs to be taken off, that I might get on board the easier. This circumstance being perceived by some of the company, who stood upon the gang-boards to see us enter, one of them called to Jack Rattlin, who was busied in doing his friendly office for me, "Hey, Jack, what Newgate galley have you boarded in the river as you came along? Have we not thieves enow among us already?" Another, observing my wounds, which remained exposed to the air, told me that my seams were uncaulked, and that I must be new payed. A third, seeing my hair clotted together with blood, as it were, into distinct cords, took notice, that my bows were manned with red ropes, instead of my side. A fourth asked me, if I could not keep my yards square without iron braces? And, in short, a thousand witticisms of the same nature were passed upon me before I could get up the ship's side. After we had been all entered upon the ship's books, I inquired of one of my shipmates where the surgeon was, that I might have my wounds dressed, and had actually got as far as the middle deck, (for our ship carried eighty guns,) in my way to the cock-pit, when I was met by the same midshipman who had used me so barbarously in the tender. He, seeing me free from my chains, asked, with an insolent air, who had released me? To this question I foolishly answered, with a countenance that too plainly declared the state of my thoughts, "Whoever did it, I am persuaded did not consult you in the affair." I had no sooner uttered these words, than he cried, "D—n you, you saucy s—— of a b——, I'll teach you to talk so to your officer." So saying, he bestowed on me several severe stripes with a supple-jack he had in his hand; and, going to the commanding officer, made such a report of me, that I was immediately put in irons by the master-at-arms, and a sentinel placed over me. Honest Rattlin, as soon as he heard of my condition, came to me, and administered all the consolation he could, and then went to the surgeon in my behalf, who sent one of his mates to dress my wounds. This mate was no other than my old friend Thomson, with whom I became acquainted at the Navy Office.

If I knew him at first sight, it was not easy for him to recognise me, disfigured with blood and dirt, and altered by the misery I had undergone. Unknown as I was to him, he surveyed me with looks of compassion, and handled my sores with great tenderness. When he had applied what he thought proper, and was about to leave me, I asked him, if my misfortunes had disguised me so much that he could not recollect my face? Upon this address, he observed me with great earnestness for some time, and at length protested he could not recollect one feature of my countenance.

To keep him no longer in suspense, I told him my name; which when he heard, he embraced me with affection, and professed his sorrow in seeing me in such a disagreeable situation. I made him acquainted with my story; and when he heard how inhumanly I had been used in the tender, he left me abruptly, assuring me I should see him again soon. I had scarce time to wonder at his sudden departure, when the master-at-arms came to the place of my confinement, and bade me follow him to the quarter-deck, where I was examined by the first lieutenant, who commanded the ship in the absence of the captain, touching the treatment I had received in the tender from my friend the midshipman, who was present to confront me. I recounted the particulars of his behaviour to me, not only in the tender, but since my being on board the ship, part of which being proved by the evidence of Jack Rattlin and others, who had no great devotion of my oppressor, I was discharged from confinement, to make way for him, who was delivered to the master-at-arms to take his turn in the bilboes. And this was not the only satisfaction I enjoyed; for I was, at the request of the surgeon, exempted from all other duty than that of assisting his mates in making and administering medicines to the sick. This good office I owed to the friendship of Mr. Thomson, who had represented me in such a favourable light to the surgeon, that he demanded me of the lieutenant to supply the place of his third mate, who was lately dead. When I had obtained this favour, my friend Thomson carried me down to the cock-pit, which is the place allotted for the habitation of the surgeon's mates; and when he had shown me their berth, as he called it, I was filled with astonishment and horror.

We descended by divers ladders to a space as dark as a dungeon, which I understood was immersed several feet under water, being immediately above the hold. I had no sooner approached this dismal gulf, than my nose was saluted with an intolerable stench of putrefied cheese and rancid butter, that issued from an apartment at the foot of the ladder, resembling a chandler's shop, where, by the faint glimmering of a candle, I could perceive a man with a pale meagre countenance, sitting behind a kind of desk, having spectacles on his nose, and a pen in his hand. This, I learned of Mr. Thomson, was the ship's steward, who sat there to distribute provision to the several messes, and to mark what each received. He therefore presented my name to him, and desired I might be entered in his mess; then, taking a light in his hand, conducted me to the place of his residence, which was a square of about six feet, surrounded with the medicine chest, that of the first mate, his own, and a board, by way of table, fastened to the after powder-room; it was also enclosed with canvas, nailed round to the beams of the ship, to screen us from the cold, as well as from the view of the midshipmen and quarter-masters, who lodged within the cable-tiers on each side of us. In this gloomy mansion he entertained me with some cold salt pork, which he brought from a sort of locker, fixed above the table; and, calling for the boy of the mess, sent for a can of beer, of which he made excellent flip to crown the banquet. By this time I began to recover my spirits, which had been exceedingly depressed by the appearance of everything about me, and could no longer refrain from asking the particulars of Mr. Thomson's fortune, since I had seen him in London. He told me, that, being disappointed in his expectations of borrowing money to gratify the rapacious secretary of the Navy Office, he found himself utterly unable to subsist any longer in town, and had actually offered his service in quality of mate to the surgeon of a merchant's ship bound to Guinea, on the slaving trade; when, one morning, a young fellow, of whom he had some acquaintance, came to his lodgings, and informed him, that he had seen a warrant made out in his name at the Navy Office, for surgeon's second mate of a third rate. This unexpected piece of good news he could scarcely believe to be true, more especially as he had been found qualified at Surgeons' Hall for third mate only; but, that he might not be wanting to himself, he went thither to be assured, and actually found it so. Whereupon, demanding his warrant, it was delivered to him, and the oaths administered immediately. That very afternoon he went to Gravesend in the tilt-boat, from whence he took a place in the tide-coach for Rochester; next morning, got on board the *Thunder*, for which he was appointed, then lying in the harbour at Chatham; and the same day was mustered by the clerk of the cheque. And well it was for him that such expedition was used; for, in less than twelve hours after his arrival, another William Thomson came on board, affirming that he was the person for whom the warrant was expedited, and that the other was an impostor.

My friend was grievously alarmed at this accident—the more so, as his namesake had very much the advantage over him both in assurance and dress. However, to acquit himself of the suspicion of imposture, he produced several letters, written from Scotland to him in that name, and recollecting that his indentures were in a box on board, he brought them up, and convinced all present that he had not assumed a name which did not belong to him. His competitor, enraged that they should hesitate in doing him justice, (for, to be sure, the warrant had been designed for him,) behaved with so much indecent heat, that the commanding officer, who was the same gentleman I had seen, and the surgeon, were offended at his presumption, and, making a point of it with their friends in town, in less than a week got the first confirmed in his station. "I have been on board," said he, "ever since, and, as this way of life is become familiar to me, have no cause to complain of my situation. The surgeon is a good-natured indolent man; the first mate, who is now on shore on duty, is, indeed, a little proud and choleric, as all Welshmen are, but, in the main, a friendly honest fellow. The lieutenant I have no concern with; and as for the captain, he is too much of a gentleman to know a surgeon's mate, even by sight."

II

AN OLD-TIME MATE

While he was thus discoursing to me, we heard a voice on the cock-pit ladder pronounce with great vehemence, in a strange dialect, "The devil and his dam blow me from the top of Mounchdenny, if I go to him before there is something in my pelly; let his nose be as yellow as saffron, or as plue as a pell, look you, or green as a leek, 'tis all one." To this declaration somebody answered, "So it seems my poor messmate must part his cable for want of a little assistance. His fore-top-sail is loose already; and, besides, the doctor ordered you to overhaul him; but I see you don't mind what your master says." Here he was interrupted with, "Splunter and oons! you lousy tog, who do you call my master? get you gone to the doctor, and tell him my birth, and education, and my abilities, and moreover my behaviour is as good as his, or any shentleman's (no disparagement to him) in the whole world. Cot pless my soul! does he think, or conceive, or imagine, that I am a horse, or an ass, or a goat, to trudge backwards and forwards, and upwards and downwards, and by sea and by land, at his will and pleasure? Go your ways, you rapscallion, and tell Dr. Atkins, that I desire and request that he will give a look to the tying man, and order something for him if he be dead or alive, and I will see him take it by and by, when my craving stomach is satisfied, look you." At this the other went away, saying, that if they would serve him so when he was dying, by G—d, he would be foul of them in the other world.

Here Mr. Thomson let me know that the person we heard

was Mr. Morgan, the first mate, who was just come on board from the hospital, whither he had attended some of the sick in the morning. At the same time I saw him come into the berth. He was a short thick man, with a face garnished with pimples, a snub nose turned up at the end, an excessive wide mouth, and little fiery eyes, surrounded with skin puckered up in innumerable wrinkles. My friend immediately made him acquainted with my case; when he regarded me with a very lofty look, but without speaking, set down a bundle he had in his hand, and approached the cupboard, which, when he had opened, he exclaimed in a great passion, "Cot is my life! all the pork is gone, as I am a Christian!" Thomson then gave him to understand, that as I had been brought on board half-famished, he could do no less than entertain me with what was in the locker; and the rather as he had bid the steward enter me in the mess. Whether this disappointment made Mr. Morgan more peevish than usual, or he rather thought himself too little regarded by his fellow-mate, I know not, but, after some pause, he went on in this manner, "Mr. Thomson, perhaps you do not use me with all the good manners, and complaisance, and respect, look you, that becomes you, because you have not vouchsafed to advise with me in this affair. I have, in my time, look you, been a man of some weight and substance and consideration, and have kept house and home, and paid scot and lot, and the king's taxes; ay, and maintained a family to boot. And moreover, also, I am your senior, and your elder, and your petter, Mr. Thomson." "My elder I'll allow you to be, but not my better," cried Thomson with some heat. "Cot is my Saviour, and witness too," said Morgan, with great vehemence, "that I am more elder, and therefore more petter, by many years, than you." Fearing this dispute might be attended with some bad consequence, I interposed, and told Mr. Morgan I was very sorry for having been the occasion of difference between him and the second mate; and that rather than cause the least breach in their good understanding, I would eat my allowance by myself, or seek

admission into some other company. But Thomson, with more
spirit than discretion, as I thought, insisted upon my remaining
where he had appointed me; and observed, that no man possessed of generosity and compassion would have any objection
to it, considering my birth and talents, and the misfortunes I
had of late so unjustly undergone.

This was touching Mr. Morgan on the right key, who protested with great earnestness that he had no objection to my
being received in the mess; but only complained that the ceremony of asking his consent was not observed. "As for a shentleman in distress," said he, shaking me by the hand, "I lofe him
as I lofe my own powels; for, Cot help me! I have had vexations
enough upon my own pack." And, as I afterwards learned, in
so saying, he spoke no more than what was true; for he had
been once settled in a very good situation in Glamorganshire,
and was ruined by being security for an acquaintance. All differences being composed, he untied his bundle, which consisted of three bunches of onions, and a great lump of Cheshire
cheese, wrapped up in a handkerchief; and, taking some biscuit
from the cupboard, fell to with a keen appetite, inviting us to
a share of the repast. When he had fed heartily on his homely
fare, he filled a large cup, made of a cocoa-nut shell, with
brandy, and drinking it off, told us, "Prandy was the pest
menstruum for onion and sheese." His hunger being appeased,
he began to be in better humour; and being inquisitive about
my birth, no sooner understood that I was descended of a good
family, than he discovered a particular good will to me on that
account, deducing his own pedigree in a direct line from the
famous Caractacus, king of the Britons, who was first the
prisoner and afterwards the friend of Claudius Cæsar. Perceiving how much I was reduced in point of linen, he made me a
present of two good ruffled shirts, which, with two more of
check which I received from Mr. Thomson, enabled me to appear with decency. Meanwhile the sailor whom Mr. Morgan
had sent to the doctor, brought a prescription for his mess-

mate, which, when the Welshman had read, he got up to prepare it, and asked if the man was "Tead or alive." "Dead!"
replied Jack, "if he was dead he would have no occasion for
doctor's stuff. No, thank God, death ha'n't as yet boarded him,
but they have been yard arm and yard arm these three glasses."
"Are his eyes open?" continued the mate. "His starboard eye,"
said the sailor, "is open, but fast jammed in his head; and the
haulyards of his under jaw have given way." "Passion of my
heart!" cried Morgan, "the man is as pad as one would desire
to be! Did you feel his pulses?" To this the other replied with,
"Anan?" Upon which this Cambro-Briton, with great earnestness and humanity, ordered the tar to run to his messmate, and
keep him alive till he should come with the medicine, "And
then," said he, "you shall, peradventure, pehold what you shall
see." The poor fellow, with great simplicity, ran to the place
where the sick man lay, but, in less than a minute, returned with
a woeful countenance, and told us his comrade had struck.
Morgan, hearing this, exclaimed, "Mercy upon my salvation!
why did you not stop him till I came?" "Stop him?" said the
other; "I hailed him several times, but he was too far on his
way, and the enemy had got possession of his close quarters;
so that he did not mind me." "Well, well," said he, "we all owe
Heaven a tithe. Go your ways, you ragamuffin, and take an
example, and a warning, look you, and repent of your misteets."
So saying, he pushed the seaman out of the berth.

While he entertained us with reflections suitable to this
event, we heard the boatswain pipe to dinner, and immediately
the boy belonging to our mess ran to the locker, from whence
he carried off a large wooden platter, and in a few minutes
returned with it full of boiled peas, crying, "Scaldings," all the
way as he came. The cloth, consisting of a piece of an old sail,
was instantly laid, covered with three plates, which, by the
colour, I could with difficulty discern to be metal, and as many
spoons of the same composition, two of which were curtailed
in the handles, and the other abridged in the lip. Mr. Morgan

himself enriched this mess with a lump of salt butter, scooped from an old gallipot, and a handful of onions shorn, with some pounded pepper. I was not very much tempted with the appearance of this dish, of which, nevertheless, my messmates ate heartily, advising me to follow their example, as it was banyan-day, and we could have no meat till next noon. But I had already laid in sufficient for the occasion; and therefore desired to be excused, expressing a curiosity to know the meaning of banyan-day. They told me that on Mondays, Wednesdays, and Fridays, the ship's company had no allowance of meat, and that these meagre days were called banyan-days, the reason of which they did not know; but I have since learned they take their denomination from a sect of devotees in some part of the East Indies, who never taste flesh.

After dinner, Thomson led me round the ship, showed me the different parts, described their uses, and, as far as he could, made me acquainted with the particulars of the discipline and economy practised on board. He then demanded of the boatswain an hammock for me, which was slung in a very neat manner by my friend Jack Rattlin; and as I had no bedclothes, procured credit for me with the purser, for a mattress and two blankets. At seven o'clock in the evening, Morgan visited the sick, and having ordered what was proper for each, I assisted Thomson in making up his prescriptions; but when I followed him with the medicines into the sick berth or hospital, and observed the situations of the patients, I was much less surprised that people should die on board, than that any sick person should recover. Here I saw about fifty miserable distempered wretches, suspended in rows, so huddled one upon another, that not more than fourteen inches space was allotted for each with his bed and bedding; and deprived of the light of the day, as well as of fresh air; breathing nothing but a noisome atmosphere of the morbid steams exhaling from their own excrements and diseased bodies, devoured with vermin hatched in the filth that surrounded them, and destitute of every convenience necessary for people in that helpless condition.

III

A SEA-DANDY

Our tyrant having left the ship, and carried his favourite
Mackshame along with him, to my inexpressible satisfaction,
our new commander came on board in a ten-oared barge, over-
shadowed with a vast umbrella, and appeared in everything
the reverse of Oakum, being a tall, thin, young man, dressed in
this manner: a white hat, garnished with a red feather, adorned
his head, from whence his hair flowed upon his shoulders, in
ringlets, tied behind with a ribbon. His coat, consisting of pink-
coloured silk lined with white, by the elegance of the cut retired backward, as it were to discover a white satin waistcoat
embroidered with gold, unbuttoned at the upper part to display
a brooch set with garnets, that glittered in the breast of his
shirt, which was of the finest cambric, edged with right
Mechlin. The knees of his crimson velvet breeches scarcely
descended so low as to meet his silk stockings, which rose without spot or wrinkle on his meagre legs, from shoes of blue
Meroquin, studded with diamond buckles, that flamed forth
rivals to the sun! A steel-hilted sword, inlaid with gold, and
decked with a knot of ribbon which fell down in a rich tassel,
equipped his side; and an amber-headed cane hung dangling
from his wrist. But the most remarkable parts of his furniture
were, a mask on his face, and white gloves on his hands, which
did not seem to be put on with an intention to be pulled off
occasionally, but were fixed with a curious ring on the little
finger of each hand. In this garb Captain Whiffle, for that was
his name, took possession of the ship, surrounded with a crowd
of attendants, all of whom, in their different degrees, seemed
to be of their patron's disposition; and the air was so impreg-
nated with perfumes, that one may venture to affirm the clime
of Arabia Felix was not half so sweet-scented. My fellow-mate,
observing no surgeon among his train, thought he had found
an occasion too favourable for himself to be neglected; and

remembering the old proverb, "Spare to speak, and spare to speed," resolved to solicit the new captain's interest immediately, before any other surgeon could be appointed for the ship.

With this view he repaired to the cabin in his ordinary dress, consisting of a check shirt and trousers, a brown linen waistcoat, and a nightcap of the same (neither of them very clean), which, for his future misfortune, happened to smell strong of tobacco. Entering without any ceremony into this sacred place, he found Captain Whiffle reposing on a couch, with a wrapper of fine chintz about his body, and a muslin cap bordered with lace about his head; and, after several low congees, began in this manner: "Sir, I hope you will forgive, and excuse, and pardon the presumption of one who has not the honour of being known unto you, but who is, nevertheless, a shentleman porn and pred, and moreover has had misfortunes, Cot help me, in the world." Here he was interrupted by the captain, who, on seeing him, had started up with great amazement at the novelty of the apparition; and having recollected himself, pronounced, with a look and tone signifying disdain, curiosity, and surprise, "Zauns! who art thou?" "I am surgeon's first mate on board of this ship," replied Morgan, "and I most vehemently desire and beseech you, with all submission, to be pleased to condescend, and vouchsafe to inquire into my character, and my pehaviour, and my deserts, which, under Cot, I hope will entitle me to the vacancy of surgeon." As he proceeded in his speech, he continued advancing toward the captain, whose nostrils were no sooner saluted with the aromatic flavour that exhaled from him, than he cried, with great emotion, "Heaven preserve me! I am suffocated! Fellow, fellow, away with thee. Curse thee, fellow! get thee gone. I shall be stunk to death!" At the noise of his outcries, his servants ran into his apartment, and he accosted them thus: "Villains! cutthroats! traitors! I am betrayed! I am sacrificed!—Will you not carry that monster away? or must I be stifled with the stench of him! oh! oh! With these interjections he sunk down upon his settee in a fit; his valet de chambre plied him with a smelling bottle, one foot-

man chafed his temples with Hungary water, another sprinkled the floor with spirits of lavender, a third pushed Morgan
out of the cabin; who, coming to the place where I was, sat
down with a demure countenance, and, according to his custom, when he received an indignity which he durst not revenge,
began to sing a Welsh ditty. I guessed he was under some agitation of spirits, and desired to know the cause; but, instead of
answering me directly, he asked, with great emotion, if I
thought him a monster and a stinkard? "A monster and a stinkard," said I, with some surprise, "did anybody call you so?"
"Cot is my judge," replied he, "Captain Fifle did call me both;
aye, and all the water in the Tawy will not wash it out of my
remembrance. I do affirm, and vouch, and maintain, with my
soul, and my pody, and my plood, look you, that I have no
smells about me, but such as a Christian ought to have, except
the effluvia of tobacco, which is a cephalic, odoriferous, aromatic herb, and he is a son of a mountain goat who says otherwise. As for my being a monster, let that be as it is: I am as
Cot was pleased to create me, which, peradventure, is more
than I shall aver of him who gave me that title; for I will proclaim it before the world, that he is disguised, and transfigured,
and transmographied with affectation and whimsies, and that
he is more like a papoon than one of the human race."

He was going on with an eulogium upon the captain, when
I received a message to clean myself, and go up to the great
cabin; and with this command I instantly complied, sweetening
myself with rose water from the medicine chest. When I
entered the room, I was ordered to stand by the door, until
Captain Whiffle had reconnoitred me at a distance with a spyglass. He having consulted one sense in this manner, bade me
advance gradually, that his nose might have intelligence, before
it could be much offended. I therefore approached with great
caution and success, and he was pleased to say, "Aye, this
creature is tolerable." I found him lolling on his couch with a
languishing air, his head supported by his valet de chambre,
who, from time to time, applied a smelling bottle to his nose.

"Vergette," said he, in a squeaking tone, "dost thou think this wretch (meaning me) will do me no injury? may I venture to submit my arm to him?" "Pon my vord," replied the valet, "I do tink dat dere be great occasion for your honour losing one small quantity of blodt; and the young man ave quelque chose of de bonne mien." "Well, then," said his master, "I think I must venture." Then, addressing himself to me, "Hast thou ever blooded any body but brutes? But I need not ask thee, for thou wilt tell me a most damnable lie." "Brutes, Sir?" answered I, pulling down his glove, in order to feel his pulse, "I never meddle with brutes." "What the devil art thou about?" cried he; "dost thou intend to twist off my hand? God's curse! my arm is benumbed up to the very shoulder! Heaven have mercy upon me! must I perish under the hands of savages? What an unfortunate dog was I, to come on board without my own surgeon, Mr. Simper!" I craved pardon for having handled him so roughly, and, with the utmost care and tenderness, tied up his arm with a fillet of silk. While I was feeling for the vein, he desired to know how much blood I intended to take from him, and when I answered, "Not above twelve ounces," started up with a look full of horror, and bade me be gone, swearing I had a design upon his life. Vergette appeased him with difficulty, and opening a bureau, took out a pair of scales, in one of which was placed a small cup; and putting them into my hands, told me the captain never lost above an ounce and three drachms at one time. While I prepared for this important evacuation, there came into the cabin a young man gaily dressed, of a very delicate complexion, with a kind of languid smile on his face, which seemed to have been rendered habitual by a long course of affectation. The captain no sooner perceived him, than, rising hastily, he flew into his arms, crying, "O! my dear Simper! I am excessively disordered! I have been betrayed, frighted, murdered by the negligence of my servants, who suffered a beast, a mule, a bear, to surprise me, and stink me into convulsions with the fumes of tobacco." Simper, who by this time I found was obliged to art for the clearness of his complexion, assumed an air of softness and sympathy, and lamented, with many tender expressions of sorrow, the sad accident that had thrown him into that condition; then feeling his patient's pulse on the outside of his glove, gave it as his opinion, that his disorder was entirely nervous, and that some drops of tincture of castor, and liquid laudanum, would be of more service to him than bleeding, by bridling the inordinate sallies of his spirits, and composing the fermentation of his bile. I was therefore sent to prepare this prescription, which was administered in a glass of sack posset; after the captain had been put to bed, and orders sent to the officers on the quarter-deck, to let nobody walk on that side under which he lay.

# THE SALVING OF THE *YAN-SHAN*

From "In Blue Waters," by H. DE VERE STACPOOLE

I

THE *Heart of Ireland* was spreading her wings to the north-west trades, making a good seven knots, with the coast of California a vague line on the horizon to port and all the blue Pacific before her.

Captain Blood was aft with his mate, Billy Harman, leaning on the rail and watching the foam boosting away from the stern and flowing off in creamy lines on the swirl of the wake. Ginnell, owner and captain of the *Heart of Ireland*, shanghaied and reduced to deck hand, was forward on the look-out, and one of the coolie crew was at the wheel.

"I'm not given to meeting trouble half-way," said Blood, shifting his position and leaning with his left arm on the rail, "but it 'pears to me Pat Ginnell is taking his set down a mighty sight too easy. He's got something up his sleeve."

"So've we," replied Harman. "What can he do? He laid out to shanghai you, and by gum, he did it. I don't say I didn't let him down crool, playin' into his hands and pretendin' to help and gettin' Captain Mike as a witness, but the fac' remains he got you aboard this hooker by foul play, shanghaied you were, and then you turns the tables on him, knocks the stuffin' out of him and turns him into a deck hand. How's he to complain? I'd start back to 'Frisco now and dare him to come ashore with his complaints. We've got his ship, well, that's his fault. He's no legs to stand on, that's truth.

"Leavin' aside this little bisness, he's known as a crook from Benicia right to San Jose. The bay stinks with him and his doin's; settin' Chinese sturgeon lines, Captain Mike said he was,

and all but nailed, smugglin' and playin' up to the Greeks, and
worse. The Bayside's hungry to catch him an' stuff him in the
penitentiary, and he hasn't no friends. I'm no saint, I owns it,
but I'm a plaster John the Baptis' to Ginnell, and I've got
friends, so have you. Well, what are you bothering about?"

"Oh, I'm not bothering about the law," said Blood, "only
about him. I'm going to keep my eye open and not be put
asleep by his quiet ways—and I'd advise you to do the same."

"Trust me," said Harman, "and more especial when we
come to longsides with the *Yan-Shan*."

Now the *Yan-Shan* had started in life somewhere early in
the nineties as a twelve hundred ton cargo boat in the Bullmer
line; she had been christened the *Robert Bullmer*, and her first
act when the dog-shores had been knocked away was a bull
charge down the launching slip, resulting in the bursting of a
hawser, the washing over of a boat and the drowning of two
innocent spectators; her next was an attempt to butt the Eddy-
stone over in a fog, and, being unbreakable, she might have
succeeded only that she was going dead slow. She drifted out
of the Bullmer line on the wash of a law-suit owing to the
ramming by her of a Cape boat in Las Palmas harbour; engaged
herself in the fruit trade in the service of the Corona Capuella
Syndicate, and got on to the Swimmer rocks with a cargo of
Jamaica oranges, a broken screw shaft and a blown-off cylinder
cover. The ruined cargo, salvage and tow smashed the Syndicate, and the *Robert Bullmer* found new occupations till the
See-Yup-See Company of Canton picked her up, and, rechris-
tening, used her for conveying coffins and coolies to the American seaboard. They had sent her to Valdivia on some business,
and on the return from the southern port to 'Frisco she had, true
to her instincts and helped by a gale, run on San Juan, a scrap
of an island north of the Channel Islands off the California coast.
Every soul had been lost with the exception of two Chinese
coolies, who, drifting on a raft, had been picked up and brought
to San Francisco.

She had a general cargo and twenty thousand dollars in gold

coin on board, but the coolies had declared her to be a total wreck, said, in fact, when they had last sighted her she was going to pieces.

That was the yarn Harman heard through Clancy, with the intimation that the wreck was not worth two dollars, let alone the expenses of a salvage ship.

The story had eaten into Harman's mind; he knew San Juan better than any man in 'Frisco, and he considered that a ship once ashore there would stick; then Ginnell turned up, and the luminous idea of inducing Ginnell to shanghai Blood so that Blood might with his, Harman's, assistance shanghai Ginnell and use the *Heart of Ireland* for the picking of the *Yan-Shan's* pocket, entered his mind.

"It's just when we come alongside the *Yan-Shan* we may find our worst bother," said Blood.

"Which way?" asked Harman.

"Well, they're pretty sure to send some sort of a wrecking expedition to try and salve some of the cargo, let alone those dollars."

"See here," said Harman, "I had the news from Clancy that morning, and it had only just come to 'Frisco, it wasn't an hour old; we put the cap on Ginnell and were out of the Golden Gate before sundown same day. A wrecking ship would take all of two days to get her legs under her, supposing anyone bought the wreck, so we have two days' start; we've been makin' seven knots and maybe a bit over, they won't make more. So we have two days to our good when we get there."

"They may start a quick ship out on the job," said Blood.

"Well, now, there's where my knowledge comes in," said Harman. "There's only two salvage ships at present in 'Frisco, and rotten tubs they are. One's the *Maryland*, she's most a divin' and dredgin' ship, ain't no good for this sort of work, sea-bottom scrapin' is all she's good for, and little she makes at it. The other's the *Port of Amsterdam*, owned by Gunderman. She's the ship they'd use; she's got steam winches and derricks 'nough to discharge the Ark, and stowage room to hold the cargo down to the last flea, *but* she's no good for more than eight knots; she steams like as if she'd a drogue behind her, because why?—she's got beam engines—she's that old, she's got beam engines in her. I'm not denyin' there's somethin' to be said for them, but, there you are, there's no speed in them."

"Well, beam engines or no beam engines, we'll have a pretty rough time if she comes down and catches us within a cable's length of the *Yan-Shan*," said Blood. "However, there's no use in fetching trouble; let's go and have a look at the lazaret, I want to see how we stand for grub."

Chop-stick Charlie was the name Blood had christened the coolie who acted as steward and cabin hand. He called him now, and out of the opium-tinctured gloom of the fo'c'sle Charlie appeared, received his orders and led them to the lazaret.

None of the crew had shown the slightest emotion on seeing Blood take over command of the schooner and Ginnell swabbing decks. The fight, that had made Blood master of the *Heart of Ireland* and Ginnell's revolver, had occurred in the cabin and out of sight of the coolies, but even had it been conducted in full view of them, it is doubtful whether they would have shown any feeling or lifted a hand in the matter.

As long as their little privileges were regarded, as long as opium bubbled in the evening pipe, and pork, rice and potatoes were served out, one white skipper was the same as another to them.

The overhaul of the stores took half an hour and was fairly satisfactory, and, when they came on deck, Blood, telling Charlie to take Ginnell's place as lookout, called the latter down into the cabin.

"We want to have a word with you," said Blood, whilst Harman took his seat on a bunk edge opposite him.

"It's time you knew our minds and what we intend doing with the schooner and yourself."

"Faith," said Ginnell, "I think it is."

"I'm glad you agree. Well, when you shanghaied me on board this old shark-boat of yours, there's little doubt as to what you intended doing with *me*. Harman will tell you, for we've talked on the matter."

"He'd a' worked you crool hard, fed you crool bad, and landed you after six months' cruise doped or drunk, with two cents in your pocket and an affidavit up his sleeve that you'd tried to fire his ship," said Harman. "I know the swab."

Ginnell said nothing for a moment in answer to this soft impeachment, he was cutting himself a chew of tobacco; then at last he spoke:

"I don't want no certifikit of character from either the pair of you," said he. "You've boned me ship and you've blacked me eye and you've near stove me ribs in sittin' on me chest and houldin' me revolver in me face; what I wants to know is your game. Where's your profits to come from on this job?"

"I'll tell you," replied Blood. "There's a hooker called the *Yan-Shan* piled on the rocks down the coast and we're going to leave our cards on her—savvy?"

"Oh, Lord!" said Ginnell.

"What's the matter now?" asked Harman.

"What's the matter, d'you say?" cried Ginnell. "Why, it's the *Yan-Shan* I was after meself."

Blood stared at the owner of the *Heart of Ireland* for a moment, then he broke into a roar of laughter.

"You don't mean to say you bought the wreck?" he asked.

"Not me," replied Ginnell. "Sure, where d'you think I'd be findin' the money to buy wrecks with? I had news that mornin' she was lyin' there derelick, and I was just slippin' down the coast to have a look at her when you two spoiled me lay by takin' me ship."

It was now that Harman began to laugh.

"Well, if that don't beat all," said he. "And maybe, since you were so keen on havin' a look at her, you've brought wreckin' tools with you in case they might come in handy?"

"That's as may be," replied Ginnell. "What you have got to worry about isn't wreckin' tools, but how to get rid of the boodle if it's there. Twenty thousand dollars, that's the figure."

"So you know of the dollars?" said Blood.

"Sure, what do you take me for?" asked Ginnell. "D'you think I'd have bothered about the job only for the dollars? What's the use of general cargo to the like of me? Now what I'm thinkin' is this, you want a fence to help you to get rid of the stuff. Supposin' you find it, how are you to cart this stuff ashore and bank it? You'll be had, sure, but not if I'm at your back. Now, gents, I'm willin' to wipe out all differences and help in the salvin' on shares, and I'll make it easy for you. You'll each take seven thousand and I'll take the balance, and I won't charge nuthin' for the loan you've took of the *Heart of Ireland*. It's a losin' game for me, but it's better than bein' done out entirely."

Blood looked at Harman and Harman looked at Blood. Then telling Ginnell that they would consider the matter, they went on deck to talk it over.

There was truth in what Ginnell said. They would want help in getting the coin ashore in safety, and unless they marooned or murdered Ginnell, he, if left out, would always be a witness to make trouble. Besides, though engaged on a somewhat shady business, neither Blood nor Harman were scoundrels. Ginnell up to this had been paid out in his own coin, the slate was clean, and it pleased neither of them to take profit from this blackguard beyond what they considered their due.

It was just this touch of finer feeling that excluded them from the category of rogues and made their persons worth considering and their doings worth recounting.

"We'll give him what he asks," said Blood, when the consultation was over, "and mind you, I don't like giving it him one little bit, not on account of the money but because it seems to make us partners with that swab. I tell you this, Billy Harman, I'd give half as much again if an honest man was dealing with us in this matter instead of Pat Ginnell."

"And what honest man would deal with us?" asked the ingenuous Harman. "Lord! one might think the job we was on was tryin' to sell a laundry. It's *safe* enough, for who can say we didn't hit the wreck cruisin' round promiscuous, but it won't hold no frills in the way of Honesty and such. Down with you, and close the bargain with that chap and tip him the wink that, though we're mugs enough to give him six thousand dollars for the loan of his old shark-boat, we're men enough to put a pistol bullet in his gizzard if he tries any games with us. Down you go."

Blood went.

## II

Next morning, an hour after sunrise, through the blaze of light striking the Pacific across the far-off Californian coast, San Juan showed like a flake of spar on the horizon to southward.

The sea there is of an impossible blueness, the Pacific blue deepened by the *Kuro Shiwo* current, that mysterious river of the sea which floods up the coast of Japan, crosses the Pacific towards Alaska, and sweeps down the West American seaboard to fan out and lose itself away down somewhere off Chile.

Harman judged the island to be twenty miles away, and as they were making six and a half knots, he reckoned to hit it in three hours if the wind held.

They went down and had breakfast, and after the meal Ginnell, going to the locker where he had stowed the wrecking tools, fetched them out and laid them on deck. There were two crow-bars and a jemmy, not to mention a flogging hammer, a rip saw, some monstrous big chisels and a shipwright's mallet. They looked like a collection of burglar's implements from the land of Brobdingnag.

"There you are," said Ginnell. "You never know what you may want on a job like this, with bulkheads, maybe, to be cut through and chests broke open; get a spare sail, Misther Harman, and rowl the lot up in it so's they'll be aisier for thransport."

He was excited, and the Irish in him came out when he was

like that; also, as the most knowledgeable man in the business, he was taking the lead. You never could have fancied from his cheerful manner and his appearance of boss that Blood was the real master of the situation, or that Blood, only a few days ago, had nearly pounded the life out of him, captured his revolver, and taken possession of the *Heart of Ireland*.

The schooner carried a whale-boat, and this was now got in readiness for lowering, with provisions and water for the landing-party, and when that was done the island, now only four miles distant, showed up fine, a sheer splinter of volcanic rock standing up from the sea and creamed about with foam.

Not a sign of a wreck was to be seen, though Ginnell's glasses were powerful enough to show up every detail from the rock fissures to the roosting gulls.

Gloom fell upon the party, with the exception of Harman.

"It'll be on the other side if it's there at all," said he. "She'd have been coming up from the s'uthard, and if the gale was behind her it would have taken her right on to the rocks; she couldn't be on this side, anyhow, because why?—there's nuthin' to hold her. It's a mile deep water off them cliffs, but on the other side it shoals gradual from tide marks to ten fathoms water, which holds for a quarter of a mile—keep her as she is, you could scrape them cliffs with a battleship without danger of groundin'."

After a minute or two, he took the wheel himself and steered her whilst the fellows stood by the halyards ready to let go at a moment's notice.

It was an impressive place, this north side of the island of San Juan; the heavy swell came up smacking right on to the sheer cliff wall, jetting green water and foam yards high to the snore and boom of caves and cut outs in the rock. Gulls haunted the place. The black petrel, the Western gull and the black-footed albatross all were to be found here; long lines of white gulls marked the cliff edges, and far above, in the dazzling azure of the sky, a Farallone cormorant circled like the spirit of the place, challenging the newcomers with its cry.

Harman shifted his helm, and the *Heart of Ireland* with main boom swinging to port came gliding past the western rocks and opening the sea to southward where, far on the horizon, lovely in the morning light like vast ships under press of sail, the San Lucas Islands lay remote in the morning splendour.

Away to port the line of the Californian coast showed beyond the heave of the sea from Point Arguello to Point Conception, and to starboard and west of the San Lucas's a dot in the sun-dazzle marked the peaks of the island of San Nicolas.

Then, as the *Heart of Ireland* came around and the full view of the south of San Juan burst upon them, the wreck piled on the rocks came in sight, and, anchored quarter of a mile off the shore—a Chinese junk!

"Well, I'm damned," said Harman.

Ginnell, seizing his glasses, rushed forward and looked through them at the wreck.

"It's swarmin' with chows," cried he, coming aft. "They seem to have only just landed, be the look of them. Keep her as she goes and be ready with the anchor there forrard; we'll scupper them yet. Mr. Harman, be plazed to fetch up that linth of lead pipe you'll find on the cabin flure be the door. Capt'in, will you see with Charlie here to the boat while I get the anchor ready for droppin'; them coolies is all thumbs."

He went forward, and the *Heart of Ireland*, with the wind spilling out of her mainsail, came along over the heaving blue swell, satin-smooth here in the shelter of the island.

Truly the *Yan-Shan*, late *Robert Bullmer*, had made a masterpiece of her last business; she had come stem on, lifted by the piling sea, and had hit the rocks, smashing every bow-plate from the keel to within a yard or two of the gunnel, then a wave had taken her under the stern and lifted her and flung her broadside on just as she now lay, pinned to her position by the rock horns that had gored her side, and showing a space of her rust-red bottom to the sun.

The water was squattering among the rocks right up to her, the phosphor-bronze propeller showed a single blade cocked crookedly at the end of the broken screw shaft; rudder there was none, the funnel was gone, spar deck and bridge were in wrack and ruin, whilst the cowl of a bent ventilator turned seaward seemed contemplating with a languid air the beauty of the morning and the view of the far distant San Lucas Islands.

The *Heart of Ireland* picked up a berth inside the junk, and as the rasp and rattle of the anchor chain came back in faint echoes from the cliff, a gong on the junk woke to life and began to snarl and roar its warning to the fellows on the wreck.

"Down with the boat," cried Ginnell. With the "linth of lead pipe," a most formidable weapon, sticking from his pocket, he ran to help with the falls; the whale-boat smacked the water, the crew tumbled in, and, with Ginnell in the bow, it started for the shore.

The gong had done its work. The fellows who had been crawling like ants over the dead body of the *Yan-Shan* came slithering down on ropes, appeared running and stumbling over the rocks abaft the stern, some hauling along sacks of loot, others brandishing sticks or bits of timber, and all shouting and clamouring with a noise like gulls whose nests are being raided.

There was a small scrap of shingly beach off which the Chinamen's scow was lying anchored with a stone and with a China boy for anchor watch. The whale-boat passed the scow, dashed nose end up the shelving beach, and the next moment Ginnell and his linth of lead pipe was amongst the Chinamen, whilst Blood, following him, was firing his revolver over their heads. Harman, with a crowbar carried at the level, was aiming straight at the belly of the biggest of the foe, when they parted right and left, dropping everything, beaten before they were touched, and making for the water over the rocks.

Swimming like rats, they made for the scow, scrambled on board her, howked up the anchor stone and shot out the oars.

"They're off for the junk," cried Ginnell. "Faith, that was a clane bit of work; look at thim rowin' as if the divil was after thim."

They were, literally, and now on board the junk they were hauling the boat in, shaking out the lateen sail and dragging up the anchor as though a hundred pair of hands were at work instead of twenty.

Then, as the huge sail bellied gently to the wind and the junk broke the violet breeze shadow beyond the calm of the sheltered water, a voice came over the sea, a voice like the clamour of a hundred gulls, thin, rending, fierce as the sound of tearing calico.

"Shout away, me boys," said Ginnell. "You've got the shout and we've got the boodle, and good day to ye."

### III

He turned with the others to examine the contents of the sacks dropped by the vanquished ones and lying amongst the rocks. They were old gunny bags and they were stuffed with all sorts of rubbish and valuables, musical instruments, bits of old metal, cabin curtains, and even cans of bully beef—there was no sign of dollars.

"The fools were so busy picking up everything they could find lying about, they hadn't time to search for the real stuff," said Blood. "Didn't know of it."

"Well," said Ginnell, "stick the ould truck back in the bags with the insthruments; we'll sort it out when we get aboard and fling the rubbish over and keep what's worth keepin'."

Helped by the coolies, they refilled the bags and left them in position for carrying off, and then, led by Ginnell, they made round the stern of the wreck to the port side.

Now, on the sea side the *Yan-Shan* presented a bad enough picture of desolation and destruction, but here on the land side the sight was terrific.

The great yellow funnel had crashed over on to the rocks and lay with lengths of the guys still adhering to it; a quarter boat with bottom half out had gone the way of the funnel; crabs were crawling over all sorts of raffle, broken spars, canvas from the bridge screen and woodwork of the chart-house, whilst all forward of amidships the plates, beaten and twisted and ripped apart, showed cargo, held, or in the act of escaping. One big packing case, free of the ship, had resolved itself into staves round its once contents, a piano that appeared perfectly uninjured.

A rope ladder hung from the bulwarks amidships, and up it Ginnell went, followed by the others, reaching a roofless passage that had once been the part alley-way.

Here on the slanting deck one got a full picture of the ruin that had come on the ship; the masts were gone, as well as the funnel; boats, ventilators—with the exception of the twisted cowl looking seaward—bridge, chart-house, all had vanished wholly or in part, a picture made more impressive by the calm blue sky overhead and the brilliancy of the sunlight.

The locking bars had been removed from the cover of the fore hatch and the hatch opened, evidently by the Chinese in search of plunder. Ginnell scarcely turned an eye on it before he made aft and, followed by the others, he reached the saloon companion-way and dived down it.

If the confusion on deck was bad, it was worse below. The cabin doors on either side were either open or off their hinges, bunk bedding, mattresses, an open and rifled valise, some women's clothes, an empty cigar-box and a cage with a dead canary in it lay on the floor.

The place looked as if an army of pillagers had been at work for days, and the sight struck a chill to the hearts of the beholders.

"We're dished," said Ginnell. "Quick, boys, if the stuff's anywhere it'll be in the old man's cabin, there's no mail room in a packet like this. If it's not there, we're done."

They found the captain's cabin, they found his papers tossed about, his cash-box open and empty, and a strong box clamped to the deck by the bunk in the same condition. They found, to complete the business, an English sovereign on the floor in a corner.

Ginnell sat down on the edge of the bunk.

"They've got the dollars," said he. "That's why they legged it so quick and—we let them go. Twenty thousand dollars in gold coin and we let them go. Tear an' ages! Afther them!" He sprang from the bunk and dashed through the saloon, followed by the others. On deck they strained their eyes seaward towards a brown spot on the blue far, far away to the sou'-west. It was the junk making a soldier's wind of it, every inch of sail spread. Judging by the distance she had covered, she must have been making at least eight knots, and the *Heart of Ireland* under similar wind conditions was incapable of more than seven.

"No good chasing her," said Blood.

"Not a happorth," replied Ginnell. Then the quarrel began.

"If you hadn't held us pokin' over them old sacks on the rocks there we'd maybe have had a chance of overhaulin' her," said Ginnell.

"Sacks," cried Blood, "what are you talking about; it was you who let them go, shouting good day to them and telling them we'd got the boodle!"

"Boodle, b'g-d!" cried Ginnell. "You're a nice chap to talk about boodle. You did me in an' collared me boat, and now you're let down proper, and serve you right."

Blood was about to reply in kind, when the dispute was cut short by a loud yell from the engine-room hatch.

Harman, having satisfied himself with a glance that all was up with the junk, had gone poking about and entered the engine-room hatchway. He now appeared, shouting like a maniac.

"The dollars," he cried, "two dead Chinkies an' the dollars."

He vanished again with a shout, they rushed to the hatch, and there, on the steel grating leading to the ladder, curled together like two cats that had died in battle, lay the China-men, Harman kneeling beside them, his hands at work on the neck of a tied sack that chinked as he shook it with the glorious rich, mellow sound that gold in bulk and gold in specie alone can give.

The lanyard came away, and Harman, plunging his big hand in, produced it filled with British sovereigns.

Not one of them moved or said a word for a moment, then Ginnell suddenly squatted down on the grating beside Harman, and, taking a sovereign between finger and thumb gingerly, as though he feared it might burn him, examined it with a laugh. Then he bit it, spun it in the air, caught it in his left hand and brought his great right palm down on it with a bang.

"Hids or tails!" cried Ginnell. "Hids I win, tails you lose." He gave a coarse laugh as he opened his palm, where the coin lay tail up.

"Hids it is," he cried, then he tossed it back into the bag and rose to his feet.

"Come on, boys," said he, "let's bring the stuff down to the saloon and count it."

"Better get it aboard," said Blood.

Harman looked up. The grin on his face stamped by the finding of the gold was still there, and in the light coming through the hatch his forehead showed beaded with sweat.

"I'm with Ginnell," said he, "let's get down to the saloon for an overhaul. I can't wait whiles we row off to the schooner. I wants to feel the stuff and I wants to divide it, b'g-d, right off and now. Boys, we're rich, we sure are. It's the stroke of my life, and I can't wait for no rowin' on board no schooners before we divide up."

"Come on, then," said Blood.

The sack was much bigger than its contents, so there was plenty of grip for him as he seized one corner. Then, Harman grasping it by the neck, they lugged it out and along the deck and down the saloon companionway, Ginnell following.

The Chinese had opened nearly all the cabin port-holes for the sake of light to assist them in their plundering, and now as Blood and Harman placed the sack on the slanting saloon table, the crying of gulls came clearly and derisively from the cliffs outside, mixed with the hush of the sea and the boost of the swell as it broke creaming and squattering among the rocks. The lackadaisical ventilator cowl, which took an occasional movement from stray puffs of air, added its voice now and then, whining and complaining like some lost yet inconsiderable soul.

No other sound could be heard as the three men ranged themselves, Ginnell on the starboard, and Blood and Harman on the port side of the table.

The swivel seats, though all aslant, were practicable, and Harman was in the act of taking his place in the seat he had chosen when Ginnell interposed.

"One moment, Mr. Harman," said the owner of the *Heart of Ireland*. "I've a word to say to you and Mr. Blood—sure, I beg your pardon—I mane Capt'in Blood."

"Well," said Blood, grasping a chair-back. "What have you to say?"

"Only this," replied Ginnell with a grin. "I've got back me revolver."

Blood clapped his hand to his pocket. It was empty.

"I picked your pocket of it," said Ginnell, producing the weapon, "two minits back; you fired three shots over the heads of them chows and there's three ca'tridges left in her. I can hit a dollar at twinty long paces. Move an inch either the one or other of you, and I'll lay your brains on the table fornint you."

They did not move, for they knew that he was in earnest. They knew that if they moved he would begin to shoot, and if he began to shoot he would finish the job, leave their corpses on the floor, and sail off with the dollars and his Chinese crew in perfect safety. There were no witnesses.

"Now," said Ginnell, "what the pair of you have to do is this. Misther Harman, you'll go into that cabin behind you, climb on the upper bunk, stick your head through the porthole and shout to the coolies down below there with the boat to come up. It'll take two men to get them dollars on deck and down to the wather side. When you've done that, the pair of you will walk into the ould man's cabin an' say your prayers, thanking the saints you've got off so easy, whiles I puts the bolt on you till the dollars are away. And remimber this, one word or kick from you and I shoot—the Chinamen will never tell."

"See here," said Harman.

"One word!" shouted Ginnell, suddenly dropping the mask of urbanity and levelling the pistol.

It was as though the tiger-cat in his grimy soul had suddenly burst bonds and mastered him. His finger pressed on the trigger and the next moment Harman's brains, or what he had of them, might have been literally forenint him on the table, when suddenly, tremendous as the last trumpet, paralysing as the inrush of a body of armed men, booing and bellowing back from the cliffs in a hundred echoes came a voice—the blast of a ship's syren.

"Huroop, Hirrip, Hurop, Haar—Haar—Haar!"

Ginnell's arm fell. Harman, forgetting everything, turned, dashed into the cabin behind him, climbed on the upper bunk, and stuck his head through the port-hole.

Then he dashed back into the saloon.

"It's the *Port of Amsterdam*," cried Harman, "it's the salvage ship, she's there droppin' her anchor; we're done, we're dished —and we foolin' like this and they crawlin' up on us."

"And you said she'd only do eight knots!" cried Blood.

Ginnell flung the revolver on the floor. Every trace of the recent occurrence had vanished, and the three men thought no more of one another than a man thinks of petty matters in the face of dissolution. Gunderman was outside, that was enough for them.

"Boys," said Ginnell, "ain't there no way out with them dollars? S'pose we howk them ashore?"

"Cliffs two hundred foot high," said Harman, "not a chanst. We're dished."

Said Blood: "There's only one thing left. We'll walk the dollars down to the boat and row off with them. Of course we'll be stopped; still, there's the chance that Gunderman may be drunk or something. It's one chance in a hundred billion—it's the only one."

But Gunderman was not drunk, nor were his boat party; and the court-martial he held on the beach in broken English and with the sack of coin beside him as chief witness would form a bright page of literature had one time to record it.

Ginnell, as owner of the *Heart of Ireland*, received the whole brunt of the storm; there was no hearing for him when, true to himself, he tried to cast the onus of the business on Blood and Harman. He was told to get out and be thankful he was not brought back to 'Frisco in irons, and he obeyed instructions, rowing off to the schooner, he and Harman and Blood, a melancholy party with the exception of Blood, who was talking to Harman with extreme animation on the subject of beam engines.

On deck it was Blood who gave orders for hauling up the anchor and setting sail. He had recaptured the revolver.

# THE SWORD OF ALAN

## From "Kidnapped," BY ROBERT LOUIS STEVENSON

MORE than a week went by, in which the ill-luck that had
hitherto pursued the *Covenant* upon this voyage grew yet more
strongly marked. Some days she made a little way; others, she
was driven actually back. At last we were beaten so far to the
south that we tossed and tacked to and fro the whole of the
ninth day, within sight of Cape Wrath and the wild, rocky coast
on either hand of it. There followed on that a council of the
officers, and some decision which I did not rightly understand,
seeing only the result: that we had made a fair wind of a foul
one and were running south.

The tenth afternoon, there was a falling swell and a thick,
wet, white fog that hid one end of the brig from the other. All
afternoon, when I went on deck, I saw men and officers listening hard over the bulwarks—"for breakers," they said; and
though I did not so much as understand the word, I felt danger
in the air and was excited.

Maybe about ten at night, I was serving Mr. Riach and the
captain at their supper, when the ship struck something with
a great sound, and we heard voices singing out. My two masters
leaped to their feet.

"She's struck," said Mr. Riach.

"No, sir," said the captain. "We've only run a boat down."

And they hurried out.

The captain was in the right of it. We had run down a boat
in the fog, and she parted in the midst and gone to the bottom
with all her crew, but one. This man (as I heard afterwards)
had been sitting in the stern as a passenger, while the rest were
on the benches rowing. At the moment of the blow, the stern
had been thrown into the air, and the man (having his hands

free, and for all he was encumbered with a frieze overcoat that
came below his knees) had leaped up and caught hold of the
brig's bowsprit. It showed he had luck and much agility and
unusual strength, that he should have thus saved himself from
such a pass. And yet, when the captain brought him into the
round house, and I set eyes on him for the first time, he looked
as cool as I did.

He was smallish in stature, but well set and as nimble as a
goat; his face was of a good open expression, but sunburnt very
dark, and heavily freckled and pitted with the small-pox; his
eyes were unusually light and had a kind of dancing madness
in them, that was both engaging and alarming; and when he
took off his great-coat, he laid a pair of fine, silver-mounted
pistols on the table, and I saw that he was belted with a great
sword. His manners, besides, were elegant, and he pledged the
captain handsomely. Altogether I thought of him, at the first
sight, that here was a man I would rather call my friend than
my enemy.

The captain, too, was taking his observations, but rather of
the man's clothes than his person. And to be sure, as soon as he
had taken off the great-coat, he showed forth mighty fine for
the round-house of a merchant brig: having a hat with feathers,
a red waist-coat, breeches of black plush, and a blue coat with
silver buttons and handsome silver lace: costly clothes, though
somewhat spoiled with the fog and being slept in.

"I'm vexed, sir, about the boat," says the captain.

"There are some pretty men gone to the bottom," said the
stranger, "that I would rather see on the dry land again than
half a score of boats."

"Friends of yours?" said Hoseason.

"You have none such friends in your country," was the reply.
"They would have died for me like dogs."

"Well, sir," said the captain, still watching him, "there are
more men in the world than boats to put them in."

"And that's true too," cried the other; "and ye seem to be a
gentleman of great penetration."

"I have been in France, sir," says the captain; so that it was plain he meant more by the words than showed upon the face of them.

"Well, sir," says the other, "and so has many a pretty man, for the matter of that."

"No doubt, sir," says the captain; "and fine coats."

"Oho!" says the stranger, "is that how the wind sets?" And he laid his hand quickly on his pistols.

"Don't be hasty," said the captain. "Don't do a mischief, before ye see the need for it. Ye've a French soldier's coat upon your back and a Scotch tongue in your head, to be sure; but so has many an honest fellow in these days, and I daresay none the worse of it."

"So?" said the gentleman in the fine coat: "are ye of the honest party?" (meaning, Was he a Jacobite? for each side, in these sort of civil broils, takes the name of honesty for its own).

"Why, sir," replied the captain, "I am a true-blue Protestant, and I thank God for it." (It was the first word of any religion I had ever heard from him, but I learnt afterwards he was a great church-goer while on shore.) "But, for all that," says he, "I can be sorry to see another man with his back to the wall."

"Can ye so, indeed?" asks the Jacobite. "Well, sir, to be quite plain with ye, I am one of those honest gentlemen that were in trouble about the years forty-five and six; and (to be still quite plain with ye) if I get into the hands of any of the red-coated gentry, it's like it would go hard with me. Now, sir, I was for France; and there was a French ship cruising here to pick me up; but she gave us the go-by in the fog—as I wish from the heart that ye had done yoursel'! And the best that I can say is this: If ye can set me ashore where I was going, I have that upon me will reward you highly for your trouble."

"In France?" says the captain. "No, sir; that I cannot do. But where ye come from—we might talk of that."

And then, unhappily, he observed me standing in my corner, and packed me off to the galley to get supper for the gentleman.

I lost no time, I promise you; and when I came back into the round-house, I found the gentleman had taken a money-belt from about his waist, and poured out a guinea or two upon the table. The captain was looking at the guineas, and then at the belt, and then at the gentleman's face; and I thought he seemed excited.

"Half of it," he cried, "and I'm your man!"

The other swept back the guineas into the belt, and put it on again under his waistcoat. "I have told ye, sir," said he, "that not one doit of it belongs to me. It belongs to my chieftain"—and here he touched his hat—"and while I would be but a silly messenger to grudge some of it that the rest might come safe, I should show myself a hound indeed if I bought my own carcass any too dear. Thirty guineas on the seaside, or sixty if ye set me on the Linnhe Loch. Take it, if ye will; if not, ye can do your worst."

"Ay," said Hoseason. "And if I give ye over to the soldiers?"

"Ye would make a fool's bargain," said the other. "My chief, let me tell you, sir, is forfeited, like every honest man in Scotland. His estate is in the hands of the man they call King George; and it is his officers that collect the rents, or try to collect them. But for the honor of Scotland, the poor tenant bodies take a thought upon their chief lying in exile; and his money is a part of that very rent for which King George is looking. Now, sir, ye seem to me to be a man that understands things: bring this money within the reach of Government, and how much of it'll come to you?"

"Little enough, to be sure," said Hoseason; and then, "If they knew," he added, dryly. "But I think, if I was to try, that I could hold my tongue about it."

"Ah, but I'll begowk [1] ye there!" cried the gentleman. "Play me false, and I'll play you cunning. If a hand's laid upon me, they shall ken what money it is."

"Well," returned the captain, "what must be must. Sixty guineas, and done. Here's my hand upon it."

[1] Befool.

"And here's mine," said the other.

And thereupon the captain went out (rather hurriedly, I thought), and left me alone in the round-house with the stranger.

At that period (so soon after forty-five) there were many exiled gentlemen coming back at the peril of their lives, either to see their friends or to collect a little money; and as for the Highland chiefs that had been forfeited, it was a common matter of talk how their tenants would stint themselves to send them money, and their clansmen outface the soldiery to get it in, and run the gauntlet of our great navy to carry it across. All this I had, of course, heard tell of; and now I had a man under my eyes whose life was forfeit on all these counts and upon one more; for he was not only a rebel and a smuggler of rents, but had taken service with King Louis of France. And as if all this were not enough, he had a belt full of golden guineas round his loins. Whatever my opinions, I could not look on such a man without a lively interest.

"And so you're a Jacobite?" said I, as I set meat before him.

"Ay," said he, beginning to eat. "And you, by your long face, should be a Whig?" [2]

"Betwixt and between," said I, not to annoy him; for indeed I was as good a Whig as Mr. Campbell could make me.

"And that's naething," said he. "But I'm saying, Mr. Betwixt-and-Between," he added, "this bottle of yours is dry; and it's hard if I'm to pay sixty guineas and be grudged a dram upon the back of it."

"I'll go and ask for the key," said I and stepped on deck.

The fog was as close as ever, but the swell almost down. They had laid the brig to, not knowing precisely where they were, and the wind (what little there was of it) not serving well for their true course. Some of the hands were still hearkening for breakers; but the captain and the two officers were in the waist with their heads together. It struck me, I don't know why, that

[2] Whig or Whigamore was the cant name for those who were loyal to King George.

they were after no good; and the first word I heard, as I drew softly near, more than confirmed me.

It was Mr. Riach, crying out as if upon a sudden thought: "Couldn't we wile him out of the round-house?"

"He's better where he is," returned Hoseason; "he hasn't room to use his sword."

"Well, that's true," said Riach; "but he's hard to come at."

"Hut!" said Hoseason. "We can get the man in talk, one upon each side, and pin him by the two arms, or if that'll not hold, sir, we can make a run by both the doors and get him under hand before he has the time to draw."

At this hearing, I was seized with both fear and anger at these treacherous, greedy, bloody men that I sailed with. My first mind was to run away; my second was bolder.

"Captain," said I, "the gentleman is seeking a dram, and the bottle's out. Will you give me the key?"

They all started and turned about.

"Why, here's our chance to get the firearms!" Riach cried; and then to me: "Hark ye, David," he said, "do ye ken where the pistols are?"

"Ay, ay," put in Hoseason. "David kens; David's a good lad. Ye see, David my man, yon wild Hielandman is a danger to the ship, besides being a rank foe to King George, God bless him!"

I had never been so be-Davided since I came on board; but I said yes, as if all I heard were quite natural.

"The trouble is," resumed the captain, "that all our firelocks, great and little, are in the round-house under this man's nose; likewise the powder. Now, if I, or one of the officers, was to go in and take them, he would fall to thinking. But a lad like you, David, might snap up a horn and a pistol or two without remark. And if ye can do it cleverly, I'll bear it in mind when it'll be good for you to have friends; and that's when we come to Carolina."

Here Mr. Riach whispered him a little.

"Very right, sir," said the captain; and then to myself: "And see here, David, yon man has a beltful of gold, and I give you my word that you shall have your fingers in it."

I told him I would do as he wished, though indeed I had scarce breath to speak with; and upon that he gave me the key of the spirit locker, and I began to go slowly back to the round-house. What was I to do? They were dogs and thieves; they had stolen me from my own country; they had killed poor Ransome; and was I to hold the candle to another murder? But then, upon the other hand, there was the fear of death very plain before me; for what could a boy and a man, if they were as brave as lions, against a whole ship's company?

I was still arguing it back and forth, and getting no great clearness, when I came into the round-house and saw the Jacobite eating his supper under the lamp; and at that my mind was made up all in a moment. I have no credit by it; it was by no choice of mine, but as if by compulsion, that I walked right up to the table and put my hand on his shoulder.

"Do ye want to be killed?" said I.

He sprang to his feet, and looked a question at me as clear as if he had spoken.

"O!" cried I, "they're all murderers here; it's a ship full of them! They've murdered a boy already. Now it's you."

"Ay, ay," said he; "but they haven't got me yet."

And then looking at me curiously, "Will ye stand with me?"

"That will I!" said I. "I am no thief, nor yet murderer. I'll stand by you."

"Why, then," said he, "what's your name?"

"David Balfour," said I; and then thinking that a man with so fine a coat must like fine people, I added for the first time "of Shaws."

It never occurred to him to doubt me, for a Highlander is used to see great gentlefolk in great poverty; but as he had no estate of his own, my words nettled a very childish vanity he had.

"My name is Stewart," he said, drawing himself up. "Alan

Breck, they call me. A king's name is good enough for me, though I bear it plain and have the name of no farm-midden to clap to the hind-end of it."

And having administered this rebuke, as though it were something of a chief importance, he turned to examine our defences.

The round-house was built very strong, to support the breachings of the seas. Of its five apertures, only the skylight and the two doors were large enough for the passage of a man. The doors, besides, could be drawn close: they were of stout oak, and ran in grooves, and were fitted with hooks to keep them either shut or open as the need arose. The one that was already shut, I secured in this fashion; but when I was proceeding to slide to the other, Alan stopped me.

"David," said he—"for I cannae bring to mind the name of your landed estate, and so will make so bold as call you David— that door, being open, is the best part of my defences."

"It would be yet better shut," says I.

"Not so, David," says he. "Ye see, I have but one face; but so long as that door is open and my face to it, the best part of my enemies will be in front of me, where I would aye wish to find them."

Then he gave me from the rack a cutlass (of which there were a few besides the firearms), choosing it with great care, shaking his head and saying he had never in all his life seen poorer weapons; and next he set me down to the table with a powder-horn, a bag of bullets, and all the pistols, which he bade me charge.

"And that will be better work, let me tell you," said he, "for a gentleman of decent birth, than scraping plates and raxing [3] drams to a wheen tarry sailors."

Thereupon he stood up in the midst with his face to the door, and drawing his great sword, made trial of the room he had to wield it in.

"I must stick to the point," he said, shaking his head; "and that's a pity, too. It doesn't set my genius, which is all for the

[3] Reaching.

upper guard. And now," said he, "do you keep on charging the pistols, and give heed to me."

I told him I would listen closely. My chest was tight, my mouth dry, the light dark to my eyes; the thought of the numbers that were soon to leap in upon us kept my heart in a flutter; and the sea, which I heard washing round the brig, and where I thought my dead body would be cast ere morning, ran in my mind strangely.

"First of all," said he, "how many are against us?"

I reckoned them up; and such was the hurry of my mind, I had to cast the numbers twice. "Fifteen," said I.

Alan whistled. "Well," said he, "that can't be cured. And now follow me. It is my part to keep this door, where I look for the main battle. In that, ye have no hand. And mind and dinnae fire to this side unless they get me down; for I would rather have ten foes in front of me than one friend like you cracking pistols at my back."

I told him, indeed I was no great shot.

"And that's very bravely said," he cried, in a great admiration of my candor. "There's many a pretty gentleman that wouldnae dare to say it."

"But then, sir," said I, "there is the door behind you, which they may perhaps break in."

"Ay," said he, "and that is a part of your work. No sooner the pistols charged, then ye must climb up into yon bed where ye're handy at the window; and if they lift hand against the door, ye're to shoot. But that's not all. Let's make a bit of a soldier of ye, David. What else have ye to guard?"

"There's the skylight," said I. "But indeed, Mr. Stewart, I would need to have eyes upon both sides to keep the two of them; for when my face is at the one, my back is to the other."

"And that's very true," said Alan. "But have ye no ears to your head?"

"To be sure!" cried I. "I must hear the bursting of the glass!"

"Ye have some rudiments of sense," said Alan, grimly.

But now our time of truce was come to an end. Those on

deck had waited for my coming till they grew impatient; and scarce had Alan spoken, when the captain showed face in the open door.

"Stand!" cried Alan, and pointed his sword at him.

The captain stood, indeed; but he neither winced nor drew back a foot.

"A naked sword?" says he. "This is a strange return for hospitality."

"Do you see me?" said Alan. "I am come of kings; I bear a king's name. My badge is the oak. Do you see my sword? It has slashed the heads off mair Whigamores than you have toes upon your feet. Call up your vermin to your back, sir, and fall on! The sooner the clash begins, the sooner ye'll taste this steel throughout your vitals."

The captain said nothing to Alan, but he looked over at me with an ugly look. "David," said he, "I'll mind this"; and the sound of his voice went through me with a jar.

Next moment he was gone.

"And now," said Alan, "let your hand keep your head, for the grip is coming."

Alan drew a dirk, which he held in his left hand in case they should run in under his sword. I, on my part, clambered up into the berth with an armful of pistols, and set open the window where I was to watch. It was a small part of the deck that I could overlook, but enough for our purpose. The sea had gone down, and the wind was steady and kept the sails quiet; so that there was a great stillness in the ship, in which I made sure I heard the sound of muttering voices. A little after, and there came a clash of steel upon the deck, by which I knew they were dealing out the cutlasses and one had been let fall; and after that silence again.

I do not know if I was what you call afraid; but my heart beat like a bird's, both quick and little; and there was a dimness came before my eyes which I continually rubbed away, and which continually returned. As for hope, I had none; but only a darkness of despair and a sort of anger against all the world that made me long to sell my life as dear as I was able. I tried to pray, I remember, but that same hurry of my mind, like a man running, would not suffer me to think upon the words; and my chief wish was to have the thing begin and be done with it.

It came all of a sudden when it did, with a rush of feet and a roar, and then a shout from Alan, and a sound of blows and some one crying out as if hurt. I looked back over my shoulder, and saw Mr. Shuan in the doorway, crossing blades with Alan.

"That's him that killed the boy!" I cried.

"Look to your window!" said Alan; and as I turned back to my place, I saw him pass his sword through the mate's body.

It was none too soon for me to look to my own part; for my head was scarce back at the window before five men, carrying a spare yard for a battering-ram, ran past me and took post to drive the door in. I had never fired with a pistol in my life, and not often with a gun; far less against a fellow-creature. But it was now or never; and just as they swung the yard, I cried out, "Take that!" and shot into their midst.

I must have hit one of them, for he sang out and gave back a step, and the rest stopped as if a little disconcerted. Before they had time to recover, I sent another ball over their heads; and at my third shot (which went as wide as the second) the whole party threw down the yard and ran for it.

Then I looked round again into the deck-house. The whole place was full of the smoke of my own firing, just as my ears seemed to be burst with the noise of the shots. But there was Alan, standing as before; only now his sword was running blood to the hilt, and himself so swelled with triumph and fallen into so fine an attitude, that he looked to be invincible. Right before him on the floor was Mr. Shuan, on his hands and knees; the blood was pouring from his mouth, and he was sinking slowly lower, with a terrible, white face; and just as I looked, some of those from behind caught hold of him by the heels and dragged him bodily out of the round-house. I believe he died as they were doing it.

"There's one of your Whigs for ye!" cried Alan: and then turning to me, he asked if I had done much execution.

I told him I had winged one, and thought it was the captain.

"And I've settled two," says he. "No, there's not enough blood let; they'll be back again. To your watch, David. This was but a dram before meat."

I settled back to my place, recharging the three pistols I had fired, and keeping watch with both eye and ear.

Our enemies were disputing not far off upon the deck, and that so loudly that I could hear a word or two above the washing of the seas.

"It was Shuan bauchled⁴ it," I heard one say.

And another answered him with a "Wheesht, man! He's paid the piper."

After that the voices fell again into the same muttering as before. Only now, one person spoke most of the time, as though laying down a plan, and first one and then another answered him briefly, like men taking orders. By this, I made sure they were coming on again, and told Alan.

"It's what we have to pray for," said he. "Unless we can give them a good distaste of us, and done with it, there'll be nae sleep for either you or me. But this time, mind, they'll be in earnest."

By this, my pistols were ready, and there was nothing to do but listen and wait. While the brush lasted, I had not the time to think if I was frighted; but now, when all was still again, my mind ran upon nothing else. The thought of the sharp swords and the cold steel was strong in me; and presently, when I began to hear stealthy steps and a brushing of men's clothes against the round-house wall, and knew they were taking their places in the dark, I could have found it in my mind to cry out aloud.

All this was upon Alan's side; and I had begun to think my share of the fight was at an end, when I heard some one drop softly on the roof above me.

⁴ Bungled.

Then there came a single call on the sea-pipe, and that was the signal. A knot of them made one rush of it, cutlass in hand, against the door; and at that same moment, the glass of the sky-light was dashed in a thousand pieces, and a man leaped through and landed on the floor. Before he got his feet, I had clapped a pistol to his back, and might have shot him, too; only at the touch of him (and him alive) my whole flesh misgave me, and I could no more pull the trigger than I could have flown.

He had dropped his cutlass as he jumped, and when he felt the pistol, whipped straight round and laid hold of me, roaring out an oath; and at that either my courage came again, or I grew so much afraid as came to the same thing; for I gave a shriek and shot him in the midst of the body. He gave the most horrible, ugly groan and fell to the floor. The foot of a second fellow, whose legs were dangling through the skylight, struck me at the same time upon the head; and at that I snatched another pistol and shot this one through the thigh, so that he slipped through and tumbled in a lump on his companion's body. There was no talk of missing, any more than there was time to aim; I clapped the muzzle to the very place and fired.

I might have stood and stared at them for long, but I heard Alan shout as if for help, and that brought me to my senses.

He had kept the door so long; but one of the seamen, while he was engaged with others, had run in under his guard and caught him about the body. Alan was dirking him with his left hand, but the fellow clung like a leech. Another had broken in and had his cutlass raised. The door was thronged with their faces. I thought we were lost, and catching up my cutlass, fell on them in flank.

But I had not time to be of help. The wrestler dropped at last; and Alan, leaping back to get his distance, ran upon the others like a bull, roaring as he went. They broke before him like water, turning, and running, and falling one against another in their haste. The sword in his hands flashed like quicksilver into the huddle of our fleeing enemies; and at every flash there came the scream of a man hurt. I was still thinking we were lost, when lo! they were all gone, and Alan was driving them along the deck as a sheepdog chases sheep.

Yet he was no sooner out than he was back again, being as cautious as he was brave; and meanwhile the seamen continued running and crying out as if he was still behind them; and we heard them tumble one upon another into the forecastle, and clap-to the hatch upon the top.

The round-house was like a shambles; three were dead inside, another lay in his death agony across the threshold; and there were Alan and I victorious and unhurt.

He came up to me with open arms. "Come to my arms!" he cried, and embraced and kissed me hard upon both cheeks. "David," said he, "I love you like a brother. And O, man," he cried in a kind of ecstasy, "am I no a bonny fighter?"

Thereupon he turned to the four enemies, passed his sword clean through each of them, and tumbled them out of doors one after the other. As he did so, he kept humming and singing and whistling to himself, like a man trying to recall an air; only what *he* was trying, was to make one. All the while, the flush was in his face, and his eyes were as bright as a five-year-old child's with a new toy. And presently he sat down upon the table, sword in hand; the air that he was making all the time began to run a little clearer, and then clearer still; and then out he burst with a great voice into a Gaelic song.

I have translated it here, not in verse (of which I have no skill) but at least in the king's English. He sang it often afterwards, and the thing became popular; so that I have heard it, and had it explained to me, many's the time.

> This is the song of the sword of Alan:
> The smith made it,
> The fire set it;
> Now it shines in the hand of Alan Breck.
>
> Their eyes were many and bright,
> Swift were they to behold,
> Many the hands they guided:
> The sword was alone.

The dun deer troop over the hill,
They are many, the hill is one;
The dun deer vanish,
The hill remains.

Come to me from the hills of heather,
Come from the isles of the sea.
O far-beholding eagles,
Here is your meat.

Now this song which he made (both words and music) in
the hour of our victory, is something less than just to me, who
stood beside him in the tussle. Mr. Shuan and five more were
either killed outright or thoroughly disabled; but of these, two
fell by my hand, the two that came by the skylight. Four more
were hurt, and of that number, one (and he not the least important) got his hurt from me. So that, altogether, I did my
fair share both of the killing and the wounding, and might have
claimed a place in Alan's verses. But poets (as a very wise man
once told me) have to think upon their rhymes; and in good
prose talk, Alan always did me more than justice.

In the meanwhile, I was innocent of any wrong being done
me. For not only I knew no word of the Gaelic; but what with
the long suspense of the waiting, and the scurry and strain of
our two spirits of fighting, and more than all, the horror I had
of some of my own share in it, the thing was no sooner over
than I was glad to stagger to a seat. There was that tightness on
my chest that I could hardly breathe; the thought of the two
men I had shot sat upon me like a nightmare; and all upon a
sudden, and before I had a guess of what was coming, I began
to sob and cry like any child.

Alan clapped my shoulder, and said I was a brave lad and
wanted nothing but a sleep.

"I'll take the first watch," said he. "Ye've done will by me,
David, first and last; and I wouldn't lose you for all Appin—no,
nor for Breadalbane."

So he made up my bed on the floor, and took the first spell,
pistol in hand and sword on knee; three hours by the captain's

watch upon the wall. Then he roused me up, and I took my turn of three hours; before the end of which it was broad day, and a very quiet morning, with a smooth, rolling sea that tossed the ship and made the blood run to and fro on the round-house floor, and a heavy rain that drummed upon the roof. All my watch there was nothing stirring, and by the banging of the helm, I knew they had even no one at the tiller. Indeed (as I learned afterwards) they were so many of them hurt or dead, and the rest in so ill a temper, that Mr. Riach and the captain had to take turn and turn (like Alan and me), or the brig might have gone ashore and nobody the wiser. It was a mercy the night had fallen so still, for the wind had gone down as soon as the rain began. Even as it was, I judged by the wailing of a great number of gulls that went crying and fishing round the ship, that she must have drifted pretty near the coast or one of the islands of the Hebrides; and at last, looking out of the door of the round-house, I saw the great stone hills of Skye on the right hand, and, a little more astern, the strange isle of Rum.

# THE REMARKABLE WRECK OF THE
## *THOMAS HYKE*

From "The Christmas Wreck," BY FRANK R. STOCKTON

IT WAS half-past one by the clock in the office of the Registrar of Woes. The room was empty, for it was Wednesday, and the Registrar always went home early on Wednesday afternoons. He had made that arrangement when he accepted the office. He was willing to serve his fellow-citizens in any suitable position to which he might be called, but he had private interests which could not be neglected. He belonged to his country, but there was a house in the country which belonged to him; and there were a great many things appertaining to that house which needed attention, especially in pleasant summer weather. It is true he was often absent on afternoons which did not fall on the Wednesday, but the fact of his having appointed a particular time for the furtherance of his outside interests so emphasized their importance that his associates in the office had no difficulty in understanding that affairs of such moment could not always be attended to in a single afternoon of the week.

But although the large room devoted to the especial use of the Registrar was unoccupied, there were other rooms connected with it which were not in that condition. With the suite of offices to the left we have nothing to do, but will confine our attention to a moderate-sized room to the right of the Registrar's office, and connected by a door, now closed, with that large and handsomely furnished chamber. This was the office of the Clerk of Shipwrecks, and it was at present occupied by five persons. One of these was the clerk himself, a man of goodly appearance, somewhere between twenty-five and forty-five years of age, and of a demeanor such as might be supposed to

433

belong to one who had occupied a high position in state affairs, but who, by the cabals of his enemies, had been forced to resign the great operations of statesmanship which he had been directing, and who now stood, with a quite resigned air, pointing out to the populace the futile and disastrous efforts of the incompetent one who was endeavoring to fill his place. The Clerk of Shipwrecks had never fallen from such a position, having never occupied one, but he had acquired the demeanor referred to without going through the preliminary exercises.

Another occupant was a very young man, the personal clerk of the Registrar of Woes, who always closed all the doors of the office of that functionary on Wednesday afternoons, and at other times when outside interests demanded his principal's absence, after which he betook himself to the room of his friend the Shipwreck Clerk.

Then there was a middle-aged man named Mathers, also a friend of the clerk, and who was one of the eight who had made application for a sub-position in this department, which was now filled by a man who was expected to resign when a friend of his, a gentleman of influence in an interior county, should succeed in procuring the nomination as congressional representative of his district of an influential politician, whose election was considered assured in case certain expected action on the part of the administration should bring his party into power. The person now occupying the sub-position hoped then to get something better, and Mathers, consequently, was very willing, while waiting for the place, to visit the offices of the department and acquaint himself with its duties.

A fourth person was J. George Watts, a juryman by profession, who had brought with him his brother-in-law, a stranger in the city.

The Shipwreck Clerk had taken off his good coat, which he had worn to luncheon, and had replaced it by a lighter garment of linen, much bespattered with ink; and he now produced a cigar-box, containing six cigars.

"Gents," said he, "here is the fag end of a box of cigars. It's

not like having the pick of the box, but they are all I have left."
Mr. Mathers, J. George Watts, and the brother-in-law each
took a cigar with that careless yet deferential manner which
always distinguishes the treatee from the treator; and then the
box was protruded in an offhand way toward Harry Covare,
the personal clerk of the Registrar; but this young man declined,
saying that he preferred cigarettes, a package of which he drew
from his pocket. He had very often seen that cigar-box with a
Havana brand, which he himself had brought from the other
room after the Registrar had emptied it, passed around with six
cigars, no more nor less, and he was wise enough to know that
the Shipwreck Clerk did not expect to supply him with smoking
material. If that gentleman had offered to the friends who generally dropped in on him on Wednesday afternoon the paper
bag of cigars sold at five cents each when bought singly, but
half a dozen for a quarter of a dollar, they would have been
quite as thankfully received; but it better pleased his depre-
cative soul to put them in an empty cigar-box, and thus throw
around them the halo of the presumption that ninety-four of
their imported companions had been smoked.

The Shipwreck Clerk, having lighted a cigar for himself, sat
down in his revolving chair, turned his back to his desk, and
threw himself into an easy cross-legged attitude, which showed
that he was perfectly at home in that office. Harry Covare
mounted a high stool, while the visitors seated themselves in
three wooden arm-chairs. But few words had been said, and
each man had scarcely tossed his first tobacco ashes on the
floor when some one wearing heavy boots was heard opening
an outside door and entering the Registrar's room. Harry Covare jumped down from his stool, laid his half-smoked cigarette
thereon, and bounced into the next room, closing the door
after him. In about a minute he returned, and the Shipwreck
Clerk looked at him inquiringly.

"An old cock in a pea-jacket," said Mr. Covare, taking up
his cigarette, and mounting his stool. "I told him the Registrar
would be here in the morning. He said he had something to

report about a shipwreck; and I told him the Registrar would be here in the morning. Had to tell him that three times, and then he went."

"School don't keep Wednesday afternoons," said Mr. J. George Watts, with a knowing smile.

"No, sir," said the Shipwreck Clerk, emphatically, changing the crossing of his legs. "A man can't keep grinding on day in and out without breaking down. Outsiders may say what they please about it, but it can't be done. We've got to let up sometimes. People who do the work need the rest just as much as those who do the looking on."

"And more too, I should say," observed Mr. Mathers.

"Our little let-up Wednesday afternoons," modestly observed Harry Covare, "is like death; it is sure to come, while the let-ups we get other days are more like the diseases which prevail in certain areas; you can't be sure whether you're going to get them or not."

The Shipwreck Clerk smiled benignantly at this remark, and the rest laughed. Mr. Mathers had heard it before, but he would not impair the pleasantness of his relations with a future colleague by hinting that he remembered it.

"He gets such ideas from his beastly statistics," said the Shipwreck Clerk.

"Which come pretty heavy on him sometimes, I expect," observed Mr. Mathers.

"They needn't," said the Shipwreck Clerk, "if things were managed here as they ought to be. If John J. Laylor," meaning thereby the Registrar, "was the right kind of a man, you'd see things very different here from what they are now. There'd be a larger force."

"That's so," said Mr. Mathers.

"And not only that, but there'd be better buildings, and more accommodations. Were any of you ever up to Anster? Well, take a run up there some day, and see what sort of buildings the department has there. William Q. Green is a very different man from John J. Laylor. You don't see him sitting in his chair and picking his teeth the whole winter, while the representative from his district never says a word about his department from one end of a session of Congress to the other. Now if I had charge of things here, I'd make such changes that you wouldn't know the place. I'd throw two rooms off here, and a corridor and entrance door at that end of the building. I'd close up this door," pointing toward the Registrar's room, "and if John J. Laylor wanted to come in here he might go round to the end door like other people."

The thought struck Harry Covare that in that case there would be no John J. Laylor, but he would not interrupt.

"And what is more," continued the Shipwreck Clerk, "I'd close up this whole department at twelve o'clock on Saturdays. The way things are managed now, a man has no time to attend to his own private business. Suppose I think of buying a piece of land, and want to go out and look at it, or suppose any one of you gentlemen were here and thought of buying a piece of land and wanted to go out and look at it, what are you going to do about it? You don't want to go on Sunday, and when are you going to go?"

Not one of the other gentlemen had ever thought of buying a piece of land, nor had they any reason to suppose that they ever would purchase an inch of soil unless they bought it in a flower-pot; but they all agreed that the way things were managed now there was no time for a man to attend to his own business.

"But you can't expect John J. Laylor to do anything," said the Shipwreck Clerk.

However, there was one thing which that gentleman always expected John J. Laylor to do. When the clerk was surrounded by a number of persons in hours of business, and when he had succeeded in impressing them with the importance of his functions, and the necessity of paying deferential attention to himself if they wished their business attended to, John J. Laylor would be sure to walk into the office and address the Shipwreck Clerk in such a manner as to let the people present know that he was a clerk and nothing else, and that he, the Registrar, was the head of that department. These humiliations the Shipwreck Clerk never forgot.

There was a little pause here, and then Mr. Mathers remarked:

"I should think you'd be awfully bored with the long stories of shipwrecks that the people come and tell you."

He hoped to change the conversation, because, although he wished to remain on good terms with the subordinate officers, it was not desirable that he be led to say much against John J. Laylor.

"No, sir," said the Shipwreck Clerk, "I am not bored. I did not come here to be bored, and as long as I have charge of this office I don't intend to be. The long-winded old salts who come here to report their wrecks never spin out their prosy yarns to me. The first thing I do is to let them know just what I want of them; and not an inch beyond that does a man of them go, at least while I am managing the business. There are times when John J. Laylor comes in, and puts in his oar, and wants to hear the whole story, which is pure stuff and nonsense, for John J. Laylor doesn't know anything more about a shipwreck than he does about—"

"The endemies in the Lake George area," suggested Harry Covare.

"Yes; or any other part of his business," said the Shipwreck Clerk; "and when he takes it into his head to interfere, all business stops till some second mate of a coal-schooner has told his whole story, from his sighting land on the morning of one day to his getting ashore on it on the afternoon of the next.—Now I don't put up with any such nonsense. There's no man living that can tell me anything about shipwrecks. I've never been to sea myself, but that's not necessary; and if I had gone, it's not likely I'd been wrecked. But I've read about every kind of shipwreck that ever happened. When I first came here I took care to post myself upon these matters, because I knew it would save trouble. I had read *Robinson Crusoe, The Wreck of the*

*Grosvenor, The Sinking of the Royal George,* and wrecks by
waterspouts, tidal waves, and every other thing which would
knock a ship into a cocked hat, and I've classified every sort of
wreck under its proper head; and when I've found out to what
class a wreck belongs, I know all about it. Now, when a man
comes here to report a wreck, the first thing he has to do is just
to shut down on his story, and to stand up square and answer a
few questions that I put to him. In two minutes I know just
what kind of shipwreck he's had; and then, when he gives me
the name of his vessel, and one or two other points, he may go.
I know all about that wreck, and I make a much better report
of the business than he could have done if he'd stood here talking three days and three nights. The amount of money that's
been saved to our tax-payers by the way I've systematized the
business of this office is not to be calculated in figures."

The brother-in-law of J. George Watts knocked the ashes
from the remnant of his cigar, looked contemplatively at the
coal for a moment, and then remarked:

"I think you said there's no kind of shipwreck you don't
know about?"

"That's what I said," replied the Shipwreck Clerk.

"I think," said the other, "I could tell you of a shipwreck, in
which I was concerned, that wouldn't go into any of your
classes."

The Shipwreck Clerk threw away the end of his cigar, put
both his hands into his trousers pockets, stretched out his legs,
and looked steadfastly at the man who had made this unwar-
rantable remark. Then a pitying smile stole over his countenance, and he said: "Well, sir, I'd like to hear your account of
it; and before you get a quarter through I can stop you just
where you are, and go ahead and tell the rest of the story myself."

"That's so," said Harry Covare. "You'll see him do it just
as sure pop as a spread rail bounces the engine."

"Well, then," said the brother-in-law of J. George Watts,
"I'll tell it." And he began:

"It was just two years ago, the first of this month, that I sailed for South America in the *Thomas Hyke*."

At this point the Shipwreck Clerk turned and opened a large book at the letter T.

"That wreck wasn't reported here," said the other, "and you won't find it in your book."

"At Anster, perhaps?" said the Shipwreck Clerk, closing the volume, and turning round again.

"Can't say about that," replied the other. "I've never been to Anster, and haven't looked over their books."

"Well, you needn't want to," said the clerk. "They've got good accommodations at Anster, and the Registrar has some ideas of the duties of his post, but they have no such system of wreck reports as we have here."

"Very like," said the brother-in-law. And he went on with his story. "The *Thomas Hyke* was a small iron steamer of six hundred tons, and she sailed from Ulford for Valparaiso with a cargo principally of pig iron."

"Pig iron for Valparaiso?" remarked the Shipwreck Clerk. And then he knitted his brows thoughtfully, and said, "Go on."

"She was a new vessel," continued the narrator, "and built with water-tight compartments; rather uncommon for a vessel of her class, but so she was. I am not a sailor, and don't know anything about ships. I went as passenger, and there was another one named William Anderson, and his son Sam, a boy about fifteen years old. We were all going to Valparaiso on business. I don't remember just how many days we were out, nor do I know just where we were, but it was somewhere off the coast of South America, when, one dark night, with a fog besides, for aught I know, for I was asleep, we ran into a steamer coming north. How we managed to do this, with room enough on both sides for all the ships in the world to pass, I don't know; but so it was. When I got on deck the other vessel had gone on, and we never saw anything more of her. Whether she sunk or got home is something I can't tell. But we pretty soon found that the *Thomas Hyke* had some of the plates in her bow badly

smashed, and she took in water like a thirsty dog. The captain
had the forward water-tight bulkhead shut tight, and the pumps
set to work, but it was no use. That forward compartment
just filled up with water, and the *Thomas Hyke* settled down
with her bow clean under. Her deck was slanting forward like
the side of a hill, and the propeller was lifted up so that it
wouldn't have worked even if the engine had been kept going.
The captain had the masts cut away, thinking this might bring
her up some, but it didn't help much. There was a pretty heavy
sea on, and the waves came rolling up the slant of the deck like
the surf on the seashore. The captain gave orders to have all
the hatches battened down so that water couldn't get in, and
the only way by which anybody could go below was by the
cabin door, which was far aft. This work of stopping up all
openings in the deck was a dangerous business, for the decks
sloped right down into the water, and if anybody had slipped,
away he'd have gone into the ocean, with nothing to stop him;
but the men made a line fast to themselves, and worked away
with a good will, and soon got the deck and the house over the
engine as tight as a bottle. The smoke-stack, which was well
forward, had been broken down by a spar when the masts had
been cut, and as the waves washed into the hole that it left, the
captain had this plugged up with old sails, well fastened down.
It was a dreadful thing to see the ship a-lying with her bows
clean under water, and her stern sticking up. If it hadn't been
for her water-tight compartments that were uninjured, she
would have gone down to the bottom as slick as a whistle. On
the afternoon of the day after the collision the wind fell, and
the sea soon became pretty smooth. The captain was quite sure
that there would be no trouble about keeping us afloat until
some ship came along and took us off. Our flag was flying, upside down, from a pole in the stern; and if anybody saw a ship
making such a guy of herself as the *Thomas Hyke* was then
doing, they'd be sure to come to see what was the matter with
her, even if she had no flag of distress flying. We tried to make
ourselves as comfortable as we could, but this wasn't easy with

everything on such a dreadful slant. But that night we heard a rumbling and grinding noise down in the hold, and the slant seemed to get worse. Pretty soon the captain roused all hands, and told us that the cargo of pig iron was shifting and sliding down to the bow, and that it wouldn't be long before it would break through all the bulkheads, and then we'd fill and go to the bottom like a shot. He said we must all take to the boats, and get away as quick as we could. It was an easy matter launching the boats. They didn't lower them outside from the davits, but they just let 'em down on deck and slid 'em along forward into the water, and then held 'em there with a rope until everything was ready to start. They launched three boats, put plenty of provisions and water in 'em, and then everybody began to get aboard. But William Anderson, and me, and his son Sam, couldn't make up our minds to get into those boats and row out on the dark, wide ocean. They were the biggest boats we had, but still they were little things enough. The ship seemed to us to be a good deal safer, and more likely to be seen when day broke, than those three boats, which might be blown off if the wind rose, nobody knew where. It seemed to us that the cargo had done all the shifting it intended to, for the noise below had stopped; and, altogether, we agreed that we'd rather stick to the ship than go off in those boats. The captain, he tried to make us go, but we wouldn't do it; and he told us if we chose to stay behind and be drowned it was our affair, and he couldn't help it; and then he said there was a small boat aft, and we'd better launch her, and have her ready in case things should get worse, and we should make up our minds to leave the vessel. He and the rest then rowed off so as not to be caught in the vortex if the steamer went down, and we three stayed aboard. We launched the small boat in the way we'd seen the others launched, being careful to have ropes tied to us while we were doing it; and we put things aboard that we thought we should want. Then we went into the cabin and waited for morning. It was a queer kind of a cabin, with a floor inclined like the roof of a house, but we sat down in the corners, and were glad to be there. The swinging lamp was burning, and it was a good deal more cheerful in there than it was outside. But, about day-break, the grinding and rumbling down below began again, and the bow of the *Thomas Hyke* kept going down more and more; and it wasn't long before the forward bulkhead of the cabin, which was what you might call its front wall when everything was all right, was under our feet, as level as a floor, and the lamp was lying close against the ceiling that it was hanging from. You may be sure that we thought it was time to get out of that. There were benches with arms to them fastened to the floor, and by these we climbed up to the foot of the cabin stairs, which, being turned bottom upward, we went down in order to get out. When we reached the cabin door we saw part of the deck below us, standing up like the side of a house that is built in the water, as they say the houses in Venice are. We had made our boat fast to the cabin door by a long line, and now we saw her floating quietly on the water, which was very smooth, and about twenty feet below us. We drew her up as close under us as we could, and then we let the boy Sam down by a rope, and after some kicking and swinging he got into her; and then he took the oars, and kept her right under us while we scrambled down by the ropes which we had used in getting her ready. As soon as we were in the boat we cut her rope and pulled away as hard as we could; and when we got to what we thought was a safe distance we stopped to look at the *Thomas Hyke*. You never saw such a ship in all your born days. Two-thirds of the hull was sunk in the water, and she was standing straight up and down with the stern in the air, her rudder up as high as the topsail ought to be, and the screw propeller looking like the wheel on the top of one of these wind-mills that they have in the country for pumping up water. Her cargo had shifted so far forward that it had turned her right up on end, but she couldn't sink, owing to the air in the com-partments that the water hadn't gotten into; and on the top of the whole thing was the distress flag flying from the pole which stuck out over the stern. It was broad daylight, but not a thing did we see of the other boats. We'd supposed that they wouldn't row very far, but would lay off at a safe distance until daylight; but they must have been scared and rowed farther than they intended. Well, sir, we stayed in that boat all day, and watched the *Thomas Hyke;* but she just kept as she was, and didn't seem to sink an inch. There was no use of rowing away, for we had no place to row to; and besides, we thought that passing ships would be much more likely to see that stern sticking high in the air than our little boat. We had enough to eat, and at night two of us slept while the other watched, dividing off the time, and taking turns to this. In the morning there was the *Thomas Hyke* standing stern up just as before. There was a long swell on the ocean now, and she'd rise and lean over a little on each wave, but she'd come up again just as straight as before. That night passed as the last one had, and in the morning we found we'd drifted a good deal farther from the *Thomas Hyke,* but she was floating just as she had been, like a big buoy that's moored over a sand-bar. We couldn't see a sign of the boats, and we about gave them up. We had our breakfast, which was a pretty poor meal, being nothing but hard-tack and what was left of a piece of boiled beef. After we'd sat for a while doing nothing, but feeling mighty uncomfortable, William Anderson said: 'Look here, do you know that I think we would be three fools to keep on shivering all night and living on hard-tack in the day-time, when there's plenty on that vessel for us to eat, and to keep us warm. If she's floated that way for two days and two nights, there's no knowing how much longer she'll float, and we might as well go on board and get the things we want as not.' 'All right,' said I, for I was tired of doing nothing, and Sam was as willing as anybody. So we rowed up to the steamer, and stopped close to the deck, which, as I said before, was standing straight up out of the water like the wall of a house. The cabin door, which was the only opening into her, was about twenty feet above us, and the ropes which we had tied to the rails of the stairs inside were still hanging down. Sam was an active youngster, and he managed to climb up one of these ropes; but when he got to the door he drew it up and tied knots in it about a foot apart, and then he let it down to us, for neither William Anderson nor me could go up a rope hand over hand without knots or something to hold on to. As it was, we had a lot of bother getting up, but we did it at last, and then we walked up the stairs, treading on the front part of each step instead of the top of it, as we would have done if the stairs had been in their proper position. When we got to the floor of the cabin, which was now perpendicular like a wall, we had to clamber down by means of the furniture, which was screwed fast, until we reached the bulkhead, which was now the floor of the cabin. Close to this bulkhead was a small room which was the steward's pantry, and here we found lots of things to eat, but all jumbled up in a way that made us laugh. The boxes of biscuits and the tin cans, and a lot of bottles in wicker covers, were piled up on one end of the room, and everything in the lockers and drawers was jumbled together. William Anderson and me set to work to get out what we thought we'd want, and we told Sam to climb up into some of the state-rooms, of which there were four on each side of the cabin, and get some blankets to keep us warm, as well as a few sheets, which we thought we could rig up for an awning to the boat; for the days were just as hot as the nights were cold. When we'd collected what we wanted, William Anderson and me climbed into our own rooms, thinking we'd each pack a valise with what we most wanted to save of our clothes and things; and while we were doing this, Sam called out to us that it was raining. He was sitting at the cabin door looking out. I first thought to tell him to shut the door so's to keep the rain from coming in; but when I thought how things really were, I laughed at the idea. There was a sort of little house built over the entrance to the cabin, and in one end of it was the door; and in the way the ship now was the open doorway was underneath the little house, and of course no rain could come in. Pretty soon we heard the rain pouring down, beating on the stern of the vessel like hail. We got to the stairs and looked out.

The rain was falling in perfect sheets, in a way you never see except round about the tropics. 'It's a good thing we're inside,' said William Anderson, 'for if we'd been out in this rain we'd been drowned in the boat.' I agreed with him, and we made up our minds to stay where we were until the rain was over. Well, it rained about four hours; and when it stopped, and we looked out, we saw our little boat nearly full of water, and sunk so deep that if one of us had stepped on her she'd have gone down, sure. 'Here's a pretty kittle of fish,' said William Anderson; 'there's nothing for us to do now but to stay where we are.' I believe in his heart he was glad of that, for if ever a man was tired of a little boat, William Anderson was tired of that one we'd been in for two days and two nights. At any rate there was no use talking about it, and we set to work to make ourselves comfortable. We got some mattresses and pillows out of the state-rooms, and when it began to get dark we lighted the lamp, which we had filled with sweet-oil from a flask in the pantry, not finding any other kind, and we hung it from the railing of the stairs. We had a good night's rest, and the only thing that disturbed me was William Anderson lifting up his head every time he turned over, and saying how much better this was than that blasted little boat. The next morning we had a good breakfast, even making some tea with a spirit lamp we found, using brandy instead of alcohol. William Anderson and I wanted to get into the captain's room, which was near the stern, and pretty high up, so as to see if there was anything there that we ought to get ready to save when a vessel should come along and pick us up; but we were not good at climbing, like Sam, and we didn't see how we could get up there. Sam said he was sure he had once seen a ladder in the compartment just forward of the bulkhead, and as William was very anxious to get up to the captain's room, we let the boy go and look for it. There was a sliding door in the bulkhead under our feet, and we opened this far enough to let Sam get through; and he scrambled down like a monkey into the next compartment, which was light enough, although the lower half of it, which was next to the engine-room, was under the water-line. Sam actually found a ladder with hooks at one end of it, and while he was handing it up to us, which was very hard to do, for he had to climb up on all sorts of things, he let it topple over, and the end with the iron hooks fell against the round glass of one of the port-holes. The glass was very thick and strong, but the ladder came down very heavy and shivered it. As bad luck would have it, this window was below the water-line, and the water came rushing in, in a big spout. We chucked blankets down to Sam for him to stop up the hole, but 'twas of no use; for it was hard for him to get at the window, and when he did the water came in with such force that he couldn't get a blanket into the hole. We were afraid he'd be drowned down there, and told him to come out as quick as he could. He put up the ladder again, and hooked it on to the door in the bulkhead, and we held it while he climbed up. Looking down through the doorway, we saw, by the way the water was pouring in at the opening, that it wouldn't be long before that compartment was filled up; so we shoved the door to and made it all tight, and then said William Anderson: 'The ship'll sink deeper and deeper as that fills up, and the water may get up to the cabin door, and we must go and make that as tight as we can.' Sam had pulled the ladder up after him, and this we found of great use in getting to the foot of the cabin stairs. We shut the cabin door, and locked and bolted it; and as it fitted pretty tight, we didn't think it would let in much water if the ship sunk that far. But over the top of the cabin stairs were a couple of folding doors, which shut down horizontally when the ship was in its proper position, and which were only used in very bad, cold weather. These we pulled to and fastened tight, thus having a double protection against the water. Well, we didn't get this done any too soon, for the water did come up to the cabin door, and a little trickled in from the outside door, and through the cracks in the inner one. But we went to work and stopped these up with strips from the sheets, which we crammed well in with our pocket knives. Then we sat down on the steps, and waited to see what would happen next. The doors of all the state-rooms were open, and we could see through the thick plate-glass windows in them, which were all shut tight, that the ship was sinking more and more as the water came in. Sam climbed up into one of the after state-rooms, and said the outside water was nearly up to the stern; and pretty soon we looked up to the two port-holes in the stern, and saw that they were covered with water; and as more and more water could be seen there, and as the light came through less easily, we knew that we were sinking under the surface of the ocean. 'It's a mighty good thing,' said William Anderson, 'that no water can get in here.' William had a hopeful kind of mind, and always looked on the bright side of things; but I must say that I was dreadfully scared when I looked through those stern windows and saw water instead of sky. It began to get duskier and duskier as we sank lower and lower, but still we could see pretty well, for it's astonishing how much light comes down through the water. After a little while we noticed that the light remained about the same; and then William Anderson, he sings out: 'Hooray, we've stopped sinking!' 'What difference does that make?' says I. 'We must be thirty or forty feet under water, and more yet for aught I know.' 'Yes, that may be,' said he; 'but it is clear that all the water has got into that compartment that can get in, and we have sunk just as far down as we are going.' 'But that don't help matters,' said I; 'thirty or forty feet under water is just as bad as a thousand to a drowning man.' 'Drowning!' said William; 'how are you going to be drowned? No water can get in here.' 'Nor no air, either,' said I; 'and people are drowned for want of air, as I take it.' 'It would be a queer sort of thing,' said William, 'to be drowned in the ocean and yet stay as dry as a chip. But it's no use being worried about air. We've got air enough here to last us for ever so long. This stern compartment is the biggest in the ship, and it's got lots of air in it. Just think of that hold! It must be nearly full of air. The stern compartment of the hold has nothing in it but sewing-machines. I saw 'em loading her. The pig-iron was mostly amidships, or at least forward of this compartment. Now, there's no kind of a cargo that'll accommodate as much air as sewing-machines. They're packed in wooden frames, not boxes, and don't fill up half the room they take. There's air all through and around 'em. It's a very comforting thing to think that the hold isn't filled up solid with bales of cotton or wheat in bulk.' It might be comforting, but I couldn't get much good out of it. And now Sam, who'd been scrambling all over the cabin to see how things were going on, sung out that the water was leaking in a little again at the cabin door, and around some of the iron frames of the windows. 'It's a lucky thing,' said William Anderson, 'that we didn't sink any deeper, or the pressure of the water would have burst in those heavy glasses. And what we've got to do now is to stop up all the cracks. The more we work, the livelier we'll feel.' We tore off more strips of sheets and went all round, stopping up cracks wherever we found them. 'It's fortunate,' said William Anderson, 'that Sam found that ladder, for we would have had hard work getting to the windows of the stern state-rooms without it; but by resting it on the bottom step of the stairs, which now happens to be the top one, we can get to any part of the cabin.' I couldn't help thinking that if Sam hadn't found the ladder it would have been a good deal better for us; but I didn't want to damp William's spirits, and I said nothing.

"And now I beg your pardon, sir," said the narrator, addressing the Shipwreck Clerk, "but I forgot that you said you'd finish this story yourself. Perhaps you'd like to take it up just here?"

The Shipwreck Clerk seemed surprised, and had, apparently, forgotten his previous offer. "Oh, no," he said, "tell your own story. This is not a matter of business."

"Very well, then," said the brother-in-law of J. George Watts, "I'll go on. We made everything as tight as we could, and then we got our supper, having forgotten all about dinner, and being very hungry. We didn't make any tea, and we didn't light the lamp, for we knew that would use up air; but we made a better meal than three people sunk out of sight in the ocean had a right to expect. 'What troubles me most,' said William Anderson, as he turned in, 'is the fact that if we are forty feet under water, our flag-pole must be covered up. Now, if the flag was sticking out, upside down, a ship sailing by would see it and would know there was something wrong.' 'If that's all that troubles you,' said I, 'I guess you'll sleep easy. And if a ship was to see the flag, I wonder how they'd know we were down here, and how they'd get us out if they did!' 'Oh, they'd manage it,' said William Anderson; 'trust those sea-captains for that.' And then he went to sleep. The next morning the air began to get mighty disagreeable in the part of the cabin where we were, and then William Anderson he says: 'What we've got to do is to climb up into the stern state-rooms, where the air is purer. We can come down here to get our meals, and then go up again to breathe comfortable.' 'And what are we going to do when the air up there gets foul?' says I to William, who seemed to be making arrangements for spending the summer in our present quarters. 'Oh, that'll be all right,' said he. 'It don't do to be extravagant with air any more than with anything else. When we've used up all there is in this cabin, we can bore holes through the floor into the hold and let in air from there. If we're economical, there'll be enough to last for dear knows how long.' We passed the night each in a stateroom, sleeping on the end wall instead of the berth, and it wasn't till the afternoon of the next day that the air of the cabin got so bad we thought we'd have some fresh; so we went down on the bulkhead, and with an auger that we found in the pantry, we bored three holes, about a yard apart in the cabin floor, which was now one of the walls of the room, just as the bulkhead was the floor, and the stern end, where the two round windows were, was the ceiling or roof. We each took a hole, and I tell you it was pleasant to breathe the air which came in from the hold. 'Isn't this jolly?' said William Anderson. 'And we ought to be mighty glad that hold wasn't loaded with codfish or soap. But there's nothing that smells better than new sewing-machines that haven't ever been used, and this air is pleasant enough for anybody.' By William's advice we made three plugs, by which we stopped up the holes when we thought we'd had air enough for the present. 'And now,' says he, 'we needn't climb up into those awkward staterooms any more. We can just stay down here and be comfortable, and let in air when we want it.' 'And how long do you suppose that air in the hold is going to last?' said I. 'Oh, ever so long,' said he, 'using it so economically as we do; and when it stops coming out lively through these little holes, as I suppose it will after a while, we can saw a big hole in this flooring and go into the hold, and do our breathing, if we want to.' That evening we did saw a hole about a foot square, so as to have plenty of air while we were asleep, but we didn't go into the hold, it being pretty well filled up with machines; though the next day Sam and I sometimes stuck our heads in for a good sniff of air, though William Anderson was opposed to this, being of the opinion that we ought to put ourselves on short rations of breathing so as to make the supply of air hold out as long as possible. 'But what's the good,' said I to William, 'of trying to make the air hold out if we've got to be suffocated in this place after all?' 'What's the good?' says he. 'Haven't you enough biscuits, and canned meats, and plenty of other things to eat, and a barrel of water in that room opposite the pantry, not to speak of wine and brandy if you want to cheer yourself up a bit, and haven't we good mattresses to sleep on, and why shouldn't we try to live and be comfortable as long as we can?' 'What I want,' said I, 'is to get out of this box. The idea of being shut up in here down under the water is more than I can stand. I'd rather take my chances going up to the surface and swimming about till I found a piece of the wreck, or something to float on.' 'You needn't think anything of that sort,' said William, 'for if we were to open a door or a window to get out, the water'd rush in and drive us back and fill up this place in no time; and then the whole concern would go to the bottom. And what would you do if you did get to the top of the water? It's not likely you'd find anything there to get on, and if you did you wouldn't live very long floating about with nothing to eat. No, sir,' says he, 'what we've got to do is to be content with the comforts we've got around us, and something will turn up to get us out of this; you see if it don't.' There was no use talking against William Anderson, and I didn't say anything more about getting out. As for Sam, he spent his time at the windows of the state-rooms a-looking out. We could see a good way into the water, further than you would think, and we sometimes saw fishes, especially porpoises, swimming about, most likely trying to find out what a ship was doing hanging bows down under the water. What troubled Sam was that a sword-fish might come along and jab his sword through one of the windows. In that case it would be all up, or rather down, with us. Every now and then he'd sing out, 'Here comes one!' And then, just as I'd give a jump, he'd say, 'No, it isn't; it's a porpoise.' I thought from the first, and I think now, that it would have been a great deal better for us if that boy hadn't been along. That night there was a good deal of motion to the ship, and she swung about and rose up and down more than she had done since we'd been left in her. 'There must be a big sea running on top,' said William Anderson, 'and if we were up there we'd be tossed about dreadful. Now the motion down here is just as easy as a cradle, and, what's more, we can't be sunk very deep; for if we were there wouldn't be any motion at all.' About noon next day we felt a sudden tremble and shake run through the whole ship, and far down under us we heard a rumbling and grinding that nearly scared me out of my wits. I first thought we'd struck bottom, but William said that couldn't be, for it was just as light in the cabin as it had been, and if we'd gone down it would have grown much darker, of course. The rumbling stopped after a little while, and then it seemed to grow lighter instead of darker; and Sam, who was looking up at the stern windows over our heads, he sung out, 'Sky!' And, sure enough, we could see the blue sky, as clear as daylight, through those windows! And then the ship, she turned herself on the slant, pretty much as she had been when her forward compartment first took in water, and we found ourselves standing on the cabin floor instead of the bulkhead. I was near one of the open state-rooms, and as I looked in there was the sunlight coming through the wet glass in the window, and more cheerful than anything I ever saw before in this world. William Anderson, he just made one jump, and, unscrewing one of the state-room windows, he jerked it open. We had thought the air inside was good enough to last some time longer; but when that window was open and the fresh air came rushing in, it was a different sort of thing, I can tell you. William put his head out and looked up and down and all around. 'She's nearly all out of water!' he shouted, 'and we can open the cabin door.' Then we all three rushed at those stairs, which were nearly right side up now, and we had the cabin doors open in no time. When we looked out we saw that the ship was truly floating pretty much as she had been when the captain and crew left her, though we all agreed that her deck didn't slant as much forward as it did then. 'Do you know what's happened?' sung out William Anderson, after he'd stood still for a minute to look around and think. 'That bobbing up and down that the vessel got last night shook up and settled down the pig iron inside of her, and the iron plates in the bow, that were smashed and loosened by the collision, have given way under the weight, and the whole cargo of pig iron has burst through and gone to the bottom. Then, of course, up we came. Didn't I tell you something would happen to make us all right?'

"Well, I won't make this story any longer than I can help. The next day after that we were taken off by a sugar-ship bound north, and we were carried safe back to Ulford, where we found our captain and the crew, who had been picked up by a ship after they'd been three or four days in their boats. This ship had sailed our way to find us, which, of course, she couldn't do, as at that time we were under water and out of sight.

"And now, sir," said the brother-in-law of J. George Watts

to the Shipwreck Clerk, "to which of your classes does this wreck of mine belong?"

"Gents," said the Shipwreck Clerk, rising from his seat, "it's four o'clock, and at that hour this office closes."

# THE RAFT [1]

## BY ROBERT TRUMBULL

THE plane struck the surface of the sea with a sound like the slap of a giant hand on the water. Two sharp bumps, and the plane settled quietly back on the long, slow swells. I had made a good landing.

As I rose from my seat in quick concern for Gene, Tony, the raft, and a multitude of things that competed for my attention in this crowded moment, I was conscious that the plane was bobbing gently up and down, but that at any second a wave might pull a wing, and we'd be gone.

I knew that our small three-man scout bomber would not float long. It is no great trick to set a land plane down on water, but these heavily armored war jobs are not intended to float.

I jumped as quickly as I could onto the left wing to receive the raft from Tony Pastula, my bomber, and he was right there to hand it to me without an instant's delay. Gene Aldrich, my radioman and gunner, was raising himself from the rear cockpit and was busy with his gear. I was already trying to open the raft's gas valve, which seemed to stick.

Suddenly there was no airplane. The next thing I knew I was hanging in my life jacket, kicking the water.

The sinking of that plane was like a magician's trick. It was there, and then it was gone, and there was nothing left in our big, wet darkening world but the three of us and a piece of rubber that was not yet a raft.

Of course the plane took with it everything the two boys in their well-disciplined haste had pulled together from emergency stores and equipment. I was soon to discover that what fight we were to make for our lives must depend upon the "junk" in our pockets, tools attached to the raft, which were

[1] Courtesy of Henry Holt and Co.

so negligible in value as to be almost frivolous, and the uses we could make of the clothes upon our backs. All these things were to stand us well until they were wrested from our grasp, one by one, by the great unseeable enemy we fought, and then our only weapon was the mind, until this too began to go in the particular corrosion to which it is susceptible.

Finally I got the raft blown up, but the thing inflated itself upside down. Fortunately there was a handrail around it, of half-inch manila line. As soon as the raft expanded to its full size we had grabbed hold of this. I was at the bow, and struggled to twist the raft right side up, with the boys holding on so that we were fighting each other's weight as well as the clumsy vessel. After I struggled for fifteen or twenty minutes, with the sea banging me in the face and filling my mouth with salt water, I did get the raft turned over once.

The handrail ran along the side, and the boys, across from me, had a grip on it. The raft weighed only forty pounds, and their weight tipped it right over again on top of them. My work had been for nothing.

By this time we had been floundering and coughing in the water for quite a while, and were all exhausted.

It was quite dark now, but our eyes were becoming accustomed to it and we could see quite well.

Gene spoke first.

"There's a way to get this thing over," he said, still a little short of breath.

"We've got to stop and dope us out a scheme," I said.

Tony chimed in.

"All right," he said, blowing sea water from his lips, "how about we take off our blouses, tie 'em together, tie one end to the line on one side of the boat, throw that up across the bottom of the boat, then we all go to the other side and pull, and see if we can't turn her over that way."

So we tied the blouses together as Tony had suggested, worked around to the other side and pulled, and boom!—over she came.

"You stay here and hold her down, while I get aboard on the other side," I said.

In the raft, I pulled the boys aboard by the wrists one at a time. I looked around and reflected that it was swell to be alive, though why I should have thought that then I don't know.

The raft was only four feet long by eight feet wide. With its sides inflated like tires, it resembled an oblong doughnut. The dimensions inside were eighty inches by forty inches. We discovered almost at once that it was impossible for three men to dispose this space so that any one of us would be comfortable.

I talked to the boys about our chances of rescue, and tried to cheer them up. This didn't take as long as I had expected. I learned that healthy young men in their early twenties are not naturally pessimistic. Gene and Tony's husky young bodies threw off the exhaustion of their struggle in the sea. The discipline in which they had been trained exerted itself now, and they were ready to appraise the situation calmly.

We thought about the things you would expect a person to think about under such circumstances. We were on a spot, and knew it. However, we confidently expected the ship to send back a search, and we knew there was a good possibility that we'd be found.

Tony was actually elated now.

"Hey, who's got a cigarette?" he demanded.

Gene jammed his hand into his sodden trousers pocket with automatic politeness, and then stopped and grinned.

"I'd like a cigarette with my coffee, if we had some coffee," he drawled.

The lack of cigarettes and coffee was to become one of our favorite topics of conversation.

Meanwhile I looked over the raft as best I could, and felt all over the fabric, wishing Gene had hung onto one of the flashlights. However, I examined the boat thoroughly, and found it to be in practically new condition and in excellent shape.

I had taken an inventory of our equipment, and tried to belittle its insufficiency by pointing out that we were sure to be rescued in the morning.

We found to our sorrow that all the necessary tools—oars, pump, and so forth—were missing. The pump was to blow up the boat if we developed a leak.

We found that all we had was this:

A police whistle;

A pair of pliers;

Another pair of pliers that I had stuck in my pocket;

An ordinary pocketknife—Gene's;

A can of rubber cement patching fluid;

A small piece of patching material;

A .45 caliber pistol which Pastula had saved;

Three clips of ammunition;

And the clothing we had on.

The two lads threw their shoes away, as I was afraid shoes would scuff the boat. We regretted that later. I kept my shoes, thinking we had better save one pair; in case we made a desert island we wouldn't want to be entirely without shoes.

We were, or at least pretended to be, very optimistic this first night as we talked over the situation.

"We'll keep a watch," I said. "Watch on, watch off, and relax in between."

None of us could more than doze. We bobbled like a cork, and to me one of the most amazing phases of this adventure was that we never became seasick.

Each little wave that struck the bottom of our rubber bubble of a boat was a jarring blow across the shoulders and the back of the head of the man lying inside. Imagine doubling up on a tiny mattress, with the strongest man you know striking the underside as hard as he could with a baseball bat, twice every three seconds, while someone else hurls buckets of cold salt water in your face. That's what it was like.

"Hey, look, it's dawn!"

I don't remember who said it, but we gave a cheer, and immediately began joking about breakfast. We chatted and shifted unwisely about the raft, and scanned our vast, expanding world for sign of ship or plane.

I judged it to be about 8:00 or 8:30 A. M. when we sighted the plane. At first I thought it was a bird, but far away as it was we could see that it was steady on its course, and in a few minutes we heard the faint sound of motors.

We jumped to our feet in our excitement, and almost tipped over the raft.

We sat down carefully, keeping our eyes on the plane. She was from our own forces, all right.

It was plain that we were being hunted. The plane approached on an easterly course at about 140 knots, never deviating from her line of flight. As she came nearer, we began to wave our arms, but there was no sign that we were seen.

Then Gene and Tony began to shout. I wished we had been able to save one of the parachutes. I would have opened it now and let it billow on the water. I made one quick search of the raft. There was not a single thing that we could use as a signaling device, except our shirts. Gene and Tony already had theirs off and were waving them wildly.

Evidently our tiny raft, being orange-yellow in color, was invisible in the silver path of the morning sun on the sea. The plane came closer, and closer, until she was within a half-mile of us.

Finally it was clear that we had not been seen. The plane was going away now, the sound of her motors dwindling to the southward like the last note of a dirge.

I sank down upon the forward thwart. Gene and Tony were leaning by their hands on the sides, still waving half-heartedly, and staring as if their thoughts could bring him back.

Now the plane was a speck in the sky, and the only sound was the lapping of the waves against the raft.

The boys sank down, their faces expressionless.

I had been sorry that I said what I did then; it was automatic, I guess, and I didn't even remember until Tony recalled it later, bitterly:

"Boys, there goes our one and only chance."

We sank back, spent by our futile effort to attract the pilot. Gene was by no means dispirited. "Shucks, maybe he saw us and is going back for help," he suggested confidently. He was enthusiastic all day. He expected any minute to see a destroyer, or another plane.

The geography of this part of the Pacific was far from a mystery to me. So I knew from the beginning just where I wanted to go. Controlling our craft's progress was my first concern because, while we were entirely without food or water, there was nothing any of us could do about this but wait for the Lord to send us a shower, and bring some food where we could catch it.

The wind blew up to a fresh breeze of about 12 knots, and I spent most of the first day observing how our boat was going to act. It soon became apparent that the raft was not only responding satisfactorily to the push of the wind, but that she had no tendency to yaw. She remained steadily lengthwise of the trough of the sea.

About eighteen hours after we went into the water, the wind shifted to the northwest and started driving us south. There were islands directly on our course now, but we were afraid the Japs had taken possession of these.

- A serious lack was head covering; the sun's rays came down like red-hot corkscrews and cooked our brains. Tony had his dungaree jacket, so I took his shirt and tore out the two front panels. With these I fashioned a sort of bonnet which gave the top of our heads some protection.

We wet our clothes almost constantly. Within fifteen minutes after a good dousing they would be thoroughly dry again. After we had soaked our clothes three or four times they would be stiff as boards from the salt.

Nights, especially when the sea was rough, we had opposite problems. Then our wet garments were clammy and cold.

On the first day I shot off a whole clip of ammunition— about half our supply—trying to kill a bird. We thought it was going to be easy to shoot a bird, because the curious creatures flocked around us by the hundreds, coming so close to inspect our strange craft that we were almost under the illusion that we could reach up and grab one. Actually, they came down within five or six feet of us.

I held the pistol until a bird was directly overhead, then I would aim and let go. The boat bobbled like a cork, and this seemed to throw off my aim every time. I finally gave up.

We were very much interested in the birds and the various tropical fishes. The boat, being orange-yellow in color, was a great attraction to the fish, and they all came up and looked it over as if it were some strange animal.

Aldrich showed at once that he was interested in fishing, so we looked around for something to use for a line. In the tool pocket there was a three-strand cotton cord perhaps fifteen feet long. This I unraveled into three thinner pieces of line, and cut them off to about ten feet. Tony had a red bandanna handkerchief, so Gene tied a piece of this to the end of the string for bait.

Gene stood over the side and flung his line into the water. It was over for only a couple of minutes when he discovered that the bait was gone—bitten clean off.

I broke the pliers trying to make a fishhook from a spring in the ammunition clip. As I took hold of the wire and clamped down, the bolt that holds the two sections of pliers together gave way, having crystallized. However, the piece of broken plier made a good sinker. With this rig Gene fished for hours, but never had another bite.

We made a game of our hardships as time went on. Talking about food and cigarettes and coffee of course accentuated our longings, but paradoxically we seemed to derive some comfort from thus torturing ourselves.

So far I had no means of controlling our progress. I thought, anyway, that it was vital to keep track of our position. To do this it was necessary to devise a way to gauge, as accurately as possible, the speed of our craft. The only navigation instrument I had was a small aerial navigator's scale of mileage. I tried several schemes for estimating our speed. One of the first was to throw a piece of rag, which was the only thing we had that would float, into the water, then counting by the one-thousand-and-one, one-thousand-and-two method, it taking just about a second to say each numeral. While we still had plenty of rags I would tear a few threads and cast them into the water, as far ahead as I could, then count as they passed the length of the raft, which was the known factor.

Thus I came to deduce that an estimated 12 knots of wind gave us a drift of approximately 2.5 knots, six knots of wind a drift of one knot.

However, I did not find the thread method very satisfactory. In the tool pocket there was also a 20-foot length of heavy cord. I cut off a length of about six feet of this, and tied to the end a flat metal identification disk from Tony's key ring, to act as a sinker. I tied the other end of the line to the center of the side of the raft, and tossed it out to drift. The metal disk was slightly concave and would flutter as we scooted along. The faster we went, the faster it would flutter, and the nearer the surface it would rise. I soon became quite expert at computing our speed with fair accuracy by this means.

At the very first we decided to keep a continuous watch, and we did throughout the first few weeks—up until the time we became too weak and exhausted to sit up for any length of time.

Discipline was well kept throughout the voyage. I took an occasion to remind the boys that I as captain held absolute authority.

"We've got to be all for one and one for all," I explained, "but when a final decision has to be made by one of us for us all, the captain's word has got to be the law."

Tony and Gene, good sailors both, readily assented, and we had no trouble on that score.

As time went on, though, our dispositions became rottener and rottener. I, being older and more experienced, blame myself more than either of the others for the times toward the last when my temper got out of control. There were occasions, I'm ashamed to admit, when my greatest exasperation was over the fact that I had nothing in the boat to throw. On the whole, though, we managed to get along very well, and even had some pleasant times with such little diversions as we could invent.

As time went on and our gallant little rubberized fabric boat showed no signs of serious wear, or deterioration of any kind, I soon acquired the greatest of confidence in her.

The only time she would take water to any important amount was when a big comber broke directly into the boat.

The bailing we accomplished by taking off our clothes, sopping up the water with them and wringing them out over the side, then wringing out our clothes again before putting them back on.

On the third day I discovered that I had a pencil. It suddenly burst upon me that this was a marvelous tool. I could make a chart!

My eyes darted about the boat. Draw it on the gunwale? No, a life jacket!

I had lost my life jacket shortly after the sinking of the plane. It leaked, wouldn't hold air, so I had just let it go in the water. But we had two left, and I seized one.

They watched with great interest as I traced the lines of latitude and longitude on the front of the life jacket, and marked with tiny ovals the approximate spot where we had landed, and my estimate of our positions in the past days' drifting.

"There's where we are, and there's where we're going," I said enthusiastically. They nodded, excited but not understanding this abstruse science.

Each afternoon just before sundown I would estimate the component direction and distance of our progress in the preceding twenty-four hours, and enter it on our chart. At the same time I would make one straight mark on the gunwale to denote one more day passed. I reckoned each day to begin and end at 7:30 in the evening, which was the approximate hour that we went into the sea.

The boys were quite proud of our possessing so useful and encouraging a tool as a chart. Our daily progress meant something when you could see it drawn each evening in a pencil line.

We were very anxious to work westward from our starting position, and now a new wind was driving us north and east, exactly the opposite of our desires.

Then I had it! Why wouldn't it be feasible to rig some sort of sea anchor to check our progress when the wind was wrong?

"Gimme that life jacket," I ordered Gene.

The half-inch manila rope life line still encircled the boat. I removed it, and tied one end to the deflated life jacket, the other to the gas inductor manifold on the pointed bow of the boat. I cast out the jacket to see how she would work as a sea anchor.

As the jacket sank in the sea and the boat pulled to the end of her tether, the tiny craft jerked, slowed, and swung about lazily, pointing her bow into the wind.

Perfect!

Under average conditions this improvised sea anchor cut our rate of drift to practically zero. Now we felt quite heartened, and more the masters of our fate.

We were beginning to notice a dryness of our tongues and throats. Though we were not yet suffering greatly from thirst, we knew our systems must be craving water, and we were worried.

Here and there, far off yet seemingly near, we could see gray and silver streaks between the waves and the darker clouds just above.

Rain.

Many times we thought one of those squalls would surely hit us and we could get a drink, and many times we seemed to sail right between two showers.

In the gray morning of the fifth day we realized, fully and definitely, that our force had left us behind.

Tony said it: "They aren't coming back, fellas."

This time I couldn't think of anything to say.

Gene looked at each of us without expression, swallowed, and stretched a grin.

"Well, shucks, ours ain't the only ship on the ocean."

He turned his sharp blue eyes back to their patient vigil.

This brought Tony's volatile spirits up again.

"Some convoy—why, hell—"

We chewed this over awhile.

Over and over I took stock of our situation. In a few hours I would make the fifth pencil mark on the gunwale. Five days without food or water. Five days of turning our suffering skins, like basting fowl, to baths of stinging salt. Five days—and how many days ahead?

I shook my head like a boxer who suddenly catches himself being counted out.

"Boys," I said.

They stared at me.

"All we've got to do now," I said, trying to make my voice strong and confident, "is keep going south and west, and we'll either be picked up or run into an island. It isn't easy, but it might be worse, and if we stick together, I have a feeling we're going to come out all right."

"Let's shake on it," Gene said.

So we shook hands all around, and things seemed better after that.

Before evening, the three of us were sitting dejectedly silent. Then Gene made a suggestion.

"It might be a good idea," he said, not meeting our eyes, "to say a prayer."

We discussed this seriously. We found that we had all been reared in some religious atmosphere, but that we had all drifted away.

We all concluded that a word of prayer wouldn't hurt anything.

So we sat in the steaming little cup that our boat had become, and bowed our heads beneath the cruel tropic sun. We each mumbled a few words of our own awkward choosing, calling on our God to bless our loved ones back home, over whom we were more concerned than ourselves, and asking for a little rain.

"Well, now we done all we could," Tony said.

"Gee, give it a chance," Gene answered impatiently.

"Well, come on, rain," Tony challenged. "Or maybe it ain't gonna rain no mo', no mo'."

We lifted our voices lustily at that and sang, "It Ain't Gonna Rain No Mo'," as far as we knew the words—which wasn't far—as if by our false cynicism we could put a reverse hoodoo on the elements.

At least we were all laughing again, which we hadn't done for some time.

Despite our elaborate irreverence, there was no denying that the prayer had made us feel better.

That night it rained.

It was Tony's watch. Gene was lying in the bottom, his long legs jackknifed. I was sitting on the after thwart, vainly trying to get some rest with my head held in my hands. Tony was sprawled on the forward seat. Suddenly he straightened, so abruptly that the boat wobbled a bit, and I glanced up.

A drop of moisture hit me in the face. I was afraid to think it might be anything but a puff of spray.

"Hey!" Tony said softly. His voice was almost a whisper.

Several more drops struck my upturned face. Then they came faster, until we were being fairly pelted by large globules of water. It was rain, sure enough, and I've never smelled a thing so sweet.

In another instant it was pouring—a tropical squall.

"Grab that oar pocket!" I ordered. As I spoke I snatched up

the life jacket and formed a hollow of its fabric between my hands.

As soon as I had a mouthful of water collected in the cup I had formed with the life jacket, I bent and sucked it up with my mouth. Immediately I spat it out. Salty.

"You've got to rinse the salt out of the fabric!" I yelled over the wind. Every fiber in our fabric boat had its coating of salt, baked in. We scrubbed furiously with our knuckles, begrudging every drop of fresh water that we had to waste in washing.

We were ducking our heads like greedy fishing birds to suck up each precious mouthful as fast as it collected.

The rain ended as suddenly as it had begun, and then we lapped up what was not too brackish in the bottom of the boat.

The small drinks we had was not enough to do our dehydrated systems much good, but for that night it quenched our thirst.

That night the wind shifted to the north and slightly east again, so we hauled in the sea anchor.

All of the sixth day we kept watching and hoping for another squall. Our thirst, whetted by that first drink, had now become intense. As for hunger—our shrunken stomachs were numb now.

That evening Gene suggested another prayer, pointing out that we hadn't done so badly on the first one.

After our prayer meeting we felt much better, and we talked until well into the night.

We were not so glad to see the dawn, this seventh morning. The sun had become our enemy.

Gene Aldrich was the most patient fisherman I've ever seen. I was not very enthusiastic when he announced he was going to try to stab a fish with the pocketknife. I figured it would occupy his mind and provide some amusement, anyway, so I made no objection.

He would lean out over the boat, poised and ready.

Tony, meanwhile, was lying in the bottom of the boat, dozing.

I was watching Gene's maneuvers warily. If the boat got punctured, we would indeed be in a bad way.

One fish, about the size of a fresh-water perch—the kind we used to call a "punkin perch"—was especially curious.

Then he came a little too close.

Gene stabbed viciously.

The fish fell from his knife and dropped on Tony.

Quick as a cat, he rolled over on top of the little fish and lay on it until it stopped struggling.

When he was sure it was dead, he lifted it by the tail, holding it gingerly and well into the center of the boat, so there would be no possibility of our losing it.

"Chow!" he said reverently.

After we had eaten as much as we could, there was a sizable portion left.

This was our lucky day.

That afternoon it rained again.

Our method of catching water hadn't been too successful the first time.

I hit upon the idea of soaking the rain water up in rags. I made the boys take off their underdrawers, and I took mine off too. I cut them along the inside seams, making of each pair one rag about thirty inches long by fourteen inches wide.

These worked quite satisfactorily. In the beginning we used the shirt rags too.

We could see this second squall coming. The rain came up very fast.

This time we all had a good drink. This, on top of our first food, made us feel very much better.

After the rain had passed, we took off all our clothes. We sloshed the sodden garments in the bottom of the boat, soaking up the excess water which was useless for drinking because it was saltier, from washing the brine-coated fabric, than the sea itself. We wrung our clothes over the side, and put them on again, refreshed.

It was Gene's watch.

I had been lying on my back for perhaps a half hour, my eyes closed, when there was a terrific explosion.

I came out of the bottom of the boat like a streak of lightning.

Gene had shot an albatross.

The impact knocked the big bird several feet into the water.

The bird's carcass was drifting slowly away from the boat, but in their excitement neither Tony nor Gene was making any move to do anything about it.

I dived over the side. A few strokes, and my fingers closed in his feathers.

I was back aboard before the boat had drifted twenty feet.

We tried to pluck the bird, but we found it impossible to pull out the feathers. So we skinned it with the pocketknife.

None of us was very hungry after eating the heart, liver, and other organs, including the entrails. We put the rest of the meat in the bow with the fish, intending to eat it for breakfast the next morning.

Naturally, we recalled the Ancient Mariner's curse.

My watch came around at about midnight. I got up and took over.

After sitting awhile on the after thwart, I noticed a glow of light in the bow. It was so strong that it illuminated the entire boat, and the sea around. It seemed to be coming from our pile of rags.

I got down and untangled the rags until I came upon the meat we had saved from the fish, and the carcass of the albatross. When I held it up, the albatross glowed like a flashlight. The fish glowed where it had lain against the bird.

I aroused the two boys.

"What do you think of that?" I said.

"Looks like it's spoiled, all right," Tony said slowly.

Gene came right to the point.

"I don't know about you fellas," he said, "but I wouldn't feel like eating any more of that."

"What makes that?" Tony asked.

I explained phosphorescence, and pointed out that phosphorus was poison.

"It might be dangerous to eat any more of it," I concluded reluctantly.

"Damn albatross poisoned the fish too," Tony said.

"Yeah, better heave it all," Gene said, looking down.

Without further talk I threw the whole mess into the sea.

Later it occurred to me that I should have saved it for bait. As a matter of fact, I found out later that it wouldn't have been dangerous to eat the albatross, at all. The flesh of an albatross is phosphorescent as a rule, I learned, because it preys largely upon luminous fish.

We were making fair time, on nothing—the nearest islands were hundreds of miles to the south, by my reckoning, but we were heading in their direction.

Physically we were not in bad shape at all, yet. Our faces were drawn, under the beards and flecks of shredded skin, but our muscles were still hard despite our almost entire lack of exercise. We couldn't swim for fear of sharks, which were thicker about the boat every morning.

We could see their black fins in the water everywhere. We watched them lie in wait, then rush and close their long jaws on luckless lesser fish that played innocently about the raft.

Gene, for a while this morning, studied the play that was going on around us. Then he conceived the idea of trying to stab a shark.

Finally, a shark swam bravely up to him.

The knife flashed out and down, and there was a sound like a punch.

Gene turned pale.

"I—I think I hit the boat," he said. He held his hand in the water where he had struck.

There was a quick, convulsive thrash and Gene's arm was yanked like a line.

"Wait! I got him," he yelled.

He had been fortunate enough to strike the shark in the gill.

That, we learned later, was the only spot vulnerable to the little knife.

Quickly, but with care, Gene hauled the shark into the boat, using the knife like a hook.

Tony again was dozing in the bottom of the boat. The shark landed right on top of him.

The yelp of surprise was hardly out of Tony's mouth, though, when he grasped the whole situation. Like a wrestler, Tony flipped over and slammed all his weight on the struggling sea beast.

In about ten minutes the shark lay still.

"Okay, let's cut him," he said, after catching his breath.

I tried to cut him, but his hide was too tough.

Finally, after considerable exertion, I got a small cut started. Using both hands, I pulled toward me as if I were hauling on a saw handle, and thus I managed to split the length of his belly.

The liver was quite large. I cut it into three equal pieces, and we devoured it before exploring the shark's possibilities any further. We had eaten just enough fish the day before to stimulate our appetites, and we were consumed by hunger at this time.

When we had eaten our fill of meat, we held up the tail and head, forming a picket in the center of the carcass in which a large quantity of blood collected. The blood was thin and watery and strong-flavored, but we downed it manfully, every drop.

With our stomachs full for the first time, we felt pretty good.

The wind was bearing out of the northeast now, and I thought things were going rather well.

We had another prayer meeting that night, and every night thereafter.

On the tenth, eleventh, and twelfth days we had almost continual squalls. At last we filled our water bottles, which held enough to keep our throats wet sparingly for a day or two. After this mean ration was safely stored, we found that the blessing of rain could turn into a curse.

The almost constant bailing, added to the considerable exertion required merely to keep ourselves inside the heaving raft, was drawing heavily upon our waning strength.

On the twelfth day the sea was still rough, with the choppy surface showing whitecaps as far as I could see. During my watch in the morning I sat on the forward thwart, scanning the glaring blue water for anything that might affect us.

Suddenly, well ahead, I saw something strange bobbing in the water. As we drew nearer, I saw that it looked like the nose of a seal.

That's strange, I thought. What in the world is a seal doing in this place?

The closer we approached, the more the thing began to look like a seal.

In a moment we were abreast.

If this is a seal, I thought, it should be frightened by the boat. Why doesn't it dive or swim away?

Suddenly something flashed in my mind.

I whipped around, looked hard, and half rose, then sat down again and cursed.

I turned to Gene.

"See that thing way out there?" I asked, pointing.

"Yeah," he said slowly. "What is it?"

"Does it look like a seal?" I asked.

Tony was in on the game by now.

"Seals don't belong down here," he declared.

"If it ain't a seal, what is it?" Gene demanded.

"Well, maybe it could have got away from home," Tony admitted.

"Well," I said, "listen. If there was room in this boat, I'd let you kick me for a damn fool. That was no seal, fellas! Damn it! It was a coconut!"

I reflected bitterly that I had as good as thrown a heaven-sent meal in the ash can.

After that we kept a coconut watch.

Early in the morning of the fourteenth day there were many small sharks playing around the boat.

Gene was vigilant with his knife, trying to repeat his feat of gilling one. Hour after hour he leaned over the side of the boat, stabbing at every swimming creature that came anywhere near his reach.

On the fourteenth day he was rewarded. A small specimen, exactly like the first, got a little too near the boat, and Gene's long brown arm sprung out like a snake's tongue. He drew it back triumphantly with the fish impaled on the knife in his hand.

Our hunger had been very intense the four or five days after eating the shark, but was now beginning to subside—a dangerous sign, I thought. We had been getting drinking water fairly regularly, thanks to the squalls, so we were able to eat this fish with relish.

A few minutes after the shower ended I lay down in the bottom of the boat to try again to rest. Suddenly I became conscious of a scratching noise on the stern of the boat, just above my head.

I opened my eyes to see what was causing the noise.

It was a bird, calmly perched there.

Neither Gene nor Tony appeared to be aware of our visitor. Very carefully and noiselessly I slid my hand up inside and as close to the edge of the boat as I could without taking a chance of causing some slight scraping sound on the fabric.

Then I quickly grabbed, and had him by the leg.

The flapping and squawking and general commotion that immediately ensued brought the boys to my assistance. In a moment Gene and Tony held it securely. Gene took his knife, grasped the bird by the beak and face, and efficiently cut off its head with a deft stroke.

We examined the bird in the gray light before dawn. It was a young tern of some sort.

We picked off his feathers, and proceeded to eat. The little fish of the previous day had reawakened our dormant appetites, and we were ravenous.

The fifteenth day dawned on a torpid sea. As the morning wore on and I saw no signs of the calm lifting, I began to wish we had some means of rowing. Our strength was a little less with each foodless day, and I felt it necessary that we should make some sort of progress. Besides, rowing would give us something to do. Activity might be a tonic to our dulling spirits.

I looked over our stock of gear for some means of improvising oars. Finally my eyes lit upon my shoes, which I was still saving.

"Gene," I said, "give me the knife."

He turned his head slowly, after a moment, without interest.

"Give me the knife," I repeated.

He handed it to me, and turned back to his contemplation of the silent sea.

With the knife I cut away the uppers of one shoe, slicing off the leather flush around the heels, but leaving about a half-inch of the uppers attached around the toe. This formed a sort of cup, and was also to act as reinforcement to keep the sole from bending backward under pressure of water.

After finishing the first shoe, I moved over to the forward thwart, sat down and tried it out.

"Glory be!" I whispered.

I could dip the shoe into the water and, pushing backward, create a perceptible forward drive.

In a few minutes I had made another "paddle" from the other shoe, and thus I created our motive power.

"Look alive, lads," I shouted, elated with accomplishment. "We're going places."

When the boys saw that my idea would work, their listlessness vanished.

"Let's get agoin'," Gene said, enthusiastic now.

I believe it was Gene and I who started. Gene was on the starboard side and I on the port. In fifteen minutes we had stretched a wake behind us.

"You rest now, Gene," I said. "Your turn, Tony."

Gene moved back to the stern to rest. I slid over to his place, Tony took my former position at port and rowed with a will. After fifteen more minutes, as nearly as we could judge, I went aft for my rest, Tony moved to starboard and Gene came in at port.

Thus we spelled each other, circling counterclockwise. All that day we rowed, never stopping, until about two o'clock the next morning—almost eighteen hours.

As I had hoped, action raised our spirits.

Fifteen minutes' rest for each man as he finished his half-hour shift kept us fresh; shifting from one side to the other every fifteen minutes kept us from straining either arm.

At about two o'clock in the morning a breeze sprang up from the east, driving us on in the direction we had been rowing all day and night.

We "shipped oars" gratefully, and composed ourselves to rest as best we could for the remainder of the night.

Before closing my eyes to try to doze, I checked our progress by the stars. We had rowed a hundred miles.

The next day, however, we lost all that we had gained.

The winds turned variable and shifted us about. Finally a steady breeze held in the northwest. This was worse, for it drove us back eastward about a hundred miles, the same distance we had so laboriously paddled to the west. We were becoming discouraged, when another flat calm descended. We took up our shoe paddles and rowed back westward for eight hours straight before the wind set in from the east, and took us westward again.

Gene was on watch. I was sitting in the bottom of the boat; Tony was lying down.

Suddenly Tony sat up.

"I feel a coconut," he said.

Gene and I watched him, stupidly, "I feel a coconut"—the statement didn't make sense.

Was Tony imagining things?

"Didn't you hear me? I felt a coconut bump me under the bottom of the boat."

That was different!

I jumped up and looked over the side. Sure enough, there was a coconut bobbing just out of reach in the water.

"Get it!" Gene said.

The water-soaked shell looked slick, so I didn't try to grab it. Instead, I dived over the side, caught the nut, and heaved it back into the raft. The boys put the nut down carefully, and helped me back aboard.

The thick, fibrous outer husk had begun to rot. Soaked as it was, the outer shell was easy to remove. I pulled it off, a strip at a time, with the pliers. First I tasted the milk inside, to see if it was fit to drink. It was a little brackish, but not too bad.

I passed the nut around, and each of us took a turn until the milk was all gone.

After we drank the milk we cracked the nut open and divided it.

We had had a strong breeze out of the west for some time. Then, on the twenty-fifth day, we again had the terrifying experience of a sudden shift of wind, this time from due west to southwest.

Noon was overtaking us when the sky began to cloud. Some distance to our left an ominously rolling mass, almost jet black, appeared in the misty gray, and for the first time we heard thunder. The sea was growing dark, and rising uneasily. The black cloud spat a thin stream of electric flame, long, thin, and forked. The burnt air crackled, and the sharp burst of thunder made us jump.

Like a great slap in the face, the rain hit. It drove down violently, in solid masses. We found, too late this time, that it didn't pay to sit together, with our weight all on one side. The lighter side was in the air; a wave struck the under edge with a loud boom! and the next instant we were in the water, the raft flying through the air over our heads.

I saw a flash of white—our rags for catching water! I let the boys look out for themselves, and made a wild grab for the rags. I got both of them, as the raft fell back and hit me on the shoulder. It was upside down.

It was fairly easy to right the boat this time. We made the wind assist us. The raft was so light that we merely had to raise the side facing into the wind, and the wind swept under and blew it right over, just as it had done a moment ago when we were in it.

We were so concerned about getting back into the boat that I don't remember that the effort was particularly exhausting. When we did get in, however, we could do nothing for a few minutes but sit and blow.

We squatted in the corners of the boat, holding on for our lives. When the rain stopped, we raised our dripping heads and were surprised to see that the clouds had broken, a mile or so away, and the sun was already shining through. The wind dropped instantly, and the sea, while very rough, was no longer in a terrifying frenzy.

"Better check the losses," I said.

The only things we lost were my head rags, the remainder of Tony's shirt, and the hammer we had made from the gun.

The sun came out strong, and had just dried our clothes when we ran into another brief squall that soaked us through again.

Tony was disgusted.

"Chief," he said, pulling off his trousers to bail and wring all over again, "it's the little things like this that annoy me."

We hadn't eaten for a week now. Our last food was the coconut we got on the twenty-first day. We began to appreciate the luck we had had when we caught the birds and fish. Those chances never came again.

Gene's eyes were the sharpest in the boat. In his afternoon watch, on this twenty-eighth day, he raised the coconut alarm again. Instantly Tony and I had out the paddles, and made our way cross-wind to where the big brown nut rose and dipped on the snapping blue waves. I shifted my shoe-paddle to the inboard hand and scooped the prize into the boat.

After the twenty-eighth day and the last coconut, we realized at last that we were starving.

On the twenty-ninth day the old gray albatross returned and began introducing bad luck to us in large doses.

The wind rose higher, and the waves came faster. They rolled beneath the raft and raised us up until we looked into a sickening depth. We shipped water, gallons at a time, and bailed frantically with our hands. We learned to shift ourselves adroitly when the crest hit, to keep the raft in balance.

But the sea is cunning. It can bide its time, and spring like a beast. The wind was its ally.

A wall of green laced with white, translucent as we saw it against the sky, collapsed all over us. Its weight made our ears ring, and filled our nostrils. Coughing and blinded, we fell across the gunwale. The wind, as if it had been waiting, blew a heavy gust that raised the raft and tipped it over.

We were in the sea again, a more fearsome sea than any of us had ever seen.

I got my hand beneath the boat and lifted. Again I tricked the wind. It swept beneath, filled the inside, and lifted the raft right side up, slamming its bottom against a slanted wall of sea.

We flung ourselves against the raft again. I somehow scrambled in, and grabbed Tony by both his wrists. I let myself fall to a sitting position, braced my feet, and pulled him in. Between us, then, we rescued Gene. All of us lay and panted, heads down.

Sometime later, maybe hours, I took the inventory. All our spare rags were gone, but the water-catching rags were there. Then—I missed the anchor.

We passed a night of misery in the brewing hurricane. Without an anchor we were at the mercy of the wind, and it blew viciously.

Toward morning the gale slackened, but the sea still boiled. When we stopped shipping water, we sat in the boat with our backs hunched against the rain and wind. We were still drifting to the northeast.

It rained steadily all morning. Shortly after noon we hit a heavy squall, with high winds and a terrifying sea, and we tipped over again.

How we got back into the raft against the waves I don't know. When we did, we found that all our gear was gone—knife, pliers, our chart, the unsuccessful sea anchor, and our last rag.

Our courage almost failed. This had been a day of horrible disaster.

About eleven o'clock the next morning we hit another shower, heavy and as cold as ice water. The raft held water over our ankles when it ended.

We had lost the last of our rags in the last tip-over, so we took off all our clothes, mopped the bottom of the boat and wrung over the side, repeating until the raft was dry.

As we finished this tiresome chore the sun appeared, for the first time that day.

"Let's take a sun bath before we put our clothes on," I suggested.

The boys assented readily.

After a while Tony spoke up nervously.

"Don't you think we'd better put on our clothes?"

I wasn't looking forward to it. They were damp.

"Well, it's pretty rough, you know," Tony argued.

The wind had risen and the waves were coming to a boil. I hesitated for a few seconds, and was just about to agree with Tony when a big comber caught us.

My head was out of the water again, and somehow my hand was on the raft. Gene, it appeared, had never let go, and was hanging on desperately. Tony had fallen almost on us. I grabbed him by an arm.

The waves were flinging us about, pulling at our legs as if with hands. The raft was upside down.

Never letting go our handholds, we grouped ourselves together and at an unspoken signal heaved the raft upward, trying to keep our grasp on the upended gunwale at the same time. A comber thundered down and almost tore it from our grip.

Quickly, before the next wave came, we pushed upward again. The light raft went over this time, and I worked my way to the opposite side to hold it down while the boys climbed in.

For a few minutes we rested, panting, each with an arm locked across a thwart in case we tipped again.

How long we lay this way I don't remember, I know that we were not in full possession of our minds.

I found myself as if awakened by a noise I half remembered from a dream. The boys were sitting up, revived but not disposed to talk. I tried to straighten on my haunches, and then the situation struck me like a blow.

All our clothes were lost—every thread and stitch, except, ridiculously, a police whistle that hung by a cord around my neck.

Now on this day, our thirty-third in the raft, our position was desperate.

This was the one time during the entire trip that I was truly disheartened. In fact, I was just about ready to give up. I knew that the end of our voyage was very near; we must make an island in a day or two, or die.

Tony shared my gloom. He considered going over the side; it would be a quick death, without the torture that the sun had in store. But he changed his mind.

"We've come this far," he argued, "and by God we'll go on!"

We all agreed that neither this nor any other disaster which could overtake us now was sufficient reason for giving up the fight we had been making. Again we shook hands all around, and vowed we'd go on.

Although we had divided our days into two-hour watches, I was up and vigilant myself most of the time until my eyes began to fail. Now, because of that and my general physical

condition, I was forced to let the man on watch take full re-
sponsibility for the boat while I conserved my dwindling
energy for my own two-hour shift. Thus I lay on the forward
thwart this thirty-fourth morning.

It was about ten o'clock.

We topped a wave, and in that brief instant while we seemed
to hang suspended before the long downward slide began,
Gene spoke for the first time since taking the watch.

"Chief," he said, "I see a beautiful field of corn."

I didn't even look up. I thought sadly that the boy's mind
had finally gone.

After a few minutes, when we had risen to the next crest,
he spoke again insistently: "Sure enough, chief!—I see something green in the distance!"

With this statement, so rationally put in his Missouri drawl,
it dawned upon me suddenly that perhaps he did see something. I looked hard, but could still see nothing in the tumbling
sea. Tony was looking too, but had not spoken. I tried to
stand up, and found I couldn't balance on my cramped and
crooked legs. I asked the boys to hold me upright.

We came to the summit of the next large swell. Sure enough,
in the distance I could see something green. As Gene had said,
it was beautiful. I instantly recognized it as an island, one
of the low, verdant atolls of the far South Sea. I let out a
hoarse whoop.

Tony took a deep breath, and let it go out noisily, trying
to repress his joy.

"Well," he said, "thank God—and it's about time."

The wind had risen strongly, making long and prominent
streaks on the water, which gave me an excellent gauge of
the exact wind direction. I took a bearing on the island, compared it with the wind direction, and found that our course
of drift was carrying us about ten degrees to the right of the
island.

We realized, of course, that this was our God-given chance
for refuge, so, weak as we were, we saw nothing for it but

to row. I took the port side of the raft, using our one remaining shoe-paddle. Gene and Tony paddled together on the starboard side, using their hands only.

We rowed all day, exactly across wind at 90 degrees to our sailing direction. By one o'clock our progress was visible.

When we were about a mile from the island I saw from the wind streaks and blowing foam that we were directly upwind, and that the stiff breeze would land us at the center of the beach without assistance.

"Okay, boys!" I said. "We can knock off the rowing."

From now on it was just a matter of drifting in the wind. I kept a close eye on the bearings by the wind streaks, to be sure that we hit the beach.

We became conscious of a steady, sullen thunder that seemed to grow in volume. I realized after a moment that it was surf breaking over a barrier reef, and I feared we were in for a little trouble.

Our only hope was to paddle over the reef ahead of the breaker—that is, in the interval between two waves.

We were fortunate enough to pass over the reef at the one brief instant when the surf was not breaking.

The breaker caught the raft behind. The heavy blow of the rushing foam against the stern sped us up the sloping rear of the smaller, shoreward-speeding wave ahead.

The three of us were in the water.

After a threshing by the water that left me only half conscious, I found myself sitting on a flat ledge of coral rock. Gene and I were close together, and we still had about three hundred yards to go to reach solid ground. Tony was about fifty yards behind us.

None of us was able to stand. I tried to raise myself on my feet, but couldn't get my balance. Then I found that the current was skidding me along on my bottom. Gene, even with me and to my right, also let himself drift and we kept abreast.

I heard a call for help, and looked back. It was Tony. Being unable to swim, he thought he was going to drown. When I waved and yelled, he realized he was out of danger, and thence-forth scooted along like Gene and me. Crawling on all fours, we dragged ourselves from the last persistent clutch of the sea.

We lay on the beach together, faintly conscious of the broken coral that was cutting our flaming, sunburned flesh as our bodies jerked in the effort to breathe.

There were several thatched huts a few yards from where we lay.

"Boys," I said, "you know there may be Japs here waiting for us."

They raised their heads and nodded.

I looked at each one closely. They were gazing steadily into my eyes. Tony gestured toward the police whistle, still on a cord about my neck.

"If we have to scatter," he suggested calmly, "two blasts on the whistle will be the signal to meet wherever you are."

It was agreed.

We were too weak to try to find food, so we decided to rest for the night in one of the shacks.

I chose three long pieces of driftwood lying about that were best suited to my purpose, and handed one to each.

"If there are Japs on this island," I said, "they'll not see an American sailor crawl. We'll stand, and march, and make them shoot us down, like men-o'-warsmen."

Using the sticks of driftwood as canes to support us, we got to our feet. Three abreast then, myself in the middle, we walked to the nearest hut and went in.

By now the rising wind was blowing gusts of rain into our shelter, so we rigged one of the coconut mats to protect us.

We spent a miserable night. The wind kept blowing the mats with which we tried to cover ourselves, and the rough, woven fiber scratched painfully against our sunburn. We were unable to sleep at all.

The next morning early, the first thing I did was to look around the shack and try to patch it where the wind, during the night, had blown off the siding.

While we were still working on the patching job, we saw a native coming toward us from the beach. It had stopped raining. I grabbed my police whistle, which I had laid on the ground the night before, and blew a loud blast. The native stopped and looked at us, evidently aghast. It was obvious that he couldn't understand our being there.

After I blew my whistle two or three more times, he finally gathered his wits and ran up to see what was going on. The native stared, fascinated. We all pointed to our mouths, trying to signify that we were hungry. He could see from our emaciated condition that we were in a bad state, so it didn't take him long to get the idea. He held up his hand reassuringly, and dashed off into the coconut jungle.

In a few minutes he was back, with several coconut kernels. As we ate, the native made signs to us that he was going for help. He pointed to my police whistle, and held out his hand, smiling encouragingly. I gave him the whistle, and immediately he turned and ran off among the coconut trees, tooting the whistle vigorously. We looked at each other in great relief. At least the natives were friendly.

Our visitor was gone for perhaps a half hour. He returned with a party of several natives and a man who seemed to be the leader. This was the resident commissioner.

The commissioner's first question was as to our nationality. Upon learning that we were American sailors, he showed his delight immediately.

He was curious as to how we had reached this particular part of the island. Had we walked there? We merely turned and pointed seaward. He was astounded. That, he said, was impossible! He could not believe we had come upon this beach from the sea. No one had ever come over that reef and lived to tell the tale!

At length the commissioner gave an order in the island language, and the husky, handsome brown natives gathered us into their arms like babies and set off with us at a swift pace.

The natives carried us a mile or more until we arrived at the commissioner's residence.

We received a warm welcome from the commissioner's wife. When I tasted my first sip of coffee I was able to believe, at last, that it was all true and not one of those nightmares I used to have when I dozed in the raft. We were really safe—it seemed impossible to believe, but that welcome cup of coffee was the convincer.

Lying there in civilized beds, we realized for the first time what an ordeal we had come through, as evidenced by the physical conditions and reactions which now pressed themselves upon our consciousness. Our skinned backs and cooked hips kept us in constant torment for many days, and we found ourselves still unable to sleep at first.

Under the kind and skillful care of the commissioner's wife we recuperated amazingly. Strength began to flow back into our muscles, and in a few days we were able to straighten our legs, then to walk with only a barely perceptible unsteadiness. We were still weak, of course, and were to remain so for some time, but mentally we seemed quite normal, all of us, and that relieved a worry I had had.

Seven days from the date of our arrival on the island, there was an American warship offshore, and pretty soon we were shaking hands with the commander.

# BATTLE IN SUBIC BAY [1]

A Story of the Motor Torpedo Boats from "They Were
Expendable," BY W. L. WHITE

"IT WAS a job we did for the army," explained Bulkeley. "A
couple of Jap ships, one of them an Imperial Navy auxiliary
cruiser with 6-inch guns had been shelling our 155-millimeter
emplacements on Bataan—blasting them with heavy stuff. The
major in charge had been wondering how to get rid of them
and had phoned Admiral Rockwell, who gave us permission
to tackle the job. We knew they were based in Subic Bay,
probably in Port Binanga. Subic is on the west coast of Luzon,
just north of Bataan. I decided to send two boats—the 31
boat, which was Lieutenant DeLong's, and the 34 boat, which
was Kelly's, now commanded by Ensign Chandler. I went
along in it for the hell of it.

"We tested everything—tuned the motors, greased torpedoes, and got under way at nine o'clock, chugging north
along the west coast of Bataan. It was very rough. We throt-
tled down to thirty knots, and even then we were shipping
water, but we got off the entrance to Subic Bay about half
an hour after midnight. Here, according to plan, the two boats
separated. DeLong in the 31 boat was to sweep one side of
Subic Bay and I the other. We were to meet at Port Binanga,
at the end. If something happened and we didn't meet there,
then we were to rendezvous at dawn just outside the mine
fields of Corregidor.

"So we separated, expecting to meet at dawn. It was the
last I ever saw of the 31 boat. But here's what happened to

[1] From "They Were Expendable." Copyright, 1942, by W. L. White. Reprinted by permission of Harcourt, Brace and Co.

our 34 boat in Subic. First, remember it was darker than
hell, and the shore line was loaded with Jap field guns. None
of us had ventured in there since the Japs took over. We had
got in just a little way when a Jap searchlight spotted us and
blinked out a dot-dash challenge, asking who we were. Since
we didn't know the Jap code reply, naturally we didn't answer,
but changed course, veering away. But the Japs were getting
suspicious by now, and from over by Ilinin Point a single field
piece opened up. None of it fell near us—maybe they were
shooting at DeLong in the 31 boat.

"When we were about abeam of Sueste light another light
came on to challenge us—this time from a ship, maybe that
cruiser. We changed course to go over and have a look, but
she was small fry—not worth a torpedo—the hell with her—
we were headed for Binanga and the cruiser.

"By this time the Japs over on Grande Island realized something funny was going on—their light challenged us, but of
course we didn't answer. Then they broke out some 50-caliber
machine-gun fire at us from Ilinin Point. We could see the
tracers feeling for us, and then the fun started—big 3-inch
shore batteries rumbling all over the bay and lights feeling
for us. We could hear the shells whistle over our heads in the
dark, and could have done without some of them. But the
lights and flashes from the shore batteries were a real help,
for they enabled us to pick out the shore line, so, in spite of
the fact that it was blacker than hell, we knew where we were.

"By one o'clock we were off the north entrance to Port
Binanga, where we were to meet DeLong in the 31 boat and
go in together for the attack, and when he didn't show up,
I began to be afraid something might have happened, yet I
couldn't be sure.

"But there was nothing to do but go on in alone. To make
the sneak, we cut the speed down to eight knots, skirted Chi-
quita Island, rounded Binanga Point, and entered the little
bay on two engines at idling speed. Everything was quiet, no
firing down here, and then we saw her ahead in the dark not

five hundred yards away. Creeping up on her, we had just readied two torpedoes when a searchlight came on and in dot-dash code she asked us who we were.

"We answered, all right—with two torpedoes—but they had hardly been fired when I gave our boat hard rudder and started away. It isn't safe for an MTB to stay near a cruiser. One torpedo hit home with a hell of a thud—we heard it over our shoulders. Looking back, we saw the red fire rising, and presently two more explosions which might have been her magazines.

"But we had no time for staring, for we were into plenty trouble. One of those torpedoes had failed to clear its tube and was stuck there, just at the entrance, and was making what we call a 'hot run,' its propellers buzzing like hell, compressed air hissing so you couldn't hear yourself think. But worst of all, a torpedo is adjusted so that it won't fire until its propeller has made a certain number of revolutions—I shouldn't give it exactly, but let's say it is three hundred. After that, the torpedo is cocked like a rifle, and an eight-pound blow on its nose would set it off—blowing us all to glory.

"So what to do? Somehow that torpedo propeller had to be stopped and stopped quick, or else a good hard wave slap on the torpedo's nose would blow us all to splinters. And at this point our torpedoman, Martino, used his head fast. He ran to the head and swiped a handful of toilet paper. He jumped astride that wobbling, hissing torpedo like it was a horse, and, with the toilet paper, jammed the vanes of the propeller, stopping it.

"We'd stopped for all this, but we couldn't afford to wait long. The cruiser's fire was lighting up the bay behind us. Ahead, all over Subic, hell was breaking loose. So we started up, gave her everything we had to get through that fire.

"With three motors roaring, and us skipping around in that rough water with everything wide-open, I guess we made considerable commotion. Anyway the Japanese radio in Tokyo, reporting the attack next day, said the Americans had a new secret weapon—a monster that roared, flapped its wings, and fired torpedoes in all directions. It was only us, of course, but we felt flattered. We got the hell out of there, and that was all there was to it."

"Well," said Kelly, "MacArthur wouldn't quite agree. He gave you the D.S.C. for what you'd done."

"But DeLong has the real story," insisted Bulkeley. "I pulled up outside the mine field off Corregidor to wait for him. Neither of us could go in until it got light, because otherwise the army on shore, hearing us in the dark out there, would think it was Japs and set off the mine field. But when the sky got light and I saw my boat was alone, I realized DeLong was in trouble. And since he's now a prisoner of the Japanese— if he's alive—we'd better tell his story for him.

"After we parted company at the entrance to Subic Bay, he started around its northern rim as we'd planned. But just before midnight he developed engine trouble—the saboteur's wax had clogged his strainers. He cleaned them and had just got under way when more trouble developed—the cooling system went haywire. They stopped, and were drifting as they repaired it when there was an ominous grinding sound under the boat—they were aground on a reef in Subic Bay. At any minute a wandering Jap searchlight might pick them up and artillery fire would blow them to bits.

"They rocked the boat, and finally started the engines to get themselves unstuck. But the noise now attracted the Japs, and a 3-inch gun on Ilinin Point opened up on them—splashes coming nearer and nearer. They worked frantically, finally burned out all reverse gears so that the engines were useless. DeLong gave orders to abandon ship. They wrapped mattresses in a tarpaulin to make a raft, and all got aboard but DeLong, who stayed to chop holes in the gas tanks and blow a hole in the boat's bottom with a hand grenade before he jumped. That was the end of the 31. Then he couldn't find the raft in the darkness, and being afraid to call out, swam to the beach.

"The raft had shoved off with all twelve aboard at three o'clock.

"He waited on the sands until dawn. Then, in the gray half-light, he picked up the tracks of nine men. He followed these until they led into a clump of bushes, where he found most of his crew. They explained they had stayed with the raft until dawn was about to break. Fearing sunrise would expose them to the Japanese, they had decided to risk a swim to the beach, where they could hide. But Ensign Plant and two men, who couldn't swim very well, decided to stay. What became of them the nine didn't know, and no one knows for sure to this day.

"But the first thing DeLong did was to post lookouts, and all day they stayed in that clump, with an eye on the Jap observation planes which flew over them in relays, watching a hot little skirmish between the Americans and the Japanese on the far shore of the bay. At one point the Japs were falling back, and there seemed to be a chance that they could make a run for it in daylight, rejoining the American lines. But never was it quite possible, and in the meantime they had spotted a couple of bancas, native boats, farther down the beach.

"Two men who were sent out to investigate, crawling on their bellies through the grass, returned to report the bancas were in fair condition. So when the sun had set they crawled to them and started getting them in shape. For rowing they had two paddles, a couple of spades, and a board. They had to work fast and quietly, for the Japs were all around them— just as they were launching the bancas they heard Japanese voices not two hundred yards away.

"But a heavy wind came up, and at nine o'clock at night, both boats capsized. They righted them, but the shovels and the board were lost, and they now had only one paddle for each banca. Yet with these they continued to fight the head wind until three in the morning, when they were so exhausted that they decided to try the shore. So DeLong landed on what he hoped was Napo Point. They picked their way through the barbed-wire entanglement on the beach, and then found themselves up against a steep cliff.

"They kept very quiet until dawn, not knowing whether daylight would find them surrounded by Americans or Japanese. But when it became light, the first thing they saw was a Filipino sentry.

" 'Hey, Joe—got a cigarette and a match?' they called out. And an hour later they were telling their story to Captain Cockburn, in the Ninety-second American Infantry's field headquarters tent. The nine were back with us at Sisiman Cove the next evening."